TABULA RASA

WRITING A NEW STORY

ANA WATERS

TABULA RASA: BEAUTY FOR ASHES: Book One

ISBN: 978-1-7351036-0-0

MOBI eISBN: 978-0-9965127-3-2

EPUB eISBN: 978-1-7351036-2-4

Library of Congress Control Number: 2020909319

Cover design and interior formatting by: Hannah Linder Designs
www.hannahlinderdesigns.com

To my three, beautiful children I get to hold
and to the two in Heaven I'll hold one day.

For Sara.

"The Spirit of the Sovereign Lord is on me, because the Lord has anointed me to proclaim good news to the poor. He has sent me to bind up the brokenhearted, to proclaim freedom for the captives and release from darkness for the prisoners, to proclaim the year of the Lord's favor and the day of vengeance of our God, to comfort all who mourn, and provide for those who grieve in Zion —to bestow on them a crown of beauty instead of ashes, the oil of joy instead of mourning, and a garment of praise instead of a spirit of despair..."

— *ISAIAH 61:1-3 NIV*

CONTACT THE AUTHOR

FOR NEW RELEASES, SPECIAL PROMOTIONS AND ANNOUNCEMENTS:

Facebook @ AnaWatersAuthor
Instagram @ anawatersbooks
anawatersauthor@yahoo.com

PROLOGUE

Five Months Earlier

"PASTOR, THANK YOU SO MUCH FOR MEETING WITH me," I said with a smile. As a member of Sycamore Bible Church for the past thirteen years, Pastor and I had endured our share of ups and downs, but we seemed to be moving forward after a recent series of misunderstandings.

"Of course, Rebecca. What can I do for you?" He returned my smile and gestured for me to sit in an empty pew while he sat in the row behind me.

"It's my family again," I sighed. "Different day, same old story."

Just then, Pastor's wife, Ashley, interrupted us. She placed a hand on her husband's arm, whispering in his ear. He frowned slightly at her, shook his head, and then followed with, "I'll meet up with you and the kids later. I need to talk to Rebecca."

Surprised at how easily he'd dismissed his wife, I watched as Ashley blasted through the sanctuary double doors in obvious annoyance. Anger flashed across Pastor's face, immediately followed by a bright smile when he found me observing him.

"You were saying?"

Fidgeting with my sweater, I replied, "I don't want to keep you from lunch with Ashley and the kids, Pastor. It's nothing you haven't heard before." I got up to leave, but Pastor's hand on my arm stopped me.

"Really, Rebecca," he said, meeting my eyes, "you can talk to me."

Even with people milling around in the nave just outside, plenty of witnesses to ensure no impropriety was afoot, there we sat, a forty-something pastor and his thirty-something female congregant alone in the church narthex. Sunlight streamed through the stained glass windows, creating delicate rainbows around us. Brushing off a sinking feeling of déjà vu, I pushed forward with my story.

"So, after the huge blow up six months ago, my father sent me an email on Thursday. He said he's ashamed I won't talk to my own family and that I'm selfishly punishing everyone for my imaginary offenses."

"Well, no family is perfect, Rebecca. When did you last reach out to them?"

Hurt, I exclaimed, "Pastor, you know exactly when! This whole mess started when I overheard my father trashing me yet again to my little sister. My father never apologizes for any of his behavior, but he acts like the burden for making peace rests solely on me."

"What about 'blessed are the peacemakers'?" Pastor quoted from Scripture. "Do you really think God wants to see the Ivy family torn apart, Rebecca? Six months seems like long enough to go without speaking to your family. I don't think there's anything wrong with trying to make more of an effort in this situation, especially since your father can be a little stubborn."

My voice rose in frustration. "Don't my feelings matter too?"

"Of course they do," Pastor said soothingly. "Would you like me to say something to your father? As your spiritual authority here at SBC, of course. We both know your former fiancé never had the guts to do it."

"Pastor, I don't think—"

Ignoring me, he continued, "One day, Jason says he can't wait to marry you, and the next, the jerk announces 'this isn't going to work' during our premarital counseling session. I don't think I'll ever forget the look on your face, Rebecca. You were so devastated."

"I was," I murmured. Though no longer brokenhearted, my mind still brimmed with unanswered questions.

"I didn't mean to open an old wound, but it's been almost three years, Rebecca. Definitely time to move on." I noticed Pastor's hand on my arm again. The nagging feeling in my gut leapt with a vengeance.

So did I, scrambling to my feet. "Pastor, I really should get going. I don't want to keep you from lunch with your family."

He stood up as well, only taller than me by a few inches. "We can talk later, Rebecca. In fact, I was thinking we could—"

"Oh, there you are!" Cynthia Russell sing-songed. Perky as a high school cheerleader, the women's ministry leader walked purposefully toward us. She acknowledged my presence with a quick look of disdain before turning her full attention to Pastor. His strained smile felt like a tacit apology for Cynthia's rudeness.

"Are Jeremy and the boys feeling better?" I asked, offering Cynthia some crumbs of kindness she rarely deigned to reciprocate. "They haven't been around lately, and somebody mentioned they'd been sick. I hope you'll tell them I've been praying for them."

"They're just fine, Rebecca," came her clipped response. "Don't you have somewhere else to be right now?"

Too stunned to formulate a reply, I simply gaped. A lengthy pause ensued as Cynthia glared at me like a presumptuous interloper. I raised my eyebrows, silently imploring my leader to address the hostility in the room.

"Doesn't our Cynthia just embody the picture of a servant's heart?" Pastor finally said, clapping her robustly on the arm. "Jeremy and the boys are so blessed to have you, and certainly, all of SBC thanks you for everything you do around here. Isn't that right, Rebecca?"

I couldn't even fake a polite nod.

Taking charge of the situation, Cynthia said, "Rebecca, we know how much you enjoy monopolizing all of Pastor's time, but we have a meeting this afternoon. Why don't you run along, and we'll see you on Wednesday for Bible study, all right?"

I jerked in surprise. "A meeting? Pastor, didn't Ashley just ask you about lunch with the kids? You said you'd catch up with her later because you needed to talk to me. Am I missing something?"

To my complete astonishment, Cynthia and Pastor turned their backs on me, disregarding my question and my existence. I stumbled from the narthex into the nave, my brain scrambling to process a proper response to the situation. I acknowledged a few lingering members with a slight nod, but the entire encounter left me shell-shocked. By the time I exited the building, the church parking lot resembled a ghost town.

A dull headache throbbed at my temples, and I paused to pray and clear my head of the confusing sequence of events.

Autumn colors beautifully adorned the trees, but the crisp air carried scents of foreboding along with burning leaves. Unable to shake my sudden anxiety, I groped for my car keys, ready to go home.

Instead, I exhaled a weary sigh.

"Just go in, get your purse, and get out," I muttered. "She can't give you another condescending lecture just because you left your purse on the pew."

I wrapped my cardigan more tightly around myself, fighting off a chill as I re-entered the building.

The crime I witnessed defied description.

CHAPTER 1

Present Day

SHIVERING AT BAD MEMORIES AND TRYING desperately to suppress them, I took another sip of my morning coffee. Blessedly, the pile of new work requests on my desk offered the perfect, immersive distraction from my dark dance with the past. I had never intended to make a career in commercial insurance, but a series of temping disasters eventually led me to Culver Incorporated. I took the job interview on a whim, and I worked my way from front desk receptionist to marketing department of one. As one of the few parts of my life untouched by the Ivy family or Sycamore Bible Church, the Culver Incorporated office suite served as my personal sanctuary.

My cell phone buzzed, and I read another frantic text from my best friend, Jessica Goldstein. While I appreciated her concern as well as the invitation to watch the newest season of *Crossbow*, if she asked me if I was okay one more time, I felt like I might scream.

"I told you I was fine three days ago," I said with annoyance. "I love you, Jessica, but you're smothering me."

After several more minutes of silence on my part, Jessica threatened to send her brother over to my cubicle to check up on me. Kyle Goldstein, Jessica's twin brother, had accepted a position with Culver Incorporated two years after I started working there. Ordinarily, I enjoyed Kyle's quick wit and overblown tales of dating drama, but the thought of the Goldstein twins playing their game of monkey-in-the-middle raised my hackles.

Sure enough, Kyle emerged from his cluster of cubicles and approached.

"Penny for your thoughts," he said, perching himself on top of my desk. When I didn't respond, he offered me his standard, sideways smile. Gesturing toward my overstuffed inbox, he added, "Looks like you're up to your elbows as usual."

"What can I do for you, Kyle? I'm pretty busy right now."

"Beck, you're going to work yourself into an early grave," he said. "Why don't you ask corporate for some back up once in a while?"

"I like my work," I said, "and it's better than being home alone right now."

Kyle's smile faded. "How are you really doing, Beck? And don't tell me you're *fine* one more time. We both know you're not."

"Just because Jessica commands you to come over and spy on me doesn't mean you have to obey," I snapped.

"My sister hasn't heard from you in three days. She has a right to be concerned."

"Look at my desk, Kyle. What does she want from me? I'm exhausted when I get home, and I pretty much fall into bed after dinner."

Kyle's eyes grazed over my appearance. "She's worried about you, Beck. We both are. Jessica says you barely eat when you guys go out, and half the time, you just sit there like a zombie. Why won't you tell us what happened instead of torturing yourself with all of these secrets?"

"I am not torturing myself."

Kyle raised a dark eyebrow over hideously large hipster glasses.

Piqued, I said, "Nothing has changed in the last five months, okay?"

"So, you haven't heard anything else from him?"

"Which *him* are you referring to?"

"The one who tried to ruin your life," Kyle said.

"Again, which *him* are you referring to? My father, my pastor, or my ex?"

Kyle removed the monster goggles to meet my eyes without a barrier. "I'm so sorry, Rebecca."

I shrugged off his pity. "I'll be fine."

Kyle stared at me for a long minute. "You got a message from one of those creeps at your old church, didn't you?" Before I could reply, Kyle corrected himself. "No, you don't get this upset when you hear from them. This has Ivy family written all over it."

My self-protective anger melted slightly at Kyle's perceptiveness. "You know me too well."

"I've known you just as long as my sister has. You learn a few things about someone after twelve years." His trademark grin reappeared along with a hint of something else in his eyes.

I shifted in my seat.

"You okay, Beck?"

"Like I said, I'm just really busy."

Kyle placed his glasses back on his nose, pale blue eyes

searching for secrets I would not relinquish. "Definitely your family. Is Aunt Eleanor back to her old tricks again?"

I conceded the point with a slight smirk.

"What did she say?"

Throwing Kyle a bone so I could get back to work, I said, "The latest is how my brother and sister are going back to my parents' church—unlike me, of course. My father is exalting Ada and Daniel to high heaven while telling everyone how worthless I am in comparison. My aunt just repeats it all verbatim to shame me back into the family."

Kyle sucked in a breath, the disparity between our families always a shock to the Goldstein twins. Their biggest family squabble centered on Kyle's bottomless stomach and Jessica's difficulty in keeping off extra weight. On my darker days, I struggled with bitterness toward a friend whose only complaint in life was how she had shared the same womb with her brother but not the same metabolism.

"Beck?" Kyle called. "Did I lose you?"

"Still here," I said. "What did I miss?"

"I asked why you gave your aunt your new phone number. I was so proud of you for finally changing it last fall."

"Wishful thinking," I replied. "Aunt Eleanor sold me a bunch of lies about how she wanted to have a relationship with me separate from the rest of the family. Stupidly, I believed her."

"I remember. Jessica thought she was sincere, but I had my doubts."

"Once I realized my aunt was just spying on me, things went back to business as usual. Frankly, I'm surprised she hasn't given my number to my parents yet. My father would be blowing up my phone if he knew how to contact me directly."

"I think your parents are waiting for you to come groveling

back," Kyle said. "They let your aunt play bad cop because it's less work on their part."

"Probably," I admitted.

Not sure what else to say, I inclined my body toward my computer monitors and the mountain of work piled next to them. Failing to take the hint, Kyle continued to stare at me as if awaiting further conversation. I frowned.

"Kyle, I have an RFP from the mighty Margolin and four other summaries that need to get done before I leave today."

My friend's expression turned sardonic. "Ah, what would life be like without another Request for Proposal from Culver's top, east coast Producer, hmm?"

"I know Ted's demanding, Kyle, but you act like he's my father."

"How many times has one of Ted Margolin's assignments kept you here until eight at night, Beck? I don't care if everyone calls him the king of commercial insurance brokerage," Kyle said. "Margolin treats you like his personal assistant."

"The entire office treats me like their personal assistant, Kyle. They remember me as the receptionist who magically taught herself how to use the ArtHut Design Suite. Ted just acts extra entitled because nobody brings more money to Culver this side of the Mississippi."

As if on cue, the sound of squeaky loafers and jangling keys announced the arrival of the mighty Margolin to my work station.

"Goldstein," Ted said, acknowledging Kyle with a quick jerk of the chin, "do you have those loss reports for me on Triple J?"

"Oh, I uh..." Kyle sputtered.

"I needed them an hour ago," Ted said, his gaze flicking over my friend still seated on my desk. "Our deadline hasn't changed just because you got distracted in the marketing department."

Heat crept into my cheeks as Kyle's eyes narrowed.

"Well?" Ted prompted with his usual arrogance.

"I'll be right on it," Kyle said, hopping down. I could almost see the steam coming out of my friend's ears as he stalked back to his cubicle. Glancing up, I noticed the mighty Margolin also tracked Kyle's progress until he disappeared from sight.

"What can I do for you, Ted?" I asked.

"Did you get those revisions I left for you last night?"

"I did."

"When do you think they'll be ready? I have a few more changes I need to send once you're finished with them."

"As you can see," I said, gesturing to my desk, "I'm absolutely swamped, but I promise I'm working as fast as I can. You've got some other people ahead of you in line, but I'll let you know how things are going after lunch."

Ending my monologue with a strained smile, I swiveled in my chair, eagerly anticipating the receding sounds of Ted's loafers and car keys. Instead, I felt the gaze of the mighty Margolin on my back. Unable to keep the edge out of my voice, I asked, "Is there something else I can help you with?"

"Rebecca, can you turn back around, please?"

I grudgingly obliged.

Checking to ensure the coast was clear, Ted leaned down toward me and said, "Culver has a very strict sexual harassment policy. If Goldstein keeps bothering you, please let me know. You should be allowed to get your work done in peace."

Irritation immediately forgotten, I said, "What are you talking about?"

"Goldstein's over here a lot and usually in your personal space. I'm not the only one who's noticed, and I want to make sure you're protected."

"Protected?" I repeated in shock.

"Nobody could handle this job the way you do, Rebecca. We can't afford to lose you. Your work speaks for itself, and I've said so for a long time."

My mouth opened and closed in disbelief. Had I not already been seated in my chair, I would have collapsed into it.

"Wow," I said. "I had no idea you felt this way, Ted."

"It's not just me," he replied gruffly. "Miss Belle, Deondre, and MacKenzie have all mentioned how often they find Goldstein loitering at your desk."

"He's not loitering."

"I saw the two of you from across the room, Rebecca. It seemed pretty obvious you wanted Goldstein to leave, and he was in no hurry to do so." Raising his eyebrows in question, he asked, "Is there some other reason you didn't tell him to go?"

Defensively, I replied, "His sister is my best friend, and they both tend to worry about me. It's not what it looks like, I promise, Ted."

"Why are they worried? Are you all right?" He reached a hand toward my arm, saw my stunned expression, and then withdrew it.

Confused, I tried to reconcile my most demanding coworker of the past six years with the man standing before me. Much to my chagrin, Ted Margolin was not wholly unattractive. Quite the opposite actually. Compassion was a very good look for him.

"What?" he asked, searching my eyes.

"Protected?" I repeated again. "Did you really just say that?"

"Does that sound anti-feminist or something? I don't mean to cause any offense here, Rebecca. I just want to help."

"I don't think I know what it's like to be *protected*," I said before thinking better of it. Countless memories flooded to the surface, all of them reminding me how often I'd been thrown to the wolves. Wrestling the old ghosts back into submission, tears of gratitude welled up from this unlikely source of comfort.

Ted's eyes widened in alarm. "Whoa, Rebecca, I didn't realize how bad the situation was with Goldstein. I can talk to Bonnie in HR or Phil if you need me to. I meant what I said. We don't want to lose you."

"It's not what you think," I said, waving him off.

"Are you sure? You seem pretty upset."

I quickly dabbed the moisture from my eyes. "You just...you made me think of something else." I rose to my feet to make purposeful eye contact. "Thank you for your concern, Ted. I truly mean that."

He nodded in acknowledgment, his hazel eyes staring back into mine. For the first time in months, a genuine smile found its way to my lips. I had finally upgraded from "personal assistant" to actual human being.

And it felt good.

I beamed at the mighty Margolin, grateful to be seen. His eyes darted briefly toward my mouth, and I jerked back in surprise. Awkwardly, Ted began coughing and stepped away from my cubicle. With his tone all business, he said, "Okay, sounds great, Rebecca. I'll just wait to hear from you then."

"You got it," I chirped.

Ted lifted his chin and turned away. The sound of jangling keys and squeaky loafers accompanied him toward his spacious, window office.

Still smiling over the word "protected," I sat back down and tackled my work with a vengeance.

CHAPTER 2

FOLLOWING AN EXTRA TWO HOURS OF OVERTIME ON
Ted's RFP, I endured the slight remains of rush hour traffic and
made myself an omelette once I arrived home. Curled up on my
sofa watching television, a knock on my apartment door startled
me out of my semi-vegetative state.

"Becca?" I heard from outside.

Disbelieving my ears, I tiptoed toward the peephole.

Time stood still as I beheld my ex-fiancé, Jason Whitmore.
Jason still had the same haircut, the same navy peacoat, and the
same face perpetually covered in five o'clock shadow.

"Becca?" he called again. "Unless you somehow gave up
Food Station and *Sliced & Diced*, I know you're in there."

Jason's presumption pulled me out of my musings. "What
do you want?" I said tersely.

"It's nice to hear your voice again, even through a door." A
slight smile touched his mouth.

Attraction pulsed through me followed by immediate
recriminations of the agony I had endured getting over him.

"You're the one who broke off our engagement, remember? I'm not taking you back, Jason, so there's really no reason for you to be here."

"I didn't come over to get back together," he said flatly, his smile falling.

"You better not tell me you're getting married to someone else, but you decided to stop by for some closure," I said.

He rolled his eyes. "Give me a little credit, would you?"

"And why should I do that, exactly?"

Jason exhaled in frustration. "This would be a lot easier if you just opened the door, Becca."

I laughed bitterly. "Making things easier for you stopped being my problem three years ago."

"It's about your precious pastor."

I flung the door open, ready to breathe fire. "Listen, whatever you have to say, I am not interested, okay?"

"I would have called you, but you changed your number."

"Five months ago," I said, steeling myself against the cold, night air. Spring took her sweet time arriving that year, even gifting us with a snow dusting in early March.

"You going to invite me in?" Jason asked, conveniently shivering for sympathy.

"No."

Jason looked me over, studying my face intently. "You're different."

"What did you expect?"

"I don't know. I just...you look...hard. Did I...I mean...did I do that to you?"

I scoffed. "You broke my heart, Jason, but you didn't ruin my life. That distinction belongs to—" I caught myself before I stumbled, glaring at Jason instead.

Forgoing all manners of etiquette, Jason shoved past me and into the apartment.

"This is not happening again!" I roared. I squashed the ghosts reminding me I had been put in this position once before.

The shock expanded from my ex-fiancé's eyes to his entire face. "What did he do to you, Becca?"

I glared at him. "What are you talking about?"

"You know exactly what I'm talking about."

"Jason, you have ten seconds to tell me what you're doing here before I call the police."

"What did *Pastor,*" he spat the word out, "do to you, Becca?"

My jaw dropped. "How did you—?"

"Becca, you clung to every word the man said like it was gospel. You sang his praises and had a million excuses for his flaws. I hated the condescending way he treated you, like some lapdog he tolerated for his own amusement."

"Don't you think that's a bit harsh?" I said, wrapping my arms around myself. Reluctantly, I closed my front door, refusing to let any more cold in my home when I already felt frozen from the inside out.

"Try telling me it wasn't true, Becca. I haven't forgotten the snide comments from Cynthia Russell and her clique of leadership peons either. You don't think that started from the top down?"

"The clones," I murmured, recalling how each member of Cynthia's posse behaved like mirror images of one another. They talked alike, dressed alike, and dieted alike. They also took perverse pleasure in humiliating and shunning me, something Jason obviously still remembered. Though five months removed from SBC, the clones continued to propagate slander about me for leaving the church.

"Becca, did you hear a word I just said?" Jason demanded.

"Honestly? No. I was thinking about Cynthia and her flying monkeys."

Jason's frown grew more pronounced, new lines appearing on his forehead. "Tell me what happened, Becca. You look like you, but you're not acting like you."

"Why do you care? You're the one who left."

Jason took a step toward me, and I took a step backward.

"Becca," he pleaded.

"You deserted me, Jason. You just up and left without a single look back. I think I have a right to know why."

"That's why I'm here," he said, his tone softening. "I've been telling myself that it's none of my business, but I had to come and see you. I couldn't let you do this to yourself, Becca. Please, don't throw your life away. He's not worth it."

My sinking resolve matched my gradual descent onto the sofa. "Jason, what are you talking about? What does Pastor have to do with why you left? What does he have to do with why you're here now?"

Wonder and compassion filled my ex-fiancé's eyes. "Are you saying you didn't know?"

"Know what?"

Jason sat on the couch with me, but a respectable two feet away. "Do you remember all of the intimate questions Pastor asked us during our premarital counseling sessions?"

"You had to expect the topic of sex to come up, Jason. We were getting married after all."

"Becca, you know what I mean. He drilled you for details, almost like he was trying to force you into confessing something that wasn't even true. He acted like you were deliberately withholding information."

Reluctantly, I let my mind travel back down that dangerous road. I frowned. "It was definitely overkill. I'll give you that."

"I also saw the way he looked at you," Jason added. "I didn't like it."

I pressed my lips together, unwilling to dignify that answer with a response. Too much pain. Too much confusion.

"He played both of us, Becca. I watched him put wedges in our relationship, made you doubt that I loved you, that I didn't want to defend you against your family."

That snapped my head back to the present. "Excuse me, but you didn't defend me against my family."

"Because he told me not to!"

"That's impossible! I sat right there when Pastor lectured you about it."

"Right before that miserable Thanksgiving, I went to Pastor privately about how to handle your family—your father especially. He said to stop enabling you and let you learn to fight your own battles."

"What!" I gasped.

Jason nodded grimly. "He said you needed to stop looking for some man to save you. No matter how ugly it might get, he told me the best way to help you was to stay quiet and force you to deal with things on your own."

I sat there stunned, hurt and betrayed anew.

Jason continued, "At our next counseling session, Pastor started in with that smug sermon about me not being man enough to protect you. I couldn't believe how he set me up."

"Why didn't you tell me?" I whispered.

"Because I knew you'd never believe me, Becca. You just looked up at him with those big, brown eyes like he was Jesus incarnate. I could never compete with that."

"Oh, Jason," I moaned in despair.

He shifted closer to me, and I felt Jason's warm touch on the blocks of ice that had become my hands. Unlike Pastor, Jason's hands didn't feel foreign or defiling.

"Did you and he...I mean, did you guys ever...?"

"No!" I jerked my hands free. "I'm insulted you would even ask!"

Eyes narrowing, Jason said, "Insulted, Becca? Why don't you explain Pastor's FaceSpace post that God provided some new, mystery woman he says is going to serve alongside him in the church?"

I felt the color leave my face.

"Nobody even knows the guy got a divorce, but he's already talking up this new chick like she hung the moon. When he called the situation an exciting opportunity for Sycamore Bible Church, I almost threw up in my mouth."

Finding my voice, I asked, "Why are you acting like I have something to do with this?"

Jason's angry expression turned skeptical. "Are you saying you didn't know anything about it?"

"I left SBC five months ago, Jason. This news is just as appalling to me as it is to you."

Looking both repentant and relieved, he said, "I didn't know you left the church, Becca. I just saw my newsfeed blow up from mutual friends of ours. As one of Pastor's most devoted follow-ers, I thought maybe he convinced you to play house with him. Even though I told myself you two deserved each other, I couldn't let you ruin your life for that sleazeball. There's not a doubt in my mind that he sabotaged our relationship so he could sleep with you."

I scoffed. "Whether that's true or not, Jason, the choice to leave was still yours. You're the one who walked out of that door. You're the one who broke my heart, not Pastor."

Jason put his hands on my shoulders, holding me steady as if fearing I'd vanish into smoke. "He robbed us of the chance to be together, Becca, of three years we could have been married. Who knows? We might have even had a kid by now—"

I cut him off as I felt the sting of tears. "No matter the reason for Pastor's despicable stunt, you chose to leave, Jason. We've both had to make new lives and move on."

Jason searched for something in my eyes. "I've missed you, Becca. I still miss you." His head angled toward mine, bringing every kiss and tender embrace into quick remembrance.

Steeling myself to avoid an excursion down that burned out bridge, I said, "Jessica told me you've had at least four new girl-friends since we broke up. I assume they were willing to give you what I wasn't."

Jason's guilty expression and sudden loss of eye contact confirmed my best friend's trolling on social media. I stood up from the couch, creating more distance between us. The temp-tation to salve my battered soul with the only man who'd ever said he loved me was growing too strong.

"I think you should go, Jason. You've made your point."

He raked a hand through his hair. "I'm so sorry, Becca. I wish I had done things differently. Sitting here with you, same apartment, same couches, it's like time stood still. Except we both know it didn't."

"No, it didn't," I said softly. "We're not who we were three years ago."

"Did I break you?" Jason asked quietly. "Broken beyond repair, I mean?"

I shook my head and tried to offer some semblance of a smile. "Not permanently broken, Jason. I got over everything a while ago. I forgave you too."

"So, have you been seeing anybody else?" he asked.

I shrugged nonchalantly.

"Don't waste your life because of me or that psycho, Becca. I know we can't go back in time and change things, but I promise I only want happiness for you. You deserve it."

My forced smile grew into a softer, more genuine version of itself. "Hopefully, we're both a little older and wiser now."

"Hopefully," he repeated, his eyes traveling over me. "You've lost weight too. A lot. What's going on that you're not telling me?"

"I'm not starving myself," I said quickly. "I just don't have much of an appetite these days. I haven't really felt like myself since I left SBC. It doesn't help that the church keeps sending their minions to preach at me about forgiveness or to fish around for gossip."

"What happened?" Jason asked, rising from the couch. "What made you finally leave?"

"You won't believe me. I don't think anybody will."

"Try me," he said. "I promise, I'll believe you."

I took Jason's hands in mine. "I know I accused you of coming over here for closure, Jason, but that's exactly what you gave me tonight. It's too easy to cling to the past, to someone who knew me before this whole nightmare started. Thank you for telling me what really happened with our relationship, but I'm going to be okay." I gave his hands a platonic squeeze before releasing them.

Jason searched my face, his brow heavy. "Nightmare? Do you know more about Pastor's announcement than what you've been letting on? You said the new woman isn't you, and I believe you, but what aren't you telling me?"

"I can't," I whispered.

Eyes widening in realization, he said, "This is the reason why you left SBC, isn't it? And I bet it involves Cynthia Russell too. That witch acted more like Pastor's wife than Ashley ever did. Is Cynthia tangled up in this thing? Is she the reason Pastor got a divorce?"

Though my mouth refused to acknowledge Jason's litany of questions, my eyes couldn't deny what they'd seen.

CHAPTER 3

THE UPTOWN, *NOUVEAU RICHE* SECTION OF MY CITY, locally referred to as "Parkview," kissed the suburbs on one side and midtown on the other. Finding its place along the city's pulse line, the Culver office suite nestled itself within the sleek array of Parkview's skyscrapers. Sidewalks teemed with affluent and urban locals, power suit executives, and stiletto-heeled business women. Sitting on my favorite bench outside of my office high rise, I welcomed the noonday sunlight on my face.

"It figures I'd find you lazing about rather than actually working at your desk."

Feigning deafness, I silently beseeched Heaven to send this man back into the abyss of bad memories. Instead, I opened my eyes and beheld all six feet of the man known to the parishioners of First United Church of Hillcrest as Pastor Bernard Ivy.

"You've taken to coloring your hair," my father noted. "I'm glad to see you finally took your mother's advice. You looked like a witch with all of that prematurely gray hair."

"What are you doing here?" I asked, squinting from the sun.

"Don't you have an apology for the poor father whose heart you've broken with your silence? This ridiculous temper tantrum has gone on far too long, Rebecca Joanne."

"I suppose my heart and my feelings don't really matter, do they?"

Predictably, my father scoffed. "Does everything have to be about you?"

I scowled.

My father sniffed haughtily. "I came here to discuss your reprehensible behavior at Sycamore Bible Church. Imagine my embarrassment receiving a phone call like that from your former pastor."

"What?" I breathed.

"Chasing after a married man, Rebecca? Fabricating stories about him and Cynthia Russell as punishment for rejecting your sexual advances? You filthy, lying harlot! How dare you besmirch the Ivy family name with your sin!"

"*My* sin?" I said, outraged by Pastor's deception and my father's eagerness to believe it.

"Yes, *your* sin," my father sneered. "I have no doubt you also used the sins of the flesh to entice that mouthy punk into a marriage proposal all those years ago. He may have been desperate enough for a tumble in the sheets, but at least he wised up before you shackled him to a lifetime of misery."

For the first time, my father's go-to sucker punch of the past three years fell short of its mark. I felt a confidence well up within me.

"Do you have any other insults you'd like to sling at me, Dad, or are we done here? I'd really like to enjoy the rest of my lunch break."

My father blinked for a moment, stunned that his favorite insult yielded indifference rather than tears. Not one to give up easily, however, he switched tactics to emotional martyrdom. "How can a man properly shepherd the Lord's flock while his children spit in the face of the Almighty? When will you renounce this godless, Jezebel spirit within you and return to the Lord, Rebecca?"

"Leaving First United back in college doesn't mean I turned my back on Jesus," I said angrily. "God can dwell wherever He wants, and He's certainly not limited to any one denomination or church building."

"Oh, you're all living in sin!" my father said, throwing up his hands in exasperation. "The gossip mongers went crazy when your brother showed up high on drugs with his stoner girlfriend last month. Now, he claims the two of them are going to be parents! How could God possibly bless that union with a child?"

Gaining a full head of steam, he continued, "And then your sister! God meant for Ada to give us beautiful, golden haired grandchildren, not suddenly become a vegetarian lesbian, flunk out of school, and then cover herself in tattoos! We already knew nobody would ever marry *you*," he spat, giving me a derisive once-over, "but, my precious Ada! What a waste!"

I found something morbidly humorous in my father's theatrics. At thirty-two years-old, I stifled the first laugh I had ever enjoyed at Bernard Ivy's expense.

With a deep growl, my father bent his hand in the air to wipe the smile from my face. The enraged monster of my childhood stood before me, and I instantly recalled a lifetime of backhanded slaps and worse. My new-found confidence disintegrated in the heat of Bernard Ivy's fury. I sat there paralyzed, screaming on the inside yet unable to move.

"Is there a problem here?" Ted Margolin demanded sharply.

He stood a few inches taller than my father, utterly unintimi-dated by Bernard Ivy.

I jumped to my feet and hid behind God's angel sent to rescue me. "What awesome timing, Ted! I meant to ask if you had new content for your RFP. I also transformed that big para-graph about flood insurance into a really cool graphic." Snatching my purse in one hand and Ted's arm with the other, I dragged him toward our office building, leaving my father to fume in my stolen sunlight.

"Thank you," I whispered, ushering Ted toward the elevators.

The mighty Margolin motioned for me to stand behind him, effectively blocking me from sight should Bernard Ivy attempt to locate me through the glass walls of our office building. I released my pent up breath once the elevator doors opened. Ted quickly ensconced us inside.

When the doors shut, he lit into me. "What in the world was going on out there, Rebecca? That guy was going to back-hand you across the face!"

Hating that I felt so exposed, more so the humiliation of having to admit my association to the monster outside, I said quietly, "That was my father."

"Your what?!"

"Yes, Pastor Bernard Ivy," I said bitterly. "I stopped speaking to him almost a year ago. Apparently, he wasn't too happy about that." Seeing that my attempt at dry humor failed, I began to resent the pity found in the mighty Margolin's eyes. "Look, I appreciate what you did out there, Ted, but let's just forget about it, okay?"

He looked ready to object, but the elevator doors dinged open to the eighth floor. I stepped out first and said a quick hello to a few of my coworkers on their way out to lunch. Ted acknowledged them with a brief nod, but his eyes never left my face.

Once the elevator doors closed, he said, "I know this is none of my business, Rebecca, but you can't just let your father treat you like that. How long has the abuse been going on?"

"You're right, Ted...it isn't any of your business," I said coolly. "Thank you for rescuing me, but I promise, I'm fine."

"You didn't look fine, Rebecca. You looked terrified."

Before I could respond, Kyle barreled through the glass office doors and into the elevator waiting area. He looked back and forth between Ted and me, brow wrinkled at the obvious tension.

"Everything okay, guys? Did Rebecca use the wrong stock photo or something?"

Kyle's half-hearted joke provided the escape I needed. "Ted, I sent you a .pdf of the latest Guildcorp draft before I left for lunch. I have to knock out summaries for Cody and Melissa before three, but I can make any revisions after that."

The way the mighty Margolin looked at me blurred the lines of my safely compartmentalized life. Of all the coworkers to see the pain beneath my placid, Culver facade, Ted Margolin seemed the unlikeliest choice. Worse yet, traitorous parts of me actually enjoyed the attention. I realized I had felt Ted's eyes on me more than once during my time at Culver, but I had never paid much attention to it. The thought of the mighty Margolin being interested in something beyond the status of his latest work request had always seemed too ridiculous to believe.

I scurried back to my desk and relayed the entire event to Jessica later that evening over dinner.

"Wow, Beck! The guy treats you like his office slave for more than half a decade, and suddenly, he's your knight in shining armor," she said in between bites of salad. "Who knew a heart actually beat underneath the $900 power suits? It almost makes me want to forgive him for being such a jerk to you all these years."

"Ted was just being nice. Let's not make a big deal about it, okay?"

"Whatever helps you sleep at night, hon. Just don't pretend you didn't swoon a little at the handsome executive rescuing you from your dastardly dad," she teased, fluttering her lashes.

"He's not handsome. He's...Ted."

Jessica arched her eyebrow at my denial. "Unless he's using someone else's headshot on the Culver website, I'm gonna have to go with smolderingly delicious. It was a shock, quite frankly, especially after all the horror stories I've heard from you and my brother."

"I don't look at him that way, Jessica, and I can guarantee the feelings are mutual."

Jessica clicked her tongue in disgust. "You can't possibly be that blind, Beck. The guy might be a jerk, but at least he has the decency to be a really good looking jerk."

"I'll admit he's not a complete troll. Except on his bad days."

"Beck, that photo looks like something out of a men's magazine. I know you're Miss Goody Two-Shoes, but it's okay to admit that your coworker is hot. If he wasn't so mean to my brother, I'd totally tell you to go for it."

Piqued, I said, "I'm sure the mighty Margolin would have done the same thing for anyone else in my situation. Can we drop it now, please?"

Jessica's mischievous grin belied her innocent shrug. Glancing over at my dinner plate, her expression sobered. "Just promise me you'll take one bite of your pizza, Beck."

"I need to stop eating out."

"You need to start eating. I know you've always wanted to lose a few extra pounds, but not like this, hon."

I took an obnoxiously large bite. "Happy now?"

Jessica grinned. "Better."

"Thanks for meeting me on such short notice, by the way. Hopefully, your brother will leave us alone for one meal. Do you know why Kyle keeps crashing our lunch dates lately? I see him all the time at work or your condo, so I'm kind of confused."

Jessica pursed her lips.

"What?"

"Seriously, Beck? You even have to ask?"

"Jessica," I drawled, "what are you talking about?"

"I figured you knew but weren't interested, so I never brought it up."

I took another bite of pizza before realization dawned on me. "I sincerely hope you're not saying what I think you are."

"Look, if Mr. RFP can pick up on it, believe me, it's there."

I groaned. "Ted on the white horse was more than enough for one day. Let's not add your brother to my list of imaginary admirers."

"Imaginary admirers? Beck, my brother's been in love with you since college. I keep telling him to say something already. Why do you think he took the account manager position at Culver?"

"Right, because his never ending parade of girlfriends proves his real feelings for me," I said sarcastically. "Between my father, Ted, and then Jason coming over the other night, I can't handle any more drama right now. I appreciate the thought, Jessica, but I think you're wrong about this one."

Jessica dropped her fork. "Did you just say *Jason* stopped by?"

"I might have forgotten to mention that."

"Were you planning on ever mentioning it? You know, before I have grandkids?"

I rolled my eyes. "Jessica, you and Nathan barely know each other. Please, don't tell me you're planning honeymoon locations already."

"Hardly. It was three dates, and it's obvious the guy only wants one thing. I don't know why I listened to my mother about signing up for LoveJewShmooze.com."

"Did I ever tell you about the time I signed up for that site?" I asked. "At my mother's behest, no less."

"Well, aren't you full of surprises today, Miss Ivy? When did you go from being a Preacher's Kid to a Member of the Tribe?"

"My grandparents on my mom's side are Jewish. My mother converted when my father told her 'no heathen could be a pastor's wife.'"

"No offense, but your dad has issues. A lot of them."

"I don't understand why my mother went along with any of it. Maybe she thought the public persona was the real Bernard Ivy."

"Like Deborah Ivy has a halo and wings," Jessica said with a sneer. "She makes your aunt harass you via text so she can pretend her hands are clean. That last message she sent was off the rails."

"I've never understood that relationship, Jessica. It's obvious what my mother gains from it, but how does Aunt Eleanor benefit from bullying me on behalf of my mother?"

Jessica shrugged. "Maybe she feels sorry for her being married to your dad."

"I don't see why. My mother practically worships my father. That whole church does. If anything, I could see my mother holding something over my aunt's head. It really doesn't matter either way. As long as Bernard Ivy never shows his face in

Parkview again, my aunt can send me all the stupid text messages she wants."

Jessica's expression turned mischievous once again. "Didn't you say the mighty Margolin put in a call to security about your father?"

"He might have," I hedged.

"So, the guy rescues you from your father, makes sure the stupid jerk can't ever stop by your office again, and then passes by your cube at least ten times this afternoon. For someone so convinced there's nothing going on, when did you find time to count how often he strolled by?"

"Just shut up and eat my pizza," I said, tossing a slice into Jessica's salad bowl. "You've been ogling my dinner like it's named Ted Margolin or something."

"Thanks," she said with a cheshire smile.

"And don't ever use the phrase *smolderingly delicious* to describe my coworker again. That's just gross."

Jessica's uproarious laugh garnered the attention of several restaurant patrons. Proud of myself for holding my ground, I lifted up my glass of water in mock salute and took a long sip. Jessica enjoyed her pizza, and I enjoyed the silence.

CHAPTER 4

"Did Aunt Eleanor give my number to everyone?!" I yelled out to the universe. Sure enough, my baby sister, Ada, appeared on the caller ID. "Let me guess," I spat to my ringing phone, "Dad put you up to this, you need money, or you need a shoulder to cry on about your latest break up. Oh, all three? Lucky me!"

Despite my sarcastic rant, I nearly answered the phone out of habit. Instead, I heeded the calming restraint in my gut. As the fog of family obligation cleared, I stared at my phone wondering why shared DNA required me to entertain my sister and her shenanigans. I waited to see if Ada would call again or leave a message. When my cell phone remained silent with no new voicemails, I instantly knew that translated to, "on a mission for Dad."

The ghosts of Pastor's sermons returned, countless homilies advocating conflict avoidance or emotional martyrdom. I pushed away the tormenting thoughts of guilt, the twisted Bible verses about suffering and forgiveness used to beat me back into submission.

"Oh, that's right," I said, replaying the bevvy of false accusations in my mind, "questioning authority equates to pride and rebellion rather than discernment from God. Of course, my spiritual authority never makes mistakes about anything. Right, Pastor?"

The leader of Sycamore Bible Church did possess a real first name and last name, but I couldn't bring myself to acknowledge them. In truth, the word "pastor" almost became a curse word, evoking memories of *that man* or my father. Thankfully, the great Bernard Ivy did not handle rejection well, so he told the entire family he finally rejected *me* instead. Naturally, he forgave my mountain of supposed sins against the Ivy family, but he woefully lamented my corrupt heart so bent toward evil.

The man deserved an acting award.

Or a lightning bolt.

Months passed, and Ted landed the Guildcorp account, largely attributing it to my RFP design work. He even recommended me for Culver Super Star over the summer. During our company's June birthday/anniversary get together, our CEO, Phil Robbins, awarded me with a $250 gift card and a three month, executive level parking permit. My modest, blue sedan stood out like a sore thumb amidst the gleaming, black luxury vehicles.

Smiling at the disparity one early August morning, I put the finishing touches on my morning routine. I pulled a clip from my wet hair and shook out the curls. After applying a coat of lipstick in the mirror, I noticed the mighty Margolin shaving in his car a few spots over. The man would probably die if he knew I saw him. Somehow, that made the whole situation even funnier.

I chuckled about my little discovery all the way to the elevators, barely containing my mirth when Ted stopped the closing doors with his hand. He looked up, surprised to see me.

"Good morning, Rebecca," he said evenly.

I kept myself from laughing out loud, but I could not withhold my signature smile. Jessica called it my "megawatt" smile, claiming it lit up the entire room. Jason said I always gave that smile to Pastor when I saw him on Sundays. That day, I bestowed it on an unwitting Ted Margolin whose only crime was being caught with an electric razor in his car.

Ted seemed bemused. "Are you always so cheerful in the morning, or can we attribute this to your new parking space?"

The megawatt smile went supernova.

In an instant, all humor vanished from the mighty Margolin's face. He visibly startled before clearing his throat and stepping into the elevator. The unbidden and almost scandalous thought pressed in that perhaps I intimidated the king of commercial insurance brokerage.

I kept my tone light as I answered Ted's original question. "I have zero complaints about the new parking spot, Ted. My hair thanks you as well."

"Your hair?"

I flipped a cluster of damp tendrils from my face. "There are some definite advantages to walking underground rather than facing tornado alley every morning," I said, referring to the partially covered walkway connecting the parking deck to the office high rise. "All of that wind is brutal on curly hair, especially right after a shower."

The strained expression on Ted's face increased, and my own smile diminished. Belatedly, I realized the less than professional picture I'd just painted of myself. Try as I might to deny Jessica's assessment of the situation, the mighty Margolin seemed uncomfortably aware he shared the elevator with a female. A very single female.

As if to prove my point, he tapped the button for the eighth floor with a note of frustration.

"Ted?"

"Yes?" he choked.

"You're going to break the button if you keep jamming it like that."

His hand dropped like a lead weight.

After a tense, silent ride to the Culver office suite, Ted escorted me to my cubicle. I glanced over at the suddenly enigmatic man, wondering if I had been blind to something staring me right in the face for six years. Instead, Ted's elevated jaw and squared shoulders suggested I had greatly overestimated the power of my feminine wiles. My coworker of old had returned *en force*.

"I have some time-sensitive documents that need to be handled ASAP. I was hoping we could go ahead and get started on them."

Strangely disappointed, I bristled at the way I had been relegated back to office slave so easily. "Do you mind if I caffeinate first? Not all of us can afford the fancy, foreign stuff," I said, pointing to Ted's to-go cup from the Italian café across the street, "but I absolutely love that french vanilla creamer in the break room."

"Do what you need to do," he said, and the sound of squeaky loafers and jangling keys faded into the morning hum of activity around the office.

Irritated once again, I silently berated myself for actually caring what the mighty Margolin thought of me. It seemed ridiculous to fault the man for treating me with the same dismissive attitude he had always used during my tenure at

Culver, but something had changed for me. Whether my own interest resulted from misplaced gratitude or simply flattering myself that I had any effect on the man, I marched toward Ted's office determined to find out.

The mighty Margolin sat behind his desk, and his eyes flew up to meet mine in surprise. I regretted my decision immediately.

"Coffee time," I sing-songed awkwardly.

Ted smirked over the rim of his own coffee cup. "Thanks for the update."

I winced, ready to crawl into the nearest hole.

As I turned away, I heard Ted call out my name. I poked my head back inside. "Yes?"

"Please, tell your hair I said 'you're welcome.' Tornado alley would hardly do it justice."

Carefully concealing megawatt, I pretended not to notice the gaze of the mighty Margolin following me down the corridor. My usual morning trek to the break room mysteriously transformed into a sashay.

Unfortunately, a tsunami of work kept my sashaying to a minimum after that, and my strappy sandals lay abandoned under my desk.

"Brilliant as usual!" Belinda Vickers, affectionately known as "Miss Belle" exclaimed. She handed back a proposal for Avatron Inc. with two minor flags for revisions. Miss Belle served as our resident spitfire grandma, equal parts sweetness and sass. So long as you didn't call her "Belinda," Miss Belle would take a bullet for you. She reminded any violator of this unspoken rule that only the late Mr. Vickers and her ninety-three-year-old Mama got to call her by her given name.

"Kayla said she'd stop by with the employee benefits guide for Avatron," she said.

"Oh, I didn't realize we got commercial and benefits," I replied, leaning back into my chair.

"Ted and Phil worked on the deal with that new guy, Joe Trautweig, in Benefits. I love when the two arms of the company work together. It's a win for everybody," Miss Belle said like a proud mama hen.

As an international insurance brokerage, Culver negotiated commercial insurance for its clients on one side and employee health benefits on the other. My job meant juggling the needs of both: creating proposals, marketing content, and client documents for CID, the Commercial Insurance Division, and beautifying digital presentations and health insurance summary booklets for the Benefits Department.

"Penny for your...oh hey, Miss Belle," Kyle said as he approached my desk.

Miss Belle shot me a knowing glance. "Baby girl, this is your best work yet. I'm so glad Phil gave you that Super Star award, because you earned it, child." Turning her attention to my best friend's brother, she added, "Kyle Goldstein, don't you go making Rebecca's life any more difficult than it needs to be, you hear? A body needs to be able to work in peace." With a self-satisfied nod, Miss Belle marched back to her cubicle.

Mildly offended, Kyle said, "What was that all about?"

I gestured to my desk covered in stacks of finished and in-process work requests. "I think she meant my workload."

"So, how have you been?" he drawled.

I raised a brow. "You all right?"

"I need to talk to you about something, Beck, and I can't do it here. Can you meet me downstairs in the lobby in a few minutes?"

"Sure."

Before Kyle could elaborate further, we both heard the sound of loafers and jangling keys approaching. Darting away from my cubicle, Kyle said, "If Margolin sees me over here again, he'll report me to Bonnie. Meet you downstairs."

Moments later, Ted's squeaking shoes halted as he checked to see if his most recent document sat up on my computer screen. "Looks like you finished those revisions I sent," he said. "I'll get you some more shortly."

I spun around to face the mighty Margolin, very aware of my bare calves and shoeless, newly pedicured feet. I crossed my legs at the ankle, pointed my toes, and smiled sweetly.

"No problem, Ted. Anything else you need?"

He inhaled a taut breath through his nose, and my smile naturally broadened in response. To my astonishment, the mighty Margolin smiled back. With a slow gaze traveling from my toes to my eyes, his expression held an appreciative gleam. Feeling the spark of something wonderful burst within me, I beamed at the mighty Margolin.

Then, panic set in. My mind flashed to that final meeting with Pastor, and the old ghosts resurrected to ruin the moment. I looked over just in time to see Kyle sneaking out the side door.

Hastily donning my sandals, I said, "Sorry, Ted, but I forgot I need to speak with someone right now. Please, excuse me."

I tried to brush past him, but the mighty Margolin refused to budge. "Are you okay, Rebecca?" he said. "What just happened?"

I forced myself to meet Ted's potent gaze, noting flecks of gold in his hazel eyes. He, of all people, might be able to unearth the secrets I kept so carefully buried. The thought terrified me to death.

"Rebecca," he said low, leaning closer to find answers in my eyes.

I shook my head and maneuvered around him. "I *have* to go."

The sensation of Ted's eyes on me hastened my sprint out of the office. I opted to take the stairs, needing the extra time to recalibrate before seeing my friend. Once I reached the lobby, Kyle hissed at me to join him in a semi-private alcove.

"I'm really worried about Jessica," he said as soon as I joined him.

"What do you mean?"

"Well, you know she's still seeing that Nathan guy, right?"

"Really? The last time Jessica mentioned him, she said he only wanted one thing. I assumed an imminent breakup."

"The one thing is marriage. Nathan wants a wife."

"Since when?" I asked. "Jessica cancelled our last three lunch dates, but I just assumed she's been bogged down with paralegal work. She said they landed Halpern Industries last month, and it means millions for the firm. I had no idea things had gotten so serious with Nathan."

"What do we do, Beck? He's one of those Messianic Jews for Jesus. He'll force my sister to convert."

"I thought Messianic Jews still practiced Judaism," I said, confused.

"You can't be Jewish and believe in Jesus," Kyle huffed.

"Well, I'm Jewish."

"Since when, Preacher's Kid?"

"Since my mother converted to marry my father, and her maiden name is Shapiro."

Kyle studied my face. "You know, I always thought you had a *yiddishe punim*."

"A what?"

"It means a 'Jewish face,' and your mother's story doesn't make me feel any better about this Nathan guy."

"Kyle, if you want someone to talk to your sister, it needs to be you. I'm done being put in the middle with you two. We're all grownups here. You need to let your sister make her own mistakes."

"Don't you care that Jessica could ruin her life? The same way your mom did?"

I sucked in a breath. "Low blow, dude."

Kyle sighed. "You're right, I'm sorry. I'm just worried about her, Beck. My rabbi calls Messianic Judaism a cult."

"Then, why don't you go scope out Nathan's church and find out for yourself?"

"Apparently, they call it a synagogue, and if I'm going, I'm taking you with me."

"Think again, pal. I'm not going anywhere near organized religion right now."

From just beyond my left shoulder I heard, "What about organized work? Are the two of you avoiding that as well?" Ted Margolin stood three feet away, controlled anger simmering below the surface.

"Margolin, we're in the middle of a private conversation," Kyle said with uncharacteristic backbone.

"Well, you promised an updated claims report to Triple J fifteen minutes ago, Goldstein, and nobody could find you." Looking between the two of us with palpable disgust, Ted added, "I would suggest the two of you exercise some self-control and save the flirting for after hours."

Infuriated at the accusation, especially after what had nearly happened upstairs, I lit into Ted. "Per our state's right-to-work laws, *Mr. Margolin*, I am entitled to one, fifteen-minute break per four hours of work. According to my cell phone," I pulled it out for good measure, "I still have eight minutes left. If you need Kyle for some sort of client issue, so be it, but don't cast aspersions on my character when you have absolutely no idea what you're talking about."

Kyle's blue eyes widened to the edges of his obnoxious glasses.

Meanwhile, the mighty Margolin looked like he'd just sucked on a lemon. "Are you quite finished, *Miss Ivy*?"

Ted and I deadlocked into an angry staring contest, neither of us willing to look away. As my eyes took in strong cheekbones, a slightly large nose, and lips angrily compressed into a thin line, I noticed an imperfection I hadn't seen earlier during our morning elevator ride together.

Tapping my left cheek, I said, "You missed a spot shaving in the car." Then, I unleashed megawatt supernova on the mighty Margolin.

Ted stood there red and speechless, and I pulled a gaping Kyle into an open elevator. As my friend burst into hysterics loud enough for the entire building to hear, I pounded the "close door" button on the elevator like my life depended on it.

CHAPTER 5

EITHER BY CHANCE OR BY DESIGN, THE MIGHTY Margolin avoided me like the plague with scheduled client meetings across the country. Kyle called our little scene the most hilarious thing he'd ever witnessed. He also found requited love in the form of our new, twenty-something receptionist, Morgan. She returned Kyle's front desk flirtation with equal gusto, giving the office gossip mill something to do other than complain about each other.

After one particularly grueling day in the office, I came home to find ten different messages in my email account and fifteen others on social media.

"What in the world?" I wondered aloud. I clicked on the first email and my stomach dropped.

Dear Rebecca,

I know you don't want to talk about what happened at SBC, and I've tried to respect that. You're still missed here, even though

Pastor and Cynthia have had a few unkind things to say
about you...

"A few? Unkind?" I said in disbelief. "That's the understate-
ment of the century."

I'm writing because Pastor made a shocking announcement after
Bible study tonight. In case you didn't know, Ashley and the chil-
dren stopped coming to church six months ago. Pastor revealed
Ashley's long term drug addiction. He seemed so broken about the
whole thing, even crying a few times. You could feel the heaviness
in the room. We all knew Ashley was irritable and unfriendly, but
this is almost too much to believe.

"Because it isn't true," I said, twisting the bottom part of my
shirt into knots.

After all of that, Pastor tells us he's marrying Cynthia Russell.
Can you believe it?! I had no idea Cynthia and Jeremy even sepa-
rated. Turns out, they got divorced two months ago. Pastor says
he tried to make it work with Ashley for the sake of the kids, but
he just couldn't negotiate with an angry addict. I don't remember
if he explained what happened with the Russells' marriage, but it
all just seems so sudden.

Pastor quoted some Bible verses about not speaking against lead-
ership, and then he told us to trust in God's sovereignty. He says
they've left their old lives behind to forge this new ministry God
wants them to do together. Maybe I'm being too sensitive, but this
really doesn't sit right with me. I'm sure that Pastor spends hours
a day praying and reading the Word, but I just can't make sense

*of this. I know you're not his biggest fan, but you've always been
so encouraging. Help!*

I shut the screen of my laptop after the fifth email, not
wanting to hear about the supposed shock of my former congregants, or worse, their actual support of Pastor. I found it uncon-
scionable for any self-professed Christian to endorse Pastor's
behavior. From the pulpit, Pastor had always extolled the benefits of marriage, of husband and wife mirroring the mysterious
nature of God. Conveniently, he never addressed how spouses
couldn't be forced to testify against one another during criminal
proceedings. My heart ached for all of those naïve SBC sheep
when the real truth would come to light.

The barrage of emails persisted over the next few days. I
finally took a social media sabbatical, needing a break from the
growing list of people coming to me for answers. To their credit,
most of the congregants didn't buy the convenient sob story.
From suspicion came accusations against Pastor, followed by
assumptions that I'd left because I somehow knew these events
would transpire.

Have they been having an affair all this time?

Have you talked to Jeremy?

Have you talked to Ashley?

*I know this isn't right, but Pastor and Cynthia are
such godly people.*

His sermons are still so anointed.

Everybody makes mistakes.

Let he who is without sin cast the first stone.

There's no way I can stay at SBC with an unrepentant sinner in the pulpit.

There's no way I could ever leave SBC. This is my home.

As best I could, I supplied generic, vague answers. If I could barely accept the truth witnessed with my own two eyes, how would anyone else? Members who had believed the slander spread about me condescended me as a would-be homewrecker in one paragraph, but then hungrily fished for details in the next.

"Make this right, Lord," I prayed, finally at my limit. "I still struggle believing the evil I actually witnessed, but I see the fruit of it in all of this deception. Open the eyes of the blind too determined to ignore the truth because they'd rather believe the lie. Oh, Jesus, please make them uncomfortable enough to finally deal with the sin in the camp. I ask for vindication for all that's been done to me, for all of the years they played with my mind and laughed at how they manipulated me. Jesus..." my voice broke as tears streamed down my cheeks. "Jesus, they need you so much, and they don't even realize it."

And then I wept.

For two weeks, I cried off and on, allowing myself to experience the grief of an illusion I had believed for thirteen years. I finally gave myself permission to be angry about the manipulation and abuse of power. My best friend sat on the phone with me for much of it, eventually inviting me over one night as respite from my tears.

We sat in Jessica's family room watching our favorite super-hero rescue Stirling City with his crossbow.

"He's so hot," Jessica groaned, practically drooling before she shoved a handful of popcorn in her mouth.

"I'm pretty sure that's why they hired him," I said with a wink and a grin.

My best friend glanced over at me, then clicked pause on the TV. "How are you doing, Beck?"

"Better," I said, adjusting my legs underneath me on her sofa. "I didn't realize how much I just needed to let it all out. I don't know how I stayed at that place as long as I did."

"Are the SBC sheeple finally leaving you alone?"

I shrugged. "I haven't been on social media in a while, so hopefully, they took the hint."

"And things at work are going well?" she asked.

I raised a brow. "Yeah. Why?"

"I've just been really worried about you is all."

"I told you. I'm doing a lot better."

"Kyle wondered if you might be uncomfortable with him dating the receptionist. He said you didn't exactly seem cool with it."

I rolled my eyes. "Totally not jealous. I actually like Morgan. She's great at what she does. Phil gave her some public kudos at the last birthday meeting."

"I can't believe you guys do those birthday things. It's so corny."

"Why? You can't go wrong with a cake from Georgie's regardless of the reason."

"True," she conceded. "Their wedding cakes are gorgeous!"

I cleared my throat. "Anything I should know about, Jessica Margaret Goldstein?"

My best friend blushed prettily. Hesitantly, she said, "Not

yet. But things look like they might be headed in that direction."

"And you're okay with the whole Messianic thing?"

"Not really, but I love him, Beck. Nathan treats me better than anyone else ever has. He makes me feel so—"

"Loved?" I finished for her.

"Yeah," she said with a sigh.

My best friend appeared radiant and happy. I expected to feel that empty ache, that pang of wondering when it would be my turn to love and be loved. Instead, absolute joy welled up within me. I was thrilled to see my best friend treated like the incredible gift she was. I returned her smile with one of my own.

"I'm so happy for you, Jessica. Please, know that."

"Well, don't go planning my bridal shower just yet," she said playfully.

I raised an eyebrow. Jessica had mapped out her dream wedding since elementary school.

"Okay, fine. But I want a cupcake tower, turquoise and silver decor, and for the love of all things holy, do not allow a shred of lingerie at that shower. My mother lives to see me publicly embarrassed."

"Done. Now put Crossbow back on."

A month later, Jessica's potential engagement became official, and the days moved quickly thereafter. My thirty-third birthday came and went. Summer still clung to the first few days of October, and I found myself back on my favorite bench outside of my office building. With my Bible open next to me, I basked in the last shards of summer sunlight.

My eyes flew open at the sound of that oh so familiar squeak and jangle. Either the mighty Margolin didn't see me, or he pretended he didn't. From where I sat on the bench, he had already walked past me and now faced Captain's Grille, one of several restaurants situated at the base of our office high rise complex. A leggy blonde approached and kissed his cheek. Ted responded with a genuine smile, one that reached his eyes. The blonde seemed perfect for a guy like Ted Margolin. Dressed in a fitted black suit and sky high, patent leather stilettos, she embodied the Parkview stereotype to a tee. I immediately felt frumpy in my red top, white skirt, and sandals.

I watched Ted for a few more moments as he and Corporate Supermodel disappeared into the restaurant. Forcing my gaze away from Captain's Grille, I picked up my Bible. To my horror, I realized I'd finished with the closing chapters of *Ecclesiastes'* wisdom and moved right into the passionate love story of *Song of Solomon*.

Glancing up at Heaven, I said aloud, "Not funny, and so not ready for this right now." I gestured toward the restaurant and added, "Like I could ever compete with that."

I skipped *Song of Solomon* and dove into *Isaiah* before my cell phone alerted me break time was over. Morosely, I headed toward the office kitchenette for a sugar fix. I found myself ill prepared when Ted walked into the room wearing a large smile. It widened when he spotted the empty, hot cocoa packages to my left.

"Hitting the hard stuff?" he teased.

Lunch with Corporate Supermodel had certainly put the mighty Margolin in a friendlier mood. I pressed my lips into a tight smile and devoted my energies to that whirring coffee machine as if I'd never beheld such a feat of human ingenuity.

"Look, Rebecca, I just wanted to say—" before Ted could finish, his hand touched my arm.

My arm that now held a very full cup of cocoa.

The jolt of electricity from Ted sent my drink tumbling, and cocoa spilled all over the counter and down my white skirt.

As I fought the urge to dissolve into a sobbing heap of mortification, my lower lip trembled. Ted took notice of both lips, and he stared longer than a man who had just enjoyed lunch with Corporate Supermodel probably should.

"Ted?" I breathed, poised to receive something much better than an RFP from the mighty Margolin.

Returning to his senses, Ted vigorously shook his head and took a large step away from me. "This," he gestured between the two of us, "is not a good idea. I don't know what exactly *this* is, but I meant it when I said I take our company's sexual harassment policy seriously. I'm sorry for anything I've done to scare you or make you uncomfortable, Rebecca. I promise, it won't happen again." He reached for the paper towels and handed a few to me as a peace offering. He began wiping the counter with a fury.

"Who's the blonde?" I blurted out, dabbing at my ruined skirt.

Ted stilled, then studied me for a moment. "Here I thought you were working on your tan and reading *Song of Solomon*."

My mouth opened and then quickly closed. "I didn't realize you saw me. Or my Bible."

"Likewise. And *the blonde* is the Loss Control Vice President from Culver's Nashville office. She's also an old friend. Not unlike your good buddy, Kyle."

Before I could respond, our mischievous CEO burst through the door. Phil surveyed my skirt, the guilty look on Ted's face, and then he grinned.

"Well, buy the girl a new outfit, would ya, Margolin? It's not like you can't afford it."

I blushed. "My fault, Phil. Bit of a butterfingers today."

"I've seen Margolin spill coffee in this room at least twenty times, but I appreciate you trying to cover for him, Rebecca. If he doesn't give you at least a hundred bucks for some new clothes, come see me, and I'll make him double it."

Not missing a beat, Ted pulled a pair of hundred dollar bills from his wallet and handed them to me. "Satisfied, Phil?" Frowning, he threw the paper towels into the trash and stormed out of the room.

Phil tipped his head back and laughed while I cleaned up the remains of my mess.

"I didn't really think Ted would go for that, but I love busting his chops and knocking the mighty Margolin down a few pegs. Sometimes, he forgets he's human like the rest of us."

I looked down at the hundred dollar bills now crumpled in my hand. "You know I can't keep this money, Phil."

"The heck you can't!" he exclaimed. "Take the money and go buy yourself something cute. Then, make sure you wear it to the office. When you see Margolin, tell him he paid for it."

I promptly turned as red as my shirt.

"He's sweet on you, Rebecca, but I'm sure you already knew that."

"Phil, you're not my fairy godmother, and I'm not Cinderella," I said, placing the two crumpled bills firmly in his palm. "Give Ted his money, and please tell him it was just a joke. I have enough drama in my life right now. The last place I need it is on the job."

Phil sobered immediately. "Did I overstep my bounds there, Rebecca? I really thought you would find this as funny as I did."

I offered a half smile. "My heart is too broken for anybody right now, Phil. I appreciate the thought, but we get paid on Friday. I can buy my own skirt. Thanks anyway."

I walked out of the breakroom, avoided Ted's office at all costs, and got back to my mountain of work. After returning from a quick bathroom break, the hundred dollar bills had migrated back to my desk along with a note that read,

Truly sorry for any embarrassment, but you deserve something nice. Keep the money. - Ted

I stared at the wrinkled bills for a long time before tossing them into my purse. Kyle made me promise to scope out Nathan's church/synagogue with him, and I had reluctantly agreed to go. Thanks to Ted Margolin, I would at least have a new outfit to wear when we went.

CHAPTER 6

PULLING INTO THE PARKING LOT OF NATHAN'S Messianic synagogue, I beheld a contemporary stucco structure not unlike many non-denominational churches in the area. The stained glass Star of David window proudly proclaimed *Congregation Beth Shalom* as a Jewish building, yet the inside boasted the same style nave and narthex, the same raised solea and podium stand as my father's church. Kyle and Nathan both feared I might suffer from culture shock based on my church upbringing, but aside from Jewish artifacts and the men wearing prayer shawls and satin skullcaps, it all felt surprisingly familiar. I waited just inside the doors as Kyle arrived ten minutes after me.

"So what do you think?" Kyle said close to my ear.

"I think you look like a deer in headlights."

"Anything screaming, 'Hey I'm a cult!' to you?"

I chuckled. "Other than the same architect apparently designing every house of worship back in the '80s, nothing yet. It looks like First United minus the green carpet."

Kyle turned to me. "Are you okay being here? I mean, no more flashbacks or triggers?"

"None so far, but I did leave SBC over a year ago. It also helps knowing my father and Pastor won't waltz through the front doors."

"Speaking of," Kyle said, glancing at his watch, "time to bite the bullet and get in there."

Moving from the nave, we nodded wordlessly at the ushers holding open the double doors to the Beth Shalom sanctuary. Inside sat twenty rows of theater style chairs in three columns, eight seats in each row. Kyle maneuvered us to the right and grabbed a spot toward the back. Just like the chairs at SBC, they outfitted the backs with a large pocket containing a Bible and what appeared to be a purple hymnal. A smaller pocket filled with tithing envelopes rested just below. Picking up the thin purple book, I flipped it over and read the word *"siddur."*

"Kyle?" I asked, holding up the purple anomaly, "do you know what a 'sitter' is?"

Surprise registered on his face. "You mean a siddur? They actually have those here?" He grabbed the book from my hand and flipped through it.

"What's the deal with the backward pages?"

Kyle finally smiled. "It's not backward. Hebrew reads right to left."

"Do the sitters in your synagogue look like this?"

"*Sih-DOER*," Kyle said slowly, "and sort of. The transliteration is a little weird though."

"The what?"

Kyle sighed. "Are you sure about these Jewish grandparents of yours?"

I rolled my eyes. "I'm sure my father is a racist anti-Semite, so please forgive me if you find my knowledge of Jewish customs somewhat lacking."

Kyle's eyes widened. "No wonder Margolin likes you."

I proceeded to choke on my own spit.

Kyle continued on unaffected. "I know we've joked about the mighty Margolin treating you like a personal assistant, but he seems more like your personal protector lately. He cracked down on CID for dropping stuff on your desk last minute, and he called you the best thing to ever happen at Culver right in front of Morgan. He told Phil he liked knowing we had someone in the office he couldn't steamroll."

Too stunned to do much else, I nodded.

Kyle noticed the look on my face and asked, "Did I say something wrong?"

"Um, no, I'm fine. Just a little surprised is all. I had no idea the mighty Margolin said all of those things about me."

"I think Margolin gained a new respect for you when you told him off by the elevators. Sometimes it takes a ballbuster to appreciate another one."

"I am hardly a..." I stammered.

"Maybe not a year ago, Beck, but you've changed. You got a lot more self-sufficient and a lot less needy."

Not sure whether to be insulted or humiliated at my easily perceived pain, I responded with a tight smile and observed the people around me. Two gentlemen donning prayer shawls and *yarmulkes* spoke quietly on the stage, what Kyle informed me they called a *bima*, and I spotted an armoire with Hebrew letters on the doors. Kyle called it an "ark," and presumably, it housed a Torah scroll inside. I knew "the Torah" as the writings of Moses, but I didn't anticipate those 3,500 year-old writings to still be penned and read in the original, ancient Hebrew. I felt

Kyle's pride in his history and heritage as I soaked in every word.

"Look, don't feel bad for asking questions, Beck. I think it's pretty awesome you want to learn about it," he said with an encouraging wink.

Before I could formulate a reply, the service leader spoke into the podium microphone. I spotted Nathan on the front row in a purple button down and gray slacks. Jessica's absence showed just how uncomfortable she still found the Messianic synagogue.

Following a few introductory remarks, the leader instructed us to open a siddur and read the Jewish liturgy responsively. I found the Hebrew chanting hauntingly beautiful. Kyle's face showed a mixture of surprise and confusion.

I leaned in and whispered, "You okay?"

"Not really."

"What's wrong? This is Hebrew, isn't it?"

Kyle grimaced. "Yeah, but not how we do it."

"What do you mean?"

"I don't know. It's just different. And there's usually a lot less people."

I surveyed the room. It seemed about three quarters full with more people entering from the nave. "Isn't it good to see people in the pews?"

"Ask the people in Waco, Texas."

I rolled my eyes. "Give it a chance at least. No red flags just yet."

We went through an extensive portion of Hebrew prayers, the English translation following afterward. Looking in the siddur and having the Hebrew words transliterated meant I could reconcile the sounds I heard with how it appeared phonetically on the page. I enjoyed the deep reverence of the prayers, the obvious devotion and awe of God by the original writers. I recognized some of the prayers as direct Scripture references while others simply offered up high praise to the God of Israel. The liturgy spoke to something deep within me, creating a longing to learn more about my recently discovered heritage.

After a series of Bible readings and accompanying blessings, the worship band played three songs, one I'd never heard followed by two, contemporary Christian songs. Kyle glanced at me multiple times hoping to gauge my reaction, and I shrugged. The song choices surprised me as well. Though they substituted the words "Jesus" with "Yeshua" and "Christ" with "Mashiach," nothing in this part of the Messianic service distinguished itself from any other church service I'd attended.

I waited expectantly to hear the rabbi offer some kind of ancient wisdom, some deeper understanding of the Bible because of the rich Jewish heritage he possessed. I wondered how much of his teaching would differ from my seminary educated father or former pastor. Sadly, the sermon consisted of lofty platitudes and pandering commentary on the state of the world. Also frustrating were the tangential anecdotes just when I thought the rabbi might finally dig into a meaty portion of his sermon.

"What am I listening to?" Kyle muttered to me.

"I'm still figuring that out," I said. "Does Rabbi Epstein give messages at your synagogue like this?"

Kyle shook his head. "Not even close."

I frowned.

Following the end of the service, several people beelined toward us. They seemed overly interested in getting our reaction, and it was clear they expected us to be as enthralled with Beth Shalom as they were. As they talked up the synagogue and all of the "exciting" upcoming events, Kyle's eyes darted toward the exit. With a practiced smile, I thanked the members for their hospitality, but I declined their offers to join them for coffee and bagels in the fellowship hall. Kyle pulled me toward the front doors, and I followed his lead.

Texting me from his car, he invited me to join him at Burger Palace to debrief about the evening. Kyle didn't seem to relax until our food arrived.

I glanced at my phone to check the time. "You said Morgan was going to meet us here, right? Did she say what time?"

Kyle took another bite of his burger. "She promised to take her son to a movie, and then she'd head over once she dropped him off at her parents' house."

I nearly gagged on a french fry. "Morgan has a son? How old is she again?"

Nonchalantly, he swallowed his bite of burger and replied, "Her son is five. Morgan's twenty-four. Did I tell you she got married right out of high school?"

I grabbed my water and took a sip to get the fry moving down my esophagus. "No, um, I don't think you mentioned that. How do you feel about being a stepdad?"

Kyle looked at me for a minute, then bent his head back and laughed. "Stepdad, Beck? Are you serious? We just started dating!"

"Does she know you're not serious? That you think it's *just dating*?"

Kyle held his hands up in self-defense. "Don't start projecting all of your man-hating angst on me, Beck."

"Man-hating angst?" I repeated shrilly. "Man. Hating. ANGST?"

"I rest my case."

I promptly threw a french fry at him.

"Exhibit A, your honor. A normal person would actually eat the best french fries available in the tri-county area. Instead, the defendant hurled this poor, unsuspecting, fried potato at my head. Clearly, she's gone unhinged."

I stuck my tongue out at Kyle, then ate a fry for good measure. "Perfectly sane, your honor."

"Speaking of, what did you think of Beth Shalom," he said with a tinge of mockery. "Weird, or what?"

"I'm assuming you want me to compare a lifetime of church weirdness with what we experienced tonight."

A side of Kyle's mouth lifted. "Good guess."

I paused, collecting my thoughts. "I really enjoyed the Jewish liturgy, but the sermon bounced all over the place. I don't know if I should blame Nathan for my sky high expectations or myself, but I don't feel like it lived up to how he advertised it. I'm kind of disappointed, actually. The members all seemed pretty into it, though."

"I have a hard time believing the Messianic rabbi has ever had any legitimate, Jewish training," Kyle said.

"Why?" I said in surprise. "How is Nathan's guy different from Rabbi Epstein? You and Jessica have attended *Beth Tefillah* your whole lives, so you know better than I do. What do you guys do in a Reform temple that they didn't do in the Messianic one?"

"Well, for one thing, Rabbi Epstein actually pronounces his Hebrew correctly. I can give this Messianic guy a pass for talking about Jesus since we all know what kind of a place it is, but how can you call yourself a rabbi and then butcher the language? Why not just call it a Jewish church instead of pretending it's a traditional synagogue? I don't know, Beck. That place just creeped me out."

"The sermon sounded exactly like my father's preaching

style. Frankly, most of the service felt like high church at First United. As we both know, that's hardly a recommendation."

"And you're absolutely sure it's not a cult, Beck? Seems like a few too many coincidences if you ask me."

"I don't know, Kyle, I'm hardly unbiased here. My father fakes his spirituality so well that anyone who reminds me of him automatically makes me suspicious."

"Have you heard from him lately?"

"Heard from who?" Morgan asked, sliding in next to Kyle and planting a kiss on his cheek. "Hey, Rebecca."

I smiled at our blonde, highlighted receptionist who barely looked a day over twenty. Kyle put his arm around her with a look of admiration I had never seen from him before. I suddenly felt very old.

And alone.

Forcing a bright smile on my face, I stood up and said, "Why don't you guys make this a date? I've got some errands to run in the morning, and I won't sleep if I eat any more food this late. Kyle, what do I owe you?"

Breaking away from his Morgan-induced trance, Kyle startled, suddenly remembering my presence. "Don't worry about it, Beck. Go have fun binge watching Crossbow and doing all of your adulting tomorrow."

I rolled my eyes, but laughed. He knew me too well.

CHAPTER 7

STILL FOUR WEEKS AWAY FROM THANKSGIVING, MY local stores had already ditched the Halloween decor and moved right into plastic Christmas trees and inflatable, front yard display items. The year before, I had spent Thanksgiving weeping into my frozen turkey dinner, secretly missing the taste of my mother's sweet potato casserole but not her constant jabs about how much food went on my plate.

I thought back to four years earlier, when the black sheep of the Ivy family had her life together. Engaged and already going through Christian premarital counseling, I hoped my parents could finally be proud of me.

"You look nervous," Jason said as we stood outside the door of my parents' massive, colonial home.

Eyeing the house that hypocrisy built, I said, "One would expect a shepherd of God's people to help those truly in need, right? You know, like giving aid to widows, orphans, and struggling families."

"One would expect," Jason said dryly. "What about your parents?"

I rolled my eyes. "My father gives nothing to anyone outside of his circle of congregational sycophants. You have to be a member in good standing to receive any benevolence money from First United."

"What exactly does that mean?" Jason asked.

"In other words, you better pay into the kitty if you want to get anything back."

"Sounds very holy," he mocked.

"My father preaches about 'storehouse tithing' almost weekly, telling people that the secret to unlocking God's blessing in their lives means pouring ten percent of their gross income into the church coffers. He belittles Judaism as backward and under the law, but he finds no problem quoting verses from the Old Testament supposedly proving his understanding of tithing as valid."

"Are you saying he's wrong?" Jason asked, searching my eyes.

"One morning, I told my father I found two passages from *Deuteronomy* describing a very different picture of tithing than the one he preaches. I showed him verses from chapters twelve and fourteen, thinking I had made this incredible discovery. Instead, my father looked at me like I was Satan himself."

While Jason mulled over my words, I took a deep breath, pushing away memories of my father backhanding me and ferociously yelling mere inches from my face.

"What happened after that, Becca?"

Swallowing back the pain, I replied, "He said only an unlearned, rebellious sinner would dare criticize their God ordained authority. For six weeks, he treated me like a ghost haunting the house, only acknowledging my existence at church to keep parishioners from gossiping. My mother finally guilted me into apologizing to him, saying I broke my father's heart with my false accusations. Not long after that, I left First United and found my way to SBC. You know the rest of the story after that."

Jason smiled down at me. "I'm glad that's all in your past, Becca. You can finally conquer your fears today."

Puzzled by his remark, I raised an eyebrow while Jason rang the doorbell.

My sister, Ada, opened the door for us. "Thank God, you're here," she breathed. "Now they can lay off of me and Tammy."

"Good to see you too, Sis."

Ada rolled her eyes. "Whatever. Just don't start preaching about homosexuality is a sin. Dad already tried that, and I threatened to leave. I still can't believe we have an entire holiday celebrating a dead animal on the table."

"Hi, I'm Jason," my fiancé said with an artificial smile. "You must be Ada. Nice sleeve by the way," he said, gesturing to the array of tattoos peeking out from her t-shirt.

Ada startled for half a second before regaining her composure. "What do you know about tats?"

Jason winked at her. "More than you think."

My lesbian sister actually blushed at my fiancé. "Thanks for not bringing home a loser," she said, turning on her smile for Jason. With ease, my baby sister both addressed me and dismissed me all in the same breath.

Jason's grip tightened in mine and he maneuvered his way past Ada, leading me into the Ivy house of horrors. He whistled as he took in his new surroundings. "This place looks like a museum," he murmured. "Beautiful, well-polished, and cold."

"I'm so glad it's not just me," I said close to his ear. I leaned in for extra warmth.

"So, here's the man who thinks my daughter is good enough to marry," my father said grandly, entering the room.

Jason raised an eyebrow. "Don't you mean 'who's good enough for my daughter'?"

My father continued as if Jason had said nothing. "Welcome to our humble abode. As you can see, we don't live like royalty, but God has faithfully provided a modest home for us." With a heaping dose of feigned piety, he added, "It's all for *His* glory, of course."

"My mother lives in a double wide in Manchester," Jason said without missing a beat. "I'm pretty sure she'd call this a mansion."

My sister overheard the exchange and gagged on her tongue ring.

"You okay, Ada?" I asked sweetly.

"Where did you find him?" she said in my ear.

"Biker bar," I quipped.

Ada looked me up and down for a minute. "You're different."

I smiled. "I'm in love."

"He's hot, I'll give you that."

"I thought you were a lesbian."

"Doesn't mean I'm blind."

Joining the conversation with my father and Jason, my mother said, "A trailer park, hmm? My, how...interesting."

"Does your mom date sweaty bikers with lots of tattoos?" my sister said with a smirk. "Jason seems to know a lot about body ink, so I thought I'd ask."

Ada faltered at my fiancé's look of disgust. "Actually, she and my stepdad have been married for almost twenty years. They like to travel, so they don't see much need for a big, fancy house," he said, his eyes sweeping over my parents' ornate furniture and artwork.

The temperature in the room dropped about thirty degrees. Ever the peacemaker, I quickly interjected, "Mmm, Mom, it smells wonderful in here. Is dinner almost ready?"

"Not here five minutes and she's already asking about food," my father said. He glared at me like a dead cockroach on the floor.

I turned to Jason, anticipating another scathing rejoinder, but he just looked back at me expectantly. After an awkward silence, my father smirked and sermonized the room at large. He commented on God's beneficence to our family

"Don't forget how hard your mother worked on the cooking," he tacked onto his lecture. "Even if the food proves average at best, we can still *act* grateful for her efforts today."

Your family is amazing," Jason said, heavy sarcasm belying the plastic smile on his lips. "I've never heard someone disguise an insult inside of a compliment inside of a guilt trip so well."

"Why didn't you say anything?" I hissed.

"When?"

"When my father made that snide remark about me and the food?"

Jason searched my eyes, too many emotions on his face to decipher. "Why didn't *you* say something, Rebecca? This is your family."

"Well, you defended your mother when my sister made that inappropriate joke."

"She's my mother."

"I'm your fiancée."

"You're a big girl, Rebecca. It's time to start acting like one. You can't keep looking for some man to save you."

Devastated by Jason's betrayal, my mouth snapped shut. I

walked to the dining room like a lamb to the slaughter, beseeching God to intervene on my behalf while emotionally distancing myself from Jason.

"You prepare a table before me in the presence of my enemies," I murmured, wiping tears from cheeks. Jason looked pained, but he remained uncharacteristically stoic.

Once the meal began, my brother ignored everyone but his latest girlfriend, and my sister boasted about her relationship with Tammy to see how far she could push my parents. I withdrew inside myself to avoid being noticed. Unfortunately, no matter how full or empty my plate remained, my mother found something to criticize.

"Oh, Rebecca, can't you save some food for everybody else? Maybe your fiancé wanted the last roll."

"Oh. I thought we had more in the kitchen," I said quietly.

"Still taking me for granted, I see. I suppose you expect me to go get them even though I just sat down from serving everyone," she said with practiced martyrdom.

"Mom, I—"

She cut me off with a wave of her hand. "The last thing you need to do is poke around in the kitchen or stuff your face with extras with nobody watching. I'll get them myself."

Again, I looked to Jason, my eyes imploring him to do something.

Anything.

He did nothing.

"You're going to have to reign that one in," my father said to Jason, cutting into his turkey with surgical precision. "Ungrateful, selfish, and gluttonous. You're actually the first man Rebecca has ever brought home. We began to wonder if she'd turn out like Ada."

"What's that supposed to mean?" Tammy said, wrapping a possessive arm around my sister.

"We've accepted Ada's, ahem, *lifestyle*," my mother said, re-entering the room with a fresh basket of rolls, "but we expected more from Rebecca since she abandoned First United for not meeting her holier-than-thou standards."

Daniel and his girlfriend watched the entire exchange like a ping pong match. Better to remain quiet and let my parents assume he agreed with them. It kept him from the line of fire.

"Would it kill you to say something?" I whispered furiously to Jason.

Inexplicably silent, my fiancé stared at his plate.

"Aren't you going to take a roll, Rebecca?" my mother demanded.

"Not that she needs another one," my father said loud enough for everyone to hear.

"I, um…" I faltered, blinking back tears.

"Just as well," my mother said primly, laying her napkin in her lap. "You hardly need any more food, Rebecca. A little self-control would do you good."

"Unacceptable!" my father bellowed seconds later. "After all of the trouble your mother went through to go and fetch them for you, Rebecca Joanne, you could at least show some gratitude rather than sit there and pout. Your mission in life seems to be ruining every family get together with your flair for the dramatic."

I closed my eyes and counted to ten. *Endure the suffering as a worker of Christ*, Pastor had told me time and again. I repeated the words in my mind, using them to console my aching heart.

"Thank you for dinner, Mom. Everything is delicious," I said brightly, willing myself to take the high road and not stoop to their petty insults.

My father jumped to his feet and snatched the basket of bread. "No need to stuff your face with more of these, Rebecca. You barely squeezed yourself into that dress as it is." Turning to my brother, he said sweetly, "Daniel, would you like a roll? Your mother bought them pre-made, so at least we know they're edible."

I suffered through the rest of that nightmarish dinner, numb and silent long after Jason dropped me off at home. I emailed Pastor later that evening and detailed the events of the dinner fiasco. Two days later at our next premarital counseling session, tears of gratitude filled my eyes when Pastor admonished Jason about a husband's role to care for and protect his wife. Jason had the audacity to look shocked and hurt, as if someone else sat at the table watching my family carve me up like the proverbial Thanksgiving turkey.

"This isn't going to work," Jason suddenly said, looking back and forth between me and Pastor.

"Now, Jason," Pastor crooned, "I understand you may feel like we're ganging up on you, but Rebecca believes in a Christian model of marriage."

If looks could kill, the scowl Pastor received from Jason should have withered him to nothing. "Spare me the phony concern about our relationship, Pastor."

"Jason!" I exclaimed.

"And you," he said, turning on me, "you're too blind to see any of it."

"What are you talking about?" I said. "My family ripped me apart, and you just let them!"

"Rebecca deserves to be loved and cared for, Jason. If pride or fear keeps you from doing your duty to protect your future wife, I have to question why we're going forward with this marriage."

"That's a really good question, isn't it?" Jason said tightly.

With a resigned sigh, Pastor said, "Rebecca, you may as well give him back the ring."

"Yeah, may as well," Jason said mockingly, his stare growing even more hateful at Pastor.

I looked between the two men, Jason radiating anger and rejection, Pastor nothing but warmth and understanding. I trusted both of these men with my heart, but only one seemed truly concerned in caring for it. Pastor's dark brown eyes met mine, compassion and encouragement in them. I *could* be strong, and with his help, I would overcome this challenge too.

Numbly, I slid my engagement ring from my finger, tears wetting my cheeks. Jason snatched it from my hand.

"Should have known this would never work," he said, stomping out of the office and slamming the door behind him.

My tears flowed without end. Pastor knelt on the floor beside me, holding my hand while grief poured unrestrained from the depths of my soul.

"He didn't deserve you," Pastor said gently. "You deserve a real man, Rebecca, a godly man who sees the virtuous woman you are."

"Oh, Pastor," I wailed, "I just want to be married. I want a family."

He handed me several tissues from his desk, and I blew my nose.

"You're a beautiful, young woman," Pastor said, his gaze intense upon me, "and you deserve so much better than Jason Whitmore."

"I love him. I thought he loved me," I said. My voice quavered, fresh tears threatening to spill. "How could I have been so blind?"

Pastor smiled softly. "Let's be thankful God spared you from a horrible marriage. I can think of nothing worse than being married to someone you can't love or respect."

Resuming my woeful sobs, Pastor lightly rubbed my back, the same way I imagined a loving father might comfort his daughter. "God has better for you, Rebecca. I'm sure of it."

CHAPTER 8

SHAKING OFF THE PAIN FROM THOSE DAYS GONE BY, I gave a silent prayer of thanks as I sat in my work cubicle rather than Pastor's office. I dabbed at the fresh tears escaping down my cheeks, patting them quickly with a tissue before taking a slow, deep breath. Jason recently emailed me about a new, serious relationship, and I genuinely congratulated him. Our tentative friendship gave a sense of finality to that painful chapter in both of our lives, and it offered hope for my own heart to heal enough to move forward. I sniffled and blew my nose.

"Are you alright, Rebecca?" the mighty Margolin asked from behind me.

I turned in my chair and looked up at him, "Getting there, thanks."

Ted inclined his head toward the balled up tissue still in my hand.

"Just some bad memories," I said quickly.

"Seems to be a recurring theme for you."

"Better to be bad memories than present reality," I said with forced gaiety.

One side of Ted's mouth lifted. "What are you doing for lunch today?"

"Oh...I...um..."

"It's not a date," he said. "Strictly professional. I wanted to treat the Guildcorp team to lunch. As an integral part of landing the account, I wanted to make sure I included you."

Touched by his thoughtfulness, I blushed slightly. "Ted, I jazzed up your RFP, but the presentation came from you guys. Besides, I'm pretty sure there's a can of soup somewhere calling my name."

"You would trade lunch at *Le Petit Versailles* for canned soup? Come on, Rebecca. This is a no-brainer." The gold in his eyes sparkled.

"You really don't need to do this, Ted."

He leaned in closer, almost conspiratorially. "But I *want* to do this, and you deserve it, Rebecca. You've been putting together these incredible documents for years, and we haven't done nearly enough to show our appreciation around here."

"Ted, I..." my voice faltered at the admiration I saw in his eyes. "It's not necessary," I said quietly.

Still in producer mode making the sale, he said, "Rebecca, I've had colleagues from at least three other firms ask me who designs our content. They've been less than subtle in asking if the right price could convince you to make a change in scenery."

"Wow."

"Exactly. So, let me take you and the team out for lunch as an incentive to keep you here at Culver."

"But this is strictly for business reasons, right?"

Ted hesitated a moment before responding. "I'd be lying if I said the prospect of sharing a meal with you didn't possess a certain appeal."

My blush deepened. "When are we supposed to leave?"

He glanced down at his watch. "Ten minutes."

No one could ever accuse Ted Margolin of lacking in the confidence department. It made him an incredible salesman. It also made him annoyingly arrogant at times.

"So, you assumed I would just drop whatever work I had going on with only ten minutes notice and all for a free lunch?" I said. "How do you know I don't already have plans?"

"Never a doubt in my mind, Rebecca."

Then he grinned.

Ted's smile was almost boyish, a slight dimple in his right cheek. His eyes were alight with playful delight.

And I was absolutely mesmerized.

For all of Jessica's talk about my own megawatt smile, when Ted truly smiled, I became sizzling butter in a hot skillet. To make matters worse, I think he knew it. I swiveled back in my chair toward my computer, closed a few windows on either monitor, and then clocked myself out as "at lunch."

Standing up, I grabbed my purse and houndstooth peacoat from my cubicle locker. "Lucky for you, I needed to take a break anyway."

"Lucky indeed," he said, clearly not buying any of it.

"Do you like my dress?" I asked.

Cherry red, knotted at the bust, and free flowing down to my knees, I felt like a million bucks in that dress. Red and gold costume jewelry adorned my neck, and nude, patent leather heels covered my feet. Rather than Corporate Supermodel, my ensemble declared "worthy of male attention."

Ted surveyed me from head to toe. "Very nice. Red definitely suits you."

"I'm glad you like it, Ted."

Dramatic pause.

"Because you paid for it."

The look on the mighty Margolin's face read initial confusion, slow comprehension, then finally, embarrassment as his face suffused with enough color to match the hue of my fabulous wardrobe piece. I sauntered to the bathroom to powder my nose, megawatt supernova my parting gift as I left a dazed Ted Margolin in its wake.

After an easy, ten minute walk to the restaurant, a little less so with my two inch heels cutting into my feet, I nearly rubbed my hands together in glee at the prospect of eating gourmet, French food. Aside from Le Petit Versailles being one of the most expensive and delicious restaurants in Parkview, I felt honored at the invitation to go as part of any Culver team. The account executives, managers, and administrators frequently ate lunch together or participated in trust building activities, usually excluding me because of my role as "the help." I maintained a friendly, superficial relationship with most of my coworkers, but the relationships began and ended with our work day.

Mercifully, Kyle also serviced the Guildcorp account, and his presence at lunch ensured things wouldn't get too weird between me and Ted. It also meant I wouldn't be excluded from conversation if Deondre and MacKenzie decided to talk shop with Ted rather than engage in standard niceties.

"*Bienvenue*," Ted greeted us, as he opened the restaurant door.

MacKenzie replied in French, as did Kyle. Deondre rolled his eyes slightly, and I just smiled. As the last to enter the restaurant, Ted's arm still stretched out behind me as he let the door close. It gave the feeling of his arm being around my waist. The room suddenly felt very warm for a crisp, early November day.

I shuffled over to Kyle who stood at the *maître d'* podium checking on our reservation.

"*Oui,* Margolin, party of five," the snooty concierge answered. I choked back a laugh at his alarming resemblance to the concierge from the teen comedy *Harris Rooney Skips School.* Even the haughty, fake accent proved right on point.

Kyle caught my eye, and we both broke into large grins. Countless viewings with Jessica meant we all quoted the movie with ease.

"Is something funny?" Ted asked close to my ear. He seemed irritated, glaring at Kyle's back as the concierge led us to our table.

I made the mistake of looking up at Ted, immediately realizing the proximity of our faces. Before I could answer, Deondre motioned for us to keep up with the rest of the group. I silently thanked God for my quick escape.

Whatever *this* was, it was alive and well.

Ted and I arrived last to the table and wound up sitting opposite one another with MacKenzie to my left, Kyle on Ted's right, and Deondre at the head of the table. I glanced over the menu, my eyes nearly bulging from their sockets at the prices, then wider still at the presence of a menu item reminding of a happier time in my life. I could barely contain my excitement when I ordered my entree, let alone when it arrived.

I released a contented sigh, twirling the long, tagliatelle pasta on my fork. "I have not eaten anything so delicious since I visited Paris twelve years ago. It tastes exactly the same!"

"That's right!" Kyle said. "The bistro!"

"Next to *L'obélisque,*" I finished. "What a find!"

"Wait, you guys were in Paris together?" Deondre said, raising an eyebrow. "This has office gossip written all over it."

MacKenzie pointed to me and Kyle. "You two? How did I not know about this? I know about everything going down at Culver!"

Kyle rolled his eyes. "Case in point why I don't tell you anything, Mac."

Ted leaned back in his chair, glancing between Kyle and me with obvious annoyance. "When were the two of you in Paris?"

"Calm down guys," Kyle laughed. "We went to college together. We also went on the same study abroad program. Beck, I don't know how you ever convinced your parents to let you go."

"That's because they still don't know," I said. "I was on scholarship already, and they didn't pay much attention when I moved on campus."

Kyle nodded in understanding while Ted raised concerned eyebrows at my parents' willful disregard. Oblivious, the rest of the Guildcorp team searched for more scintillating details.

"Oooh, *Beck*, is it?" MacKenzie purred, taking a bite from her *coq au vin*. "Keep talking."

"You guys are ridiculous," I said. "It was a semester at Oxford, and his sister went too!"

"Hold up," Deondre said. "What were you guys doing in Paris if you were studying in the UK? Sounds like something happened."

Ted's eyes zoomed in on me from across the table. It reminded me of his angry outburst when he accused Kyle of hitting on me months earlier. Realization dawning at the source of Ted's foul mood, I tried not to smile wider. If envy had an aroma, the unflappable Ted Margolin had steeped himself in a cologne bath of *Eau de Jalousie*.

"Everybody took weekend vacations while we were over there," Kyle said. "Beck always talked about going to Paris, and we had both finished our research papers. My sister got sick, so Beck and I went on one of those bus tours. We took a ferry over to Calais and then drove into Paris on the London bus."

Ted's tone softened from suspicious to genuinely curious. "What did you think of Paris, Rebecca?"

I smiled and sighed. "So beautiful! I remember walking past the *Louvre* and buying Paris postcards from some of the gypsies there. I kept looking down at my postcard and then up at the real Eiffel Tower. Pictures and movies make it seem so majestic, but in real life...I don't know."

Ted leaned in slightly, "Go ahead."

"It looked kind of like...well... Constructo blocks."

At that, Ted burst out laughing. Kyle and Deondre seemed amused, but twenty-five-year-old MacKenzie was utterly lost.

"Constructos were a toy from the '80s," Kyle said, filling in the gaps for her. "You could build with them."

Like a dog with a bone, MacKenzie said, "Forget the stupid toy! I want to know how you and Rebecca wound up on a romantic dinner date."

I rolled my eyes. "It was not romantic, and it wasn't dinner."

"Beck got lost from the tour group," Kyle said. "I decided to go searching for her because I knew she didn't speak French. I thought she might freak out being alone in a foreign city."

Picking up the story, I said, "Kyle didn't know I got bored watching the other girls on the tour try on fancy French dresses that would never fit me, so I snuck off to have my own Parisian adventure. Eventually, though..." my voice trailed off.

"Yes?" MacKenzie said, clearly hoping for some juicy details.

I shrugged my shoulders. "I had to go to the bathroom."

After a brief pause, the entire table dissolved into hysterics.

Deondre recovered first. "That is not what I was expecting to hear. TMI!"

I smirked. "If I'm lying, I'm dying."

That elicited another round of laughter.

Once the merriment died down, I continued on. "I found this hole in the wall bistro close to L'obélisque and knew enough French to get me into the ladies room. Practically starving, I figured why not stop and eat?"

"That's when I spotted her in the window of the restaurant," Kyle said. "I thought Beck would be traumatized, but she looked so happy with her bowl of french onion soup."

"French onion soup? In Paris?" MacKenzie scoffed. "That's so American!"

I shrugged. "If you're going to eat that soup anywhere, it may as well be in the place where they invented it."

Ted gestured toward my near empty plate. "Can we safely assume you enjoyed *salmon tagliatelle* for the first time in that restaurant as well?"

I smiled in response.

"She got some really cool artwork too," Kyle said around a mouthful of that same pasta dish. "Bought it straight from a street artist along the Seine."

"You have that picture hanging in your cube, don't you?" MacKenzie said. "I've always wondered about that."

Deondre looked over the rim of his glass at me and Ted seated across from each other. "Our Rebecca never ceases to amaze, does she?"

Embarrassed, I buried myself in the remains of my lunch while Ted started an in depth discussion about Guildcorp claims and losses.

CHAPTER 9

With an early afternoon team meeting, Deondre, McKenzie, and Kyle left the restaurant shortly thereafter. Ted asked if I wanted dessert, but I politely declined. No need to turn my gorgeous dress into pseudo maternity wear with a lunch bump.

Ted helped me into my coat, then pulled his wool trench around himself. "Care to take a walk with me?"

I smiled. "We can make it a leisurely stroll since these shoes are absolutely killing my feet."

Ted opened the door, and I ducked under his arm. He caught up quickly and asked, "What do women seem to love so much about uncomfortable shoes?"

"Aesthetics over functionality. I used to wear these shoes to church regularly."

"You don't wear them to church now?"

"I don't go to church now."

Ted looked down at me. "The aforementioned bad memories?"

"Yeah, you could say that."

"Does your father have anything to do with that?"

"Yes and no," I said, following his lead across a side street when the crosswalk light changed. "I thought I'd left my father's pretentious church into a place with genuine warmth and love."

"Not what you thought?"

"I made excuses for things I never should have, and I turned a blind eye to a lot more since it didn't impact me directly. Then, one day, it did, and I'll never be the same because of it."

Ted laid a hand on my arm to stop my forward progress. "How is it," he said, "that you've experienced so much heartache and grief, yet you sit in our office like this perpetual ray of sunshine?"

"I just try to treat people the way I want to be treated," I said with a shrug. "Jesus taught that. People treated me like garbage, but that doesn't mean I need to unleash my pain on the rest of the world."

Ted took both of my hands in his. He stared intently at me, then down at my lips. I inhaled a shallow breath, the air thick between us. His golden gaze traced every feature on my face, eventually returning back to my eyes and captivating me where I stood.

"I've never met anyone like you, Rebecca Ivy. You take what's wrong with the world and transform it into something beautiful. Sort of like my RFPs."

I chuckled softly.

"And," he said, his face inching closer to mine, "I think many a man has lost himself to that smile of yours."

Megawatt could not resist such an invitation. "Are you going to report yourself to Bonnie?" I teased.

"Why, do you feel harassed?" Ted said, suddenly serious. He

pulled back to better see my face. "Rebecca, did I misread something here? I was under the impression the attraction was mutual. Did I make a mistake?"

I shook my head. "I like you, Ted. A lot more than I probably should. But I'm not interested in some office fling."

"Neither am I," he said, his eyes never leaving mine.

I smiled. "So what do we do now?"

"How about a real date? Better yet, I'll cook for you."

"You? Cook?" I asked, incredulous.

"I'm a huge foodie. Beautiful gourmet kitchen with nobody to cook for."

"I guess I'm not the only one full of surprises," I said playfully, "but I think we should get back to the office before MacKenzie creates some new gossip. Deondre looked suspicious too."

"Hence, I altered the course of our lunch conversation."

"Has anyone told you how perceptive you are, Mr. Margolin?"

He grinned. "It's been mentioned a time or two."

I returned his smile with a large one of my own.

"Put that thing away, Rebecca, or I can't be held responsible for what happens next."

"I don't think Bonnie will see it that way."

"You leave her out of this."

We looked at each other and laughed. This felt *right* somehow. I had no idea if Ted believed in God, let alone Jesus, and it went against every bit of training I'd received regarding Christian dating and relationships. After the disastrous situation with Jason, I wondered at my own foolishness. However, one look into Ted's sparkling eyes provided the answer I felt in the depths of my soul. I looked away before my own eyes revealed too much.

Ted released my hands, but he walked close to me all the way to our office building. By the time we exited the elevator, Miss Belle greeted him with an emergency for our new client, Avatron, and four new proposals sat on my desk. Even with my workload free of Margolin projects at the moment, the familiar squeak and jangle found its way to my ears several times that afternoon.

A cryptically worded message to Jessica about my impromptu lunch date ensured an invite to her condo that evening. With my best friend so excited about the possible change in my love life, she didn't mind me playing the role of third wheel on her own date.

"I can't believe Mr. RFP asked you out!" Jessica squealed.

I blushed. "Yeah. He even offered to cook for me. Now, can we put Crossbow back on, please?"

"I want more details," Nathan said, winking at me. He pulled Jessica closer to him as they put the "love" in loveseat.

I rolled my eyes. "It's just a date, guys. He didn't ask me to provide him with an heir to the Margolin insurance dynasty."

"But he offered to cook for you," Jessica said.

"I doubt I'm the first female he's tried to impress with his culinary prowess."

"Beck, you've seen every episode of Sliced & Diced in triplicate. Stop pretending you aren't impressed."

"Sounds like a match made in Heaven," Nathan said, planting a kiss on Jessica. "Just like us."

Jessica sighed contentedly then held up her engagement ring to watch it catch the light from her floor lamp. The glittering diamond cast rainbows around the room.

The rainbows released the ghosts from that SBC sanctuary over a year ago.

Tell your story.

I blinked, then nearly fell over. My mind cried out, *Tell my story? To whom?*

To Ted.

Ever the optimist, I countered, *So he can reject me before he has a chance to get to know me?*

So he can help you.

"Beck?" Jessica said, alarmed. She sat up from Nathan's embrace. "Beck!" she called louder, but it sounded muffled, like I heard it from underwater. Then, everything went black.

What felt like seconds later, I woke up flanked on either side by EMTs and ambulance lights flashing from outside of Jessica's sliding glass doors. I tried to sit up, but the paramedics urged me back down.

"What happened?" I said groggily.

"You passed out, Beck," Jessica said. She clung to Nathan like a wet rag just a few feet behind the EMTs.

"When you didn't wake up, we called 911," Nathan finished.

"How many fingers am I holding up, ma'am?" one of the EMTs asked.

"One."

"And now?"

"Two."

"Do these fainting spells happen often, Rebecca?"

"Only when I have a PTSD trigger."

The two EMTs exchanged glances. The second EMT asked, "How long has that been going on?"

Not thinking, I blurted out, "Ever since I walked in on my Pastor and the women's ministry head trying to—"

"Trying to do what, Rebecca?"

"I...I don't want to talk about it. I'm fine, really. Can I sit up now? I promise, I'm okay. Please," I begged.

Grudgingly, they allowed me up. They scooted me over to the couch so I could rest my back against it.

"How long ago was the incident?" the first EMT asked.

"I really don't want to talk about it. I buried it in the past, and I'd like it to stay there."

"And are you seeking any type of counseling to deal with the trauma?"

"She prays like nobody I've ever met," Jessica said in my defense. "Look guys, I don't think you need to interrogate my friend about an incident that causes her PTSD episodes. Obviously, Rebecca's fine now. Thank you for coming out."

The EMTs exchanged glances again. The second one, a blonde in his late twenties said, "Look, we can't force you to go to the hospital, but at least consider some kind of counseling to deal with this thing eating at you."

I nodded. "I'll think about it. I have some online support groups I'm a part of. It helps."

"Well that's better than nothing," the first EMT said. "Can one of you drive her home, or will she spend the night here?"

"Beck is spending the night," Jessica said emphatically, "and you're taking the day off of work tomorrow."

"Jessica, they need me at Culver. I can't just take a sick day because I blacked out for half a second."

"You blacked out for fifteen minutes," she responded shrilly. "I can't stand to see my best friend like this anymore. Look, if Culver can't understand your health matters more than their stupid RFPs and summaries, then they don't deserve you!"

The EMTs looked back and forth between Jessica and me, then grinned.

The first one said, "Well, I guess that's settled then. Miss, uh—"

"Goldstein," Jessica said tersely.

"Miss Goldstein," he finished, "You're a good friend. Make sure Rebecca gets some fluids and plenty of rest."

Jessica nodded. Nathan escorted the EMTs outside while Jessica sat next to me on the floor.

"When are you going to tell me what happened, Beck? I'm your best friend. Let me help you. How can you ever heal if you don't let this thing go?"

"This isn't my story to share, Jessica. I witnessed it, but it didn't happen to me. If the victim doesn't want to come forward, I would be outing them. It could destroy their entire life."

Nathan closed the front door and rejoined us. "I'm confused. I thought the big scandal was your pastor and Cynthia Russell having an affair, and you walked in on them doing the deed."

I shook my head.

"Beck, what are you saying?" Jessica asked, dread in her voice.

"They were involved in illicit activity," I said slowly, realizing that speaking it aloud made it more real.

"Okay," Jessica said. "But there's more, isn't there?"

I nodded.

Nathan put a hand over his mouth. "Oh no..."

Tears spilled from my eyes.

"Who else?" Jessica demanded, visibly shaking with anger.

"One of the boys from the youth group," I whispered.

Nathan plopped down on the couch in shock. "Beck, you're absolutely sure of what you saw?"

"I wish I could unsee all of it!" I said angrily. "They ambushed that poor boy in the church narthex! The narthex! That is supposed to be God's holy ground, and they defiled it with their...their..."

"Their perversion," Nathan said with disgust.

"What about all of the weird stuff between you and Pastor?" Jessica said. "You told me he deliberately messed with your relationship with Jason, that Jason thinks he planned to seduce you."

I drew another shaky breath. "I don't think Jason is wrong. The more I look back and remember, the clearer it becomes. The scary part is that it wasn't just me, Jessica. Pastor had this weird, controlling vibe with a lot of people there. He'd make these inappropriate or out of place comments, and we all brushed it off as some kind of social awkwardness or just a harmless faux pas."

"He runs the place like his own harem," Jessica said, outrage evident on her face. "Sick!"

"They made me look crazy, that I tried to seduce *him*—that perverted, piece of trash! Do you know how much I wish I had imagined the whole thing?"

"What about Ted?" Nathan said quietly.

Jessica whipped her head around. "Nathan, what are you talking about? Rebecca barely knows the guy. Do you want her to ruin things before they even get started?"

"Hear me out on this, Jessica. Ted's bound to know a good lawyer or investigator or something. Even if nothing comes of it, he cares about Rebecca. I think he'd want to help."

"Look guys," I said, answering before Jessica could respond, "I just want to be happy. I want to forget that SBC ever existed, that Pastor ever existed, and that the entire Ivy family is nothing more than a figment of my imagination."

Jessica leaned in and put an arm around me. "Beck, I know I'm not religious like you or Nathan, but I don't think I could survive something like this and still believe in God. But you do. No matter what drama and garbage your family spews on you, you always find a way to be better in spite of it. You deserve to finally be happy, Beck. You deserve to be free. Legally, I don't know what you can do about SBC, but if you believe Pastor has more victims, we need to make them come forward."

"I don't know," I said, pulling up my knees to rest my head against them. "I'm tired, and I just want to go to bed."

Jessica stood up, then reached out an arm to pull to my feet. "I still have your spare toothbrush in the guest bathroom and the pajamas you left from the last time you crashed here."

"Thanks."

"Hey, where's your cell phone?"

"Why?"

"I can call work for you and let them know you're sick. One less thing for you to worry about."

Too groggy and emotionally spent to think better of her offer, I agreed and then padded my way to her guest bedroom. Nathan would be moving in after the wedding, and I was thankful for the opportunity to enjoy my best friend's hospitality before the room inevitably became a nursery.

"Good night, Jessica. And thanks for everything."

She nodded, then whispered furiously to Nathan about something. Forgoing the tooth brushing, I collapsed on the bed and slept for the next twelve hours.

CHAPTER 10

I awoke to the sound of pounding on Jessica's front door followed by a male voice entering the condo I didn't immediately recognize. Then, I heard the squeak of loafers and jangle of keys. I gasped in horror, realizing I'd slept in my makeup, my breath could wake the dead, and I'd flung my bra across the room two seconds before I crashed into bed the night before.

"Beck?" Jessica called, knocking on the door. "Ted came over to see you. I told him you would need a few minutes to get presentable. Can I get you anything?"

"Other than a new best friend?" I snapped. "I can't believe you did this."

Jessica peeked her head in the room. "Beck, he said he dropped four client meetings to be here."

"Look at me!" I hissed.

"I don't think he expects you to look like a fashion model, hon. Just take a shower, get dressed, and come out when you're ready. He can wait a few minutes." Jessica offered a smile of encouragement before closing the door.

"He's really in there?" I said quietly to myself. "To see me? Like this?" I could hear my mother's voice shrieking in my head, the nitpicking of every flaw, every pimple, every dark brown hair on my face that wasn't an eyebrow or an eyelash. With a shudder, I realized I would not only bare my unadorned face to the mighty Ted Margolin, but my very soul.

"I can't do this Lord," I whispered.

I can do all things through Him who strengthens me.

"But I'm...I'm so ugly. I can't see him without makeup on. He'll see every imperfection."

You are fearfully and wonderfully made.

I felt a challenge in my gut, a nudge revealing my own fear of rejection, of daring to hope one man in the entire universe could see my faults, flaws, scars and all, and still find me beautiful. After Jason's desertion, I had convinced myself no man like that existed outside of my inspirational romance novels.

With God, all things are possible.

I recalled one of the first Bible verses I had ever memorized to help cope with my family dysfunction. Speaking the familiar words aloud, I said, "The Lord is with me; he is my helper. I look in triumph on my enemies. It is better to take refuge in the Lord than to trust in humans. It is better to take refuge in the Lord than to trust in princes."

As much as it pained me to admit, Pastor counseled me correctly about one thing regarding the Ivy family. I *had* been looking for some man to save me, for a knight on a white horse to stand against my family's abuse and defend my honor. Jason couldn't do it. Pastor never intended to do it. Even though he'd probably sacrificed multi-million dollar deals to be there, Ted Margolin couldn't save me either. My savior was Jesus of

Nazareth, the One who saw everything and would vindicate my life and reputation.

I could either trust what God said about telling my story, or I could cling to my fear of rejection. At that moment, accomplishing God's will meant entrusting a piece of my heart to Ted Margolin.

In pink, polka dot pajamas.

I quickly tackled my morning grooming and located my wayward brassiere. Taking one last breath for strength, I marched into Jessica's family room barefaced with my curls pulled into a messy topknot. Ted rose from the couch, his eyes searching my face.

"Are you okay, Rebecca? Jessica called me and told me some of what happened. Do you need to go to the hospital?"

I inched closer to Ted, willing to let him see underneath the makeup mask. I braced myself for revulsion or disgust on his face. I saw neither. Instead, he smiled.

"I didn't know you had freckles," he said softly.

I smiled back at him.

"I'm going to leave you guys alone," Jessica said. "I told work I needed a personal day, so I'll be doing some early Hanukkah shopping online if you need anything. Beck, I made you a bagel. It's on the kitchen table."

"Thank you," I said.

"No problem. You guys behave," she said, winking at both of us as she walked off.

I gestured toward the kitchen. "Care to join me? Knowing Jessica, she made extra coffee too."

Ted followed me and sat at the tiny table. "For someone who claims she's unfairly treated like a personal assistant, I find it ironic you're offering to bring me coffee."

I grinned. "Cream and sugar?"

"Black is fine."

I pulled down two mugs from a kitchen cabinet, fixed my own cup of coffee, and then poured Ted's. I set the mug in front of him and placed mine near the plated bagel.

"French vanilla?" he asked. "It's my understanding you can't begin your mornings without it."

I folded my legs underneath me on the chair as I chuckled. "I'm surprised you remembered that."

"I don't miss much, Rebecca. Why don't you eat, and then we can talk about why I'm here."

I closed my eyes to say a quick prayer of thanks before taking a bite into one of Jessica's gourmet bagels. I offered the other half to Ted. "You hungry?"

"Yes, but I'd feel guilty eating part of your breakfast."

"I don't mind. If you're still here in a few hours, you can make it up to me by buying me lunch."

"In your pajamas?"

I grinned. "There's an amazing, twenty-four-hour diner not far from here. I don't think they'd bat an eye at my awesome jammies."

"You seem in remarkably good spirits considering your best friend had to call 911 to revive you last night."

My jovial expression turned quickly to surprise. "Wow, Jessica didn't leave out any details, did she?"

"Other than why you fainted, no she didn't. She said I needed to hear the story directly from you, that maybe I could help."

I gave a long sigh. "I don't know if you'll want to have anything to do with me if I tell you everything. Frankly, I'm still trying to believe you're really here. How many clients are bemoaning your absence because of me?"

Ted waved me off. "Phil mentioned Deondre's aspirations of

becoming a producer, so I provided him a great opportunity to prove himself today. No need to worry, Rebecca."

I placed my hand over Ted's on the table. "From the bottom of my heart, thank you. You being here means more than I can say. It's more than my ex ever did."

"Your ex?" he said warily. "Is this ancient history or recent history?"

"A little bit of both. Jason stopped by my apartment six or seven months ago after ending our engagement four years earlier."

"What did he want?" Ted asked, his voice tight.

"When word got out about Pastor leaving his wife for a woman in the congregation, Jason showed up on my doorstep hoping to talk me off the ledge. He knew how much I had practically worshiped the man. He thought Pastor might be leaving his wife for me."

"Why would he think you'd get involved with a married man? Does this Jason guy even know you at all? Regardless, why was it any of his business?"

Warmed by the passion and outrage in Ted's voice, I said, "Jason broke off our engagement because..."

"Yes?"

"Because Pastor sabotaged it."

Ted was incredulous. "Your pastor deliberately tried to ruin your relationship? Doesn't that violate some sort of moral code?"

"More than one," I deadpanned. "Pastor knew how much I wanted someone to shield me from my abusive family, but he counseled Jason to make me fight my own battles. Worst Thanksgiving ever that year."

"What do you mean?" Ted asked.

I took a deep breath. "My family performed their usual

shaming and public humiliation, and Jason's silence just emboldened them. They took it as a tacit agreement. I begged Jason to open his mouth and say something, but he parroted back the same words Pastor liked to preach at me. He blindsided me with his silence, and my father went above the call of duty to remind everyone of my complete unworthiness. I went home and sobbed hysterically, crying to Pastor about all of it, of course."

"I see."

"The old ghosts from that Thanksgiving came back when you caught me crying before Le Petit Versailles. I was remembering the counseling session we had with Pastor after the dinner disaster."

"What happened?" Ted asked.

"Pastor manipulated both of us, acting like Jason didn't want to defend me, trying to look like the hero who did. Jason called off our engagement and stormed out of the office. I never saw him again until a few months ago."

Ted's expression was grim. "Say no more. I get it."

I took a sip of coffee to brace myself. "Jessica says my life sounds like a made-for-television movie. People struggle to believe this kind of crazy actually exists, and sometimes it sounds insane coming out of my own mouth. I'll completely understand if you want to leave. I know it's a lot to handle."

"I'm not a little boy, Rebecca. I've seen a lot in this life, too, many things I wish I could unsee. I hate the idea of anyone deliberately treating you this way. To know you is to love you."

I gulped.

When I didn't respond, Ted continued, "Rebecca, I've been in love with you for the past eight months, probably longer if I'm being honest with myself. When I saw how much my attention bothered you, I tried to convince both of us my feelings were platonic. I didn't want to scare you, and I was convinced you had zero interest in me. During the few times we flirted, you panicked, so I tried to put some extra distance between us."

My eyes widened, suddenly piecing together my recollection of events with Ted's behavior. "I freaked out because I liked the attention...and you. I was just too scared to admit it."

"Are you scared now?" he said. "I know relationships don't usually start off this way, and I certainly didn't plan to tell you like this."

The realization of what bloomed in my own heart created a dazzling smile on my lips. "No. I'm not scared at all, actually."

"When I heard Jessica's voice mail, I knew I had to come here. Rebecca, I can't go on pretending I don't feel this way about you. When I told you I wanted more than just some office fling, this is what I meant."

Ted searched my eyes for a long minute, the earnest, silent pleading warming my heart. The mighty Ted Margolin helped me overcome my fear of rejection by exposing his own. I could do no less.

Shyly, I asked, "So, you don't think I'm ugly? You don't care that this is what I look like without any makeup on?"

Ted's bewildered expression confirmed the thought had never occurred to him. "Rebecca, when you smile, I find it hard to form coherent sentences. With or without makeup."

"Really?" I squeaked.

The gold in his eyes sparkled like jewels. "And as far as no makeup goes, that's how I plan to wake up next to you."

I flushed straight down to my toes. "Ted, I don't know how else to say this, but I don't believe in premarital sex."

The brilliance of Ted's smile sent a surge of warmth throughout my entire body. "I'm very well aware of that," he said, inching his chair closer to mine, his face closer to mine.

"Are you saying what I think you're saying, because this feels like one very large hallucination."

"This isn't a dream," Ted said. "I'm not looking to play games or mess with your head, Rebecca. I know what I want, and it's you. I've known for a long time. I just never thought you'd see me as anything other than the Culver ogre making life more difficult for you."

I blinked back tears, my brain scrambling to process the words not even my former fiancé had ever uttered so directly or so passionately. The gold in Ted's eyes sliced through every shred of self-preservation and denial about my own feelings toward him.

"I'm scared, but not of you, Ted. I don't want to get hurt again."

He reached out and cupped the side of my face. "Rebecca," he said, my name rolling off his tongue like a caress. He drew closer to me, his lips a breath from mine. "I don't want to hurt you. I love—"

"Jessica!" Kyle said, bursting through the front door. "Is Beck here? Is she okay?"

Ted and I jumped to our feet, chairs scraping against the tile floor. I knew exactly what Kyle would see, a cozy *tête-à-tête*, and me in my pajamas no less. Ted pulled me behind him just as Kyle entered the kitchen. The shock of seeing both of us together sent Kyle staggering back into the family room.

CHAPTER 11

"KYLE, PLEASE DON'T JUMP TO CONCLUSIONS," I SAID.

"Do you think I'm stupid, Beck? Margolin tells Deondre to handle Guildcorp and Triple J, and then, I find him here with you in your pajamas."

Ted took another step in front of me, shielding me from Kyle. "Think for a minute, Goldstein. Why would I be in your sister's condo? She doesn't even know me."

"Perfect place for your little office affair, right? I can't believe you threatened me with an HR write up for sexual harassment, you lying hypocrite! You just wanted to eliminate the competition!"

"Kyle!" I said, trying to rein him in. "Jessica is down the hall. She invited Ted here. She and Nathan thought Ted could help me with the SBC mess."

That gave my best friend's brother pause, but I watched him assess Ted's protective stance in front of me. "Nice try, Beck. You almost fooled me for a second there."

I put a hand on Ted's arm, letting him know I felt safe to

proceed forward. Grudgingly, he stepped aside, and I walked toward Kyle.

"There's more to the SBC story than what I've shared. After I blacked out last night, I finally told everything to your sister and Nathan. Jessica called Ted because she thought he might have some legal connections that could help me or other victims."

Ignoring the implication of my last statement, Kyle studied my face. "You're not wearing any makeup."

I blushed. "Nope."

"I haven't seen this version of you in a while, Rebecca. I've missed this face."

Ted cleared his throat from behind us.

"How much does he know?" Kyle said, gesturing back toward Ted.

"Enough to know that Rebecca deserves better than how she's been treated. I met her father earlier this year. The man is a holy terror. Literally."

Kyle looked back and forth between the two of us in shock.

"My father showed up at work back in March. He tried to attack me, but Ted intervened."

Palpable anger emanated from Ted as he relived the moment. "I was early for a Triple J meeting when I saw him about to slap Rebecca. I wouldn't let that monster lay a finger on her."

I stepped back and looped my arm through Ted's for support.

"Beck, is this why you acted so weird when I told you Margolin talked you up with Morgan and Phil? I uncovered your dirty little secret, didn't I? How long have you guys been sneaking around?"

"Goldstein, we—"

Kyle raised a hand. "You don't get to call me that. Not here. Not in my sister's house. Not when you're standing there with the woman I—"

"The woman you what?" Ted demanded.

Kyle looked at me with sad, blue eyes. "Beck, I've been thinking about that time in Paris. We had so much fun together. Morgan broke up with me three weeks ago to get back together with her ex. She said she wanted to give her son a chance to grow up with both parents."

"And now you think you're in love with Rebecca," Ted said dismissively. "How convenient."

Kyle glared at Ted. "You've known Rebecca for what, five seconds? Yet, here you are, swooping in like her savior just so you can get in her pants. Beck, he's using you!"

I grabbed onto Ted's arm before he hurled himself at Kyle. Ted looked back at me, his eyes intently questioning mine. Whispering, he asked, "Do you feel the same way about him?"

I shook my head and replied, "Try to understand what a shock this must be for Kyle, probably to anybody who knows the two of us. Let me talk to him."

"I think he wants to do more than talk with you, Rebecca."

I smiled reassuringly. "This is Kyle, not my old pastor, and he just found out about us in the worst way possible. Please, just give me ten minutes."

"I'm not leaving you alone with him."

I held Ted's gaze steady with mine. "I will be fine, I promise. I've known Kyle for twelve years, and his sister is down the hall. Trust me," I said.

Ted kissed my forehead while Kyle glared at the two of us. "I'm coming back in ten minutes whether you're done talking or not," he said. Walking a wide circle around Kyle, he closed the condo door behind him.

Once the door slammed, Kyle crumbled on the couch. I sat next to him, wanting to comfort him, but knowing it would send the wrong message.

"Kyle, I had no idea you felt this strongly about me. It's kind of a shock, especially since you and Morgan couldn't seem to keep yours hands off each other at Burger Palace. What was I supposed to think?"

He looked at me, face awash in tears. "Did I ever have a chance with you, Beck?"

"Kyle, you had a million girlfriends in school. You were always unavailable, and eventually, I grew to see you as my best friend's brother."

"Didn't Jessica ever tell you how I felt?"

I sighed. "It wasn't your sister's responsibility to tell me. That's middle school behavior. If you were interested, you should have told me directly."

"I don't know how I could have been more obvious!" he moaned. "I bought you meals all the time. I spent way too much time at your desk or bringing you french vanilla coffee in the morning. Everybody saw it. Even Ted-freaking-Margolin saw it. Everybody but you!"

I exhaled a slow breath, realizing my own blindness. "Kyle, I just assumed the behavior went along with being your sister's best friend. After I left SBC, I interpreted everything as extra kindness because of my depression. Truly, I didn't know."

His blue eyes held hope as they met mine. "And now that you know?"

He leaned his face in, and I instinctively jerked back. Kyle frowned, reaching a hand to cup my face and physically pull me closer. Having witnessed the same seduction maneuver with Morgan, I jumped from the couch in disgust.

"Kyle, a month and a half ago, you were totally goo-goo eyed in love with somebody else! I had no idea you and Morgan broke up, only that she took another job closer to home. You've had twelve years to say something, but you never did. Why now? Why only when I'm suddenly unavailable, and so is Morgan?"

"Well, I'm saying something now," he said, offended. "Doesn't that count for something?"

"I'm sorry, but I just don't feel that way about you."

"Couldn't you try?" he asked.

Exasperated, I said, "What do you want from me, Kyle? You're acting like I should drop everything going on in my life because it's suddenly convenient for your social calendar. It makes me feel like the spare tire you've kept around in case you got lonely. Is any of this real, or is it just about being jealous that Ted got here first?"

His eyes widened in shock, then narrowed. "How long have you two been sleeping together?" he said bitterly.

"Don't insult me by asking something so stupid," I snapped.

"It's a pretty simple question, Beck."

"Grow up, Kyle! Just because you're changing partners more often than some people change socks doesn't mean that everybody else does."

He glared at me. "I see."

I folded my arms over my chest. "Was I supposed to telepathically guess that sleeping with half the girls in the metro area actually meant you secretly loved me?"

A sheepish smile appeared on Kyle's face. "I may have exaggerated. Slightly."

"To do what?"

"To make you jealous," he said. "So you would see what you were missing. Of course, I didn't expect you to fall in love with Jason or that the bastard would break your heart. After that, I just kept waiting for the right time, but it never seemed to happen."

"Kyle, we're not kids. I understand why you did what you did, but it's so—"

"Juvenile?" he finished for me. "Yeah, I see it too. I hate myself right now, but I see it. Kind of want to crawl into a hole and smack myself with a stupid stick."

I sat back down on the couch, but put more space between us.

"Are you in love with him?" Kyle said.

I sighed. "Ted told me how he felt about me ten minutes before you walked in the door. We haven't been sleeping around or anything like that."

"But you like him, right?"

I allowed myself only a small smile out of respect for Kyle's fragile state. "I do. I wish you could have seen Ted with my father. He went Culver beast mode on him."

"Beck, how do you know Margolin's not just playing you because he knows you've been hurt?"

"I misjudged him, Kyle. Badly. Ted has more honor and integrity than any man I've ever met."

"If he does anything to hurt you, Beck, so help me, I will tear him apart. I don't mean metaphorically either."

I smiled at Kyle's protectiveness. "I'm pretty sure Ted knows that too."

After a pause, Kyle changed the topic to the real matter at hand. "So, you told my sister and Nathan everything that happened at SBC? About why you really left?"

Not sure how much longer I had before Ted returned, I summed things up briefly for Kyle. Shock, revulsion, and disbelief all appeared on his face.

"Beck, I don't even know what to say. I remember how you used to talk about this guy all the time."

I exhaled in disgust. "It's a struggle forgiving myself for being so blind and stupid."

"He deceived you and everyone else," Ted interjected from the now open doorway. "Who wants to believe their trusted leader is a sexual predator?"

"How long have you been standing there?" I said.

"Long enough." Ted pushed off the doorframe, entered the family room, and then closed the door behind him. His brows raised slightly at Kyle's bloodshot eyes. "Did you guys sort everything out?"

Kyle stood up to meet Ted face to face. Though several inches shorter, Kyle's ramrod posture communicated his intent unmistakably.

"Look, if you have something to say, Gold...er Kyle, then go ahead and say it."

"If you're just messing around here, *Ted*, then don't waste your time or Rebecca's. She doesn't need another lowlife scumbag trying to screw her over."

"Duly noted," Ted said coolly.

Hoping to defuse some of the tension, I said, "Kyle, are you going to be okay?"

He pinched the bridge of his nose and took in a slow, deep breath. "Beck, it's a lot to process. You said my sister is here?"

"In her room with headphones on, apparently, since she missed all of the excitement."

Kyle nodded, then exited down the hallway.

Ted approached me slowly, his eyes full of concern. "How are you?"

Standing up from the couch, I offered a tentative smile. "Other than breaking the heart of one of my closest friends? Of finding out that I completely misread all of his attempts to woo me as friendly gestures?"

"Was Goldstein crying? It sure looked like it."

"Ted, I never suspected a thing! As long as I've known Kyle, he's had this revolving door of girlfriends. I told him he should have come right out and said something, but it's like he expected me to be a mind reader."

"Good for you, Rebecca! I'm glad you didn't let Goldstein get away with trying to lay a guilt trip on you. I've known quite a few people who operate like that."

"Like what?"

"The ones who always manage to be the victim of their own decisions. They act like your world revolves around theirs, that you've got nothing better to do than sit around and figure out what they want. It's all a bunch of mind games and manipulation. Kudos to you for seeing through it."

"I don't know, Ted. That sounds a lot more like my old pastor or my family."

Considering my words for a moment, he replied, "Maybe Goldstein's not as narcissistic, but there are plenty of horrible people out there, Rebecca. They'd gladly get in line to take advantage of someone like you."

"Someone like me?"

"Yes, someone exactly like you. When you give, Rebecca, you do it with your whole heart. You get joy from helping people, and unfortunately, I've seen too many associates in our office, myself included, who let you take on responsibilities and projects that never belonged on your shoulders. We dumped stuff on you at the last minute because of our own negligence or disregard. We selfishly made our problems *your* problem to fix. I get the impression your own family treats you the same way. For my part, I want to apologize and tell you how sorry I am. It was wrong. You don't deserve to be taken advantage of by me or anyone else."

"Wow," I said. "You know, I never thought I'd feel this way with you, Ted."

He raised an eyebrow in question, a soft smile on his lips. He gestured for me to finish my thought.

"I feel safe. Even my two best friends in the other room have made excuses for how I've been treated over the years. The Goldstein family isn't perfect by any means, but they can't comprehend the level of dysfunction in my family. The idea of family members deliberately hurting one another is totally foreign to them."

Ted nodded in understanding. "My father escaped from a family that sounds very similar to yours. My mother's warnings all came true when I reconnected with my grandparents in my late twenties. I discovered just how ugly people can be, and it was eye opening."

"I always assumed it was just me. Just my family."

"You're not alone, I promise you," Ted said solemnly.

Before me glimmered golden eyes that sent my heart pounding like a drum in my chest. Ted pulled me gently toward him, wrapping his arms around my waist. He kept his eyes steady with mine, and my heartbeat thundered in my ears.

"I'd like to kiss you, Rebecca."

I grinned.

"But the last time I tried that, Goldstein burst through the front door. Out of respect for both of your friends down the hall, I think we should wait."

I took his face in my palms and unleashed megawatt. "Thank you, Ted. Truly, I don't think I've known a better man than you."

"Rebecca," Ted said in a pained voice. He very reluctantly peeled my hands from his face. "Not helping."

With a playful sigh of disappointment, I dutifully kept my arms at my sides.

"Can we get out of here?" Ted asked. "Maybe grab some food and go for a walk? I overheard the tail end of your conversation about what you witnessed with your pastor. I'd like to talk to you in more detail, but I'm thinking Goldstein could use some space."

"Sounds like Deondre is going to have his hands full today."

"Like I said, he's been itching to prove himself at Culver."

I laughed softly. "Between the three of us being out of the office today, it sounds like he'll get his chance."

CHAPTER 12

I stopped by Jessica's room to let her and Kyle know I needed to leave. Kyle sat on her bed, shoulders stooped, head bent down in utter dejection. Not sure what to say and fearing I might just make things worse, I said a quick farewell before changing back into my old clothes in Jessica's guest room. I drove back to my apartment, Ted following in his car, and he waited in the parking lot while I freshened up. As soon as I climbed in the passenger side, Ted set down his phone and greeted me with a warm smile.

"Thanks for waiting," I said.

"You're worth the wait."

I blushed.

Butter sizzled in the pan.

I blushed harder.

Amused, but aware of my discomfort, Ted changed the subject and asked, "Do you have any favorite parks or nature trails close by?"

"Well, I know this isn't Parkview, but there's a couple of nice spots," I said, buckling myself in.

"Why did you mention Parkview?"

"You don't live there? I figured you did."

"What is it they say about making assumptions?" he teased, gold twinkling in his eyes.

I rolled mine in response. "Guilty as charged."

"I don't live that far from here, actually. I'm still in the same house I had when I was married." Before I could express my surprise, he said, "I'm a widower. My wife, Annie, died in a car accident eight years ago."

"Oh Ted!" I exclaimed, placing my hand on his. "I had no idea."

He offered a sad smile. "It's not something I share often. I keep a picture of Annie hidden in my office. When you don't have pictures, people don't ask questions, and I'd rather not answer them. Right before she died, Annie and I talked about starting a family. We had planned to start trying later that year. Fate had other ideas," he said, his voice hardening.

"Fate? So you don't believe in God?"

"It took me a long time to accept what happened. Annie and I were childhood sweethearts. I never knew life without her in it. It seemed cruel for any loving God to take her away like that, to let her linger for days in a coma." He turned to study my expression. "Rebecca, is this a deal breaker for you? That I'm agnostic at best?"

My eyes filled with tears on his behalf. "Ted, my best friend told me she would understand if I turned my back on God because of everything I've been through. Suffering either drives us toward God or away from Him. We either cling to Him with everything we have because He's all we have, or we get angry and disillusioned and tell ourselves He doesn't exist. To accept the idea that God could love us as much as the Bible says He does, yet He allows us to experience hell on earth confounds the human mind. It requires us to trust Him even when we don't understand, even with pain and grief so unbearable, we just want Him to take us out of our misery. It takes faith to trust He's still good."

"You remind me of my mother," Ted said softly.

"How so?"

"My father is Jewish, and my mother converted for him when they got married. She says she found Jesus while she was pregnant with me. My dad tolerates it because he loves her, but Mom talks about God a lot like you do. She tried to comfort me after Annie died, but I didn't want to hear it. I told her to save all of that Jesus stuff for her friends at church."

"What did she do?"

"She told me she understood and would respect my wishes. She also said God would comfort me in His own way and His own time."

"Did He?"

"Almost seven years ago, Phil hired this twenty-something gal to fill a void in our office. He said she possessed a certain *je ne sais quoi* perfect for Culver."

Stunned, I could think of nothing to say. Clearly, I had underestimated my worth at Culver.

Ted continued, "I remember the first time I saw you, Rebecca. Your hair was shorter, and you sat in the breakroom reading your Bible and eating your lunch. You were so engrossed in whatever you were reading that lunch seemed like an afterthought."

"Sounds like me."

"I watched you for three years. I saw you reading your Bible in the breakroom or outside on the bench, cheerful and friendly to everyone, staying late when you needed to, and always able to handle whatever last-minute monkey wrench I threw at you."

"Did you do it on purpose?" I said, surprised.

Ted shook his head. "No, not intentional at all. Just thoughtless and selfish. When you got engaged, I remember how you glowed. It was the first time I noticed you as a woman rather than the graphic design girl who worked on my RFPs."

"Wow, Ted. I had no idea you studied me for so long."

"Am I creeping you out?" he asked. "You can be honest, because I've never seen you this quiet."

"I just assumed nobody at Culver noticed my existence outside of work requests. My family treats me that way, ignoring me unless they need something or they can elevate themselves at my expense. Looking back, the people of SBC treated me the same way. When I taught in the children's ministry or didn't ask questions, they treated me well. Maybe too well," I said ruefully.

"What do you mean?" Ted said.

"Like I told you earlier, Pastor deliberately sabotaged my engagement. He was also there to help pick up the pieces. Jason thinks he did it so he could groom me for an affair."

Ted was aghast. "The man is evil incarnate! How could anybody do those things, let alone a pastor?"

Warmed by Ted's protectiveness, I said, "You don't know how grateful I am that the idea of using and abusing someone seems totally foreign to you."

"How can you say that considering how much I took you for granted in the office?"

"Ted!" I gasped. "It's hardly the same thing!"

"Still, I don't want any part of me or my behavior equated with that degenerate."

"Not even close! I thought men like you only existed in fairytales and movies."

He scoffed. "Did you miss everything else I've told you today, Rebecca? I'm hardly Prince Charming."

"No, but you've been my guardian angel on more than one occasion. I think that's gotta count for something," I said with an encouraging smile. After a brief pause, I added, "Can we stop talking about all of this depressing stuff and find something better to do with our time? Please?"

"Excellent suggestion," Ted said, and he bestowed me with another butter sizzling grin.

We set off for our first official date, and Ted performed the role of "total gentleman" better than any Regency novel hero. The day sped by in a blur of hand holding, meaningful glances, and an overwhelming sense of peace. Ted took me to an outdoor art fair, asking pointed questions about my tastes and preferences as if studying for an exam. Following that, he drove me to our city's famous farmer's market, promising to cook my favorite meal. Since I couldn't make up my mind, Ted said he would surprise me.

I smiled as Ted pored over an array of herbs, smelling and testing different varieties. He seemed so relaxed and happy, and I paused to savor feeling the exact same way.

"Rebecca? What are you doing here?"

I whirled around at the familiar voice, but I barely recognized its owner.

"Ada?"

She shrugged. "So, the whole lesbian thing didn't really work out for me."

"I thought you said you were born that way, but you didn't realize it until college."

"I just said that to tick off Mom and Dad," she said with a

dramatic hair flip. Even with faded, blue tips and honey blonde roots, my sister turned heads.

"How did Tammy take the news?"

"Gosh, you remember her?" Ada laughed. "We broke up forever ago. I tried calling you. Aunt Eleanor gave me your number, but I guess you were busy. Probably better though. Dad grills me all the time if I've heard from you."

My plastered on smile thinned into a line. "No doubt."

"Rebecca, who's your friend?" Ted said, slipping his arm around me.

Ada eyed Ted appreciatively. "Definitely an improvement over the last one. Took you long enough too! Let's hope it goes better this time."

If looks could kill, I would have turned my sister into a chalk outline on the ground.

"Nevermind," Ted said, quickly surmising my connection to the woman before us. "I'm Ted, and you must be Rebecca's sister, Ada."

She smiled prettily for him. "I can't believe I found my workaholic sister downtown at four in the afternoon. Just so you know, Ted, Rebecca can't live without her job. That's all she ever talks about: Jesus, Culver, and Pastor," she said mockingly.

Unable to fake any more pleasantries, I said, "Well, Ada, it was nice seeing you. You can tell Dad I'm alive, well, and enjoying a day off. I'll leave you to your new life as a vegetarian non-lesbian." I turned to leave, holding onto Ted like a lifeline.

Ada rushed in front of us. "Don't you turn your back on me, Rebecca!"

"Why? Can't handle a taste of your own medicine?" I shot back.

Ada's eyes narrowed into slits. Turning her focus to Ted, she said, "Has Rebecca given you one of her little pity parties where she cries at nothing just to get attention? She's a total drama queen. It's pathetic."

Ted's jaw clenched, and his chin rose gradually in the air. At the sound of his slow and deliberate inhalation of breath, I braced myself for the Category 5 hurricane brewing.

Thinking she'd gotten the upper hand, Ada continued, "Oh, and Rebecca likes to chase after married men. She's a home-wrecker. Her old pastor knows all about that, right, Rebecca?" She grabbed a cluster of grapes from a nearby display and ate them one by one, drawing attention to her full lips. Looking seductively at Ted, she said, "Get out while you can. Better yet, you can always trade up."

The thunderous expression on Ted's face was what had earned him the title of *mighty Margolin*. The smirk dropped from my sister's mouth.

"You've done nothing but sling insults at Rebecca in the scant, three minutes we've been forced to endure your grating company," he began.

"*Endure* my company?" Ada repeated in disbelief.

Hurricane Ted made landfall.

"What kind of emotionally clueless, sadistic hypocrite taunts her own sister with homewrecker accusations and then follows with soliciting the attention of her date? You should be down on your knees begging for Rebecca's forgiveness."

"Don't flatter yourself," Ada interrupted.

Ted talked right over Ada, louder and more forcefully. "Then, you have the gall to feign moral outrage because your sister won't roll over for more of your abuse. I'm not Jason, and I won't stand idly by while some vicious, little vulture tries to peck Rebecca to death. Your father showed up unannounced at our office park earlier this year, and I stopped him from assaulting your sister. If you think I'm scared of some snot nosed punk at the produce stand, you have another thing coming." Giving Ada a quick once over, he said, "Also, I would hardly call you a trade up. Your smile doesn't hold a candle to your sister's."

"Rebecca!" Ada screeched. "How can you let your boyfriend talk to me that way?!"

"What did he say that you didn't deserve, Ada? I'm done with the verbal abuse and public tantrums."

"Abuse?" she scoffed.

"Look, I sincerely wish you well on your new journey, but I am walking out of this store and away from every toxic member of the Ivy family. Good-bye, Ada."

Desperate, she said, "Dad was right about everything he's ever said about you, Rebecca. You really are crazy! How dare you call our family toxic! Have you seen your own, train wreck life?"

I turned to Ted, ignoring Ada's final blow as well as the stares of multiple onlookers. "I'm not so hungry anymore. Ready to go?"

"Excellent idea, Rebecca."

Like the triumphant end of a movie, Ted slipped my arm through his, and we exited the farmer's market. I felt guilty leaving our cart full of groceries behind, but Ted took care of it. He explained the situation to one of the managers, apologized for any inconvenience, and gave them $100 for groceries we never purchased. He also mentioned a certain blue-tinged individual who had sampled food from various displays.

When I objected that our public set down of Ada seemed punishment enough, Ted said, "People need to feel the consequences of their actions, Rebecca. They never learn if we always protect them from the results of their own choices."

I had no rebuttal for that.

CHAPTER 13

MY FEET BARELY HIT THE GROUND THE NEXT DAY AT the office. Nervous, excited, and scared, I didn't know how to interact with Ted in a way that didn't inform the entire office he told me he loved me yesterday, and I was well on my way to being in love with him too. My heart ached at the embarrassment and pain for Kyle, but I overheard Deondre complaining on his way to the breakroom, saying, "Goldstein up and decides to take off the rest of the week. So not cool!"

I shot a quick text over to Jessica. *Is your brother okay?*

No, but he just needs time to sort things out. Stop feeling guilty, and just enjoy being happy with Ted. You deserve something good in your life, Beck.

You know me too well. Thanks for the tough love, I wrote back.

I told Kyle he needed to move on a long time ago. Not your fault or Ted's my brother never opened his mouth. Date go well?

Really well. Run-in with Ada. Fill you in later. You'll want to hear this in person.

Can't wait. I hope Ted put that little brat in her place.

And then some. Thanks for the pep talk.

No problem. TTYL.

Smiling down at my phone, I realized the mighty Margolin had made quite an impression on my best friend. Having her blessing on my relationship with Ted helped alleviate the guilt I felt for rejecting Kyle.

"Good morning," Ted said from behind me. "I brought you coffee." He handed me a to-go cup from *Vincenzo's*, the gourmet, Italian coffee shop across the street.

"You know, I usually just mix in the flavored creamer from the breakroom," I said.

Ted grimaced. "I know. Hence, I bought you the real thing."

I laughed. "Thank you. That was very thoughtful."

"Rebecca!" Phil said, quickly standing alongside Ted. "I didn't know if we'd see you back in the office this week. How are you feeling?"

Blushing at the attention, I responded, "Much better, thank you. By the looks of my inbox, I came back not a moment too soon."

"Speaking of, I need to speak with you in my office." Before I could reply, Phil took note of the cup in my hand, then noticed the matching container in Ted's. Those mischievous blue eyes twinkled. "Once you finish your coffee, of course."

"Don't even say it, Phil," Ted warned.

"Not a word. Scouts honor," he said with a salute. "Just make sure all extracurricular activities remain extracurricular."

Phil being Phil, he tipped his head back and laughed at his own joke.

Ted rolled his eyes, but he escorted me to our CEO's office a few minutes later. I rapped on Phil's doorframe once Ted departed to his own office two doors down.

"Have a seat, Rebecca," Phil said as he closed the door

behind me. "You don't need to look so concerned. I didn't ask you here to get a reprimand in the principal's office."

I smiled at Phil's skillful knack for disarming people with humor. He leaned casually against the edge of his desk while I occupied an office wing chair.

"What's going on?" I said.

"I could ask you and the mighty Margolin the same question, but that's none of my business."

"Phil, we're just—"

He held up his hand, his mirth quickly fading. "You don't owe me any explanations, Rebecca. You have always been a young woman of exemplary character and morals, so I have no worries of either of you behaving like anything other than adults. Frankly, I've already seen your positive influence on the mighty Margolin. Before Ted ever lectured CID about their treatment of our marketing department, he received quite a stern lecture from yours truly. I knew something had changed when I heard him defend you and sing your praises to the entire office."

I stared at Phil in gratitude, overwhelmed by all he'd done for me since the day he had hired me. God had sent me more than one guardian angel at Culver.

"And now, for the real reason I called you in here," Phil said, his expression brightening. "I want to let you know we will be expanding your job position."

"Expanding?"

"We plan to hire two new associates to support you, Rebecca. You will be the team lead, handling the larger accounts and potential acquisitions. Bonnie mentioned a girl named Taylor she's ready to hire, and we have more candidates set up for interviews later this week. Obviously, this helps you directly, but it also ensures we don't get caught in a total panic like we did yesterday."

"Phil, I'm so sorry."

He waved me off. "Don't apologize for being human or needing to take a day for yourself. However, the overall madness yesterday showed me how much we depend on you here and how critically we need back up. Rebecca, you've done the work of three and four people, never once complaining about it, and you've spoiled all of us. That's also why you will receive a $10,000 raise effective immediately, and we will move you to an actual office to afford you some more privacy. The mighty Margolin mentioned how the location of your cube left you too easy for interruption, particularly from those who may be paying you some unwanted attention."

"Phil, I...I'm speechless."

Speechless, but not tearless.

"I'll give you a few minutes to put yourself together," Phil said with a fatherly smile. "I hope you don't mind if I tell the news to Margolin myself. The look on his face will keep me in stitches for the rest of the day."

I laughed through the tears. "Do whatever you need to do, Phil. I'm just trying to figure out when I can wear Ted's $200 dress to celebrate."

Phil laughed so loudly, a few heads turned from their cubicles to peek into the windows of his office.

"I need to get these soundproofed," he muttered to himself as he closed the door behind him.

Containing my elation following my meeting with Phil proved easy enough. Aside from many grateful coworkers glad to see me feeling better, they were even happier to see me back in the office to help meet their various deadlines. My cell phone buzzed with a new text message from Ted just after two in the afternoon.

Just wondering if you plan to take a lunch break before today becomes tomorrow, Miss Ivy. Might I suggest the cafe downstairs?

Are you stalking my eating habits, Mr. Margolin?

No...just you. Insert heavy breathing.

I laughed out loud. This was followed by chuckling from the window office belonging to Culver's top, east coast producer.

I wrote back, *Totally slammed over here. Still playing catch up. Probably just going to grab some Chick-A-Yum, eat at my desk, and work through. Lucky if I get out of here by 7.*

Can I be of assistance?

I always wondered what having a personal assistant would feel like.

I grinned, waiting for Ted's response.

Will it get you to come to dinner with me after work? he wrote back.

You're going to bribe me with food...in order to get me to eat more food????

If it means I get to spend more time with you, then yes.

I found it difficult to wipe the smile from my face. *Meet you downstairs in 5. And you're not paying.*

Why's that?

Didn't Phil tell you? I got a raise today.

At Ted's uncharacteristic bark of laughter, several heads poked up from their cubes like gophers in a game of whack-a-mole.

"What in the world?" Miss Belle said from the set of cubicles behind me. "I have never heard the mighty Margolin laugh like that."

Ducking my head down, I blushed furiously.

"Hey Rebecca!" Miss Belle called across the aisle.

My reply came out as a very strangled sounding, "Yes?" I

didn't dare turn around lest she very astutely piece the puzzle together. I cradled my cell phone in my lap.

"You know what's going on with Margolin? That boy's in a mighty fine mood today. Did we land another new account or something?"

"You'll have to ask him yourself," I said, unapologetically throwing Ted under the bus.

My cell phone buzzed immediately with a message from the mighty Margolin. *You're paying for that, Miss Ivy.*

I hope you accept currency in waffle fries.

Ted's uproarious laughter pulled the gopher heads up once again. It also induced a visit from Miss Belle who took my advice to ask the man himself. I threw my phone into my desk drawer to hide the incriminating evidence.

Miss Belle returned from Ted's office and stopped at my cubicle. Taking a sip from my water cup and hoping to cool the blush from cheeks, I inhaled deeply before making eye contact.

"That man is in love," she said in wonder.

I gagged on my water.

"You okay?" Miss Belle asked, raising an eyebrow.

"I'm fine," I coughed. "What makes you say that?"

"Because I have never seen the mighty Margolin look so happy. And good for him, you know? Even folks like Ted deserve somebody."

"Folks like Ted?"

"Oh, you know, those high and mighty types who want the world at their beck and call. Can you believe the mighty Margolin lectured CID about respecting your time when he treats you like his personal assistant more than anybody else in this office?"

The blush cooled from my cheeks as my heart filled with compassion for Ted. I wanted to defend him and talk about how much he'd changed. However, I also knew Ted's previous behavior hardly matched his recent role as guardian angel over the past year. Not so long ago, I openly referred to him as demanding, self-absorbed, and too big for his own britches.

"Rebecca? Where'd you go, baby girl?" Miss Belle asked. "I asked if you know about this mystery woman the mighty Margolin's been seeing. Vicky said something about the Loss Control VP from Nashville, but I think she's married with kids. For all of his faults, Ted ain't that kind of guy. Least, I don't think so anyways."

"Mighty interesting conversation we're having here," Ted said, leaning against the outside wall of my cube.

Miss Belle looked mortified. I tried to keep my expression as neutral as possible.

"Miss Belle, if you have any questions, you can ask me, but please don't speculate with Rebecca or anybody else. We've known each other too long for that." His smile was sincere, as was the encouraging pat on Miss Belle's arm.

To her credit, Miss Belle appeared contrite. "Sorry, Ted. I wouldn't want folks flapping their gums about my personal life either. Rebecca, thanks for not going there with me. You're a lot better than most of the kids around here."

I offered a comforting smile, amused by Miss Belle's reference to pretty much anyone under the age of fifty as a "kid." Even properly chastised, her unofficial role as Culver's mother hen remained intact.

"Rebecca, can I talk to you in the lobby, please?" Ted said, his tone all business.

Miss Belle scurried off meekly, and my smile faded. I knew she'd probably beat herself up about the entire situation, or worse, worry that she got me in trouble.

I followed Ted into the elevator. As soon as the doors shut, he closed his eyes and released a heavy sigh.

"Ted, I—"

He cut me off. "Just wait til we get to the restaurant."

I frowned. "Are you okay?"

He met my eyes, his expression softening. The elevator doors dinged open before he could respond to my question.

"My treat, by the way," he said, gesturing for me to step out of the elevator ahead of him.

"What are you talking about? I told you I'm paying, and I meant it."

A smile finally broke through his earlier grim expression. "You forgot your purse."

Offering a tentative smile in return, I followed him through the revolving lobby door and over toward the fast food chain. Ted told me to sit and relax outside while he took care of the order. I enjoyed the familiar sounds of rushing traffic, thankful for a respite from the hectic work day. Mr. Margolin became the delighted recipient of megawatt once he arrived with sustenance.

"I didn't expect to feel this way so soon," Ted said while I bit into my chicken sandwich. "The last twenty-four hours feel like warp speed. I should have thought through how our relationship would look at work, specifically how it affects the working environment."

My stomach dropped. "So what are you saying, Ted? Yesterday was a mistake?"

Thankfully, the ambient noise outside muffled Ted's loud denial. His outburst didn't garner the attention it might have otherwise.

He held my free hand while my sandwich remained suspended in the other. "You changed me, Rebecca. I want to do backflips and cartwheels through the office, and it's barely been a day!"

Not the answer I expected.

Ted took my motionless hand and pushed the sandwich toward my open jaw. "Eat."

I nodded and obeyed, too overwhelmed by all of the good that had transpired that day to do anything else.

CHAPTER 14

"I HAVE TO SAY, THIS WILL TAKE SOME GETTING used to."

I looked at Ted inside of my tiny, galley kitchen, sweater sleeves rolled up to his elbows, as he cooked on my ancient, electric stove.

"Pretty hot, right?" he said with a cheeky grin.

"Literally. Your sauce almost boiled over twice."

The mighty Margolin actually stuck his tongue out at me.

Responding with my own grin, I said, "I can't believe Culver's golden boy is standing in my apartment cooking spaghetti and meatballs. Don't you dare send me a text tomorrow at work asking what I ate for dinner."

Ted laughed as he stirred the marinara sauce. "I'm used to a bigger work space, but the cookware was a nice surprise. Quality pans, Rebecca. I'm impressed."

"As a huge Food Station nerd, I took advantage of some Black Friday sales last year. Not as much fun cooking a feast for only one, though."

"*Touché.*"

After an awkward pause, both of us lost in thought about our respective losses, I gave a tight-lipped smile and then moved about the kitchen and dining area. I prepped my tiny table for not one, but two occupants.

Ted twirled the vermicelli on each plate like a restaurant chef before adding his "famous" meatballs and ladling on the marinara. He sprinkled fresh basil on the plates for garnish, and I marveled at how such a simple meal could suddenly feel so gourmet. The handsome chef in my kitchen felt like dessert.

Ted brought the plates to the table, and I poured cabernet for both of us. After we sat down, I silently said a quick prayer of thanks, opening my eyes to see glimmering gold before me. Finding myself short of breath, I lifted a shaky hand to my wine glass.

"What?" Ted asked.

"Nothing," I said, staring at my exquisite dinner. The man did *everything* with excellence.

"Rebecca," Ted coaxed, "what's wrong?"

Fighting back tears, I took a deep breath before responding. "I'm just overwhelmed, Ted."

"Is this too much?" he said, gesturing toward dinner. "Am I moving too fast?"

I laughed through my tears. "Ted, you haven't even kissed me yet! So much has happened in the past forty-eight hours, and my head is spinning. Two days ago, I passed out on the floor of Jessica's condo from a panic attack. Today, I have Ted Margolin sitting across from me at my garage sale dining room table with designer spaghetti, and you've hinted rather heavily at your intentions for the future. On top of that, I'm finally getting extra help in the office, I can barely focus because I have so much fun flirting with you over something as stupid as lunch, and I just don't know how to contain this much happiness."

I promptly burst into tears.

Ted came around the table and kneeled down next to me, rubbing my back. It reminded me piercingly of Pastor's comfort following the disastrous marital counseling session with Jason. Unwilling to let the old ghosts ruin such a glorious day, I shooed them away, focusing on the man beside me instead.

"You're beautiful," Ted said quietly, almost reverently. He used a thumb to wipe away the tears that had escaped. "Do you know what I see when I look at you, Rebecca?"

I shook my head.

"I see intoxicating dark eyes, eyes that see into people beyond the masks they wear. I see a perfect button nose, high cheekbones, full lips, and a very determined little chin."

"Ted, I—"

"Did you think I was done?" he asked.

"You're not?"

"Do you have any idea how beautiful you are? Why do you think Goldstein started looking for another job? He asked me for a reference this morning. I couldn't begrudge him that after what happened the other day."

"Wow," I breathed.

"Between grief over Annie and trying to make something of myself, I didn't really notice you until after you got engaged, Rebecca. You have a rare innocence and kindness, even with everything you've suffered. Goldstein was a selfish idiot for not telling you how he felt. I was a selfish idiot for taking advantage of your kindness when I should have been on my knees thanking you."

"I guess you're doing that now, huh?"

Ted cupped the back of my head, his fingers tangling in my

curls. My breath caught, especially as I saw his eyes lower to my lips.

"You know, every time I try to kiss you, we somehow get interrupted."

"The door's locked," I whispered.

Ted's face inched closer, and I closed my eyes. Months of longing finally seemed ready to culminate in that eagerly awaited kiss.

Instead, I felt Ted pull back. Confused and frustrated, I opened my eyes. I found Ted staring intently at me.

"Rebecca, I don't want to cause any PTSD triggers for you. You said you're waiting until marriage for everything else, but you *have* been kissed before, right?"

About to explode from anticipation, I launched myself at Ted. For a pulse pounding, glorious, ten seconds of bliss, electricity surged through my every extremity. I clung to Ted as if searching for air underwater.

Right until I fell out of my chair.

I toppled onto Ted, knocking him backward onto the floor, and sending my plate of spaghetti flying in the process. I landed on top of him with an embarrassing thud. Horrified, I sat up immediately, burying my face in my palms.

Ted pulled himself up to a sitting position beside me and chuckled softly. "Should I mention you have spaghetti all over the carpet?"

I expelled a sigh of disgust. "I'm glad one of us finds this funny."

Ted cradled my face with his hands. He kissed me softly on the lips, then rested his forehead against mine. "Warn me next time, okay?"

"That bad? It's been a while."

Ted gave a low, sultry laugh. "Just don't kiss me like that

unless you're prepared to finish what you start. I respect your beliefs, Rebecca, but I'm still human. It's also been a very long time."

"Oh," I said, surprised.

"Oh," he playfully mocked. "If this is you out of practice, I have a lot to look forward to."

My cheeks burned crimson.

Eyeing my mouth for a tenuous moment before ultimately deciding not to throw either of us back into the path of temptation, Ted stood up. He extended a hand to help me to my feet. As we both took in the damage from my upended dinner, we laughed at the mess.

"I'll help you clean it up," he said, turning toward the kitchen.

I grabbed onto his arm, holding him there. "Clean up can wait. We still have one perfectly viable plate of food left. I'm so hungry, I'm about to gnaw on my own hand. Dinner first. Cleaning later."

"Yes ma'am," Ted said, pulling out the chair next to him. He grabbed my silverware from across the table.

I shared a plate of spaghetti and meatballs in my apartment with Culver's top, east coast producer. We cleaned spaghetti from my carpet, wall, and baseboards when we were done, and we enjoyed every second of it.

The next week passed by quickly. Ted flew out of town for several client meetings, and the work environment began to feel like "work" again. Miss Belle apologized repeatedly for what had happened with Ted, and as expected, she feared she had endangered my job. I quickly reassured her by informing her of my promotion. Miss Belle looked relieved, and it helped allay any suspicions regarding our relationship. I wanted to protect that precious pearl as long as possible.

Kyle put in his two-week notice the Monday he came back to the office, surprising everyone except me, Ted, and Phil. Phil wished him well, though Deondre and MacKenzie grumbled loudly about his sudden departure.

I admired Kyle's courage to leave an emotionally unhealthy situation rather than stay for the sake of appearances or white knuckle his way through unnecessary pain. I had labored under that false teaching for too long, shamed and humiliated for "being negative" or "lacking faith" because I committed the cardinal sin of being unhappy and actually admitting it.

I questioned Pastor's application of *rejoicing in our trials* after a sermon one day, unsure of his assertion we simply needed to "claim our blessing" and "not allow Satan to steal our joy."

"Pastor, why would the Bible talk about comforting those who mourn if we could just remove all suffering with a simple attitude adjustment?" I asked. "How does a positive attitude resurrect a dead loved one or stop a bill collector from demanding money owed? We can name and claim all the blessings we want, but a broken arm still needs a cast, doesn't it? I don't see how tackling problems realistically gives Satan any kind of power. We still have to deal with the reality of our circumstances even if we don't like them."

"Oh, Rebecca," Pastor said, placing a hand on my shoulder. "You're being a tad legalistic here. I'm not saying people don't experience pain, but dwelling on it just glorifies the Enemy. We overcome our circumstances by choosing to move on. Do you really think God wants a bunch of whiny complainers for followers? Look how well that worked for the Israelites in the desert. Jesus promised us an abundant life. If we really trust in God, then we shouldn't be talking about our problems, but rather, focusing on *Him* as the solution."

I shrugged my shoulder away, uncomfortable with the heavy

hand on me. "I agree, Pastor, but I didn't mean the people who enjoy complaining or playing the perpetual victim. All of the psalms of David and Asaph deal with their issues openly and honestly. They lay it all out there for God, finding comfort in the end because they confess their struggles and bring them into the light. Nobody would accuse King David of lacking faith because he felt overwhelmed by Saul trying to kill him."

Pastor stood unblinking for a moment, his mouth pinched into a straight line. Just as quickly, though, he regained his usual, cheery demeanor. "As a preacher's kid with that secular, university degree, I'm sure you feel you have more scriptural insight than the rest of us mere mortals who simply attended seminary instead," he said.

My brow furrowed.

"Sometimes spiritual pride can be very deceptive, Rebecca. We confuse serving God and rightly dividing the Word with setting ourselves above our brothers and sisters in Christ. Or worse, we elevate ourselves above our God ordained, spiritual authority."

"Pastor, I—"

He cut me off, "This is exactly what I mean, Rebecca. Rather than heed the counsel of your trusted leader, you rush to defend yourself. I've had quite a few people come to me regarding your self-righteous attitude, but I've always tried to show you grace in this area. Apparently, I underestimated your struggle."

My heart dropped. I wracked my brain trying to think of an instance when I'd tried to talk over someone or assert my interpretation of the Bible above theirs. My mind went around in circles replaying recent church events, wondering if I had inadvertently caused someone else to stumble. Did my spiritual pride make me so insufferable that people felt they couldn't talk to me directly? Had I offended God while deceiving myself that

I was honoring Him by speaking up? Shame covered me like a heavy cloak.

Pastor broke through my thoughts as he said, "Now that you're aware of your sin, Rebecca, I know you'll work hard to correct it. Sit back and listen next time, or pray for humility before having conversations like these. I know you would never want to hurt someone else or wind up looking like a fool."

I could only nod dumbly, so grief stricken I had apparently hurt "quite a few people." Pastor concluded our conversation with a pat on the shoulder and jerk of the chin. He then turned his attention to a new congregant, inquiring about her two teenagers in the youth group.

I went home that day and sobbed, broken before the Lord, humiliated and scared I had blasphemed His Name somehow. I begged Jesus to show me the sin in my heart, to show me anyone I had hurt or offended so that I could repent and make things right.

Heaven remained silent.

Depressed, I spent the next few days scrutinizing and over-analyzing everything I said and did, wondering if everyone else saw this pride Pastor claimed had blinded me.

Reflecting on the incident years later, I finally recognized that my so-called, spiritual pride originated from the man projecting his own condition onto me.

CHAPTER 15

"PENNY FOR YOUR THOUGHTS," KYLE SAID QUIETLY.

Blinking back the memories, grateful to have them fade away, I took in the sad visage of one of my oldest friends. His anguished eyes tore at my heart.

Musing aloud, I said, "It's amazing how the human mind works sometimes. Bouncing here to there, connecting dots we wouldn't ordinarily make."

Kyle brightened some. "Okay, now you have me intrigued, Beck."

"Well," I said, lowering my voice, "I was thinking about your decision to leave and how glad I am you're doing what's best for yourself. I wasted too much time second guessing myself and letting other people make those decisions for me."

Kyle's gaze became intense. "Please, tell me there's someone else out there like you, Beck. I can't find her. Believe me, I've tried."

Unnerved, I glanced away. "I don't know if I necessarily believe in *the one* anymore, Kyle. Maybe it happens for some people, but I've only ever seen it in fiction. I do know that people can love more than one person. I think it's possible to fall in love with someone and then to fall in love again later in life."

"Are you speaking from personal experience here?" Kyle said. "Because I really don't want to hear about you and—"

I stopped him before the cubicle walls carried word of our conversation. "We can take this to the break room, or we can finish another time. I didn't mean to get started on a topic like this in the middle of the office."

"I heard you're getting a room with a view soon," Kyle said.

"You did hear correctly."

"Margolin's doing?"

I caught the bitter edge in Kyle's voice but ignored it. "All Phil actually. Amazingly, it just took one fainting spell and an unexpected day off of work."

"I'm genuinely happy for you, Beck. As far as the job stuff anyway."

I looked into Kyle's clear, blue eyes, wanting to offer comfort but not undue encouragement. "It does get easier, I promise. You've never had problems getting a girl, Kyle."

He scoffed. "Yeah, only one."

"Hey guys," Phil said, approaching with two Vincenzo's coffees in hand. "Sorry to see you leave, Goldstein, but I think you'll do well at Cooper & Jaye. They have a nice set up over there with plenty of room to grow."

"Thanks Phil," Kyle said morosely, his eyes still on me. I cringed, feeling the weight of his disappointment and unmet expectations.

"Here," Phil said, handing me one of the Vincenzo's cups. "Margolin asked me to grab you a coffee so you don't drink anything from the break room. He seems to find the Culver offerings subpar."

Kyle exhaled in disgust and left without a backward glance.

"He'll get over it eventually," Phil said with a slight roll of the eyes.

I took a sip from my coffee. "I think so too. Kyle's never been long without a girlfriend."

"How'd I do on the order?"

I grinned. "Perfect! Ted's right about Vincenzo's tasting better than the break room coffee. No offense meant, Phil. I'm very thankful Culver provides us with caffeine at no charge."

"None taken. Just don't tell Margolin he was right. Gotta keep that ego in check."

"It's just coffee, Phil. I have to let him win a few."

Phil leaned in and whispered, "See, but first it's coffee, and then it's baby names."

I shook my head and laughed. "You are incorrigible! And I'm telling Ted you said that."

Phil gave one of his trademark guffaws. "Will you make sure I'm in the room when you tattle on me? The look on the mighty Margolin's face will be worth his wrath."

"You're lucky he likes you," I teased, taking a sip of my delicious, Italian-roasted java.

"He's lucky I'm his boss," Phil retorted and sauntered to his office with a spring in his step.

Kyle didn't stop by my cubicle the remainder of his two weeks at Culver. In fact, he became a virtual stranger even before he left. Though I missed my old friend, I couldn't say that I blamed him. Jessica took it all in stride, perhaps too excited about her own wedding plans to give it much thought. Kyle backed out of the wedding party a day after our final conversation at Culver, unintentionally easing Jessica's conscience in choosing her best friend over her brother.

With Ted still out of town on business a week after our first date, Jessica and I began the age old tradition of wedding dress shopping. After stalking several boutiques online, Jessica finally found *the dress*. She offered an arm, a leg, and possibly her first-born child to make the down payment, then rushed to try on the hoop skirted gown. My heart overflowed seeing my best friend twirl around in her beaded, princess masterpiece. The sales women seemed appropriately happy and supportive, especially since the dress commission would probably pay for a semester of college.

"Beck, isn't it stunning?" Jessica squealed with an appropriate bridal glow.

"It's gorgeous, but who's performing the ceremony?"

Jessica sighed. "We can't seem to agree on it."

"Well, it's no use having the most beautiful dress in the land without an officiant."

"But that's just it," she said, turning to catch another angle of herself in the mirror, "Nathan wants his rabbi to do it, and I want Rabbi Epstein. Nathan's guy isn't crazy about me not believing in Jesus, and Rabbi Epstein told me if it wasn't for my parents being lifelong members of Beth Tefillah, he wouldn't perform the ceremony at all."

"How does Nathan reconcile the fact that he believes in Jesus and you don't?" I said. "I remember everything they taught me about believers and unbelievers getting married."

"Not that you're following your own advice," she said, bringing the train of her dress forward to admire the beadwork.

I stuck my tongue out at her. "Look, I don't get it either. I thought I'd fall in love with a youth pastor or something."

Jessica rolled her eyes. "We just need to get you away from pastors in general."

"I won't argue with you there."

Jessica turned to see another angle of herself. It reminded me of staring into my Parisian postcards of the Eiffel Tower, glancing down and then glancing up, trying to reconcile reality with the picture. Jessica studied the glittering sequins and pearls, the lace overlay on the bodice, and then back up into the mirror just to be sure her eyes did not deceive her.

She was utterly adorable.

For the first time in four years, I allowed my mind to wander down that path. I cautiously considered my own wedding day, especially with Ted's unequivocal intentions in pursuing me. However, I no longer thought of marriage as a goal in and of itself, as my one opportunity to accomplish something my siblings likely wouldn't. My parents had treated my engagement to Jason with all the enthusiasm of a papercut.

Thankful the memory no longer carried the pain of disappointment and rejection, I chuckled at the thought of how much more they'd disapprove of the mighty Margolin than they ever did of Jason.

"What are you snickering about over there?" Jessica asked.

"Just admiring you...admiring yourself," I said.

"Beck, I don't think I am ever going to take this dress off."

"When is the big day?" one of the salesgirls asked.

"June 5th," Jessica said before breaking into a fit of giggles.

The salesgirl smiled tolerantly, apparently used to this level of giddiness.

"Jessica," I said, glancing at my phone, "we're supposed to meet Nathan and his brother in five minutes, and it takes fifteen to get to the restaurant."

"Too bad you're not single," Jessica said. "Because Matty is cute."

"Definitely taken, my friend."

"For all of a week," she retorted. "Just don't rule anything out, okay? Office relationships can become disasters."

"Gee, thanks," I said, rolling my eyes. "Weren't you the one who called Ted smolderingly delicious? Besides, I'd thought you'd be happy for me."

Focus temporarily off of herself, Jessica met my eyes in the mirror. "You guys are really serious, aren't you?"

I nodded. "I know this day is all about you, Jessica, but it would be great if you could be happy for me too."

"Sorry, Beck."

I smiled at her, forgiveness granted.

"Now, can you help me out of my dress? I've had to pee for the last thirty minutes, and I'm not going to make it without some help."

I laughed and performed my maid-of-honor duty.

Officially, we arrived thirty minutes late. According to Jessica, the laws of time, space, physics, and finances did not apply to her as a bride-to-be. Nathan seemed mildly irritated but very happy to see his bride. Conversely, Nathan's older brother, Matty, did not temper his general dislike of my best friend. Matty's barrage of cutting and sarcastic barbs eventually caught Nathan's attention.

"Enough Matty!" Nathan barked. "Knock it off, or just leave."

"This is a farce," Matty said, glaring at the two of them. "Nathan, you're engaged to a self-absorbed airhead who isn't even a believer, and you can't get anyone to perform the ceremony. Not that it's stopped the Jewish princess from acting like the entire world revolves around her little fantasy."

"What's your problem?" I asked, irritated. "They're getting married. Jessica's allowed to be excited about it."

Matty rolled his eyes with an air of longsuffering. "And here comes the perpetually single best friend ready to read me the riot act."

"Could you possibly be any more rude?" I snapped. "How dare you look down your nose at Jessica with the way you've been acting! Deal with your own logs before you start judging me or my friend."

Matty's blue eyes narrowed. "Look, I appreciate your loyalty to Jessica, but you can't tell me they're not making a mistake, Rebecca."

"Mistake or not, it's their mistake to make. Jessica will be a part of your family in seven months. You can keep acting like a self-righteous toad, or you can get to know one of the most generous and thoughtful people on the planet."

"Thank you, Beck," Jessica said tearfully.

With a mixture of hurt and anger, Nathan said, "Matty, just go. I'll find another best man...one who actually supports our marriage."

"You can't even find a rabbi who supports your marriage. Why should anybody else?"

Whatever Jessica found "cute" about Matty at the bridal boutique ended when she splashed her cup of water on her fiancé's brother. Matty barreled past me out of the booth, drenching a good portion of my own outfit in the process.

"He stepped on my foot," I said, annoyed.

Nathan wrapped his arm around my sobbing best friend.

"What if he's right?" Jessica said through her tears. "Nathan, why are you marrying me? You know I don't believe in Jesus, and I have no idea what you see in me."

As Nathan poured his heart to my best friend, I quietly

excused myself and allowed them their privacy. Shaking water droplets from my coat, I pulled out my phone and texted Nathan to drop Jessica off at home.

Keys in hand and about to enter my car, I heard Matty say, "I'm sorry about your coat. And your foot. And for pretty much everything in there."

I whirled around. "Why didn't you say any of that inside the restaurant? You humiliated my best friend!"

Matty exhaled a heavy sigh and rubbed the back of his neck. "Look, I'm trying to save them both the pain and embarrassment of an elaborate wedding and a very short marriage."

I scoffed. "Spare me the noble intentions, Matty. You need to stop projecting your own experiences onto your brother and Jessica."

Matty's gaze came up sharply to meet mine. "What did they tell you about me? Jessica wanted to play matchmaker for you and me, but Nathan finally shut her up about it. Apparently, I became available as soon as I signed my divorce papers."

Sighing wearily, I said, "Sounds like Jessica and I need another conversation about personal boundaries. How long did she push for a relationship?"

Relief filled Matty's face. "Months, I think. Nathan also encouraged it, but now, he's trying to reverse course since you started seeing that guy from work. I told them I had planned to ask you out back in September, but obviously, I never got around to it. When I mentioned it again yesterday to Nathan, he said you were dating a coworker and to back off."

"So, the elaborate show of disdain was meant to reassure them somehow?" I asked incredulously. "And that still doesn't explain why you were so mean to Jessica."

Matty's eyes shifted away. "It's complicated."

I tapped my foot impatiently when he didn't elaborate.

"What?" he said, exasperated.

"You tell me. What part of any of this is complicated? Your brother loves my best friend. Why can't you just be happy for them?"

"It's not that simple."

"Why not?" I demanded.

"It just isn't, okay?"

I shook my head in disgust. "I really don't get you, Matty. Whatever you hoped to accomplish back there failed miserably. Frankly, it's an embarrassment as a Christian. Why would Jessica have an interest in knowing Christ with the pitiful example you just displayed for her?"

Matty kept his eyes glued to the concrete, properly chastised but not willing to own his mistake.

"I think it was an act of God that kept you from asking me out, Matty. Even if I wasn't in love with Ted, I would never subject myself to someone who could be so cruel."

Matty smirked. "You can't be in love with someone that fast."

Unfazed, I replied, "I don't need your permission or your approval for my feelings, and neither does your brother."

"I wasn't always like this, you know."

"That's for you and God to sort out, Matty. Meanwhile, go fix things with your Nathan and Jessica. You owe them that much."

Not waiting for a response, I climbed into my car and sped off. Matty still stood in the restaurant parking lot as he faded from my rear-view mirror.

I called Ted, eager to hear his voice, even if just his voicemail recording.

I needed to tell him how I felt.

CHAPTER 16

"I've missed you," Ted said into my hair.

I smiled, equally enjoying the embrace. "Tell me again how it's only been three weeks," I said dreamily.

"You gave me quite a surprise this morning, Rebecca. I didn't expect to find you standing in my parking space with matching cups from Vincenzo's."

"Thanks for not hitting me," I said, laughing. "The look on your face was worth the near collision."

Ted pulled back to look in my eyes. His hands cupped my face chilled from the November air. "How are you doing? How are Jessica and Nathan?"

I sighed. "Jessica's now questioning whether she's in love with Nathan or just in love with getting married. She's freaking out that there's no way to bridge the gap between the two of them. Matty, to his credit, did go back in and apologize."

"And he didn't try to hit on you or anything? Seven years I waited, and apparently not a moment too soon."

I grinned. "Definitely not interested in Matty, no matter how cute Jessica seems to think he is."

"Jessica actually said that? I have a hard time imagining that after the stunt he pulled in the restaurant."

"She wanted me to keep him around as a backup in case things don't work out between you and me."

Golden eyes glowed at me. "I'm not going anywhere, Rebecca."

I wanted to declare my own feelings for Ted, the ones that had been building steadily over the past year. My heart certainly felt it, but I felt an urging to hold back. Instead, I closed my eyes and just savored Ted's arms shielding me from the cold, concrete walls of the parking garage.

As Thanksgiving approached, I ignored five mammoth text messages from my aunt, all laden with increasing doses of emotional manipulation. She waxed on about the importance of family, but for the Ivy's, this simply meant the *appearance* of it. After one final text about the possibility of my father dying tomorrow, Ted snatched the phone from my hand and deleted the entire thread of messages.

"Well, that was rather heavy-handed," I said once he'd returned my cell phone.

"Did you plan to respond to her garbage or simply torment yourself by wondering if her emotional vomit had any merit?"

"You're angry," I said, studying his face.

"You're right."

"Why?"

He sighed. "Rebecca, you're meeting my parents in two days, and you don't need any added stress. While I have no doubt they will love you, you've also been dealing with training Taylor and Eric and all of the ongoing Nathan-Jessica-Matty drama."

My lips upturned slightly. "It's scary how well you know me."

"I had a lot of time to study. Also, it turns out I'm not an idiot."

I laughed.

"Why don't we go for a walk on your lunch break?" he asked.

"And add more gossip fuel to the fire? Leave it to Kyle to get completely wasted after his last day at Culver and spill his life story to MacKenzie."

"Wish I could burn that recommendation letter," Ted said under his breath.

"On the upside, most of CID is too scared of you to ask me any inappropriate questions."

"Thank goodness for small favors then, eh?"

I offered a half smile. "You're very attractive when you're being sardonic."

"I think that's the most intelligent compliment I've ever received," he said with a wink.

Phil picked the perfect moment to interrupt our hallway conversation. Grinning ear to ear, he said to Ted, "End the agony, and just marry the girl already! CID placed bets to see how long before you two either break up or get hitched."

"This weekend soon enough for you?" Ted snapped.

Phil cackled. He either had a death wish or zero fear of the mighty Margolin. No matter how much money Ted brought to Culver, Phil reigned supreme as commander-in-chief, and they both knew it.

"Rebecca, how about it? Sounds like Ted's cleared his calendar."

I chuckled and rolled my eyes. "Phil, don't you have trouble to start somewhere else in the office? Leave Ted alone."

Culver's CEO whistled *Married in the Chapel* as he re-entered the office through a side door.

"So, what are your plans for this weekend?" Ted asked playfully. "You know, if I wanted to fly us to Vegas or something?"

"Eager to be married again, are we?"

"Eager for a lot of things," he said, his gaze intense.

My face suddenly matched my crimson sweater.

"Aside from that!" Ted laughed. "I miss the companionship, the adventures, the 'us against the world' feeling as you go through life together. I miss the little things that people can sometimes take for granted in a relationship. Annie used to finish my sentences or interrupt me and say the exact words sitting on the tip of my tongue. It annoyed me how well she knew me, especially early on in our marriage during a fight. Nine out of ten times, she ripped apart my argument because she already knew what I would say." Ted smiled, momentarily lost in happy memories.

My own ghosts returned, replaying the old tapes of my parents, my siblings, Pastor, even Jason. They taunted me with how worthless, useless, and disposable I was.

Voice quivering, I said, "I know I might be pushing things here by saying this, and maybe it's too soon, but..."

Ted raised an eyebrow. "You okay?"

Frustrated that tears found themselves in my eyes, I stomped my foot. "Ugh, I hate this!"

Ted gently touched my arm. "Come with me downstairs. Our new receptionist looks like she's taking notes. It's impossible to get any privacy in this fishbowl."

"Nevermind. I have two RFPs going and a stack of proposals to get through. I...I probably shouldn't have said anything. I'm sorry," I said, hastily wiping the tears from my face.

"Rebecca," Ted said slowly, "what's wrong, and how can I help?"

Barely above a whisper, I replied, "I just hope I'm good enough for you."

Fleeing before Ted could respond, I buried myself under a mountain of work projects and training my new team.

I ignored my buzzing cell phone the rest of the afternoon, not sure if Ted had checked in on me or Aunt Eleanor launched another steaming pile of guilt. Either way, I kept my head down and immersed myself in my job. I needed the escape, a place where I felt confident and in control. I barely registered when Taylor and Eric took off for the day, let alone when the cleaning crew arrived to vacuum and empty out the trash cans.

"It's almost eight," Ted said from my new office doorway. "How long did you plan to hide from me?"

"I did say I had a lot of work," I said coolly, putting the finishing touches on a Benefits presentation for Joe Trautweig. I clicked save, closed the document, then finally leaned back into my chair.

"Is this how you normally deal with conflict?" Ted asked.

Sighing, I stood up from my chair, wobbling initially after sitting for so long. I found myself being steadied by Ted's outreached arm.

"Everybody else gone?" I asked.

"Hours ago, Rebecca."

"Then why are you still here?"

"Take a guess."

"Triple J?" I quipped.

Ted frowned. "Why did you say what you did by the elevators? Have I dumped too much work on you? Did I start treating you like I used to? Rebecca, I watched you step into your Culver shell right in front of me. You did this last year too after you left your old church. Did you panic because I talked about Annie? Are you scared of not measuring up to memories?"

He stepped closer and ran his hands up and down my arms. "I told you I love you. I meant it. Nothing has changed for me. Not Phil and his stupid jokes. Not all of the whispering whenever I walk by the CID cubes. Rebecca, please. Talk to me."

I didn't know how to express thirty-three years of inadequacy in words, thirty-three years of never being good enough to be loved, never being seen, always being used, manipulated, or treated like a doormat. I was the empathetic sap people came to when they wanted to wipe their problems off the bottom of their shoes and then forget my existence once they'd finished. I didn't know how to verbalize the pain of a heart so broken, beat up, and discarded that loving Ted felt like a miracle beyond description.

So I wept.

And Ted held me until I couldn't cry anymore.

Three days later, a ball of panic welled up as Ted drove me to his parents' house for Thanksgiving. I recognized the neighborhood as the same subdivision where Pastor and Ashley had summoned me to dinner two years earlier.

Pastor only invited the elite, inner circle to his home once he became installed as senior leader. People like Cynthia Russell bragged about those coveted invitations, effectively creating a distinction between themselves and those deemed unworthy of inclusion. They treated a welcome into Pastor's home as a tremendous privilege, Pastor himself remarking how special it was for me to be selected. I found the entire situation overblown to the point of absurdity, but I still felt flattered to receive it.

"Welcome," Ashley said, opening the beveled glass front

door for me. "Pastor's getting ready, and I let Connor and Olivia hang out in the backyard. Can I get you something to drink?"

"Water is fine," I said, stepping inside.

My eyes feasted upon perfectly appointed furnishings, and a sudden disquiet filled me. The house seemed too immaculate, too perfect, like a staged, model home rather than a place where *people* actually dwelled.

"Why don't you come into the kitchen?" Ashley said. "I'm putting the finishing touches on dinner, and I would appreciate the company."

Warmed by Ashley's change in demeanor from her usual SBC frost, I followed after her, observing that she seemed a little rounder in recent months. When I first arrived at SBC some thirteen years earlier, Pastor and Ashley were newlyweds, happy and in love. I remembered Ashley always being quiet, though kind. Pastor had inherited the congregation from his old mentor and founding leader, Pastor George Shipley, four or five years after I became a member of SBC.

"Your home is beautiful," I said once we entered the kitchen. I noted the contemporary design and state-of-the-art appliances.

The sparkle died in Ashley's eyes. "Pastor says God has blessed us mightily."

I startled, remembering the false modesty my father employed with Jason, even more so at Ashley's choice of phrasing. She seemed so unhappy even though everything around her screamed, "I'm living the dream!"

"Do you entertain a lot?" I asked, hoping to thaw the refrozen ice.

"Not as much as you might think," she said cryptically, pulling a lasagna from the oven.

My smile strained at my lips, not sure how to ease the

awkwardness. "Dinner smells amazing, Ashley. Pastor used to brag about your cooking all the time in youth group."

The heavy cloud sitting on my pastor's wife lifted slightly. "Those were the good old days," she said quietly. "We loved having you in our youth group, Rebecca. You always asked such great questions. You made us think too, especially when you told us the kinds of things they taught in your religion classes at college. Pastor took several of those questions to his own professors at seminary."

"Really?" I asked, returning her soft smile with one of my own. The old Ashley still lived and breathed somewhere within this current shell of a person.

She nodded, then glanced up at the entryway, her smile growing artificial at the arrival of Pastor. Clad in jeans and a cable knit sweater, he eschewed his standard church apparel of a suit and tie. He no longer looked like "Pastor," but a regular, flesh and blood man.

"Do I meet your fashion standards, Rebecca?" he said with a wink.

Embarrassed and horrified he noticed my appraisal, I blushed.

Pastor's smile grew into a conspiratorial grin, giving the impression of a private joke shared between the two of us.

Ashley choked, then coughed violently.

Strangely, Pastor just stood motionless while he watched his wife struggle. Circumventing him, I found my way to Ashley's side and patted her on the back. "Are you alright?"

"Fine," she replied once the coughing fit subsided. "Pastor, would you mind getting the children from outside?"

"Not a problem," he said cheerfully. He exited through a door leading to their deck and backyard.

Ashley stared into my eyes, holding my gaze for several uncomfortable seconds. "Be careful, Rebecca. Be very careful."

CHAPTER 17

I STARTLED. "EXCUSE ME?"

Suddenly aware she had said something out of place, or perhaps because we heard the approaching voices of Pastor and the children, Ashley distanced herself from me. She busied herself rearranging and refolding the already perfect kitchen towels.

Olivia and Connor entered the kitchen with Pastor, both of them the spitting image of their father. At eleven years-old, Connor stood almost equal in height to his petite mother. His temperament matched Ashley's, being generally very mild and unassuming. In total contrast, nine-year-old Olivia played the part of a spoiled princess, fully aware of her elevated rank as a Pastor's Kid.

"What's for dinner?" Connor said, offering his mom a hug.

Ashley visibly relaxed as soon as Connor entered the room. I smiled at the obvious connection between the two of them.

Before she could answer, Pastor said, "Well, this is a very special evening, children, and I hope we will be on our best behavior tonight." He gave a pointed look to Ashley and then to Olivia.

Olivia pursed her lips, but said nothing. Connor rolled his eyes.

"Connor, why don't you see about getting Miss Rebecca something to drink?" Ashley said brightly. "Olivia, can you grab the salad and the tongs, please? We're eating in the dining room tonight." She glanced briefly at Pastor who nodded his approval.

"Why do we need to eat in the dining room just for her?" Olivia said, looking over my outfit with obvious disdain. "It's not like she's gonna write one of those big checks like everyone else we invite over for fancy dinners."

"Olivia!!!" Pastor bellowed.

Something slithered into the room, something dark, ugly, and oppressive.

"You will remain silent the rest of the evening, or you will spend it hungry and alone in your room!" He towered over his daughter, yelling full volume a mere two inches from her nose. "Do you hear me, you ungrateful little Jezebel?!"

Olivia burst into tears as Pastor's face contorted into an angry, demonic mask. The nightmarish monster that haunted my dreams stood before me, except Bernard Ivy looked exactly like my pastor. I shuddered and stumbled backward, bumping into a barstool at the center island.

Ashley sprang into action, calming things immediately as she wrapped an arm around the now hysterical Olivia. I heard Olivia's wails long after Ashley escorted her from the room.

Glancing from their retreating figures to Pastor, I observed how lightning fast his countenance transformed back to its usual serenity.

"I can understand how Olivia's childish outburst might have caused some discomfort on your part," Pastor said, addressing me in soothing tones, "but let's not be so sensitive we hold onto offenses caused by a fourth grader, for goodness sake!"

I did a double take, convinced I'd misheard him.

Continuing, Pastor said, "Rebecca, you have a golden opportunity to rise above your history of rejection and demonstrate how much you've matured in this area. Please, don't allow Olivia's behavior to ruin your evening with us. I, for one, am very glad to have you here tonight."

From behind me, Connor snorted in disgust. "I can't believe you're ignoring how you just screamed at Olivia like a—"

"Connor!" Pastor barked. "Don't you have some food to bring to the dining room?"

Connor stormed from the room, muttering under his breath.

Pastor offered me the kind of indulgent smile given to placate a child afraid of the dark. Beneath the plastic expression, however, dark eyes glittered with tenuously controlled rage. My heart pounded as old memories of my father resurfaced again, memories of picture frames flying at my head for how I'd spoken up one too many times during a youth meeting or "shamed the family" by eating too much at a potluck luncheon.

"Rebecca," Pastor said, standing even closer than a few moments earlier, "I can see you're very distraught about the thoughtless words of a nine year-old, but I promise, you don't need to be. Quite candidly, it's a bit beneath you."

Realizing Pastor had me pinned against the bar stool, his face uncomfortably close to mine, my brain scrambled to find a means of escape. Years of abuse from Bernard Ivy had taught me to maintain a wide distance from this kind of emotional volatility. I spun away from Pastor and loudly called to Ashley that I would help set the table.

A silent war waged between my head and my heart. My brain implored my heart to look at the facts, the undeniable similarities to my own family, the same ominous presence that often encircled my father. It screamed shrilly about the family dynamics that proclaimed a far different narrative than the one presented at church. My heart fired back with numerous instances of warmth and kindness from Pastor, of countless hours of counsel and emails. Trying to reconcile the two felt like wading through cement. My heart refused to accept the painful contradiction to everything I had believed about Pastor and his family for almost thirteen years.

I felt a hand on the small of my back, and shivers involuntarily coursed through my body.

"Is everyone ready for dinner?" Pastor said with a sunny smile.

As if nothing unusual had occurred in the kitchen.

As if I merely imagined the presence of something evil that certainly didn't belong in the home of a man of God.

As if his wife didn't blink back tears when she noticed how long Pastor's hand remained on my back.

All of Jason's suspicions about Pastor's intentions toward me finally made sense as the memories resurfaced and replayed. The ghostly tango did not occur to torment me, but to shed light on a confusing and troublesome part of my past.

"Rebecca? Rebecca!" I heard Ted yell, seemingly through a tunnel.

My eyes blinked rapidly, my mind feverishly trying to transition from that horrible evening to the present day. Stuck in a nightmare where I couldn't wake up, my body too heavy to move, my mind cried out in blood curdling screams my lips refused to release. I heard the screech of tires and Ted's frantic voice as everything faded to black.

I opened my eyes to unfamiliar surroundings, a child's bedroom with striped, navy wallpaper, an oversized desk covered in sports trophies, and a clunky computer straight out of middle school.

"Oh, thank God!" a female voice said next to me.

I stared into familiar hazel eyes, though this pair belonged to a woman in her early sixties. Her tiny hands clutched mine, and I saw Jesus reflected in her gaze.

"Ted wanted to call 911. I told him we should pray. He mentioned you had another episode like this recently." At my confused expression, she said, "I'm Rose Margolin, Ted's mother."

I rubbed my eyes and tried to sit up. Rose placed an arm around my shoulder to help prop me up against a pillow.

"Where am I?" I asked groggily.

"Ted's old room," she said with a welcoming smile. "Obviously, we haven't changed much since 1995."

"Where is—"

The man of the hour appeared in the doorway before I could finish my question. His mother stood up so Ted could take her place in the chair next to the bed. She looked back and forth between the two of us absolutely beaming.

"What happened?" I said.

"You blacked out in my car," Ted answered grimly. "We were a few blocks from my parents' house, and I carried you inside."

I cringed at the thought of Ted carrying me anywhere. The words flew out of my mouth before I could think better of it. "Do you need a chiropractor?"

Ted's gaze turned hard. "You are not what they say you are. Turn the voices off, Rebecca."

Deliberately changing the subject, I said, "So, I just met your mother. Lovely woman. I see where you got those beautiful eyes."

If possible, Rose's grin grew larger. "Why don't I give you

two a few minutes? Ted, I asked your father to keep an eye on the turkey, but you know how focused he gets when he's watching football. Hopefully, it won't be jerky by the time I get in there. Rebecca, I look forward to meeting you properly in just a little bit." She patted my hand then quietly left the room.

Ted stood up from the chair, then motioned for me to scoot over on the tiny, twin bed. He wrapped an arm around me, and I snuggled my head against his heart. Pulling me closer to him with his free arm, he held me firmly.

His voice rumbled under me as he spoke. "First, are you okay? You hit your head hard against the door when you passed out."

"That would explain the knot above my right ear."

"Did the same thing happen in Jessica's condo too?

"Basically. Bad memories triggered a total panic attack and PTSD blackout."

"My folks are harmless, Rebecca."

"But Pastor lives off the first street in this neighborhood. They built that new section ten or twelve years ago, I think."

Ted's heartbeat accelerated under my ear.

"Don't get any stupid ideas, Ted. Pastor may not even live there anymore, and I honestly don't know what I would do if I saw him right now. It's a miracle I haven't run into any of them considering we all live in the same city."

"Why didn't you say something, Rebecca?"

"I didn't remember until we drove past the strip mall on the way over here. All of a sudden, the ghosts came back. I remembered being in his home."

"What were you doing there?" Ted said tightly, obviously drawing ugly conclusions.

"They invited me over for dinner. I remember being surprised because Ashley always acted so aloof and unfriendly.

She really changed after Pastor transitioned into the role of senior leader of the church. Suffice to say, it was not a pleasant evening."

"And that's it?" Ted said. "Just the idea of running into your pastor here?"

"No," I admitted, "but it will completely ruin Thanksgiving if I tell you right now."

He sighed, resigned to wait for answers. "Are you ready to meet my parents, or do you need a few minutes to get yourself together?"

"Well, I don't need to worry about embarrassing myself since they've already seen me unconscious and you lugging me around like a caveman."

"The second my mother saw us coming, she said God asked her to pray for you all morning. She said you were under attack, and God has a purpose for all of your pain."

Betrayed, I pulled away from Ted. I sat up and turned to confront him. "How much did you tell her about me?"

Ted held up his hands in innocence. "I told her we work together, I'm in love with you, and I'm going to ask you to marry me as soon as I think you'll let me. That's about it."

My anger melted quickly into a beautiful smile. "Thank you for explaining."

"Which part?" he said, returning my grin.

"All of it. Your mother's comments just caught me off guard."

"Mom's pretty serious about her Jesus stuff. Sometimes she just *knows* things. It's uncanny."

"Ted, you know I'm pretty serious about this Jesus stuff too, don't you? I saw the Lord in your mother's eyes. As soon as I recognized it, I felt God's peace wash over me. The panic completely vanished."

Ted held my gaze, sitting up and searching for something. "Is that what always shines in these beautiful eyes of yours, Rebecca? Your Jesus?"

"He doesn't just have to be *my* Jesus," I said gently.

"I want to understand how he let Annie die the way she did. I want to know why he allowed you to go through all of the pain and suffering you have. How could any of that be the work of a loving God?"

A quick rap on the door interrupted our conversation. Steve Margolin, Ted's father, peeked his head in the room. Bald, with silver hair at the base of his head and a full beard, he reminded me of a cap-free Santa Claus.

"Everything okay in here?" he asked. Looking at me, he said, "Rebecca, now that you're conscious, it's nice to finally meet you. Theodore, your sisters just arrived with their families, so get into the dining room before I have to explain the birds and the bees to my grandchildren."

While I audibly gasped, Ted grimaced. "Thanks, Dad. Not awkward at all."

Steve wore the same cheeky grin he'd passed along to his son. Megawatt appeared as soon as I recognized the smile. After a visible startle, Steve chuckled to himself and closed the door.

"Remind you of anyone?" Ted said. He stood off the bed and offered me a hand up.

Leaning on him as I tested out my balance, I replied, "No wonder Phil gets under your skin so much. He acts just like your father."

"They've been best friends since college. Phil jokes he was there for my *bris,* and now he watches me run circles around him in business."

"What's a bris?"

"It's a Jewish ceremony for a baby boy when they circumcise him."

I stopped dead in my tracks. "There's a ceremony for that? They don't just do it in the hospital?"

"Jews do it on the eighth day. Big party. Beaming grandparents. Plenty of lox, bagels, and embarrassing stories your mother brings up at inopportune times."

"Wow," I said. "You learn something every day."

CHAPTER 18

IN A MATTER OF MINUTES, THE FIVE MARGOLIN grandchildren turned their grandparents' family room into a warzone of baby dolls, crayons, and coloring books. I laughed at the mess and the chaos, at the gathering of people who seemed to truly enjoy one another's company. My heart constricted at the possibility of calling these people my own family one day.

"You okay?" Ted asked, putting an arm around me. He followed my gaze to the two youngest grandchildren jumping from couch to couch. "The kids are kind of noisy."

I looked up at him and smiled. "Best Thanksgiving ever. I can't keep track of which kids belong to which sister, but I'm sure I'll sort it out eventually."

Ted grinned. "Jen and Barry's kids are Addison, Riley, and Jordyn. Addison usually plays mother hen since she's the oldest of the grandchildren. Jen's the oldest of the three Margolin kids, and Amanda is only a year older than you."

"So we're both middle children?"

"So it would seem," he said. "As you can see, Amanda will finally even out the score with our big sister in a few months."

"And they have the two little girls?" I said, pointing to a kindergartener and toddler fighting over a doll.

Ted chuckled. "Anneliese and Blakeley," he said. "Jeremy nearly did cartwheels when they found out they're having a boy."

I glanced over at the expectant parents, Jeremy scrolling on his phone next to his wife. The two Margolin sisters shared a video with Rose.

At the sound of a blood curdling scream, all grown up eyes scanned the room to locate the afflicted child. Exhaling a weary sigh, Jeremy shoved his phone in his pocket and broke up a fight between his daughters.

Ted grimaced. "Sorry."

"For what? I think it's fantastic!"

"The noise?" he asked, incredulous.

"All of it! I can't imagine all of these children running around the Ivy palace, knocking over my father's prized possessions or breaking up the reverent silence he demands."

"Sounds miserable," Ted said.

"Exactly. The only real talking on Thanksgiving happened once my family got bored picking on me and found something else to discuss."

"I'm so sorry, Rebecca."

"Don't be. I'm thoroughly enjoying the silent treatment. I don't know what version of the truth my sister painted after the farmer's market, but Aunt Eleanor called you a psychopathic deviant, and she says I deserve no less after what I've done to the family."

"Ah, good old Aunt Eleanor. I suppose I have to give your

family points for their persistence, even if I find their behavior reprehensible."

I squeezed his hand. "Thank you for everything, Ted."

"Well, this is very cozy," Steve said as he navigated his way around the jumping grandchildren. "If I'm not being too much of a *buttinsky* here, you two make a very handsome couple."

I grinned while Ted forced the corners of his mouth to pull ever so slightly.

"Smile, would ya?" Steve said, clapping his son on the shoulder. "And no comments about food from the box this year. Not all of us can afford to remodel our kitchen because we want to be the next Robert Fray."

"Dad, it's Bobby—"

Steve burst into laughter while Ted released an exasperated breath. The flicker in Ted's hazel eyes alerted me to pain behind the forced smile. Steve referred to Ted as "Uncle Big Shot," and it underscored a playful disregard for his son's feelings. I suddenly understood Ted's petulance toward Phil's goading at work.

"Dinner's ready!" Rose called, the sound of cheering children meeting her in response.

Ted's littlest niece, three-year-old Blakeley, tugged on my pant leg.

"Me sit wichoo," she said, her doe eyes absolutely irresistible.

I glanced at her mother, Amanda, to translate.

"Blakeley has been going through this phase where she only wants to eat meals in Mommy or Daddy's lap," she explained. "Please don't feel obligated, no matter how cute this little stinker is."

I smiled, bending down to enjoy that cherubic face. My heart squeezed at the thought of my own children, of time lost with

Jason, but the possibility of a real future with Ted. After dinner, Blakeley stuck to me like glue. She curled up in my lap, kissed my cheeks repeatedly, and told me she loved me.

Throughout the course of what turned out to be a wonderful Thanksgiving celebration, several pairs of matching hazel eyes watched me.

But only one pair glowed golden.

After dinner and hugs to the entire Margolin clan, Ted drove me back to my apartment rather than his house as originally planned. Hoping to avoid any other triggers after my earlier blackout, he said I could come over for some "real Thanksgiving food" the following day. Ted pulled into the parking space next to my car, and we both saw a note placed conspicuously under the windshield wiper of my sedan.

"Stay in the car," Ted warned.

"Ted, I—"

"Look, I've already been scared half to death watching you pass out, and I'm not letting it happen again. I don't know which one of the narcissistic vampires in your life tried to ruin your Thanksgiving, but you don't have to face them alone anymore. Stay in the car, and I'll be right back."

Ted's decisive tone cooled my arguments. I watched him through the windshield as steam practically poured from his ears. He balled the note into his fist as he let loose a string of profanity that would make a sailor blush.

Ted looked up, suddenly aware of his audience. He shoved the note in his coat pocket, and reentered the car, taking several calming breaths before he dared making eye contact.

"Your father seems hell-bent on your imminent destruction since you refuse to allow him the satisfaction of slowly torturing you to death instead."

Stunned by his vehemence, I said, "I know you hate my

father, Ted, but do you think you could be overreacting?"

"Rebecca," he said urgently, grabbing me by the shoulders, "I'm concerned for your safety! Your father overtly threatened you!"

"Do I even want to know what the note said?" I asked weakly, dread filling me from head to toe.

"Some not so subtle threats, plenty of Bible verses condemning you to the worst types of punishment and hell for rejecting him, followed by promises of more to come. He used the word *unsubmissive* at least five or six times. Apparently, that's a big thing for your father. That and this supposed shame you've cast upon him."

I blanched. "I don't understand. Why now? He has all of First United believing I'm some kind of demonized lunatic. Why the sudden need to pretend all is well in the Ivy clan?"

"It always comes back to control with these psychos, Rebecca. They want to play God and tinker with you like you're their own little puppet. My grandmother did it to my father his entire life and used him for emotional support because of how badly she poisoned her own marriage. She constantly nitpicked my grandfather, then played the victim when he acted sullen and resentful because of it. Witnessing it firsthand felt like standing in the middle of a chemical waste spill."

"That's awful."

"My grandmother trained my father to feel responsible for her happiness. If *mommeleh* wasn't happy, my father's job meant fixing it. She cried on his shoulder about being married to someone who didn't really love her. Not like how my father loved her, of course. She treated him like the golden boy so long as he did whatever mommeleh wanted. It was so twisted, Rebecca. My grandmother even tried the same shenanigans with me and Annie. Annie didn't put up with it, and I knew my grandmother would never change. I never saw my grandparents after that."

"All things considered, how did your father wind up so normal?" I said.

Ted raised an eyebrow.

"Oh, stop! Annoying you with dad jokes hardly compares to whatever baloney my father put on that note."

"Rebecca, could you stay somewhere else tonight? I know you said Jessica went out of town to meet Nathan's parents, but would she mind if you crashed there for a little while? Do you have a spare key to her condo?"

"No, but Kyle might. I can text him and ask."

"I don't like the idea of Goldstein knowing you're alone in his sister's house."

"How is that different from Kyle knowing I'm alone in my own apartment?"

"Because his sister doesn't have an alarm system like you do. Because it looks a lot less suspicious if Goldstein shows up at his sister's place rather than yours."

I sighed. "I hate the fact you're probably right about that."

"You may not like this idea, Rebecca, but what do you think about staying—?"

"I can't sleep under the same roof as you!" I protested loudly.

"My parents' house," Ted finished with a wry smile. "I'm suddenly so repulsive now?"

I scoffed. "More like too tempting. Total recipe for disaster."

"How do you feel staying in the same neighborhood where your Pastor lives?"

"About that," I said.

"Yes?"

"I made a few inquiries via your parents' neighborhood

directory, an online search, and a real estate site while the rest of you lathered up your pumpkin pie in whipped cream."

"To do what?"

"To confirm if Pastor still lived there. They sold the house not long after I left SBC. If the internet is to be trusted, Ashley moved with the kids to Kentucky. I know her folks live there. I can only assume Pastor shacked up somewhere locally with Cynthia Russell."

"And did you research that as well?"

"Eh, sometimes ignorance is bliss. If I knew where they lived, I'd be fighting anxiety any time I drove in the vicinity."

Suddenly changing the topic, Ted said, "Rebecca, when does the lease renew on your apartment?"

"February, why?"

"What do you think about getting married and moving in with me once your lease is up? Better yet, I'll pay for any exorbitant, early termination fees your lease stipulates, and we can get married this weekend. I'll move you into my house, and I can rest easy knowing you're safe."

"What?" I whispered.

Ted took my hands in his. "You look horrified, Rebecca. Can I get a chance to try it again, or have you suffered enough trauma for the day?"

"Ted, this is crazy!" I said, finding my voice. "We've known each other as coworkers for seven years, but we just started dating a month ago! I know you understand the challenges of marriage, but you also married someone you knew your entire life!"

"Rebecca, I—"

Ignoring him, my panic level rose with each word. "There are things you have to know about Pastor before we even talk about marriage. Ted, this feels like a runaway freight train!"

"I'm not going anywhere, Rebecca. Talk to me."

I leaned back in the passenger seat and closed my eyes. "Ted, I'm being bombarded in every area of my life, and I can barely catch my breath. If it's not something with Jessica, or work, then it's my family, or Pastor, or you."

"Am I overwhelming you with my own selfishness because I want to get married? Even if it's to protect you?"

I pinched the bridge of my nose. "Ted, our relationship just shot to light speed."

In a painfully subdued voice, he asked, "Rebecca, what do you really want?"

My eyelids flew open. There was Ted's vulnerability again, that fear of rejection hidden underneath all of the "Uncle Big Shot" bluster. Turning my head to the side, I drank in Ted's profile, handsome despite his pinched features. Gently, I placed my hand on the side of his face and turned it toward mine. He cupped my palm in his.

Ted's voice came out low and raw, "Rebecca, I don't know how much longer I can stand this. I want you. I want to be with you. I can't imagine my life without you in it, and I want it to be legal. I'm tired of waking up alone, thinking about you, wondering what you like to talk about first thing in the morning, wishing I had you there with me. In the interest of transparency here, I've wanted this longer than just the past four weeks."

"Me too," I confessed. "I think it started the day we shared an elevator in the parking garage."

"Earlier than that for me," he said huskily, squeezing the hand still held against his face. "I would have started 'the rest of our lives together' four weeks ago in Jessica's kitchen. If you need me to wait, then I will. I will suffer in complete agony, but I'll do it if that's what you need."

CHAPTER 19

WHILE MY HEART FLUTTERED LIKE A CAGED BIRD, I felt the peace of God wash over me.

It's not good for man to be alone, I heard the Lord say.

My mind cried, *Lord, I love him. I don't have any doubts he loves me, but this is insane! Crazy! We haven't done any premarital counseling, and this is just happening too fast!*

The Lord began to speak to me in memorized Bible verses. *Forget the former things; do not dwell on the past. See, I am doing a new thing! Now it springs up; do you not perceive it? I am making a way in the wilderness and streams in the wasteland.*

Tears stung my eyes. I had grown so accustomed to the desert, of being parched and thirsty for love, that I felt overwhelmed by the Ted Margolin deluge raining down on me.

The Lord spoke again, *I will take away your shame and disgrace and cause you to live happy as a mother of children.*

My mind protested under the weight of a lifetime of religious teaching. *This man doesn't know you. He says he doesn't want to. How can this possibly be Your will?*

I know the plans I have for you. Plans to prosper you. Plans for a future and a hope.

"This is nuts. Absolutely nuts," I whispered aloud, no longer able to keep my thoughts private.

Trust in Me with all of your heart, and don't rely on your own understanding.

"God, this is impossible," I murmured. "How can this even be happening?"

No longer will they call you Deserted, or name your land Desolate. But you will be called Hephzibah, and your land Beulah; for the Lord will take delight in you, and your land will be married.

Ted studied my face. He watched me pray and also listen for a response. His eyes filled with wonder and tenderness.

"God is very real to you, isn't He?" Ted asked.

I smiled through my tears. "Yes, but I'd be lying if I said I wasn't scared. I'm scared of all of this being real, not just wanting to see my prayers answered, but actually walking in it. Does that make sense?"

"Perfect sense. I saw that incredible smile of yours when you thanked me for protecting you from Goldstein, and I knew right then I wanted to marry you. It scared me half to death."

Tears slipped down my cheeks. "This all feels like a dream. Too good to be true."

I heard the smile in Ted's voice. "Is that a yes?"

Supernova answered in the affirmative.

As Ted leaned in for a celebratory kiss, the crinkle of Bernard Ivy's note reminded us how we had reached this place in our relationship so quickly. Pulling back, Ted suggested we attend to business first, and he escorted me into my apartment to grab clothes and other essentials. He gave me a few minutes to read my father's note but insisted we give it to his attorney should we need it later for a restraining order.

I scanned the single page letter quickly, my mind unable to endure more after he said,

You can't keep hiding from me, Rebecca Joanne. I will find you, and you will pay for all of the shame and embarrassment you've brought to the Ivy family name.

Ted and I drove back to his parents' home in silence, both of us consumed with the precipice on which we now stood. The pastor's daughter in me could not rationalize marriage to a man so angry at the Lord he didn't want to acknowledge God's existence. The pastor's daughter could not explain the peace that far surpassed my own understanding despite the whirlwind pace of our relationship. For all of the youth group and singles ministry classes on the importance of "being equally yoked," I knew in the depths of my being I would grow old and gray with this man.

When we pulled up to the Margolins' house a scant ninety minutes after we'd left, I felt a fresh wave of courage. I watched Ted as he turned off the engine and unbuckled his seatbelt. Turning to me, his mouth curved into a slow, sizzling smile as megawatt greeted him.

"We're really going to do this, aren't we?" I said.

"I have three different justices of the peace and another two judges ready to go on speed dial," he said. "I suppose now would be a good time to ask if you want a fairytale wedding like Jessica."

I shook my head. "Just you, Ted. And I love you."

Not missing the clear invitation, the mighty Margolin proved himself a very perceptive man as well as an exceptional kisser. His parents also witnessed Ted's kissing prowess when the outside lights turned on. We hurriedly explained the situation once we got inside.

Sitting in the Margolins' kitchen, Steve said, "You two realize how fast this is happening, don't you?"

"Yes," Ted and I answered in unison. We exchanged glances and smiled. Ted's hand found mine under the table.

"Theodore, you two barely know each other," Steve continued. "Rebecca's family situation makes it seem more romantic, but it has the two of you running high on emotions."

Rose made meaningful eye contact with both of us. "Ted, Rebecca has wounds she may not even be aware of yet. Your father and I struggled for the first ten years of our marriage because he wrestled with denial about his family. Your grandmother schemed and tried to usurp my role every chance she got. When I refused to appease her, she went crying to your father, playing the victim. She deliberately pitted the two of us against each other. Rebecca's father sounds even worse than Phyllis Margolin, and those are words I never thought I'd utter about another living soul."

"Mom, I can't explain it," Ted replied. "I have an urgency in my gut to do this as soon as possible. I can't shake the feeling."

She reached across the table and grabbed Ted's free hand. "And that's why I believe you two should get married."

"Rose!" Steve said, outraged. "You just finished telling them how much our marriage suffered because of my family." Turning to Ted he said, "Son, I don't want you to struggle the way your mother and I did by rushing into marriage. I know you've been lonely since Annie died, trying to fill the emptiness by working yourself to death—"

"That's enough, Dad!" Ted said, jumping to his feet. "This has nothing to do with Annie and everything to do with Rebecca. I loved Annie, but she's a part of my past. I moved on a while ago. I can barely put into words what I feel for the woman beside me."

"Because you don't even know her!" Steve yelled, rising from his chair with equal vehemence as his son. "Ted, listen to yourself! You don't even sound like you. I know this all seems very romantic, swooping in to rescue the damsel in distress, but you can't marry someone after only a month of dating! How do you know she's not some gold digger trying to rope you in with a sob story?"

"Gold digger?" I mouthed incredulously.

"Rebecca and I are getting married with or without your approval, Dad. You can be there to support us, or you can miss out on the best thing that's ever happened to me. Regardless, I won't allow you to disrespect my future wife. Are we clear on that?"

Rose joined the other two standing Margolins, her arms outstretched between father and son locked in a scowling contest.

"Steve! Ted! Enough already! This isn't accomplishing anything, and Rebecca has endured more than enough excitement for one day. Sit down, act like adults, and let's try to make the best of this."

Steve and Ted plopped down into their chairs almost petulantly, neither of the six foot giants a match for the five foot Margolin matriarch. Rose Margolin embodied the quiet self-assurance of an army general with scars and stories aplenty.

"Rebecca, you mentioned you had more to tell about your former pastor," she said. "I still can't believe they lived just a few streets down from us. It's amazing we never met them."

"More like a miracle," I said. "Pastor could sell snake oil to a boa constrictor. He can be absolutely charming when he wants to be."

"Most sociopaths are," Ted said. "To see my grandmother on her best behavior, you'd never know what lurks beneath."

"That's still my mother you're talking about," Steve said defensively.

Ted and Rose both turned and glared at him.

"Oh, the stories I could share," Rose said.

"Is she still alive?" I asked.

"As far as we know," Rose said. "Steve's father passed away several years ago, but his mother remained a very active member in the Jewish community. I have no doubt she still terrorizes her mahjong club."

"Tell us the story, Rebecca," Steve said, eager to change the subject. "It may take me a while to accept this marriage, but I'd rather know what we're getting ourselves into here."

I took a deep breath. "Ted, even though I shared my suspicions about Pastor seeking a physical relationship with me—"

"And by *physical* you mean...?" Steve said, his voice trailing off.

I blushed, ashamed, but determined to finally share my story.

"I see," he said, his mouth a thin line.

Ted nodded for me to continue.

"I began attending Sycamore Bible Church in college, but the dynamics of the congregation were very different with Pastor Shipley in charge. He retired sort of suddenly, but they had already groomed Pastor to take over years earlier."

"Mysterious disappearance?" Rose asked.

"Yes. It seems odd, huh? Given what happened with Pastor, it certainly makes me wonder."

"Do you think the old pastor and the new pastor shared similar offenses?" Rose said, finishing my unspoken thought.

Murmuring loud enough for all to hear, Steve said, "And she wonders why I want nothing to do with her Jesus *shtick*."

"You really want to go there?" his wife fired back. "Do you want to talk about your old rabbi who hit on me when I was pregnant with Amanda? Sin is sin, Steve. It doesn't matter if you're Jewish, Christian, or anything in between."

"Dad, is that true?" Ted asked.

"Rabbi Epstein had a reputation back in the day," Steve grudgingly admitted, "but he cleaned up his act. I still think your mother misread his meaning."

Rose exhaled an exasperated sigh. "Steven, he stared at my neckline for at least half a minute before commenting on how much the new baby would enjoy nursing. I can't believe you think he meant anything innocent by that, even thirty-five years later!"

"Did you say Rabbi Epstein?" I asked, suddenly realizing why the name sounded familiar.

"Yes, he's still the head rabbi at Temple Beth Tefillah over in Danbury," Steve said.

Ted and I exchanged glances. I wondered if the Goldstein family knew the truth about their rabbi.

"Leviathan," Rose spat the word like a curse.

A shudder ran through my entire body. "Rose, what do you know that I don't? God mentions this mythical sea monster during His rebuke of Job, but I never understood why."

"This thing always shows up the same way," Rose said, "slithering around and infecting congregations and people of all denominations and sizes. You have the strong, alpha leader with an engaging, yet highly manipulative public persona. They always have an enabling spouse who publicly supports the leader with any manner of lies, no matter how small or grandiose. They'll sacrifice everything to protect the leader's image to the outside world."

"Yes," I whispered, my eyes huge. "How did you know?"

She continued, "The ringleader surrounds themselves with an inner circle of flying monkeys who jump to do their bidding, all competing for favor from this leader they practically worship. The worker bees dwell on the fringes, the ones who long to be accepted by the elite crowd and are always eager to please."

"Rose, this is scary," I said, leaning in and looking directly into her eyes. "You're reaching into my mind and pulling out the details."

"Oh, there's so much more, honey. They fast track certain folks into the upper ranks, usually because they're beautiful, talented, or bring wealth and prestige. Most people stand on the outside desperately wanting access to that elite core. The leader and their minions deliberately withhold acceptance, causing the outer circle members to endure one humiliating exercise after another to prove their loyalty to the leader. Eventually, the outsiders either wake up and leave, or they sell their soul to gain the approval of the leader and their inner circle minions. They'll overlook and excuse any manner of abuse so long as they don't lose their place in line."

"Mom," Ted said, "you just described fifteen different scenarios that happened in our office, with our clients, or even on the news. Are you telling me this *Leviathan* causes all of that too?"

Rose turned to Ted. "That's exactly what I'm saying, son, because you can set your watch to how it all manifests the same way."

CHAPTER 20

AT LONG LAST, I KNEW THE NAME OF THE MONSTER tormenting me since childhood. I stuttered and stammered trying to process the information as old ghosts collided with revelation and truth.

"Rose, there's something cultish in how Pastor and my father run their respective churches. They treat any recognized leader in almost godlike fashion, and they shame and marginalize all dissenters as 'unsubmissive,' 'having a Jezebel spirit,' or my father's personal favorite, 'having issues with authority.' I trained myself to believe I just imagined the similarities, but this all sounds like the same demon showing its ugly face."

"All right, I've had enough of this Leviathan mumbo jumbo," Steve snapped. Turning to Ted and me, he said, "Your mother has talked about this demon thing for the last forty years. Tonight is about Rebecca's past, not Rose's spiritual warfare theories."

Unfazed, Rose turned to me with an intense gaze. "You're not crazy, imagining things, or too sensitive, Rebecca. I'm sure they've told you some variation of those lies because I've heard them all myself."

I stared into Rose's hazel eyes for a long minute, deep understanding reflected in the flecks of gold she shared with her son. My own heart pounded as countless memories morphed from fuzzy balls of confusion into well-ordered patterns of behavior. A lifelong cloud of pain and abuse dissipated to reveal the truth underneath.

Taking note of my rigid posture, Ted said, "You know what, why don't we table this discussion until we've all gotten a good night's sleep? This may be the longest Thanksgiving in recorded history."

The senior Margolins spoke in hushed, fervent tones. For some reason, Rose's mention of Leviathan irked Steve to the depths of his soul. His palpable agitation seemed such a far cry from the teasing jokester I had met earlier that day. We left them alone to hash things out.

"I don't know if I've ever met another person who fully understood my mother and all of her Leviathan theories," Ted said as we walked to his childhood bedroom.

I plopped down into his old desk chair. "It seems like Rose and I share quite a few common experiences. As much as I love Jessica, she has no frame of reference to understand this level of dysfunction. I don't think she sees how malicious, calculated, and deliberate the behavior is."

Ted fell back against the bed, his legs hanging off the front at the knee. He shaded his eyes with his arm. "I feel like I could sleep for a week."

I chuckled low. "We're not sharing a bed, so find another room, buddy. I'm commandeering your old one."

Ted groaned. "That's assuming I can move my ancient carcass from the bed."

"If you're ancient, that puts me just behind you at medieval."

He cracked open one eye and grinned at me. "You're very cute, you know."

Megawatt appeared in response. "So I've been told."

"Marry me?" Ted said playfully.

"Did you have a particular time frame in mind, Mr. Margolin?"

"Tomorrow too soon?"

"Yes, but only because it's Black Friday. I doubt any of your speed dial friends will want to perform a ceremony when they could be out trampling each other for a new, flat screen television instead."

"Do you want to go look for wedding bands?"

I laughed. "Are you serious?"

He opened both eyes and stared at me for a long minute. The gold in his eyes told more than words ever could. I felt loved, truly loved for *me*.

Peeling my tired body off the chair, I crawled next to Ted and wrapped an arm around his chest. He responded by pulling me closer to himself and kissing the top of my head.

"Does the future Mrs. Margolin prefer white gold, yellow gold, or platinum?"

I suddenly remembered Phil's admonition to Ted that past Monday, the quick jab meant to keep the mighty Margolin in check. I laughed until tears streamed down my cheeks.

"Is this sleep deprivation induced hysterics, or can you share what has you so tickled?" he asked.

In between peals of laughter I gulped for air. Finally able to reply, I said, "Ted, do you remember the last thing Phil said to us before Thanksgiving? By the elevators?"

"Yeah, he told me CID took bets on our relationship."

"He asked when you were going to 'go ahead and marry the girl.' Do you remember what you told him in response?"

After a brief pause, we both burst into raucous laughter. Following such an emotional rollercoaster of a day, it provided the perfect stress relief for both of us.

We promptly fell asleep ten minutes later.

Rose found us in the same position the following morning when she opened the bedroom door. "Rebecca, are you...oh!" she exclaimed, her eyes landing on the two of us.

Ted remained completely unconscious on the bed, but I yawned and stretched, pushing tangled curls from my face.

"We, um, fell asleep," I said sheepishly. "I promise, I am not that kind of girl."

Rose smiled. "Since the two of you are wearing exactly what you had on last night, I'm not worried about hanky panky going on under my roof. Steve has slept through an actual hurricane, so I don't expect him to be up for a while. You'll find out soon enough Ted and his father share quite a few similarities. Why don't you join me in the kitchen once you've had a chance to freshen up? I can make us some pancakes and coffee. I don't think the men will be up for a few more hours."

I returned her smile with one of my own. "I'd like that, Rose. Thank you."

Rose closed the door, and I slowly shifted away from Culver's top, east coast producer and my personal, makeshift pillow.

"Where are you going?" Ted rasped behind closed lids.

I startled. "I didn't realize we woke you up."

"I heard Mom lure you away from me with promises of her world famous pancakes."

"World famous?"

"She'll never admit to it, but she adds something to those

pancakes. She refuses to tell me her secret, but she doesn't make these pancakes for just anybody."

"Well, I'm glad to know she doesn't think I'm 'just anybody' then."

Ted opened his eyes then winced at the light pouring in through the blinds. "What time is it?"

I glanced over at the bedside clock. "Eight thirty. Do you want to go back to sleep, Ted? I know your mom wanted to talk to me about a few things, and we're going to have a very busy few days on our hands."

He grunted in response, then rolled over onto his side.

I snickered quietly to myself and said, "More pancakes for me."

After a short stack, scrambled eggs, and probably the best two cups of coffee I had consumed in my entire life, I sat back contentedly in the kitchen chair. I placed a hand on my belly. "I don't think I need to eat for the rest of the day."

Rose grinned. "Not even my out-of-the-box Thanksgiving leftovers?"

"Are you guys ever going to let that go? Ted just enjoys good food. I can't say I blame him."

"Uncle Big Shot doesn't always realize how he comes off sometimes. As his mother, I know Ted doesn't mean to sound arrogant, but he can be so rigid and dogmatic about things. Most people are too intimidated by all of the bravado to contradict him."

"Is that why everyone teases him so much?"

"I'll admit that Steve can carry it too far, but we just want to see our son loosen up, smile, and not take life or himself so seriously. He was a lot more carefree before Annie died. Understandably, her death changed things. Phil offered to take Ted under his wing, and my son never gives a half effort to anything.

Obviously, you've seen the results at Culver. Speaking of, Ted showed us several of the documents you designed. You're incredible, Rebecca. Truly!"

I blushed. "Ted showed you my work?"

Rose stood up and opened a kitchen drawer. Pulling out a manila folder, she dug inside, finally handing me the RFP I'd designed for Triple J a few years earlier. Staring at the four-year-old document caused me to wince at some design skills I had honed sharper in the past few years, but I still felt pride in a job well done. I knew how much work went into pulling that document together.

"Ted raved about 'the graphic design girl' at the office. He said that he never saw someone work so well under pressure or with such attention to detail. Apparently, your predecessor did not possess the same dedication to her craft."

I laughed. "No, she certainly didn't. It took me over a year to clean up her mistakes on our existing documents." I handed the RFP back to Rose. "Thank you for showing me this. It's hard to believe I made such an impact on Ted, even back then."

Rose put the folder away and rejoined me at the table. "Honey, I've wanted to meet you for so long. Your name came up every so often, sometimes about business, sometimes about how you read your Bible at work every day. You intrigued Ted. It gave me hope that my son might one day move on from the pain of losing Annie. Even though I'd never met you, I started to feel like I already knew you."

"I'm speechless. I had absolutely no idea."

"Just so you know," Rose said, "Ted told me about what happened with your father and how he had to intervene. The Lord put a burden on my heart to pray for you ever since. I finally discovered the name of the graphic design girl."

"Why did Ted mention the incident?"

"He wanted to know if pastors normally behaved that way, if *my* pastor treated his congregants or family that way. I told him of course not and began praying for you. I asked Ted for your name since I saw how much he admired you. I don't presume to know you or the horrors you've endured, Rebecca, but I do pray for your healing. I know the Lord wants you free from your past so that you can embrace a beautiful future. Hopefully, with my son."

I smiled, warmed and comforted by genuine, motherly love.

"I see so much of my own story in you, Rebecca. I know that's one of the many reasons God brought you into our lives."

"Tell me more about this Leviathan thing, Rose. Everything you said last night felt like you'd lived my life. I could barely keep my jaw off the table."

"Leviathan, at its core, is the same narcissism we see in the Devil himself. I would best describe it as Satan's counterfeit version of the Holy Spirit. This thing wants everything the Bible says belongs to God: loyalty, deference, power, control, and praise. It's an all-encompassing selfishness so ruthless in its quest for domination, your head will spin at its cruelty. We see it in entitled, spoiled brats, but that foul spirit often takes root due to trauma or rejection from a parent or other authority figure. 'My pain' eventually becomes 'me, me, me.'"

Pondering her words for a moment, I said, "If most narcissists have truly suffered their own wounds, why do they go around like self-obsessed maniacs, and we don't? What if they've lived a charmed life? Rose, what made me want to treat people better than my own experiences, rather than perpetuating the cycle?"

"Rebecca, your family never allowed you to be selfish like them. They never permitted you to dwell on your own pain because they made it your responsibility to feed into theirs instead. Despite the literal hell you've been put through, you can think about other people rather than just yourself. Your family's selfishness gifted you with the capability for empathy and compassion. In that respect, it was a blessing in disguise."

"A blessing, Rose? A lifetime of shame and self-loathing was a blessing?" I said angrily. "Look, I know you mean well, but sugarcoating the trauma I've wrestled with, am *still* wrestling with, just adds insult to injury. Maybe we should just stop this conversation."

I stood up to leave the table, but Rose's petite hand settled on my arm. She looked up at me imploringly. "Please, forgive my careless choice of words, Rebecca. I'm not trying to minimize the pain you've endured. I just want you to see God's hand in all of this, even through the incredible suffering. Rebecca, you broke free from the toxic cycle of your family. Do you see that?"

I removed myself from her reach and folded both arms over my chest. "I'm listening."

Rose smiled, hazel eyes twinkling with tiny flecks of gold. "You're more of a fighter than they've led you to believe. That's why they worked so hard to beat you down. For all of his bravado, Ted has always respected strength and courage, and I see why he admires you so much. From the way you're looking at me, you think I'm flattering you and stalling for more time so I can come up with an answer to your earlier question."

I had to grin at her frankness. "You're not wrong."

She chuckled. "I called it a blessing in disguise because you're the only member of your family with any perspective outside of your own worldview. They gave you the ability to consider the feelings and needs of others. Although completely warped and meant to keep you in lifelong servitude to them, your family gave you the keys to the jail cell. They made you feel unworthy of love, so you looked for ways to improve and grow. Meanwhile, they just stagnated, remaining the perpetual victims to avoid responsibility. Because you never stopped growing, you finally outgrew the need for their approval. That's how you eventually escaped, my dear."

I sat back down.

I needed to hear more truth.

CHAPTER 21

"Tell me your story, Rose. How did you get to be so smart about all of this Leviathan and narcissism stuff?"

Rose flexed her fingers and offered me a sideways grin. "It's been a long time since someone asked to hear my story. Just to put the disclaimer out there, I don't have some personal vendetta against my husband's mother. The running joke in our old synagogue was that Phyllis Margolin was the only person ever born with two faces."

I whistled low. "Wow."

"It's a miracle Steve ever escaped that nightmare," Rose said. "Since her nice, Jewish boy married a *shiksa*, Phyllis spread umpteen rumors about me so none of the ladies at synagogue would acknowledge my existence."

"What does...?" I paused as Rose waved me off. "Okay, this is apparently a Yiddish word I don't need to learn?"

"It's a less than flattering word meaning non-Jew. In fact, Phyllis took great delight in reminding me I was a gentile. It's how she consoled herself over the loss of Steve as her husband."

"Wait, what? Steve is her son."

Rose rolled her eyes with a note of long held irritation. "Phyllis leeched onto her one and only child to get the love and attention she couldn't receive from her husband. Harold Margolin had plenty of his own faults, but Phyllis steamrolled him for so long, he finally gave up trying. You could never please Phyllis because she always wanted more. Everyone knew Harold as a miserable man, and he got crankier with age too."

I sucked in a breath. "Ugh, that's so awful. I can't imagine how much strain that put on your marriage to Steve. Did he eventually catch onto his mother's antics?"

Rose chuckled sarcastically. "You're kidding, right?"

I raised an eyebrow.

"Honey, I used to say that woman wrote the rule book on manipulation. You'd confront her about punching you in the face, but by the end of the conversation, she made you apologize for injuring her fist with your nose."

"Now *that* I am very familiar with," I said wearily. "As long you did whatever Bernard Ivy told you to do, thought whatever Bernard Ivy told you to think, and said whatever Bernard Ivy allowed you to say, things generally went smoothly. He still picked me apart mercilessly for some reason, much more than my brother and sister. Usually, he didn't throw things at my head unless I argued with him."

"Oh, Rebecca!" Rose said, aghast. "That must have been traumatizing as a child! How did you manage to get out of there?"

"College. My parents convinced me I would never survive out from under their roof. I consider my first act of rebellion to be transferring to a state university rather than the local college where I commuted from home. My parents barely paid any attention to me outside of my performance at church, so imagine their shock when the university offered me a full ride scholarship because of my grades and community service."

Rose beamed at me. "You must have been so proud of yourself."

"I even majored in religion, but they trivialized all of it. Graduating magna cum laude meant nothing since I didn't graduate with an engagement ring."

"After all of that hard work? That's so sad."

"A religion degree made it impossible to find a job outside the world of academia or ministry, but it helped me as I studied the Bible apart from my father's influence. As sad as this feels to admit, a part of me always wanted to be a pastor's wife."

"It's not sad, honey. It was all you knew," Rose said, patting my hand.

"Some days, I want to reach back in time and slap my twenty-year-old self for being so naïve. In my mind, you went to college because everyone did that after high school. You took your classes, met the love of your life, graduated, got married, and then became a stay-at-home mom. I had no concept of life outside the version my parents sold me."

"They deliberately sheltered you, Rebecca, to keep you dependent on them and unable to function outside of their help. I feel like I raised Steve more than his own mother did. He still lived at home when we got married and couldn't even boil water. Phyllis waited on him like a little prince, all while ignoring her own husband. Steve expected me to pamper him exactly how his mother did."

I squeezed Rose's hand. "I'm glad I'm not the only person on the planet who's survived this kind of insanity. I really thought I was crazy, or maybe I did something wrong and deserved to be treated this way."

"They want you to believe that, honey. They're professionals at blame shifting and making their problems somebody else's fault. I loved Steve when I married him. I even converted so we could be married in the synagogue, but things deteriorated so quickly with Phyllis. As soon as she realized I wouldn't share my husband with her, the claws came out. She was so vicious, Rebecca! She'd say something awful just before Steve entered a room so he would see me get upset with her while she feigned innocence. He always defended his precious mommeleh against the horrible wife who didn't treat him as well as she did."

"Ted mentioned something about that to me. How did you or your marriage survive?"

"Jesus," she answered plainly. "I cried out to God, desperate and wanting to die from a broken heart. I had no place to turn but Him. My parents barely spoke to me because they said I abandoned Christ by converting to Judaism. My own husband rejected me time and again to defend or excuse his mother's appalling behavior. We had a tiny daughter and Ted on the way, and I thought I would lose my mind."

"Oh, Rose, I'm so sorry."

She wiped tears from her eyes. "Don't be. I reconnected with God on this very kitchen floor. I devoured my Bible, prayed to Jesus, and finally found a church that felt like home. After Ted was born, things soured in Steve's relationship with his mother. She never paid much attention to Jennifer since she was a girl, but Phyllis practically worshiped Ted. Steve saw the impact on Jennifer, the callous way his mother dismissed her like some mosquito pestering her."

"Does Jen remember any of this?"

"No, thank God. I tried talking to Steve about Jesus, especially when he noticed the changes in me, but he wasn't interested. I did, however, hear the word 'Leviathan' one night in prayer. There isn't much to be found in the Bible, at least not on the surface, but I felt God asking me to trust Him and watch things unfold."

"So, what happened?" I said, totally engrossed in Rose's story.

"I begged the Lord for wisdom because I knew my heart was too raw and broken to be objective. The Bible calls Solomon the wisest man who ever lived, so I read *Proverbs*. Not just one time, honey, but over and over for almost a year."

"What did the Lord show you?"

Rose smiled. "He showed me Phyllis, Steve, even myself on the page. He showed me how to recognize the lies before they came, how to recognize the manipulation and attempts at bribery. He also taught me to fast, pray, and wait expectantly for a response. New Agers like to talk about the power of prayer, but I found the real power in trusting God to do what He said He would. The power of God to heal my heart and restore my hope came when I finally surrendered my marriage and my future to Him."

"Did Steve ever confront his mother?"

I received a throaty chuckle in response.

"This sounds like a good story," I said with a smile.

"It started when Phyllis presumed to lecture my husband about our married life, specifically how fast we had children."

I put my hand over my mouth. "Please, tell me she didn't."

Rose laughed. "Oh, honey, you know she did! He said Phyllis pressed him for details about our love life, nagged him about using birth control, that her precious little Teddy didn't need any competition."

"That's um, some nerve."

"In Yiddish, it's called *chutzpah,* and Phyllis Margolin has it in spades. Steve told me a veil ripped off of his eyes. He finally recognized all of the meddling and manipulation. He saw the blatant favoritism between the grandchildren and everything else I'd been saying for years.

"When he confronted Phyllis, she tried the blame game, the 'woe is me' card, even told my husband he owed his first loyalty to his mother because she gave him life. For the first time ever, Steve stood up to his mother. He told her exactly what she could do with her worrying and her advice, and that was the end of it. We never mentioned Phyllis again until Ted wanted to meet his grandmother twenty-five years later."

"What do you mean you never mentioned her?" I asked.

Rose sighed. "Exactly what I said. Steve knows the real Phyllis behind the sugary mask and manipulation, but he struggles admitting it out loud. I think he's ashamed of her...and himself, probably more than anything. He feels like a fool in many ways."

"So, what happened after all of that?"

"The longer we stayed away from his parents, the more clearly Steve saw things, especially the disastrous state of our marriage. When we finally cut the cord from his parents, we began to love each other beyond infatuation and our physical relationship. My husband isn't perfect, but he is my best friend. I've prayed for Steve to accept Jesus as his Savior for thirty-six years, and I will continue praying and believing God will work this miracle. I haven't seen all of my prayers answered yet, but we're happy."

After a moment of silence, both of us enjoying a few sips of coffee to help digest breakfast and all of the information shared, Rose said, "Now, enough about me. I'm pretty sure I asked to hear about your story, Rebecca. Tell me how you finally got free."

Daring to trust this woman I had met less than twenty-fours earlier, I began my own tale.

"For all of the sermons my father gives about gossip in the congregation, he and my mother commit that offense more than anyone else. Image means everything to my father. Occasionally, the mask slips, and people see the real Bernard Ivy. That's when Pastor and Mrs. Ivy immediately launch their smear campaign. The feathers sure flew when Pastor Ivy's daughter fled First United of Hillcrest to attend another church across town."

"Ah," Rose said. "Since your father portrayed himself as perfect to his devoted flock, any ripples in the family facade might cause people to question what they saw."

"Exactly. My father punished me at every opportunity after that, even more than before. Any chance he or my family had to pick at me, shame me, or humiliate me, they took with relish. With my brother constantly battling drugs and my sister going through her lesbian phase, it gave my siblings a way to win brownie points with my parents and avoid lectures about their own life choices. Ripping me apart for the tiniest infraction, real or perceived, became a game to them. If I finally cracked under the pressure or did anything other than roll over, they used that as proof of my supposed, emotional instability."

"How awful! I thought I had it bad with Phyllis, but I can't imagine being ganged up on like that. How did you survive? What did you tell your new pastor?"

"Oh, I told him everything. Cried on his shoulder. Sent huge emails pouring out my heart and wondering what was wrong with my family. Without fail, Pastor always found something wrong with *me*. Ostensibly, he disapproved of their behavior, but he always focused on improving my reactions to the abuse without ever addressing their latest stunt. Everything I endured he called an opportunity to grow."

Rose's lips thinned into a single thread. "In other words, he completely invalidated you. Rather than offer you any kind of support or encouragement, he kept the focus on everything negative and wrong with *you* instead of with them. His behavior reinforced all of the shame and false guilt you had already received from your family. With you pouring your heart out like that, trusting someone who pretended to be trustworthy, your pastor made you a victim all over again."

I took a steadying breath. "This whole situation is even more demented and twisted than I realized."

Rose smiled sadly. "Better to know the truth and be free, honey, than to think you're somehow to blame for what they knowingly did to you."

"Knowingly?" I croaked.

"Believe me, they knew what they were doing, Rebecca. That's how I've seen this thing operate for almost forty years."

"I just want to be free, Rose. So badly!"

She patted my hand. "I know you do, honey. I need you to understand that your old pastor took advantage of your vulnerability and used that to learn plenty of information about you."

"You make it sound so calculated. And cold."

Rose's expression indicated I didn't misread her meaning.

"You mean he didn't care about me?" I said, stunned. "*All* of it was a lie?"

"Why don't you finish telling your story from last night? You said you had more to share regarding why you blacked out yesterday."

Confused by the two realities battling in my mind, I pressed onward, hoping to uncover the truth and finally put some old ghosts to rest. "The night Pastor and his wife invited me to their home, I noticed similarities between him and my father. Pastor terrorized his nine-year-old daughter for some flippant remark, and I saw my own father screaming at me the same way."

"How did your pastor try to cover his behavior?"

"By blaming everyone else, including me."

Rose was horrified. "How were you responsible for his behavior?"

I smiled ruefully. "Because Pastor and my father have mastered the 'you're just offended/you're too sensitive' technique."

"Gaslighting," she said. "A page out of the old, Phyllis Margolin playbook. I know it well."

"That's what I gathered from your own story."

"So, what happened after the altercation with the daughter?"

I sighed. "He made a pass at me later that night. I felt absolutely blindsided, but Pastor said it was all my fault."

CHAPTER 22

ROSE'S FACE HELD ALL THE DISGUST I FELT INSIDE. "How could he possibly justify his behavior toward you, Rebecca?"

"Pastor insisted I sent him signals, and he finally succumbed to my many temptations."

Rose uttered a very unladylike word followed by a few more.

I continued, "He said he noticed how I looked at him, claimed to be flattered, but told me nothing like that could ever happen again. He said we shouldn't sully the work of the Lord by acting on our impulses."

"Despicable!" Rose exclaimed. "What a disgusting pig!"

"Pastor kept pressing me to admit my feelings for him, except I had nothing to confess. He told me God couldn't forgive me if I refused to repent of my sin. When I began to argue with him about the circumstances, Pastor changed tactics and told me we could both learn a valuable lesson in over-coming temptation by denying our so-called, *mutual attraction*."

"The Bible tells us to flee from temptation, not throw

ourselves in front of the truck hoping it doesn't hit us," Rose said. "Rebecca, please tell me you understand what he tried to do to you."

"I realize now he wanted to seduce me, if that's what you mean."

She shook her head. "No, honey. Your pastor tried to brain-wash you into believing that you're the one who instigated an affair. He planted the seed, knowing you'd dwell on it and beat yourself up about it. Any overture he made toward you after-ward, he could pass off as *your* sin and *your* struggle. Your pastor wanted to seduce you while making you believe you tried to seduce *him*. Rebecca, all of this behavior just screams Leviathan. This thing contorts and twists the truth beyond human under-standing."

The light exposed the face of darkness, and I shuddered at the ugliness before me.

Rose plowed on, "Your pastor noticed your vulnerability after he attacked his own child. From your description, he spent the evening invading your personal space, right?"

I nodded, unable to do much more.

"Honey, think back to that night even if it hurts. Every sin your Pastor committed, he projected onto you. He turned his own sin into accusations against you. He wanted to confuse you to the point of believing you wanted what *he* really wanted. You would ultimately assume the blame while he looked like the innocent lamb. He'd label you with every accusation as he pretended to have no control over his own libido."

"Wait," my voice broke, "I meant nothing to him at all?"

Rose looked at me sympathetically. "You presented a chal-lenge to him, Rebecca, not a person. He wanted to see you controlled, conquered, and eventually discarded once he got bored with you. Your pastor would have sloughed you off like yesterday's trash and then left you broken, ashamed, and racked with *his* guilt as he moved onto his next victim."

My head began to throb.

"Oh, honey," Rose said, seeing the devastation on my face. "You didn't know."

I talked around convulsing sobs. "Do you know how long I've lived with this guilt? Thinking I needed to confess to your son that I caused a married man to stumble? That I somehow welcomed his advances?"

"Rebecca, the married man played the role of stumbling block. Not the other way around."

The sobs came faster and louder, the full realization of all I had believed about myself as nothing more than demonic manipulation tactics. Rose wrapped her arm around my shoulders while I cried ugly tears.

"How do I tell Ted?" I wailed.

"What's there to tell?" Rose said against my hair. "Rebecca, you trusted a master con artist. These people operate in the currency of shame. They shame you for having normal, human reactions to their abuse. They shame you for their own behavior. When the dust settles, if and when you actually escape, they shame you for leaving. Then comes the later shame of realizing just how horribly they deceived you. You battle with constantly second guessing yourself or why you didn't see it sooner."

I nodded through my tears.

"Honey, look at me," Rose said, holding my chin up gently with the side of her finger. "Shame does not come from our Lord. It comes from the same evil one who tried to destroy your life through your family and your old church. 'Therefore, there is now no condemnation for those who are in Christ Jesus,'" she quoted. "I know you believe God has forgiven you of your sins, sweetheart. You have to forgive yourself. Letting go doesn't mean pretending nothing happened. There's a reason why God allows us to have scars, to remember what we've survived. Letting go means you stop tormenting yourself, and you stop accepting responsibility for what others did to you. You stop trying to find ways you could have controlled or changed the outcome."

She spoke the truth my heart feared to accept. A lifetime of conditioning trained me to believe all of the abuse was somehow "self-inflicted," or at the very least, my responsibility to fix. As each successive layer of betrayal and abuse came to light, I repeated the same four words to my battered heart, mind, and soul. I repeated them until I finally believed them.

It.

Wasn't.

My.

Fault.

Rose pressed on, "Rebecca, these villains held a position of authority over you. They knew your weaknesses, and they took full advantage of them. They accused you of playing the victim to hide the fact that you really *were* a victim...of them! Those horrible people gaslighted you and convinced you to discard your own perception of reality and accept their distorted version instead. By treating you like a lunatic and shaming you for seeking or speaking the truth, they controlled you and used you for whatever selfish need they had in mind."

My tears dried as I sat in awe of Rose's hard-fought wisdom. Despite the initial agony of reopening my most ancient wounds, I finally experienced peace. Rose spoke to the deepest parts of my soul, the broken pieces I had either ignored or simply accepted as "I'll never know why." Freedom came from hearing the truth, facing the ugly, and rejecting the comforting mirage of denial.

With freedom from the guilt and condemnation also came anger. I uttered quite a few unladylike words as the full scope of my abuse crystallized before me.

"Whoa! Do you kiss my son with that mouth?" Steve Margolin said from the doorway.

I turned to face him, and Steve's expression sobered at my puffy face awash with tears.

"Belay that," he amended. "I assume you finished your story for Rose?"

"Steve, why don't you see if Ted is awake?" Rose said. "I'm sure Rebecca would like to talk to him."

Opting to go myself, I found Ted already alert and on his phone. I relayed everything, finally exposing every shred of ugly I'd kept hidden out of fear. Perhaps to help keep me calm, Ted reined in his reactions, though his anger slipped through in acidic quips.

"Are you absolutely certain your old pastor doesn't live in that house anymore, Rebecca? Because a grease fire can completely destroy a home if someone doesn't know how to properly deep fry a turkey. We hear stories like this on the news all the time. I'm just saying."

"Murder by failed Thanksgiving cookery, Ted?"

"Not murder, just arson. Less jail time that way. I'm furious, Rebecca, but I'm not totally irrational," he said.

It felt good to laugh, even at macabre humor.

Sitting down next to me on the bed, Ted said, "You're holding up remarkably well considering the sadistic horrors you just laid out for me. I'm guessing you got a lot of the crying out with Mom?"

"I'm currently functioning within the realms of sarcasm and wrath. I'm sure the tears will return, but for now anyway, I'll just fantasize about a flaming ball of turkey grease and then repent for it later," I said with a smirk.

"Obviously, we'll postpone ring shopping. What else would you like to do today?"

"Why wouldn't I want to go ring shopping?"

Ted's expression matched the incredulity in his tone. "Rebecca, you just discovered Pastor Sociopath is even more of an amoral deviant than either of us realized. I know we're making light of it right now, but the last thing I want to do is cause you more stress. I feel like a selfish jerk for proposing yesterday. I'm normally not this impetuous, but it seemed like the best solution to protect you from your father."

"Ted, I can give the world the middle finger, or I can show the world my ring finger. This seems like a no brainer. I can think of no better revenge against my parents or even Pastor than to—"

"Pastor Sociopath," Ted corrected.

"Fine. Pastor *Sociopath*, than to accomplish exactly what they set out to prevent. Let's not forget that I want to marry you. Can one of your friends still perform the ceremony today?"

"We have to go down to the county clerk's office and get the marriage license on Monday since they're still closed for Thanksgiving. Then, we take it over to my friend Brian's office so he can marry us. All of my other potential officiants asked me if you were pregnant because of the rush to get married. I told them the real reason, and they respectfully declined."

"They can do that?"

"Sure can."

"Bummer. I wanted to rush to the courthouse with a swelling orchestral number that reinvigorates everyone's faith in life and humanity. Ooh, or maybe some '80s power ballad!

We could burst into the judge's office declaring our passionate love and lifelong commitment to one another."

My very recent fiancé looked at me like I had lost my marbles.

I pursed my lips and rolled my eyes. "Realm of sarcasm and wrath, babe, and right now, I'm leaning heavily in the sarcasm direction. I can't believe Mr. Grease Fire is looking at me like I'm the crazy one in this relationship. Since Jason and I never made it past the initial counseling phase with Pastor Sociopath, I missed out on the legalities involved in getting married. Clearly, I filled in the gaps with a few too many chick flicks."

Ted grinned at me. "I'm afraid so, *babe*. The real world involves a lot more red tape and bureaucracy. Definitely a 'no' on the '80s hair bands. You have the fun of waiting at the Social Security office and DMV to change your name and driver's license once we get our marriage certificate in the mail."

"Ted, you're killing the romance here. Let me think about paperwork after I enjoy my unexpected bachelorette weekend. Although, I never quite imagined it happening like this."

He grimaced. "My fault again."

"No, Ted, I'm just thinking out loud. I feel like I'm on the outside watching my life like a movie." I reached out to hold his hand. "I've wasted so much of my life letting everyone dictate the ideal or dream situation. I have to shake myself sometimes and say, 'Rebecca, this is *your* life. *You* get to live it.'"

Sparkling gold and sizzling butter appeared. "If I believed in God, I'd be thanking him you never realized Goldstein was in love with you."

Megawatt appeared for the first time that day. "God is real Ted. You and I are together because of Him. And speaking of Goldsteins, Jessica comes back to town on Sunday. I want her to be there for the wedding."

"Gotta make sure you make it to the altar before your best friend, right? Is that why you want to marry me so fast?"

I picked up a pillow and knocked Ted upside the head. He laughed and kissed my forehead.

Transitioning to business mode, Ted said, "Is your leasing office open today? I want to talk to your landlord about your contract and then to a moving company about getting everything out as soon as possible."

"You really did think of everything, didn't you?"

"I know I asked you to marry me yesterday, but I've thought about the details for a while. I needed something to preoccupy my thoughts at night other than wishing I had you next to me."

"We're really going to do this, aren't we?" I said, my voice filled with wonder.

"Yes, we are really doing this," Ted said. He gave me a smile so dazzling, it was all I could do to keep myself from launching at him again.

"Do you remember that kiss in my apartment?" I asked.

Ted's eyes lingered on my mouth before he released a low groan. He rested his forehead against mine.

He remembered all right.

Smiling, I said, "I waited thirty-three years to kiss somebody like that, and I'm so happy the wait is almost over. I'm tired of trying to do everything perfectly, of thinking God will love me more if I go through life mistake free. I've followed rules my whole life that had nothing to do with the Bible and everything to do with pleasing my father or Pastor Sociopath."

Ted lifted his head so he could look in my eyes. "I'm confused, Rebecca. Do you think getting married is a mistake, but you're just throwing caution to the wind here?"

"Ted, none of this makes sense, but I know God wants us to get married. Even better, I know what I want, and it's you."

Ted's fingers tangled into my curls as he leaned his face in close to mine again. "I've waited a long time to hear you say that."

"I'm breaking free, Ted, and I want to do that with you. I don't care if we have to buy rings from a gumball machine at the grocery store, but we are getting married. Maybe we can do a regular ceremony down the road, but I want it legal and binding as much as you do. I don't want to fight all of these battles all alone anymore."

"You're not alone, Rebecca."

CHAPTER 23

By the time Ted and I finished talking, planning, and making various phone calls, we'd missed the bulk of the Black Friday deals. Rose served up a dinner platter of cold turkey, wheat bread, sandwich fixings, and leftover sides while Steve and Ted discussed the easiest way to relocate all of my worldly belongings into Ted's house. Realizing that I had never actually set foot in Ted's home felt like a throwback to a time gone by. It harkened to an age of arranged marriages where the bride and groom barely knew each other, and the groom made his house ready for the bride to live. In this case, I prepared to step into Ted's old memories, the footsteps Annie once trod. Ted seemed preoccupied with my ability to accept the reality of a hasty marriage, but I wondered at his ability to cope if reminders of his old life resurfaced. I posed the question to his mother.

"Ted gutted the entire house," Rose said after finishing a bite of her sandwich. "He always made excuses to delay renovations because he and Annie never agreed on what to do with the house. After she passed, Ted used the renovations and physical labor as a stress relief. It kept the focus off of missing Annie. I don't even recognize the inside of the house as the same one they bought after they got married."

"Why didn't Ted just sell the house and move?"

"Annie wanted to buy the house originally. Maybe Ted thought of it as a final way to give her the win."

"I see we're talking about me," Ted said dryly, entering the room and making himself a sandwich. He leaned back against the wall, sandwich in hand.

"I'm just trying to figure out how my apartment will fit into your house," I said. "I've never seen your home, so I'm flying blind. Your mother kindly offered some assistance."

Ted glanced from this mother to me, then smirked, not totally buying my explanation. "I have an empty guest room, so if need be, we can use it for storage. There's also a basement rec room we can convert, plus another bedroom currently used as an office. I figured we could share it."

"Will that be weird for you, Ted? Seeing me in your old house? Old memories and all of that?"

"I gutted the house for a reason, Rebecca. I kept the walls bare minus a few paintings I acquired after our trip to the art festival."

I grinned. "You're joking, right?

His sizzling smile answered first. "You have good taste, Rebecca. I happened to agree with you."

I blushed. "You went back and bought them just because I said I liked them?"

"I told you," he said, leaning down close to my ear, "I've been thinking about this for a while." Standing back up, he said, "With my house looking like a *tabula rasa* for so long, it seemed like the right time to start painting on the canvas, so to speak."

"A what?" Rose asked.

"A blank slate," Ted translated.

"Which pieces did you choose?" I said.

The gold in Ted's eyes glimmered with mischief as he sat down next to me at the table. "You wanna guess?"

"If memory serves, I found two pieces reminiscent of the Kandinsky paintings I fell in love with at the Paris Museum of Natural Art. I couldn't get enough of the colors and intersecting swirls and lines."

"'Organized chaos' you called it," Ted said before taking a bite of his sandwich.

"Sort of like your relationship," Rose said, wiping some mayonnaise from the side of her mouth. "It seems like a total mess, but God is right there orchestrating all of it."

"Okay, Mom," Ted said with an air of impatience.

"Don't roll your eyes at me, Theodore. What are the odds of me coping with all the *tsuris* I endured from your grandmother only to help your future bride forty years later?"

"I'm getting a Yiddish dictionary," I said. "The lost in translation is killing me."

"Stick around long enough, and it'll grow on you," Rose shot back with a wink. "They have an old saying, 'If you can't say it nicely, say it in Yiddish.' Sometimes, the English language just can't quite do it justice."

I chuckled. "I wish I could have asked my grandparents."

"Your grandparents are Jewish?" She asked excitedly. "On your mother's side, I assume, since your father is such a self-righteous, anti-Semitic *schm*—"

"Mom!" Ted exclaimed. "Don't teach her all the bad words first!"

I laughed while Rose waved off Ted. Answering her question, I said, "My mother rarely talked about her parents, but I finally learned their names a few years ago: Marvin and Leah Shapiro. Those are Jewish names, right?"

"Definitely Jewish," Rose said with a grin. "Was she born here or in the mother country?"

"You mean in Israel?"

"No. New York," she said, affecting a Brooklyn accent.

Ted rolled his eyes. "Cute, Mom."

I searched my mental archives for the lone conversation where my mother had shared something meaningful about her past. "I mentioned going to the Goldsteins' for a Hanukkah party, and my mother got weepy and nostalgic. The perfect little mask briefly slipped off, and she acted like a human being instead of my father's number one sycophant."

"Did your grandparents disown her for converting?" Ted asked.

"More like the other way around. From all accounts, my father absolutely detested my grandmother. Reading between the lines, it seems like she had his number long before anybody else did. My grandmother tried to stop him from marrying my mother."

Catching the end of our conversation, Steve said, "Rebecca, you know there's always public records to see if we can find anything on your grandparents. Even if they're not local, you could try to phone them and reconnect. Would they know who you are?"

I shrugged. "I don't know, but it's worth a shot."

Two hours later, I stared bleary eyed at the Margolins' family computer, finally slumping back into the leather office chair in defeat.

"How goes it?" Rose asked, coming up behind me. "Ted and Steve waged war over a game of Tile Scramble. I needed a break from the unbearable level of testosterone."

"Rose, I've tried at least ten different sites, and I can't find anything. I'm beginning to wonder if my mother made up some names to keep me from ever finding my grandparents. It certainly wouldn't be the first time she's lied to me."

"Can you access your mother's birth certificate somehow?"

"That's just it. I keep searching for Deborah Shapiro and found about seven million of them. Literally. As far as I know, my mother was born in New York. So again, we're talking needle in a haystack. The site in front of me has over 20,000 different records."

"If God wants you to meet your grandparents, then you will, Rebecca. Why don't you take a break and join us out in the family room? Steve and I are here to help with moving and anything else we can do to make this marriage work. If you need us to keep quiet and just let you two figure things out, we will respect that too."

"Is this what a real family does, Rose? My perception of normal is so skewed."

"Honey, I don't think there's such a thing as 'normal.' People are people. Maybe a better word to use would be *healthy*. Our family has its quirks just like any other. I'm sure you saw some of the dynamics yesterday with Amanda and Jennifer competing about their birthing stories or the cousins' accomplishments. I've tried teaching my children about God, but none of them seemed particularly receptive. That makes you a welcome change for our family too, you know."

A soft knock on the office door kept me from responding.

"Any luck?" Ted said, ducking into the room.

"Other than determining how long I can go before straining my eyes? No."

Ted extended his hand to me. "Why don't we go for a walk? It will spare me from hearing my father gloat all night."

"So he beat you, eh?" Rose said, grinning.

"Barely, and I still maintain he cheated."

"I will definitely take you up on that walk," I said to Ted. "My back won't tolerate another minute in this chair."

"Stay safe," Rose warned, "and please avoid setting anybody's house on fire with flaming turkeys, Theodore."

"Tattletale," Ted whispered into my ear.

He offered me a hand out of the chair and never relinquished his grip. We strolled across the lamp lit sidewalk of his parents' subdivision in companionable silence for a while. Our joined hands served as a lifeline for both of us.

"Is Mom smothering you, or is she behaving?"

"Why would you think I feel smothered?" I asked.

Ted glanced up at the night sky and sighed. "I don't know, maybe it's just me. Ever since Annie died, I feel this pressure every time I'm around her. I know what she wants me to do, but I'm not ready."

"What do you think that is?"

Ted held my gaze for a long moment. "Forgive God. Forgive myself."

I stopped walking and searched Ted's face. He looked weary. The bits of silver at his temples glistened as if attesting to his struggle. "Why do you need to forgive yourself, Ted? What do you think you could have done differently?"

He sighed heavily. "I guess we should talk about this now rather than later."

"I don't like the sound of this."

"I didn't think you would, Rebecca. If it makes you change your mind, I will understand that too. I know how important your faith is to you."

"Look, Ted, I don't want to get into a debate over semantics, but this isn't about my faith or my religion but my relationship with Jesus. I know that sounds really corny, but I'm tired and I don't have any better words in my vocabulary arsenal at the moment."

Ted's chuckle broke the somber mood. "Yeah, about that *vocabulary arsenal*..."

"You know, if I ever used that phrase in front of my family, I'd never hear the end of it," I said. I imitated my mother's condescending tone and sneer. "Oh Rebecca, so much smarter than the rest of us with her *vocabulary arsenal*."

Ted wrapped his arms around my waist and looked down at me. His expression held nothing but tenderness and sympathy. "Don't take this the wrong way, Rebecca, but your family really sucks."

I laughed out loud.

That irresistible, boyish grin made an appearance.

Megawatt returned the greeting.

Ted took a deep breath. "Three more days. I can do this for three more days."

Blushing, I looked away. "I'm not sure I have a word in my vocabulary arsenal for how you make me feel, Ted. You look at me, and all of the horrible things I've been fed my entire life just vanish into smoke."

He rested his head on mine. I pressed my cheek against his heart, and it quickly became my favorite place on earth.

"I told you Annie and I were childhood sweethearts, but we didn't always get along. We butted heads a lot. Mom says we fought like brother and sister."

"When did you get married?"

"I was twenty-four and Annie was twenty-three. We dated in high school, broke up to go to different colleges, but got back together at a Christmas party her parents hosted a year later. One night of heavy flirting over the eggnog punch bowl led to the two of us moving in together and eventually getting married."

"So, why the regret, Ted? Why do you need to forgive yourself?"

"Because of how we left things. Because her death was my fault. Because I told God if He brought Annie back, I would follow Him, but He didn't. Please, don't try to comfort me by telling me it's not my fault, Rebecca. I've heard it too many times, and I don't believe it any more now than I did eight years ago."

"Ted," I said softly. "Look at me."

He leaned down, tears and pain on his face. I smoothed back a hair at his temple, then let my hand rest there.

"I don't know why God does what He does, why evil people prosper and good people suffer, but we can't bargain with Him like little children making promises to avoid pain or punishment. Ted, I want you to be free from your past just as much as you want me to be free from mine."

He removed my hand from his face and his arms from my waist.

"I shouldn't have brought it up," he said morosely.

"Why? I'm not rejecting you because you don't believe like I do. I'm not condemning you either, Ted. I don't have all the answers, but I can promise I won't give you some Pollyanna, 'God is in control' response. You told me that Annie's crash was your fault. Were you in the car with her?"

"I was on the phone with her."

CHAPTER 24

IT TOOK A MOMENT FOR THE WEIGHT OF TED'S WORDS to sink in, to realize the absolute horror of the situation. I finally understood why Ted had blamed himself. Unfortunately, all that came out of my mouth was a very stunned, "Oh."

"Oh," he mocked.

I frowned. "Ted, I'm not the enemy. Is this what you do when you're upset? I go into my Culver shell, but you push people away with your anger so you can lick your wounds in private?"

He glared at me.

I glared right back.

"I'm not letting this go, so you may as well talk to me." At his sullen expression, I added, "And to be completely honest, all of the homes in this neighborhood look the same. Unless you want me traipsing around knocking on doors to find your parents' house, you need to stop being mad at me long enough to take me back."

Ted's clenched jaw softened slightly. "You're cute when you're angry."

"You're not."

"I probably deserve that."

I smiled slightly. "You're cute when you're self-deprecating. You're so larger than life and in control most of the time."

He took a step toward me. "Larger than life? Is that how all of you see me?"

"Yeah. Confident, self-assured, and on your not so good days, kind of a pompous jack—er um, pompous jerk."

He sucked in a pained breath. "Truth hurts."

I held his gaze. "Sometimes it removes weights never meant for us to carry. Even when it pains us to admit our worst fears, the truth always sets us free."

"What is this truth you think I need to believe about Annie and how she died?"

"You tell me, Ted. You clammed up. You said you were on the phone with her. Was she distracted or not paying attention?"

"I heard the whole thing," he said, his voice anguished. "One second, we're fighting over what color to paint the dining room. The next, I heard her scream, the crash, and my own voice screaming."

I closed the distance between us and held his hands in mine. "So, you blame yourself?"

"It was such a stupid fight, Rebecca! She wanted to paint the dining room eggshell blue. I told her the color looked like a public bathroom. Annie called me ridiculous and insisted on picking the color since she usually handled all of the cooking and entertaining."

"You weren't kidding about brother and sister. I've heard Jessica and Kyle go at each other like that."

"We went back and forth about it, and then she screamed. I will never forget it as long as I live. One second we're going twenty rounds about how I liked to entertain just as much as she did, we both accused each other of being pig headed, and then she was gone. Annie died because I couldn't stand to lose a fight over something as meaningless as paint color. My wife would still be here," his voice cracked as he wiped tears from his eyes against his shoulder.

Ted didn't let go of my hands.

I took that as a good sign to proceed.

"When Jason broke my heart and left me, I thought my last chance at marriage, at motherhood, went with him. I beat myself up for almost two years wondering what I did wrong and if my parents were right about me this whole time. I begged God for answers that never came. I finally hit my limit when I overheard my father cataloguing all of my faults to Ada, telling her that Jason escaped a life of misery being married to someone like me. I don't even remember what microscopic infraction offended my father that day, but he consoled himself by putting me down to my sister."

"Is that when you cut them off?"

"Yes. First time I ever openly defied Pastor's counsel as a member of SBC."

"Pastor Sociopath," Ted corrected.

"Yes, Pastor Sociopath. The dinner incident at his house happened about six months prior. After that night, every time my father took his cheap shots or projected his own behavior on me, I saw myself standing in the kitchen as Olivia. I didn't want to be that scared little girl anymore. I ignored the 'go low' counsel since I knew firsthand it just emboldened my father. I finally turned my back on all of the lies the Ivy family said about me."

"Why didn't you turn your back on God? He allowed you to suffer at the hands of your father and that deviant psycho who calls himself a shepherd of the Lord. I don't understand, Rebecca."

"Jesus was all I had, Ted. No comforting mother or father held me after Jason abandoned me. Instead, they all joined in the unending parade of cutting, snide remarks, and I-told-you-so's. More than anyone else, my father, relished the opportunity to list all of the reasons nobody would ever marry me. Pastor Sociopath expected me to get over the heartbreak instantaneously, and he minimized my struggles or ignored them altogether. Jessica, God bless her, never liked Jason, so she thought bashing him would make me feel better. Unfortunately, I felt like even more of an idiot for almost marrying him. Kyle always seemed on pins and needles around me. I just assumed he didn't know how to handle that much emotional pain."

"Rebecca, you've survived so much heartache, and I just want to do right by you. I failed Annie. I won't make that mistake again."

"You didn't fail her!" I shouted. "Stop blaming yourself! You weren't behind the wheel of that car. Annie could have compromised on the paint colors too. It was an *accident*. Stop trying to control the past by acting like you're responsible for it. Look, I can't go back and erase all of the times I ignored my gut about Pastor and his intentions toward me. I saw the weirdness *for years* between him and Cynthia and his bizarre attachment to anything youth related. Does that make me responsible for his behavior? He *chose* to do those things, Ted. Annie chose to get behind the wheel of a car. You can't have a fight with only one person. She chose to continue the argument with you too. You're not responsible for Annie's decision."

"It's not the same thing, Rebecca."

"The heck it isn't! You're mad at God because you want answers for the injustice, and you want to know why. I know because I've asked those same questions myself. I've yelled and screamed at Him because of all of the abuse He allowed me to go through."

"Did you get an answer? I know I didn't."

My phone buzzed at that precise moment.

"Is it Jesus?" Ted said mockingly.

Ignoring his remark, I turned away from him and pulled my phone from my coat pocket. Aunt Eleanor had finished with her own Thanksgiving festivities and moved right back to manipulating me on behalf of my mother.

Our argument momentarily forgotten, I felt Ted's presence as he read over my shoulder. "Don't delete it," he said.

"Why not?"

"Have you responded to any of her other diatribes?"

"Not yet."

"Do me a favor, and ask her what Leah and Marvin would think of how she's carrying on. Ask if her parents would be happy with her doing your mother's dirty work."

"What? Why would I...? I paused, as realization dawned.

"It's worth a shot."

Not even bothering to read Aunt Eleanor's monstrous guilt trip, I replied, *Do you think Marvin and Leah Shapiro would approve of how you're abusing your niece?*

Who in the world are Marvin and Leah Shapiro?

My grandparents.

Who told you that? Your grandparents don't even know you. Why would they care about some ungrateful, selfish brat who gets her kicks from stomping on her mother's heart and ruining holidays?

My thumbs flew so fast across my phone, Ted said he

expected smoke. I heard the words to respond as if whispered in my ear.

Like mother, like daughter, right? Mom can't even remember the names of her own parents, the same ones whose hearts SHE stomped on to marry my father. Did she ever bother to apologize, or are they still lying cold in their graves waiting for an apology from their beloved Deborah?

Ted whistled. "Two can play at this guilt game, I see."

"I just hope it gets the answer I'm looking for."

I could hear Aunt Eleanor's clipped and haughty tone as I read her reply. *My parents are alive and well, thank you very much. They bear no ill will toward my sister. I can't say the same for you and your parents, however.*

Unfazed by the passive aggressive barb, I wrote back, *So, Marvin and Leah still live in New York, and things are all peachy keen with them and Mom? I find that hard to believe since I don't even know their real names. Mom wouldn't cover it up if she had nothing to hide. When are you ever going to stop working as Deborah Ivy's personal flying monkey and grow a backbone, Aunt Eleanor?*

Ted and I stared at the phone for a solid ten minutes waiting for a response. He rubbed my shoulders as we stood close together in the chilled air.

"Maybe you pushed her too far?" he said.

Louis and Tabitha Wasserman. They live in Cordele, about an hour from your parents' house. You didn't get this information from me, and I will deny everything if you tell your mother.

Even more shocking than Aunt Eleanor's defection of loyalty, the senior Margolins actually knew my grandparents. Rose and Steve read over the text messages to be sure they recalled the correct people.

"Honey, we've known Lou and Tabby for almost forty years," Rose said. "They were members of Beth Tefillah until they had a falling out with Rabbi Epstein. We lost touch over the years, but I'm sure they'd remember us."

"Did they know Grandma?" Ted asked. "I mean, how close to six degrees of separation are we here?"

Steve shrugged. "It's possible. My parents left the synagogue ages ago, but your respective grandparents probably knew one another."

Ted and I stared at each other in wonder. For all of his anger directed toward Heaven, he couldn't deny God's sense of irony.

"This seemed like a dead end just a few hours ago," I mused.

"Technically, it was yesterday," Steve said, glancing at the oven clock. "I don't know how any of you stay up so late anymore. I wake up feeling hungover."

"Seriously, Dad?"

Steve rewarded his son with a cheeky grin. "I wasn't always this old, Theodore, and your mother isn't the only one with stories to tell."

I laughed at Ted's look of horror.

Rose hugged me tightly. "I prayed for both of you after you left. I asked God for a miracle, Rebecca, and He answered! He's so faithful!"

Tears welled in my eyes. For all the pain I had endured from the mother who bore me, God brought me a mother-in-law who loved me like her own daughter. He'd also brought me the possibility of a grandmother denied to me for my entire life. The blessing felt so much sweeter having first known the agony of its absence.

Yawning, Rose said, "Ted, I'm going to join your father in bed, but don't stay up too late, okay? Rebecca, we have a lot of packing to do tomorrow, and I know my son wants to buy you the fanciest rock you'll let him put on your finger."

"Thanks a lot, Mom."

"Oh, and Theodore?"

"Yes, Mom?" he said, not hiding the irritation in his tone.

"I better find you asleep on the family room couch when I wake up in the morning. Rebecca doesn't have to share her bed with you for another forty-eight hours. I'm sure you can manage to keep your hands off of her for another two days, hmm?"

I laughed while Ted turned slightly pink. We changed separately before reconvening in his old bedroom.

"I'm getting pretty sick of these pajamas," I said, sitting cross legged on Ted's old bed.

He exhaled a slow breath. "Any response to that statement will get me into trouble."

"Are we going to finish our discussion from earlier?" I asked.

"Well, that's one way to kill the mood," he said.

"That's the last thing we need, Ted. My aunt interrupted a pretty important conversation."

He sat down next to me. "It's late, Rebecca. Can we talk about it tomorrow?"

I looked into his eyes, noting the lack of golden sparkle and the slight lines around the corners of his eyes and on his forehead. "We're doing ourselves a disservice by ignoring this, Ted. How are we supposed to stand against my father or SBC as a united front, as husband and wife, if your head and your heart are still tied up with Annie?"

Fervently, he cupped my face in his palms. "I love you, Rebecca. You have to know that. I'm not still in love with my first wife. This isn't a competition if that's what you're afraid of."

"I'm not afraid for me, Ted. I'm afraid for you. I'm afraid you're going to see me walking through the house you shared with Annie and remember all of your regrets in how she died. I'm afraid of seeing you torment yourself because you wish you could change what happened. I love you for wanting to rescue me and protect me from my demons, but have you considered that God brought me into your life to do the same for you? Burying the pain and pretending it no longer exists doesn't mean you've moved on."

His expression hardened. "Isn't that what you did with SBC? Aren't you just blindly trusting God to handle things instead of taking action?"

"What do you mean? I don't blame myself for what I saw, Ted. I'll openly admit that I've struggled with what to do about it. I think that's why the Lord gave me the greenlight to marry you so soon."

"Care to clue me in?"

"Not if you plan to mock me or brush me off."

Ted sighed, releasing my face and burying his head against my shoulder. "I'm so tired, Rebecca. It always comes back to Jesus. I just want Him to leave me alone."

I stroked the hair at the nape of his neck. "He loves you, Ted. You don't want to believe it, but you know He does. I don't think He brought us together by chance, as broken as we both are. We have strength the other one needs to overcome our demons and put the ghosts to rest. I need your strength to do what I believe God is asking of me."

Ted lifted his head and met my eyes. "What do you think that is?"

"I'm calling Child Protective Services on Monday to report what I witnessed. Chase didn't get a say in what happened to him, but I know he's protective of his little brother. Hopefully, the Derdens will do what's right to keep their boys safe. Regardless of whatever Pastor Sociopath or Pastor Psycho Dad have planned, I'm going to need your strength when I'd rather just give up and stop fighting."

"You're amazing, Rebecca Ivy."

I smiled. "How so?"

"You trust me to help you face your biggest fears. I'm honored."

I gazed at Ted meaningfully. "Will you please allow me to do the same for you?"

CHAPTER 25

Ted never answered my question from the night before, instead promising to think about it. I asked the Lord for easily the five hundredth time if He truly wanted me to marry Ted so soon. Doubt and confusion crept in, whispering how I'd gotten caught up in the moment after seeing my father's note. The answer I received from Heaven was simply, *Stop doubting.*

Ring shopping went fairly smoothly. As Ted and I squabbled over the dollar amount, Rose whipped out a department store coupon to placate both of us. Steve captured our lovers' spat on his cellphone, calling my reaction to the price tag "priceless." He earned three, well-deserved groans for his one liner.

After grabbing a quick bite of lunch at the mall, we drove to my apartment. Rose piled the Margolins' car with every shopping bag, suitcase, or box she could find in her house. I found the fuss unnecessary, but I could not gainsay the Margolins. Steve stopped off at a local grocery store for extra boxes while Ted and I continued on toward my apartment complex. Even with my meager, three-day relationship with my future in-laws, they already felt like family. I could no longer imagine my life without them in it.

"Something's not right," Ted said, pulling into a parking space.

Looking around, I saw no new note on my car, no sign of forced entry near my apartment.

"What's wrong?" I said, disquieted by Ted's anxious profile.

"I don't know, Rebecca. I have this really bad feeling in the pit of my stomach. Do you see any cars you recognize? Or for that matter, cars you don't?"

Then, I saw *him*. He stood on the small playground next to my apartment building, texting on his phone.

"Rebecca!" Ted shouted.

Black shadows clawed at my mind, and my head began to pound and throb. I moaned, not wanting another black out or a trip to the emergency room.

Scrambling out of the car, Ted rushed to the other side and opened the door to catch me in case I fainted.

"Stay with me," he said, cradling me in his arms.

"Is everything okay?" Rose asked, her worried voice coming from behind Ted moments later.

"It's Pastor," I said, fighting to keep myself conscious. "He's by the playground on his phone. He's...he's wearing a red sweater and jeans. Salt and pepper hair."

"We saw him when we pulled up, but it looks like he took off," Steve said, turning around and scanning the immediate area. "Are you sure it was him?"

"Look at her, Dad!" Ted barked. "Of course it was!"

Nodding, Steve replied, "Rose, why don't we go for a stroll and see if we can find anyone who doesn't belong around here?"

"We need to get a restraining order," Ted said, turning his attention back to me. "Now!"

"On what grounds?" I said weakly. "He didn't commit any crime against me, and I'll look like the crazy one if I tell the police I think I saw him here. He never threatened me, at least not overtly."

"Has he ever been here before?" Ted asked.

I didn't want to answer his question.

"Rebecca," Ted said more forcefully, "has Pastor Sociopath ever been to your apartment?"

I didn't want to confess anything, the shame of my own naïveté too much to bear. I closed my eyes and shook my head in denial.

Straining for patience, Ted said, "Rebecca, you told me that nothing physical ever happened between the two of you. Was that a lie?"

I fought back the ghosts and demons of the past, the ones hissing accusations of perversion in my own heart. I countered with the truth, of the married man who dropped by my home unannounced after I spent two weeks stuck at home with the flu and an upper respiratory infection.

"Jessica, I...oh, hi Pastor," I said, surprised to find him standing outside my door.

"You've missed church three weeks in a row," he said, surveying me from head to foot. "I came by to make sure you didn't abandon SBC and your responsibilities there. I could understand your embarrassment after I exposed your little crush on me, Rebecca, but running away from the situation just screams of cowardice. Frankly, I expected more from you."

Groggily, I shook my head, the congestion still interfering with my equilibrium. "You stopped by to check on me? Is

Ashley with you?" I glanced past him to the parking lot, hoping to find her, but somehow knowing I wouldn't.

"Aren't you going to invite me in?" Pastor demanded. "It reflects poorly for me to be seen outside the doorway of one of my single, female congregants. We don't need to provide the gossipers with any fresh material simply because your hospitality skills could use some work."

Too unsettled by his presence to censor myself, I blurted out, "Don't you think it looks worse to invite you in? Especially since I'm in my pajamas?"

"Rebecca, why do you insist on tormenting me?" he wailed dramatically. "I'm a married man. Do you normally wear such provocative clothing when strangers come calling? Have you welcomed other men the same way?"

I glanced down at my faded shirt, plaid shorts, and mismatched socks. His definition of 'provocative' and mine differed vastly. "Pastor, I didn't invite you here. I've been sick for the past two weeks. I don't understand why you came over or why you think I wanted you to be here."

He wagged his finger in my face. "Don't think I'm unaware of your little game, Rebecca Ivy. First, you attempt to seduce me while as a guest in my home. Then, you skip church, knowing full well I'd come over here to find you. Now, you answer the door deliberately dressed like you just got out of bed. What do you think that does to a man, Rebecca? Will you stop at nothing to tempt me?" He searched my eyes for confirmation of his misplaced suspicions.

"I really think you should go," I said before doubling over in a fit of coughing spasms. Pastor seized the opportunity to enter my apartment, closing and locking the door quickly. He placed his arm around me as if comforting me.

I shrugged him off, backpedaling into my kitchen in search of a glass of water.

"Cute place," he said as if he hadn't invited himself inside. He looked far too comfortable and at ease. "Ah, look at this picture of you at the SBC Fall Festival with the children."

"Pastor, you don't need to be here," I said after a long sip of water. "You should leave before anyone gets the wrong idea."

His dark eyes bored into mine. "So, you're finally admitting you manipulated me into coming over."

Bewildered, I said, "Pastor, what are you talking about? I did *not* invite you over here! I have bronchitis! I spent last weekend practically coughing up a lung."

He looked at me like a crumb covered child alleging they knew nothing about missing cookies. "Bronchitis, Rebecca? Surely you can do better than that."

Irritated, I shot back, "Do you want to see my amoxicillin prescription?"

Pastor glowered at me. The unleashed anger I had witnessed against Olivia slithered right into my apartment. Pastor's eyes glittered almost black.

Hoping to placate the beast, I said, "Pastor, I appreciate your concern for my church attendance, but as you can see, I'm recovering from an illness. I really think you should go, or I can call Ashley and have her trade places due to your concern for propriety."

"You may continue to fool the rest of the world, Rebecca Ivy, but I know the truth about you. You make such a show of innocence at church, but before me is the real dragon you hide at home."

"Dragon?" I said incredulously.

"Even your unbelieving ex knew to run from a Jezebel when he saw one. There you sat, crying in my office like Jason broke your heart. You used all of those tears for my benefit, didn't you, Rebecca? You wanted me to let my guard down while you planned your next move," he said, his eyes gesturing down the hall toward my bedroom.

God, help me! I pleaded to Heaven. My head spun in circles, the confusion and my congestion so thick, the room felt in motion. I stumbled backward until I landed against my dining room wall. I held my head in my hands.

"Oh, Jesus!" I cried, slowly rocking myself. Why did Pastor twist everything I said into the opposite of what I meant? Why did he bombard me with ridiculous accusations based in some alternate reality? I felt strangled, choked by the inability to be heard, understood, or believed.

Pastor sniffed haughtily. "I'm glad to see you haven't totally given over to the Evil One, Rebecca. I expect to see you in church this Sunday, fake illness or not, and you will dress yourself in an appropriate manner when you enter the house of the Lord. Are we clear on that?"

Too confused to do anything other than nod, I gave him the win. Nothing he said made any sense, as if he had me confused with someone else. Pastor looked me up and down one last time, the mere thought of me suddenly a stench in his nostrils.

"I'm glad you've learned your lesson," he said, chest puffed, chin elevated in the air. "Don't bother showing me out as I'm sure you'd only concoct more ways to keep me trapped in this lair of iniquity."

"Rebecca," Ted's voice broke through, "come back to me."

Clawing through my living nightmare, I blinked and focused my eyes on the shimmering gold before me. I sighed in relief at the face that held concern for me rather than lust masquerading under a facade of moral outrage.

"Pastor was here," I finally said. "He tricked me. Well, he tried to anyway."

"Did he touch you?"

I shook my head. "I had been sick for two weeks. Pastor stopped by wanting to know why I wasn't at church, trying to throw his botched seduction in my face. He probably assumed I told someone what happened or left SBC. He used a coughing fit as an excuse to sneak into my apartment. He kept accusing me of trying to manipulate him, of insinuating I wanted..."

"You wanted what?" Ted said tersely.

"He did exactly what your mother said he did. He tried to seduce me while confusing me into thinking it was the other way around."

Whatever paltry words I used with Rose Margolin twenty-four hours prior paled in comparison to the string of obscenity unleashed by my soon-to-be husband.

"If I find him, I'll kill him. So help me, Rebecca. I will kill that son of a—"

"No sign of him," Steve said, interrupting Ted's colorful outburst. "We're looking for a squat little guy in the red sweater, right?"

I nodded weakly.

"Rebecca, why don't you give me the keys to your apartment, and we'll handle the packing?" Rose said. "Ted, are you absolutely positive you two need to do this right now? Rebecca doesn't need the extra stress."

"Mom," Ted said with irritation, "in the last three days, Rebecca's father and that sociopath have stalked her apartment for God only knows what. She's not safe here, and I won't compromise Rebecca's reputation by having her stay at my house without a ring on her finger. We don't know where Pastor Sociopath and his mistress are holed up, but if there's any chance he still lives in that old house, I don't want Rebecca anywhere near him. My friend, Titus Locke, works in SVU, and I'll call him as soon as we get back to my place."

"You have friends everywhere," I said with a bemused smile. Ted's protectiveness and fearsome expression felt like a warm blanket driving the chills away.

"Rebecca, can you come inside and let me know what you need now and which things we can box up?" Rose asked.

Ted shook his head emphatically before I could answer. "If that degenerate is lurking anywhere around here, I don't want him seeing Rebecca or following her. I'll ask Titus to come back with me in a squad car to pick up Rebecca's car. Hopefully, the blue lights will keep the stalkers on the run. Dad, are you okay here with Mom, especially if sociopath number one or number two decide to make a repeat appearance?"

"I have a concealed carry permit," Steve said, gesturing toward the holstered gun on his hip, "and I haven't forgotten how to use it either."

My eyes widened.

"We also have Jesus on our side," Rose said, looking meaningfully at me. "Leviathan fears exposure more than anything else. Obviously, these charlatans fear Rebecca will pull back the curtain on their sin. The battle isn't just against flesh and blood here, and we need to bear that in mind."

Steve rolled his eyes. "Enough with the spiritual talk, Rose. Let's get everything packed up, and we'll meet at Ted's once we're done."

"Rose!" I called.

She turned around. "What do you need, honey?"

"When you get to my pajama drawer, you'll see a set with a purple shirt and matching plaid boxers buried in the back."

"Oh, do you want me to get them for you now?"

"I want you to burn them."

Ted looked at me questioningly.

Rose nodded, understanding at least in part, of some negative association tied to the clothing. Rose and Steve began the process of lugging suitcases, bags, and boxes up to my second floor apartment. I watched everything as I sat securely in Ted's car, feeling safe for possibly the first time in my life.

CHAPTER 26

WHILE THE VISIT WITH TED'S FRIEND, DETECTIVE Titus Locke, initially started as a friendly get together, Titus radioed for back up to take a formal statement. He told Ted he didn't trust himself to be impartial, nor did he want to provide any loopholes used to potentially exonerate Pastor or Cynthia. In between the three hours Ted and I gave statements to Titus' partner Detective Nichols, Rose and Steve filed in and out with boxes, bags, and suitcases.

"So, what happens now?" I asked Detective Nichols.

"We'll start the investigation process," he said. Glancing at his notepad to be sure he had the names correct, he continued, "We'll pay a visit to the Derdens along with a CPS worker specifically trained in child sexual trauma."

"And then they arrest Pastor, right? Once Chase corroborates my story?"

"Well, Miss Ivy, that's up to Chase's parents."

"What do you mean? A crime was committed."

Titus shook his head. "Technically, we can't have a crime

without a victim, Rebecca. Most crimes like these rarely get reported, and even fewer ever go to criminal proceedings. Some parents don't want the shame and embarrassment to the family. Others don't want their kid interrogated on the witness stand, especially since they have to see the abuser and face cross examination by the defense attorney."

"But there are more victims!" I insisted. "I'm sure of it! Look, I've researched the warning signs, and SBC has all of them—the grooming, the love bombing, the mind control and brainwashing. Pastor even tried it on me!"

Locke and Nichols exchanged glances. "Did your pastor ever assault you or threaten to? Has he shown up to your apartment other than the incident several years ago and again today?"

My shoulders slumped. "No. He just...he twisted everything to make me think I wanted a sexual relationship rather than the other way around. He's sick!"

Detective Nichols answered first, saying, "Miss Ivy, I don't doubt everything you're telling me. As far as being an eyewitness to the crime with the Derden boy, that's solid evidence we can use to start a case. However, you need to be prepared for the worst."

"What do you mean?" Ted said, putting his arm around me as he finished a quick conversation with his parents. "What's the worst here? We find out Pastor Sociopath has a longer list of victims than anticipated?"

"No, Ted," Titus said. "We've seen too many cases where the abuser buys the family's silence. It's similar to settling out of court in a civil lawsuit. When the perp has a lot to lose personally or professionally, they usually find a way to negotiate with the victim's family. Morally, it's reprehensible, but it's not illegal."

I shook.

Not from fear, but from anger.

"So are you telling me," I said through gritted teeth, "that this sick pedophile could keep preaching his twisted, brainwashing sermons from the pulpit with no one the wiser? Are you seriously telling me that?"

Detective Nichols met my eyes, "Miss Ivy, that's exactly what I'm saying."

"What about the parents?" Ted said. "Don't they have any responsibility to protect their kids? How can there be no accountability or recourse here?"

Titus smiled at both of us sympathetically. "We live in a pretty messed up world, guys. When we've talked to the parents and told them about the dangers and evidence of a predator but they choose not to press charges, we warn the parents of child endangerment. In that case, the parents go to jail if we discover they've allowed the predator near the victim again."

"Which means the law punishes a rotten parent for not protecting their child, but it does nothing to remove the predator from the streets," Ted said grimly.

I fought back tears of frustration. "I witnessed a despicable crime with my own two eyes. I can give you details about everything. But unless the Derdens decide to press charges, there's absolutely nothing that can be done?"

Detective Nichols shook his head. "Miss Ivy, I wish I had better news for you. You could always contact a religious board if the pastor has any higher ranking leadership who can hold him accountable, but I think we're all familiar with scandals like this being covered up. Parents don't want to believe abuse happens around *their* kids. Unfortunately, many of them would rather take a few thousand dollars than pay an attorney or deal with all of the gossip and additional trauma of a trial and police proceedings."

"These are innocent children!" I shouted. "They don't deserve this! Nobody does! He'll just keep abusing people because no one will stop him!"

Detective Nichols replied, "Again, I understand you're upset, Miss Ivy, and we'll call the Derdens on Monday to hopefully get the ball rolling. If you can talk to other parents and see if this happened with other minors, we can build a case regardless of what the Derdens ultimately decide to do. Getting people to come forward is always our biggest obstacle in a case like this. Victims are embarrassed, ashamed, or just flat out in denial."

"This is just so hopeless!" I said. "They practically worship Pastor in that church! When he married Cynthia a few weeks ago, the members posted all sorts of photos and congratulations on social media. They just don't want to see it. They complain and gossip to me, but at the end of the day, they just bury their heads in the sand and make their excuses."

Having caught the tail end of our conversation, Rose put a comforting hand on my shoulder. "Nothing is impossible with God, honey. *Ecclesiastes* says He judges everything we do, the good, the bad, and the things done in secret. You spoke up, Rebecca, and I'm proud of you. If nothing else, we now have a police report on file. Pastor Sociopath can try to spin that however he wants, but let's hope the Derden family does what's right. If, God forbid, other cases exist, they might be encouraged to come forward too. We just need to trust the Lord no matter what happens."

Locke and Nichols broke off into quiet conversation while Ted and Rose consoled me. Ted held me as I wept, and Rose prayed quietly beside me.

"Ted, why don't we pick up Rebecca's car?" Titus said, approaching us. "I can talk to some friends on road patrol and have them look for anyone casing the apartment. The letter from Rebecca's father doesn't threaten violence, but if he attempts anything else, we have proof of intent."

"Titus, I'd rather stop the crime before it happens."

"It doesn't usually work that way, my friend. With no prior convictions, we can only act after he commits a crime. I know it's not what you want to hear, but that's the system."

"Sorry, but the system sucks," I said through my tears. "I just don't understand why you guys can't do more to protect these innocent children."

"Miss Ivy, I totally understand where you're coming from," Detective Nichols said, "but we do have laws and regulations in place for a reason. You have no idea how many times we get phone calls from ex-wives and girlfriends making up stories to get more money or custody of the children. Maybe one in twenty cases we investigate involves an actual crime. We can't arrest someone on suspicion without proof or real, probable cause."

"But I saw it!" I said. "I watched it happen! They burned that image into my retinas!"

"But the crime wasn't against you personally," Titus said gently. "We can't force a victim to press charges. Our job is to serve and protect. If the victim asks us to serve them by doing nothing, we have to respect that. Now, if *we* witness a crime happening, that's different."

I sighed, utterly dejected and defeated. "So unless the Derdens press charges against Pastor, then the world goes on like nothing ever happened?"

"Let's just hope they do," Titus said. "I wish I had better news for you, Rebecca, but we see this happen every day. Off the record though, I hope they lock the bastard up for a long time."

"Let's get going," Ted said. "The sooner we leave, the sooner we get back."

The officers agreed, and they left with Ted. Steve and Rose stayed behind with me at the house.

"Don't be discouraged, honey," Rose said patting my knee. "I hoped the police might have better news for us, but you took the most important step. We need to pray for God to move on the hearts of the Derdens, and they put the welfare of their children over their own pride."

"Rose, I'm not worried about pride. I'm worried about Pastor manipulating the Derdens once he knows law enforcement got involved. No wonder he and Cynthia worked so hard to smear my reputation. They needed to completely destroy my credibility in case I started talking."

Steve joined us with two mugs of tea. Handing one to Rose and then one to me, he asked, "What about the ex-wife?"

"Gosh, I haven't even thought about Ashley," I said. "Pastor ruined her reputation the same way he did to mine. I wouldn't be surprised if he threatened her with calls to Child Protective Services just to keep her from exposing him."

"That makes no sense, honey." Rose said. "They wouldn't give her full custody of the children and let her move out of state if any of that drug abuse slander held up in court."

After taking a sip of tea, I set the mug down on a coaster and sighed wearily. "It's difficult seeing how the sin and corruption extends so far beyond my own situation. Sure, what Pastor did to me was wrong, but—"

"Don't you dare minimize the trauma or injustice done to you!" Rose interrupted. "That pervert screwed with your head for almost fifteen years, Rebecca. Pastor Sociopath would have robbed you of your innocence the same way he did to that Derden boy."

"I'm beginning to understand why Ted acts so protective of you, Rebecca," Steve said. "How does your father fit into all of this?"

"I cut things off with my entire family six months before I witnessed the incident between Pastor, Cynthia, and Chase Derden. My father showed up at my job a year after I ended all communication with him. Ted stopped him from assaulting me in the office park."

Steve raked a hand over his bald head. "Unbelievable! How can these men behave worse than animals, then get up and preach in a pulpit? Shouldn't they fear being struck by lightning?"

"That's just it, my dear," Rose said, patting Steve gently on the thigh. "They don't fear God at all. Even Satan can quote Scripture. Many of these frauds believe their own shtick and justify their immoral behavior. Others knowingly sin and simply assume they're too smart to get caught."

Steve shook his head in disbelief.

Rose continued, "My heart breaks thinking about the people in the pews blindly trusting in these leaders. Everyone thinks a sexual predator looks like the creepy guy on the television show rather than the normal looking person next to them. Steve, we both know Rabbi Epstein slept with his secretary and two other women at the synagogue, but the members didn't care. They didn't want to deal with anything unpleasant, so they just stuck their heads in the sand."

"Why do you always bring up Rabbi Epstein?" Steve said, jumping to his feet. "You can't compare cheating on your spouse to abusing a child!"

"How do we know Rabbi Epstein didn't abuse one?" Rose argued. "Just like Titus said, they can't have a crime without a victim willing to speak up. It doesn't mean nothing happened.

When men or women hold positions of authority with no accountability, they always surround themselves with lemmings willing to lie and cover up for them. They get drunk on their own power and follow after the lusts of their eyes. They turn their sins into everyone else's problem of perception rather than their own wrongdoing."

"Now, you're contradicting yourself," Steve said, stalking away from the couch and pacing in front of the fireplace. "One second, you tell me that God's in control and God sees all. Out of the other side of your mouth, you say that God just lets this stuff happen. What about justice, Rose? You call Rabbi Epstein a hypocrite who blasphemes God's Name, but I haven't seen the man get struck by lightning or even lose his job as rabbi."

Rose stood and walked toward her husband. "Steve, I don't always know why God does what He does. I don't know why He allowed your people to suffer 430 years as slaves to Pharaoh, why Rebecca has suffered so much, or even why He took Annie the way He did. I don't have an answer that would satisfy either of us because I'm not God."

"I just don't understand why your loving God would allow any of this to happen. It makes no sense, Rose."

"This is exactly why Jesus died on the cross for us," she said.

"Don't you start with your Jesus *chazarai*," he said, turning his back on her.

Quietly, I said, "It's faith in Jesus that helped me survive what I've been through, Steve. God's promises in the Bible kept me from becoming a mirror image of the people who abused me. If that isn't a miracle, I don't know what is."

"You're just a good person, Rebecca," he said. "A sweet girl."

"Who do you think made her that way?" Rose fired back. "She certainly didn't learn it from her parents or her old church. What you see as 'sweetness' in Rebecca is the work of the Holy

Spirit in her. No explanation apart from God Himself could explain why Rebecca didn't become a narcissistic monster just like the rest of them."

Steve threw up his hands in frustration. "I can't take any more of this Jesus shtick! I'm going outside for a few minutes."

The front door opened and slammed shut.

Rose sat down next to me on the couch. She wrapped her arms around me, and I leaned my head on her shoulder.

"God knows what He's doing, Rebecca. You, my dear, are the best thing that could have happened to the Margolin family. If nothing else, honey, please know that God answered my prayers by sending you into my son's life."

CHAPTER 27

WHILE STEVE AND ROSE HASHED THROUGH THEIR disagreement on Ted's front porch, I busied myself unpacking in the guest room and acclimating myself to my new surroundings. Despite the walls devoid of artwork or photos, Ted's home still felt inviting with soft, warm tones.

I rummaged through Ted's refrigerator, not surprised to find it well stocked with imported cheeses, fresh fruits and vegetables, several bottles of wine, and all of the fixings for the Thanksgiving meal he had promised me a few days earlier.

Hearing the squeak of loafers and jangle of keys behind me, my grin widened.

"Everything to your liking?" Ted said close to my ear.

I turned around, quickly noting our close proximity and the immediate electrical current between us. Ted took a step backward, but he looked me up and down with a large smile.

"I like you in my kitchen."

Megawatt emerged. "I think you mean *our* kitchen."

The distinct feel of butter sizzling in the pan nearly sent my knees knocking. I took a deep breath, knowing Ted and I could act on all of our suppressed feelings in less than forty-eight hours. Blushing at the thought of married life, I sidestepped away from the fridge and put more distance between me and my fiancé.

In two days, I would see my complete metamorphosis from Rebecca Ivy, unloved daughter and human punching bag, into Mrs. Ted Margolin. I braced myself with a hand on the counter.

"Rebecca, are you all right?" Ted asked, his smile falling into a frown. "Do you need to sit down?"

I looked up at him and smiled. "Pinch me, Ted. Seriously. Even with everything we've been through the past three days, even with the threat from my father and Pastor Sociopath, I see God's hand all over this. I never imagined myself living in a house so beautiful."

"And it looks great on you," he said, his gaze intense on me. "I saw you standing in front of the refrigerator, and it suddenly felt like you've been here the whole time. Strange, huh?"

"Do you know how badly I want to kiss you?" I said breathlessly.

Ted's jaw clenched and unclenched as he traced my cheek with his fingertips. "I think I might have an idea."

His eyes zeroed in on my mouth, and I forced myself to inhale oxygen.

"Do we need to get a chaperon to ensure you'll survive until Monday?" Rose said, barely concealing the laughter in her voice. Conflict apparently resolved, she and Steve stood just outside the kitchen threshold sporting large grins.

I ducked under Ted's arm and embraced the woman who had become far more mother than mother-in-law. She winked at me while Steve approached his son and whispered something in his ear. My husband-to-be suddenly matched the red porcelain bowl on the center island. Steve clapped him on the back with a hearty chuckle.

"Knowing my husband as I do," Rose said, wrapping an arm around my waist, "Steve just offered a birds and the bees pep talk."

I felt crimson steal into my own cheeks. "Oh dear."

Rose laughed next to me. "I pray the Lord blesses you both mightily in every area of your marriage, including parenthood. Ted wanted that for a long time, but Annie pushed it off. She said she wanted to live a little before being tied down with a family."

"Tied down?"

Rose blanched, realizing her faux pas. "Excuse me, Rebecca, I've said too much. When, and if, you and Ted start a family is for the two of you to decide. I shouldn't have said anything."

Overhearing the last bit, Ted gently pulled me toward him, replacing his mother's arm around my waist with his own. "You're already talking about grandchildren, Mom? How about we just get married first, okay?"

Rose nodded in agreement, apologizing again for the slip, and Steve announced the departure of the senior Margolins to recover from the day's festivities. As their car pulled out of the driveway, I became very aware of Ted and I alone in his beautiful house. Diverting my thoughts from temptation, I worked on a simple dinner for the two of us.

I navigated my way easily around the kitchen, locating cheese, crackers, and fruit for a light bite. We sat down at the kitchen table, Ted seated at the head with me to his right. He held my gaze for a long minute before breaking eye contact and swallowing half the contents of his water glass.

"This might just be the worst kind of torture," he finally said.

"Maybe we can find a documentary about animals being ripped apart on the Serengeti or some shark special. Nothing kills a mood like shark bait, right?"

Ted's immediate laughter helped ease the tension in the room. "You're a clever one, Rebecca Ivy."

I grinned. "Why don't we work on Thanksgiving dinner together? It turned out to be our rehearsal dinner."

"Speaking of, have you heard back from Jessica or Nathan? Are they coming?"

I shrugged. "Jessica sent me a really weird text. Sounds like things didn't go very well. She'll stop by tomorrow once she gets back into town."

"Do you think something happened between her and Matty?"

"What a crazy thing to say! Matty practically hates Jessica."

Ted raised an eyebrow then popped a grape in his mouth.

"You can't be serious! Matty told me himself how much he resents her."

"Rebecca, I know a thing or two about jealousy. If you may recall, you caught a bit of it earlier this year with Goldstein and again at Le Petit Versailles. Are you absolutely sure Matty detests his brother's fiancée, or could he possibly detest himself for being interested?"

I groaned. "Can I just have one drama free day? Maybe not even a whole day? Like a half of one, maybe?"

Finishing another bite Ted replied, "You know what, I'm probably way off base here. Yes, even the mighty Margolin can make a mistake," he said, rolling his eyes at my feigned shock.

"I hope you're right, Ted. Meanwhile, stop hogging all of the gouda. Half of that belongs to me as of Monday."

"Fair enough," he said with a laugh. "Now, hand me that

notepad on the counter, so we can figure out where to put all of your stuff."

Ted and I discovered a mutual love for home design and decorating, and we stayed up until almost one sketching out the different rooms in his house. We listed off all of my apartment furniture and then solved the puzzle of where it should go. After finally calling it a night, or rather, an early morning, Ted dropped me off at the guest room door.

"This was really fun," I said shyly. I averted my eyes like a high schooler coming home from a prom date.

Ted chuckled, casually crossing his arms over his chest and leaning back against the opposite wall in the hallway. "I can't believe you're actually in my home, sleeping under my roof."

I grinned. "You and me both. And seriously, this house is stunning. I feel like I'm walking through a magazine spread. How much of this did you do yourself?"

"I helped a lot with the demo," he said. "Very cathartic, as I'm sure you can imagine. Obviously, I contracted out the major construction and electrical work, but I helped with drywall, laying down all of the floors, and anything on the walls."

"Ted, is there anything you don't do well?"

He exhaled a heavy sigh laden with meanings I would be unwise to ponder for long. Blushing, I said simply, "Okay, um goodnight then."

"What? No goodnight kiss?" he said.

I swallowed nervously. "Do you really think that's a good idea?"

His eyes never left mine. "No, but I'm having a hard time convincing myself I shouldn't anyway."

Before I could protest, before my heart could tell my brain to shut up and not protest at all, Ted pulled away from our brief, simmering embrace. He bolted for the master bedroom, and my weak knees nearly sent me to the floor. I shakily opened the door behind me and stumbled inside the guest room.

Seeking to cool the longing in my heart, I located my Bible and flipped to *Proverbs*, reminded of Rose's testimony in overcoming Leviathan. I read for a few minutes before changing into flannel pajamas. Grabbing my toiletry case, I headed for the hallway bathroom.

I startled when I saw Ted standing in the open door frame of the master bedroom.

"Hi," I said, waving awkwardly.

"I keep thinking the second I close my eyes, I'm going to wake up and find you gone. Like I imagined you here."

"I don't think anybody could imagine these ugly pajamas," came my caustic reply. "Unless you've got a snowman and penguins fetish, I think we're safe."

Ted's smile reached his twinkling eyes. "Have I told you today how much I love you, Rebecca?"

I deposited my grooming payload into the hall bathroom before responding. Poking my head out, I said, "I love you too. Now, let's try to get some sleep so we can cook up that massive feast in your fridge."

I retreated into the bathroom and commenced with my tooth brushing.

"How much longer do we have to wait?" Ted called in a pained voice.

Spitting out a mouthful of toothpaste I yelled back, "Go to bed, Uncle Big Shot!"

Ted's laughter sent me to sleep with a sweet smile on my lips. The next morning found me feeling rested and refreshed, not remembering the last time I had woken up free of a sore back. Daylight streamed in through the two front windows, and I indulged in the quick thought of the guest room serving as an idyllic, future nursery. My buzzing cell phone interrupted my sweet reverie with a text from Aunt Eleanor.

Been thinking a lot about what you said. Here's the address for your grandparents. It'll save you a few minutes searching online. And for what it's worth, Rebecca, I'm sorry for everything. I would love to hear what's going on in your life rather than listening to your mother's version of it. Just let me know.

"Ted!" I cried, scrambling out of the room. I ran down the hallway and banged on his bedroom door. "Ted?"

He jerked the door open, his hair flattened on one side and sticking straight up on the other. If God ever gave us a son, I imagined him waking up looking the same way. I grinned.

"Rebecca! Is everything...oh...you're smiling," he said. "What's going on?"

I shoved my phone into his face. "Look! Look, what my aunt wrote!"

Blinking the sleep from his eyes, he scanned her text quickly, his brows lifting in surprise. Wow," he murmured.

"I know!" I said. "Can you believe it?"

"Are you sure she's not manipulating you?"

"Ted, in the thirty-three years I have known this woman, Aunt Eleanor has never apologized for anything. This is groundbreaking!"

"Which is why I'm suspicious," he said, scanning over her text again. Glancing down at me and my own messy appearance, his grim expression gave way to a boyish grin. "Oh, and good morning by the way."

I returned his smile. "As your future wife in less than thirty-six hours, this is a good look for you."

Ted brushed back a loose curl from my temple, anchoring his hand at the base of my head. He held me like a plate of the finest china. "Rebecca, I don't remember the last time I had something to look forward to beyond making money or closing a deal. You make me happy, and I want to see you just as happy. Can we put aside the family shenanigans for now?"

Too excited and oblivious to catch his hint, I carried on. "But we have something unprecedented here! What do you think? Do I go in guns blazing, or do I go in with an open mind?"

Ted's smile flattened into a straight line. "Your aunt has deliberately hurt and manipulated you repeatedly. I'm glad you received your first ever apology, Rebecca, but the timing concerns me. With your father overtly threatening you, I don't doubt he ratcheted up the pressure on your mother, and de facto your aunt, to get you back in the family fold. What if we put a reply on hold until after we're married? Do you think that's fair?"

I shrugged. "Yeah, I guess."

He raised an eyebrow. "What's the rush, Rebecca? Why can't this wait until Tuesday?"

"Ted, I might finally solve the mystery surrounding my mother and her family. This could change my life!"

He dropped his hand from me.

I frowned. "What did I say wrong?"

Ted sighed wearily, running a hand through his hair. He grimaced as he realized the state of it. "Rebecca, I thought we would use today to focus on our own relationship rather than your family. Why can't you put aside the Ivy family chazarai for one day and just enjoy being happy and in love?"

"Your father said the same thing last night."

"What? That we should be happy?"

"No, that cha...cha...whatever that Yiddish word was. He told your mom he didn't want to hear her Jesus cha...well you know, *that* word."

"It means 'garbage.' *Mishigas* works too because it means

'craziness,' but chazarai seemed more appropriate as regards to your family."

"Oh," I said, suddenly realizing Steve's implication from the night before. "I guess your dad really hates hearing your mom talk about Jesus. In fact, he seems even angrier about it than you. Do you know why?"

Ted shrugged. "Probably something to do with my grandparents. Jews don't believe in Jesus."

"Well, that's not true. Look at Nathan."

Patronizingly, Ted said, "He's not really Jewish, Rebecca."

"How can you be 'not really Jewish,' Ted? He's more religious than you are! He invited me over to celebrate the Feast of Tabernacles right after my birthday. Did you have a *sukkah* in your backyard too?"

"When did you suddenly become an expert on Judaism?" he snapped.

"Just a second there," I said, holding up my hands. "I didn't come down here to start a fight. Maybe we should caffeinate and then reconvene."

"Fine with me," he said curtly. After a brief pause, Ted closed his bedroom door.

I sighed wearily and got dressed.

CHAPTER 28

"THANKS FOR BREAKFAST," I MUMBLED AS TED SET A plate of fried eggs and rye toast in front of me.

He exhaled slowly. "I hurt you."

"Yeah, you did."

He sat down across from me at the table with his own plate. Per my custom, I said a quick prayer of thanks. Opening my eyes, I found Ted watching me.

"You really believe in all of this praying, don't you?"

"I'm not like my parents or Pastor Sociopath, Ted. You should know that better than anybody."

He winced at my response. "I never thought you wanted to impress anybody when I saw you pray before meals, Rebecca. Seeing you at my kitchen table, praying with no one else around, it made me realize you behave the same way behind closed doors too."

I looked at him for a long minute. "Are you apologizing?"

"No, I'm explaining."

I frowned and took a bite of my toast.

After a few, uncomfortable minutes, Ted blurted out, "Are you giving me the silent treatment because I refuse to deal with any Ivy family drama today?"

I glared at him.

He exhaled in frustration. "Can you even try to see my side of things, Rebecca, or are you going to just throw some Bible verses at me for being an unsupportive fiancé?"

Stunned and hurt, I jerked up from my seat. "Throw some Bible verses at you, Ted? That was low. Maybe you should just eat by yourself. I've suddenly lost my appetite."

Before Ted could utter another hurtful word, I turned on my heel and stormed down the hallway. I slammed the guest room door for good measure.

With nowhere else to go but up, I prayed. "God, are you really, really, *really* sure we're supposed to get married? This feels like one colossal disaster waiting to happen. Are we going to raise our kids like Steve and Rose raised theirs? God, I don't want that! You know I don't."

"Rebecca?" Ted called through the door.

"I'm praying," I said, my voice tight, "and nobody's here but me and Jesus to see how religious I am."

"Can I come in?"

"Why bother? I might preach at you or something."

Not waiting for my permission, Ted opened the door, his forehead lining at my impressive scowl.

"You're mad at me."

"Ya think?"

"I, um, I don't think I've ever seen you like this, Rebecca. Angry? Yes. Lashing out and hurt? No."

"Well, now you have. Congratulations," I clipped.

He took a deep breath. "I get it. I screwed up. Then, I compounded the problem by sticking both feet in my mouth.

I'm sorry I hurt you, Rebecca. I'm frustrated with how this morning started, and I took it out on you. The jab about the Bible verses was unnecessary and mean."

"Your assumption about why I pray hurts the most, Ted. When we sat at Jessica's kitchen table, you told me you respected my beliefs. Was that a lie just to sleep with me, even marrying me to get the deed done? I promise, I won't live up to the hype."

Ted's eyebrows drew together in confusion. "What do you mean, Rebecca? You told me you're a virgin."

"I am. I just mean...I don't know what you or Pastor or Jason think will be so amazing about me other than the novelty of being the first. If that's all you're after, Ted, I'll go back to my apartment and get a restraining order against Pastor and my father. I refuse to be anybody's conquest."

Ted held me by the shoulders. "Slow down! I have no idea what's gotten into either one of us this morning. I acted like a total grouch earlier, and your question about Judaism caught me off guard. Rebecca, I love you. That hasn't changed. I am not looking to hoist up your virginity like a trophy. I'm shocked and honored you still have it. Annie already had a few boyfriends before anything ever happened between the two of us."

Curiosity won out over defensiveness. "So, you never slept together before hooking up at that Christmas party?"

"That's what I'm saying."

"Were you...you know...when you and Annie...?"

"No."

"Was it a lot of other women?"

Ted shifted uncomfortably. "Why do you want to know?"

"Don't you think I have a right to know?" I said. "You want me to spend the rest of my life with you, but I don't know much about your past other than Annie." Testing out my Yiddish, I added, "With all of the *mishigas* happening with my father and Pastor Sociopath, the last thing I need is some psycho ex-girl-friend stalking you or a college one-night stand claiming you fathered her child a hundred years ago."

"A hundred years ago?" he croaked, a sliver of sunshine peeking through the thunderous expression on his face.

I snickered. "Fine, slightly less than a hundred, but you know what I mean."

"I'm not ashamed of my past, Rebecca, but why can't we just leave it there?"

"Because this matters to me!" I said. "I know about Annie. How many other women have also slept with my fiancé? What about after Annie passed away?"

"There was nobody after Annie died," Ted said gruffly, his eyes delving mine. "I didn't live like a priest before she and I got married, but I certainly lived like one afterward."

Mollified, I nodded. "And before?"

"Why does this mean so much to you?" he said, exasperated.

"Because it just does, okay?"

"I've tested negative for STD's, if that's the big concern here, Rebecca. Can we drop it now?"

"Don't you get it?" I said, desperation in my tone.

"Get what?" he said, equally as frustrated.

"I just...I won't be able to compete with any of your other partners," I said. "How do I know you won't be holding me and thinking about someone else? How do I know you won't compare me to them, wishing for something better?"

Ted's expression softened. "Sweetheart, I'm not asking you to compete with anyone. I never felt about any of them the way I do about you."

I searched his eyes. "What about Annie?"

"What about her?"

"You're telling me that you love *me*, the woman you've been semi-dating for a month and engaged to for basically a long weekend, more than your childhood sweetheart? Ted, that's not only crazy, but it's impossible!"

"Says who?"

"Says me. Says everybody! This seemed like such a good idea three days ago. Ted, what the heck are we thinking?"

I slumped down onto the bed. Cautiously, Ted sat next to me.

"Are you afraid of me?" he asked. "Of yourself? Do you think I'll look at you and find something lacking?"

"You wouldn't be the first," I muttered.

"Rebecca," Ted drawled, "What's this really about?"

"How many?" I repeated, unwilling to let the matter rest.

He gave a resigned sigh. "Five. Four other girls and Annie. Can we move on?"

I knew I had deliberately caused Ted pain by prying the information out of him. Moreover, I created a new way to torture myself with thoughts of *five* other women who surely had more to offer the mighty Margolin than I ever could. Dejectedly, I said. "I don't know why you want to marry me, Ted. I'm a mess. You deserve better. You have four women out there who proved themselves worthy of you. Please, don't waste any more time worrying about me."

Ted tried to kiss me, but I turned my face away, recoiling further into myself. "You don't need to do that," I said, "to try to prove to me or to yourself that you want me."

Ted dropped his hands to his sides, but he held my eyes with a searing gaze. "I told you my intentions when I first shared my feelings with you, Rebecca. That hasn't changed. When Annie died, everything in my past died with her, including any other female. I hope you believe me."

"But our fight," I protested. "How can we make a marriage work when we can't get along under the same roof for twenty-four hours?"

"Rebecca, I don't expect us to agree on everything, but I won't run away from our relationship just because we have an ugly fight. Marriage doesn't mean walking blissfully into the sunset with your soulmate. It's two people learning to live together and still like each other by the end of it. You grow together, but you also experience growing pains as part of the process. Your entire worldview changes because you have someone else to consider, not just yourself. I imagine the sensation becomes even more intense with children."

"I wouldn't know," I said bitterly. "I have yet to witness a healthy marriage."

Ted wrapped an arm around me. "I don't want to belabor the point by apologizing again for this morning, but I really am sorry I hurt you, Rebecca. What else can I say here?"

"Ted, you belittled me in the hallway. You tried to shame me for not being as Jewish as you, acting like I'm some complete ignoramus. Then, you mocked me and called me a fraud at the breakfast table."

"I didn't call you a fraud, Rebecca. I never used those words, nor would I."

"You didn't have to! Do you really think I bless God for my food to impress you? A self-professed agnostic?"

He sighed deeply. "Can we wipe the slate clean and start over? You show me the text from your aunt, I encourage you that it's a great start, and then we skip the part where I treated you like 'graphic design girl' rather than my soon-to-be wife. Please?"

I matched his sigh with one of my own. "Ted, I'm scared. Other than knowing God wants us to get married, I feel like a complete lunatic."

His expression hardened. "You told me yesterday you want to get married. Did you lie to me and to yourself, Rebecca? Do you think you get a merit badge from Jesus for going through with it? Is that why you wanted to know about my sex life? Do you collect extra brownie points in Heaven for sacrificing yourself on the altar to a total heathen?"

Jolted by Ted's choice of words, the weight of something oppressively heavy shook loose from me. The resentment I felt creeping up my spine moments earlier completely dissipated. Clear as day, I heard the word "Leviathan" from the depths of my soul, and I shuddered.

I blinked once, then opened my eyes to see Ted's face, his jaw set, mouth grim. In my own pain and selfishness, I knew I had hurt him deeply. Quickly recalling the progression of events that morning, I saw how easily things had escalated. It was almost as if a third party sat behind us whispering words of rejection in our ears.

"Ted," I began, my voice cracking, "I'm so sorry. I do love you, and I do want to marry you. I have never felt this way about anyone. Before you object that you don't have much competition, please remember I had another fiancé. You can thank Pastor Sociopath for breaking it off."

The thin line forming Ted's mouth softened, and the familiar glint of gold appeared in his eyes. "Apology accepted. Annie never admitted her mistakes so quickly. It usually took a lot of convincing before she apologized or owned what she did wrong."

I smiled tentatively. "So, even if I don't cook or clean as well as Annie, you won't wish it was her in this house instead of me?"

"I've had eight years to move on from that part of my life, Rebecca. You captured my interest a long time ago. I never dated because I didn't need to. I had my work, and then I had you. I didn't know you were exactly what I wanted until you suddenly became unavailable."

"Did you hope Jason and I would break up?" I asked.

"No, I sincerely wished you every happiness, Rebecca. If you had chosen Goldstein over me, I would have felt the same way. I've loved you for a long time, Rebecca, and I've respected you for longer. I don't even recognize the schmuck I acted like before."

"Is that the word your mother didn't want to say in front of me? I'm pretty sure everybody uses that word."

Ted chuckled. "I'm sorry I said it. For my grandparents and even my father, it's not exactly nice. Most people assume it means the same as 'jerk.' The actual definition means something closer to an old nickname for Richard."

"Wait...oh...ohhhhh!" I exclaimed. "Never using that one again! And you better clean up your potty mouth, mister. I think this room will be a great, future nursery, and I don't want any bad language spoken in it!"

Flecks of gold glittered at me. Leaning his head close to mine, Ted said, "So, are we still on for tomorrow? And then the rest of our lives after that?"

I nodded. "They're not kidding when they call marriage hard work, are they?"

Ted shook his head before inching closer for a makeup kiss. "Sort of like calling childbirth really painful."

I gave a throaty laugh. "God willing, we'll find out about both soon enough."

CHAPTER 29

"IT'S DONE! WE'RE OVER!" JESSICA WAILED, PACING IN Ted's living room as tears wet her cheeks.

"What happened?" I said.

"Nathan cheated on me! Over and over!"

"What?!" Ted and I exclaimed together.

"I can't believe I got engaged to a lying, manipulative pig!"

Confused, I said, "But Nathan is Messianic. They don't condone that kind of stuff do they?"

Ignoring me, she said, "I'm such an idiot! He kept hiding his phone or slamming the laptop cover down whenever I came up behind him."

"Do you know who it is?" I said.

"Thousands of girls!"

"Wait, what?"

"Nathan is a porn addict. I'm not even sure how much of it is legal. Those girls look like actual *girls*."

I nearly choked. "As in child pornography?"

"Okay fine, more like exhibitionist high school cheerleaders, but get this," she said, sitting down in Ted's stuffed chair. "That whole mishigas Matty pulled at the restaurant, you know, trying to make it sound like he objected to our wedding because I don't believe in Jesus, yada yada...you remember, Beck?"

"How could I forget?" I said dryly.

"Matty's known about Nathan's porn issue for years. It's why he never had a girlfriend. Heck, it's why Nathan never wanted to have sex with me. He used the pristine, Messianic Jew persona as a front."

"Jessica, did you try to sleep with him?"

She shushed me with a wave of her hand. "Yeah, early on, but he sold it to me so well, Beck. I can't believe I even wanted to visit that crackpot, Jewish church of his."

Ted glanced at me as if to say, *I told you so.*

"What did Nathan say when you caught him?" I asked.

Jessica rolled her eyes dramatically. "Every excuse you can think of. It's not what I thought it was, it only happened one time, and so on. At first, he tried to pass it off like I imagined the whole thing, and he accidentally clicked on a pop-up ad."

"Coward," I said under my breath.

"Is this a deal breaker for you, Jessica?" Ted asked. "Will Nathan get help for his addiction? Did his parents or his brother try to intervene?"

Jessica pressed her lips into a sarcastic smile as if contending with the village idiot.

Coming to Ted's defense, I said, "You do realize Ted just wants to help, don't you? Don't attack us just because you're furious at Nathan."

"Well, excuse me for not being perfect like you, Pastor's Kid," she retorted.

I put a restraining hand on Ted's arm before he could respond. "Honey, why don't you give us a few minutes to hash through this?" Whispering, I added, "She just spent more on the down payment for her wedding dress than you did at the jewelry counter yesterday. You follow what I'm saying here?"

Voice tinged with sarcastic cheer, Ted said, "I think I'm going to check on the turkey and then get started on the pie. You ladies enjoy the rest of your conversation." He squeezed my shoulder for support before heading into the kitchen.

"Of course, he can cook too!" Jessica said with a flick of the wrist. "What's it like living in a fairytale where all of your wildest dreams come true?"

"Excuse me?"

"Must be fun to rub your happy little life in my face, Beck, especially since you had nobody for so long."

"Jessica, what are you talking about?"

"Oh, come on! Rich, handsome guy? Cushy job? Beautiful house? Big, fat diamond on your finger? I guess holding out really does get you all your heart's desires, right?"

My patience for Jessica's pity party died a quick death. "You know what, Princess, let's talk about my fairytale life with a rage monster father and a child molesting, former pastor who wanted to get into my pants too. How utterly selfish of me to be dumped by a fiancé four years ago because my pastor deliberately sabotaged the relationship. What a fairytale to have to call the police because I have not one, but *two* psycho fraud pastors stalking my apartment. But please, tell me all about how your fiancé struggles with something half the men in this country do, and then have the chutzpah to be jealous of my amazing life. How dare you begrudge me this one bit of happiness!"

Disbelief covered my best friend's face. "Did you just say *chutzpah?*"

"Are you freaking kidding me?! Did you hear anything I just said, Jessica?"

She wrapped her arms around her middle as fresh tears appeared. "He lied to me, Beck. He made me feel ashamed, like I wasn't good enough for him. Turns out, he's just a hypocrite and a liar. Even though Matty behaved like a complete jerk about the whole thing, at least he tried to protect me by keeping me from marrying his brother."

I softened at the brokenness beyond Jessica's bitter exterior. "Matty's version of protection meant shaming you the exact same way Nathan did. He tried to cover his brother's sin by making it look like he objected to *you*. He protected Nathan, not you, Jessica."

"Matty also admitted to having some feelings for me," she said with a slight blush.

"I knew it!" Ted called from the kitchen.

Jessica scowled.

"Not helping, honey," I said through gritted teeth.

"You want a traditional pie crust or lattice?" he asked.

"Whichever one puts the commentary on silent," I said.

"Lattice it is."

Jessica chuckled, despite herself. "You guys are cute. And it definitely seems more real than whatever I thought I had with Nathan."

I eyed my best friend carefully. Something didn't quite add up. "Jessica, did anything happen between you and Matty?"

"What do you mean?"

I pursed my lips. "Don't play dumb, Jessica. You said Matty was cute before I even met him. You're defending his abusive behavior in the restaurant and somehow have this smitten look on your face. Nathan's porn addiction shattered your dream wedding. I hope you can understand my confusion here."

Jessica sighed. "You and me both. Matty let me cry on his shoulder about everything."

"How convenient."

"It wasn't like that!" she protested. "Matty's ex-wife cheated on him."

"If Matty wanted to play the role of upstanding citizen, why didn't he warn you about his brother? More than that, don't you think it's hypocritical to pursue his brother's fiancée when his own marriage fell apart because of cheating?"

"Beck, you make him sound like some kind of psycho. Don't lump Matty in with all of these other crazies in your life, okay?"

"Doesn't every eventual abuse victim believe she's *different* when the relationship first starts? When they love bomb you and treat you like you're the greatest thing in the world? When they swoop in to pick up all the broken pieces and act like your savior?"

Jessica glanced around Ted's house. "Speaking of hypocrites, Rebecca, care to explain how you got here with Ted?"

Irritated, I said, "Jessica, you need to stop this pity party at my expense. Nathan lied to you and betrayed you. What my father and Pastor Sociopath have done is illegal and potentially life threatening. Picking me apart won't ease your pain."

Jessica sighed wearily. "You're right. I'm sorry. Just don't judge me, okay? Matty had just finished up the divorce proceedings when Nathan and I met. Nathan said Matty was jealous of us being happy, but it always seemed like more than that. Me pushing Matty to date you didn't exactly help. I know Matty and I spent too much time together, but Nathan disappeared a lot too. He always claimed he had IT stuff for work. Obviously, I know better now."

"So, you really had no idea, Jessica?"

"None! Nathan told me he had struggled with porn in the past, but God did so much in his life." She choked back a sob, "He told me God could do the same thing for me. What a joke!"

I shook my head. "People think of Christians as lying hypocrites because of stuff exactly like this. For some reason, I thought the Messianics had a one up on the rest of us, you know, since they fuse the Jewish and Christian stuff together."

Jessica scoffed. "Oh, please! Nathan's knowledge of Judaism comes from what he researches online. He reads one article, and suddenly, he's an expert on it. Nathan and Matty grew up going to church and got into all of this 'Jewish roots' stuff three years ago. He talks a good game about Jewish this and that, but all those hours on porn sites don't exactly jive with the Torah. That lying dirtbag actually told me he just needed an *outlet* for his desires and didn't want to take advantage of me."

"Because porn will really help with that," Ted said from the kitchen.

"How's the pie going, dear?"

"Almost done," he said too cheerfully.

"So, everything is good with you two?" Jessica asked, gesturing toward the kitchen. "I thought Nathan and I took it fast, but you guys went crazy fast. Are you sure you know what you're doing?" Bringing her face closer to mine she whispered, "Nathan had me completely fooled, Beck. How do you know Ted isn't doing the same thing? Kyle thinks Ted wants to prove he can get what nobody else could."

"Kyle actually said that?" I whispered back, horrified. "Doesn't he have a new girlfriend already? Why does he care?"

"Beck, she looks exactly like you, except she does the whole drunk, party girl scene. Mom and Dad call her the Beck LMD."

I shook my head. "My Life Model Decoy? Jessica, I don't

understand why he would do this. Morgan really messed him up, didn't she?"

Jessica shrugged. "He barely knew Morgan. She doesn't have that power over him. Seeing you with Ted Margolin sent Kyle over the edge. I don't recognize my own brother right now."

"Jessica, Kyle made these choices, not me. I feel bad for him, but it doesn't change anything between me and Ted. I have peace that God wants us to get married."

"Does he treat you well?" Jessica asked. "You know, when other people aren't around? Are you sure Ted isn't playing you for sympathy with the dead wife story?"

"I've talked to Ted's mother at length about all of it. I saw the pictures myself. I'm not the Annie Margolin LMD or anything like that."

"That just proves she existed. How do you know he's not using you?"

"Jessica, look at what Ted did for me even before he told me he loved me. For all he knew, my father could have been some bum off the street, but Ted jumped in to protect me. I know you don't want to hear this, but sometimes Kyle made me uncomfortable at work. I never believed he could really be interested in me, so I stayed in denial. Ted finally spoke up and did something about it."

Jessica scoffed. "Because he was jealous of my brother."

"No, Jessica. Ted saw I didn't know how to say 'no' to Kyle. To hear Deondre or MacKenzie tell it, your brother spent a lot of time inventing reasons to be at my desk."

"Beck, you broke my brother's heart! I'm watching him self-destruct, and he won't listen to anybody. You have to help!"

"What do you want me to do, Jessica? Kyle dropped twelve years of hidden feelings in my lap and expected me to jump. Maybe something could have happened back in college or even before Jason, but Kyle waited too long. I'm sorry that he's having such a hard time accepting my relationship with Ted, but it's not my problem to fix."

"Beck!" she exclaimed, hurt. "You guys have been friends for so long. How can you be so cold about it? Don't you care about my brother at all?"

"Of course I do!" I said, irked by the accusation. "I feel bad for Kyle's situation, but I need both of you to consider my perspective too. I know your brother thinks his interest in me was super obvious, but I could never get a read on him. One second, Kyle loiters half the day in my cube, the next, he brags about his latest hook up in disgusting detail. Nothing ever made sense. Obviously, Ted saw what I couldn't, but that doesn't make him a bad guy. It just makes him an observant one. Look, I don't pretend to understand this crazy relationship, but I know I will spend the rest of my life with this man. I just hope you can be happy for me. Ted and I both feel strongly that we need to get married as soon as we can."

"And you're really sure about this?"

"Jessica, you know how much I've been through with my family after the heartbreak with Jason. It would mean so much if you could support me now. I finally have someone who loves me and actually wants to protect me."

Jessica took my hand into both of hers. "I'm happy for you, Beck. I really am. But I hope you understand why I can't be there tomorrow. It's just too much. I have to see about some kind of store credit at the bridal boutique since I don't have a reason to wear the dress anymore." The words came out choppy as Jessica started another round of tears. "Why did this happen to me?" she wailed.

Well acquainted with the agony of a broken engagement, I didn't begrudge Jessica her pain. For all of Nathan's appearance of goodness, we later discovered his deep seeded need to convince the world of his facade. I thanked God my best friend didn't become another Ashley or Deborah Ivy.

Secrets and lies in any relationship work as a slow acting poison. The result is always its eventual demise.

CHAPTER 30

SITTING DOWN TO A BEAUTIFUL TURKEY DINNER, Jessica laid out the remaining details of her Thanksgiving disaster. I did my best to tone down any lovey-dovey behavior on my part, but Jessica's pain remained too fresh. She excused herself before dessert. Ted and I simply stared at the lattice crust apple pie with homemade whipped cream.

"More for us?" I asked with a shrug.

"Since it's our rehearsal dinner, I guess I can indulge," Ted replied.

As he carved into the pie, I said, "Do you have anything you need to tell me?"

The pie slicer stood in midair.

"I can't deal with any more deception. I'm thankful we don't need to cancel a florist or photographer, but I'm trusting you to be completely honest with me here."

Ted cleared his throat and set down the slicer. "Rebecca, I thought we covered this earlier today."

"Humor me," I said, not breaking eye contact. "What about pornography?"

"I did look at porn in college, but not much once Annie and I got together. One of Annie's ex-boyfriends shared photos of her with his friends."

I gasped. "That's horrible!"

"After we got married, the bastard threatened to post them online. I dabbled with porn occasionally, but I quit cold turkey after that. The idea of looking at anything made me physically ill."

"And you've never been tempted since? Maybe when you were feeling lonely or depressed after Annie died?"

"Do you see this house, Rebecca? I put all of my energy into this place and Culver. I came home and worked on the house until I collapsed in bed. Then, I started over again the next day. I kept myself busy so I wouldn't have time to think about sex. On the rare occasion I indulged, I found something to distract myself. It took me four years to finish the work on the house."

"Four years?" I squeaked.

He smiled. "I changed my mind fifteen times about the color of the walls, the building materials, or I'd go back and redo something to make it more perfect. Phil told me to stop working on the house and start working on my love life."

"Why doesn't that surprise me?"

"Phil also scolded me for treating you like my personal slave at the office. He said he noticed the way I watched you and told me to find a better excuse to be around you."

I responded with a throaty chuckle. "Oh, I can only imagine how that went over."

Ted's wry smile communicated all I needed to know.

Suddenly, a ghost resurfaced, a memory buried away as odd, but innocuous regarding SBC. "Ted?"

"Yeah?"

"Pastor made this huge deal about not taking pictures during services. He claimed he wanted to guard our children from sexual predators by keeping images of them off of the internet. It made him look super protective, even though the teens and college age always lacked adequate adult supervision. Parents complained constantly about the kids making out or getting caught with drugs or alcohol at youth retreats."

"What are you saying, Rebecca?"

"Pastor acted super weird about two things: money and teens. Even as a member of the college program, I found his attachment to it incredibly bizarre. As far as money, any time I asked him about irregularities or things that didn't make sense, he pinched his lips, or changed the subject. If I persisted, he stonewalled me, or as I'm realizing now, flat out lied about it."

"Keep going, I'm with you."

"Since we both know about his actual abuse of teenagers, why pretend to defend them publicly? Is it just to throw people off the scent, or could it be something worse?"

Ted looked as if suddenly struck by lightning. His eyes widened, and he spoke almost too quickly for me to follow. "Rebecca, you may be onto something even bigger than we realized!"

"What do you mean?"

"Titus told me how many churches and nonprofits use their pristine image as a front for sex trafficking. They not only abuse these kids, but they also make money selling that trash online to deviants just like them. What if Pastor Sociopath didn't want online pictures because he didn't want clientele or the police to recognize any of the victims?"

"I suddenly don't want pie anymore," I said wearily.

Ted sighed then slumped back into his chair. "Rebecca, this

situation gets more deranged by the minute. I may be agnostic, but I consider it a miracle you escaped from SBC when you did. That psycho had a bullseye on you."

"He had to finish grooming me first, Ted. I read about brainwashing techniques used on POWs and the similarities scared me. The predators either love bomb you with gifts and flattery, or in my case, they break you down into a bloody pulp. Then, they start offering scraps of human kindness. It's called *intermittent reinforcement*. They train you to do just about anything to be treated like a human being again."

We sat in a few moments of silence, the grim possibilities of SBC corruption going far beyond the worst episode of any procedural crime drama.

Breaking the silence, I finally said, "Total downer for our rehearsal dinner. Sorry, I brought it up."

"Rebecca, I want you to get a white dress for tomorrow. I don't care if you buy a traditional wedding dress, but I want you to wear white."

"Care to explain, Mr. Margolin?"

Leaning forward and grabbing my hands, Ted said, "I don't want those Pastor Sociopath groupies making comments about sin or anything idiotic like that. You are pure, Rebecca. It's the rest of them with blood on their hands for their willful ignorance and denial." Ted stared meaningfully into my eyes and then down at his watch. "You've got about an hour before the stores close if you want to run out and go shopping now. I can call my mom, mistress of the store coupons, if you want a second opinion or moral support. Dad can spare her for a few hours."

Grabbing Ted's face in my hands, I kissed him longer and more thoroughly than I probably should have. Releasing him and making a run for the guest bedroom, I grabbed my purse and coat, already pulling up his mother's name on my cell phone by the time I reached the front door.

Ted walked over to meet me, handed me a credit card and said, "Also, make sure you buy something red."

My eyebrows raised in question. "I already have a red dress. I thought you wanted me to wear something white."

The sizzling butter in Ted's grin nearly caused a grease fire. Catching his meaning about our wedding night, a supernova smile emerged. Ted ordered me out the door with a reluctant, but necessary push.

On Monday, November 30, a judge pronounced us "man and wife." An hour later, we sat at Le Petit Versailles clothed in our wedding finery. I wore a lace overlay dress with a wide, satin ribbon tied just below the bust. My curls were pinned on each side with jeweled combs. Ted wore a black suit with a white shirt and tie. Steve claimed our "something borrowed" would be the memory stick from his camera as he snapped photo after photo of the two of us. Our photography session before, during, and after the proceedings eclipsed the time of the actual ceremony by three to one. The "something blue" came in a velvet box containing the Margolin family Hanukkah menorah.

Along with Ted's parents, his younger sister, Amanda, joined us with little Blakeley.

Phil dropped by and clapped Ted on the back with loud guffaws. He warmly embraced the senior Margolins, then held me at arm's length to appraise my ensemble.

"You're a beautiful bride, Rebecca Margolin," he said, "and I'm so glad I hired you."

I beamed at Phil, warmed by the fatherly love I had never experienced from Bernard Ivy. My own 'tabula rasa' began with a new name and a new story to unfold.

"So, who won the office pool?" I asked, trying to laugh away the tears smarting in my eyes.

Phil offered his trademark, mischievous grin. "Let's just say the office may know of today's ongoings."

Ted came to stand beside me. "Phil, what did you do?"

My CEO smiled wider than I thought physically possible.

"Phil," Ted warned.

"A little birdie mysteriously found a marker and updated the name outside of Rebecca's office. What was I supposed to do?" he said with faux innocence.

"You didn't!" I gasped, covering my mouth.

"Also, you might discover your office decorated with several gifts of congratulations on your desk."

"Well, that's sweet," Ted said, eyes twinkling down at me.

"Not her desk, Margolin. *Yours.* You can enjoy our handiwork tomorrow, assuming you can actually get in there."

Ted and I both looked questioningly at Culver's very naughty CEO.

"What do you want? I like streamers and balloons, and I encourage the use of both as part of boosting office morale."

"Phil Robbins master of subtle," Ted deadpanned.

"You can at least thank me for shooting down the baby rumors. Teasing you both, I enjoy. Slander about Rebecca's reputation, I won't tolerate. Also, since I won the pool, here you go," Phil said, handing me an envelope.

"What is this?" I asked.

"Ironically enough, two hundred dollars. Not that the mighty Margolin lacks the resources, but go get something engraved or monogrammed. Leslie and I would also love to invite you over for dinner at your earliest convenience. She's heard a lot about both of you over the years. She even suggested the possibility of you two finding love."

Ted kissed the top of my head. "Remind me to thank your wife."

I smiled and planted a ruby red lipstick mark on Phil's cheek. "Thank you so much, Phil. You're the closest thing I have to a father, and I'm so glad you came to celebrate with us."

Phil's blue eyes shone with tears to match my own. "Did you know Leslie and I never could have children?"

I shook my head.

"If we had ever been blessed with a daughter, I'd wish for one just like you, Rebecca."

Thanking God I had put on waterproof mascara that morning, I released Ted's hand to briefly embrace Phil.

"What's with all the tears here?" Steve said, joining the fray. "Did I miss a funeral?"

"Don't mock me, old man," Phil fired back. "I've waited a long time to see this girl happy and settled with someone who treats her the way she deserves. I can't tell you how happy I am to see your son with my girl."

"Don't make me cry again!" I said, wiping hasty tears from my eyes. "Keep it up, and I'll have to blame something besides the french onion soup."

"French onion soup? In a place like this?" Phil asked.

"Rebecca has a very charming story regarding her fondness for it," Ted said, wrapping his arm around my waist. "Speaking of, I think Mom and Amanda could use a hand with Blakeley."

While Amanda protested about Blakeley ruining my dress, I gladly welcomed my Thanksgiving buddy back into my lap. The little girl happily played with the lace and ribbon. I handed her back to her mother once Blakely's fancy, French mac and cheese arrived.

"This looks good on you," Rose whispered in my ear.

"What? Future grandchildren?"

"Happiness, honey. You're glowing."

"I *am* happy, Rose. Truly. I didn't plan things this way, but everything has been absolutely perfect."

Rose patted my hand. "You deserve it, sweetheart. My son, for all of his faults, absolutely adores you and will be faithful to you. I'm not just saying that because I'm his mother, either."

I chuckled softly. "You and Steve are such a blessing to me, Rose. More than you can possibly know."

"Likewise, honey."

I soaked in every single minute of our intimate gathering, trying to memorize the details of everyone's faces and the plethora of jokes from Phil and Steve. Ted, to his credit, took most of it in stride, genuinely laughing at a few of the corny one liners.

As Phil and Steve continued to yuk it up, their jokes turned to Ted's choice of venue. A flicker of pain on my husband's face communicated hurt beneath the tolerant smile. Ted's desire to succeed had just as much to do with Annie's memory, though I doubted his father or Phil knew such private details. I squeezed Ted's hand under the table in support.

"Are you okay?" I said.

He leaned in close to my right ear. "Suddenly tired. I can only take so much of those two magpies. The bald one especially."

I frowned slightly. "Have you talked to your father about it?"

He rolled his eyes. "Do you think he cares?"

Glancing back over at Steve and Phil regressing like college boys, I could safely hazard a guess. "Part of me wants to say something, the other part says stay out of it and don't get in the middle."

"Well, you're family now, so if the opportunity arises, I certainly won't stop you. Just not on our wedding day."

"Look at the two lovebirds secretly whispering over there," Steve said, clearly feeling the effects of his champagne. "Got some names for grandkids picked out for me yet? Amanda won't tell me anything."

"Dad!" she shrieked. "Could you possibly be any more inappropriate right now? Leave Ted and Rebecca alone."

Ted winked at his baby sister in thanks, and I suddenly knew what to do with Phil's office pool money.

Amanda had mentioned several unpurchased items on her baby registry, playfully lamenting how mothers of small children prefer practicality over cute outfits the kid will outgrow in a month.

I took notes for future reference.

CHAPTER 31

"Good morning, Mrs. Margolin," Ted said across the breakfast table. "I would ask how you slept last night, but I already know the answer."

I blushed.

Butter sizzled.

I leapt from my seat and gave my husband a very emphatic good morning kiss.

He didn't seem to mind.

Finally coming up for air, I pushed back a lock of hair from his forehead. "How much humiliation do you anticipate when we walk into the office today? Maybe I should wear my favorite red dress to match my face."

Ted sighed. "I wish I'd planned this part better. We should be on our honeymoon, not heading back to the office in an hour."

"Have you talked to Titus yet?"

"No, no, no," Ted said, cupping my face and returning my earlier kiss with gusto. "We have enough to focus on today without adding any sociopaths to the mix. Hold off on changing your name on social media too."

"Why?"

"Both of the psychos have spies everywhere. They can link you to my house. The avalanche of accusations will begin as soon as you announce your sudden marriage to one of your coworkers. One fire at a time, okay?"

"You're really cute when you're being protective, you know."

Ted combed his fingers in my hair, tangling them in my curls. "I wish we could pretend the world doesn't exist outside of our front door, but we both know it does. Speaking of, I have a client meeting and two team strategy sessions in the afternoon. I can only imagine what your desk looks like because I know what I asked my AE's to put together for me."

I groaned. "Thanks, dear."

"I'll make it up to you by taking you out to lunch and kissing you extravagantly and inappropriately in public. Sound fair?"

"We're married. What would be inappropriate?"

"How little we'd be eating, and how much we'd be kissing. Do you want a sample?"

I did not refuse his offer.

Forty-five minutes late, we stepped off the elevator and into a Culver office buzzing with electricity. Miss Belle practically tackled the two of us, insisting she knew all along. She prattled on about a "married glow" until Ted finally coughed loudly. MacKenzie and Deondre said they suspected something at our Guildcorp team lunch, while Ted's unmistakable shout alerted everyone he'd discovered Phil's office prank.

Ted stood a good six feet from his office door as mounds of white balloons spilled out like soapsuds from an overflowing washing machine.

"He doesn't do anything in half measures, does he?" I said to no one in particular.

"Thought you'd like that!" Phil guffawed, coming up behind us. "Oh, and here's a coffee for the mister and the missus. I figured a little Vincenzo's might get me back into your good graces. Although, you two might be slightly distracted this morning."

"Phil," Ted growled.

He extended his coffee peace offering to my husband first. "Fine, fine. Drink your java, then give me the evil eye later, Margolin. We have a few things to go over for the presentation in an hour." Turning to me with an overly elaborate bow, he said, "For you, my dear."

I shook my head and laughed. "It's impossible to stay mad at you, even though I should. What did you guys do to my office?"

"See for yourself," Phil replied with a wink.

Ted met my eyes. "Time to get to work."

From the office to our home, Ted and I spent the next few weeks merging our lives together. The moving company he hired seamlessly transitioned my belongings from my apartment, and Ted escorted me on the final walk through with the leasing office manager. She promised to keep a look out for Pastor and my father, not wanting to jeopardize the safety of the neighboring tenants or any future occupants of my old apartment.

The passion and emotion of our engagement slowly dissipated into the day-to-day grind of married life. Ted grumbled about the cornucopia of feminine toiletries swallowing up the bathroom counter and medicine cabinet. Our first fight about the thermostat settings occurred within two weeks.

Settling into bed on New Year's Eve, a recent text from my

aunt rescinded any good will she'd felt over Thanksgiving. She reverted back to her usual barrage of guilt and shaming, proving Ted's earlier suspicions. Regardless, I finally confirmed the existence of Louis and Tabitha Wasserman. Another few dollars accessed a birth certificate of one Deborah Rachel Wasserman, otherwise known as my mother. In that at least, my aunt had been truthful. Now armed with concrete information about my grandparents, I felt one step closer to understanding the madness behind a lifetime of abuse from Bernard and Deborah Ivy.

Ted turned to me, lowering his glasses as he skimmed through the local newspaper. "Not as exciting as the annual Goldstein New Year's Gala, huh?"

"Meh, not the same since Kyle became all mopey and weird. The tension between Jessica and her parents because of the wasted wedding money doesn't help either."

"Any change with that situation?"

I sighed. "I wish. I still have a hard time picturing Nathan as an unrepentant porn addict, but it just goes to show how easily appearances can be deceiving. I guess I should know better than anyone about that, huh?"

"Speaking of not maintaining appearances, I need to tell you something."

"What's up?"

"Titus left a voicemail earlier today. They won't be pursuing the Derden case anymore."

Dread filled me. "What do you mean?"

"The Derdens stopped cooperating with the police. They said Chase made a mistake, and their beloved pastor could never do such a thing. They called you a scorned woman looking to ruin Pastor Sociopath's good name. Titus never revealed who tipped off the police about the abuse, meaning the information had to come from Pastor Sociopath. Titus thinks he probably bought off the Derdens."

"I didn't imagine what I saw, Ted! And I most certainly did not want some kind of relationship with that psycho!"

Ted held up his hands. "I know, sweetie. For the record, the police believe you too, but without a victim willing to press charges, they can't pursue an investigation. The Derdens' silence keeps that sociopath out of jail."

"What about obstruction of justice? How can he legally coerce potential witnesses?"

"They don't consider it obstruction without an active investigation. I'm so sorry."

I jerked away from Ted, too upset to be touched. Adrenaline and anger surged through me. "This isn't justice! That child molesting, brainwashing animal got away with traumatizing a boy, and nobody is stopping him!"

"Since his record is clean, law enforcement can't do anything about him until after a proven crime has been committed."

"This is so hopeless!" I said. "Why did I think anything would happen? That he would ever get caught?"

"Rebecca, you always tell me God sees everything and is in control. You and Mom prayed together about a Hanukkah miracle happening, remember? You said it felt like the perfect time to see a breakthrough in the case."

"I don't know what to think anymore, Ted. My worst nightmare came true. It's no different than everything my father gets away with at First United, only that's all financial fraud, as far as I know."

Ted's eyebrows raised above his glasses. "Whoa! You've never shared this before."

Glad to change the subject, I said, "My father's right hand man is his elder, Bud Riley. Bud rubber stamps whatever my father needs to push through the church board. The congregants sleep better at night knowing Bud approved it. They resent how much money my father allocates for himself and his so-called, living expenses, but the congregants do nothing more than complain. No one dares to openly defy my father, so they just gossip amongst themselves."

"Does your father know they talk?"

"Of course! He has spies in the congregation who love nothing more than tattling. They're usually the eager-to-please types who take their authority way too seriously."

Ted looked disgusted. "So, he's basically grooming new sycophants to see if they'll be loyal to *him* rather than their own common sense."

"Exactly," I said. "Anyone who questions things at First United is socially ostracized or given menial labor to do around the church. If my father finds out they want to be a part of a specific ministry, he'll intentionally withhold the position as punishment. Eventually, the people leave, or they get with the program, so to speak."

"What happens when people tell *the program* to take a flying leap?"

"The First United leadership team spreads some plausible rumor about why the people left. Their favorite excuse is stylistic differences or doctrine. There's also the phony grief routine I've seen my father perform a million times."

"Phony grief?"

"Oh, he'll turn on the tears and talk about how sad it is that people care more about their personal preferences rather than unity in the church."

Ted scoffed. "And people actually believe him?"

"You'd be amazed! Who wants to believe that my father is lying and putting on a show?"

"True," he admitted.

"Usually though, people left First United because of tithing."

"Tithing? I've never heard of that."

"That's because you're not religious, Ted."

He shook his head. "Look, my mother dragged me to synagogue all the time. I've attended umpteen bar mitzvahs since I had my own a million years ago. I'm telling you, I've never heard of it."

"I always thought of tithing as a Jewish thing," I said. "I've read about it in the Old Testament. The Israelites brought the best, ten percent of their crops to the food storehouse every three years. Pastor Sociopath, my father, even Nathan's rabbi believe in *modern tithing*. They claim God wants us to bring ten percent of our income to the 'storehouse' aka to the congregation whenever you get a paycheck or some kind of financial increase. They quote this verse from *Malachi* how God will curse the people if they don't bring their tithes, but He'll pour tremendous blessing if you do. In the Bible, though, it was actual food, and it actually went to the people who needed it." Seeing Ted's bewildered expression, I said, "Are you telling me you guys don't do that in synagogue?"

Ted shook his head. "Nope. If you go to a traditional temple, you pay dues."

"Ah. Nathan's rabbi made a big deal about how Messianics don't charge money for High Holiday services. You guys have to buy tickets, right?"

"Yes, but nobody demands we hand over ten percent of our income or face hellfire and damnation. That's absolutely nuts! Nathan's rabbi doesn't charge for tickets because he extorts money from people all year long."

I exhaled a weary sigh. "The Messianic rabbi definitely had a haughty attitude toward traditional Judaism. I heard a lot of the same talking points from Nathan when we first met. During the sermon, Rabbi Lebow said that Messianics practice *Biblical Judaism*. Coming from my background in church, it sounded pretty amazing. Kyle said the rabbi didn't know what he was talking about."

"This Rabbi Lebow doesn't sound much different than the other two sociopaths we're contending with right now."

Frowning, I said, "As the daughter of a pastor, I totally understand needing money to keep the lights on and paying your leader a salary. Unfortunately, I've seen too much abuse. Pastor Sociopath and his elite SBC team went on retreats and conferences all the time—and always on the congregational dime."

"That's not illegal, Rebecca. I can't fault them for that. I do the same thing for business trips and training."

"Do you get up in front of a group of clients and tell them they're under God's curse if they don't open up their pockets to 'sow seed' into your business?"

Ted gave a caustic laugh. "Different sales pitch. I tell potential clients they can save money by working with our firm instead of Cooper & Jaye. Of course, these guys are supposed to be spiritual leaders, not businessmen."

"Exactly. Both of those men act like kings of their church castle with subjects to rule. My father and Pastor would—"

"Pastor Sociopath," Ted corrected.

I smiled ruefully. "Old habits."

"Well, let them die, Rebecca, because he's not your pastor anymore."

"Thank God!"

An enthusiastic thunder of fireworks accompanied my declaration. Ted and I both startled at the window rattling boom.

"I think God agrees with me," Ted quipped. "Oh, and Happy New Year, Mrs. Margolin. Can we put the talk of pastors and tithing and all of that other chazarai aside and find a better way to celebrate?"

The golden glow in Ted's eyes brought me to the present rather than the past. His tender embrace ensured my mind focused solely on the man with me rather than the ones wreaking havoc on the outside world.

CHAPTER 32

WHILE I HOPED TO PUT THE PAST YEAR BEHIND ME, IT followed me right into January. Once the Derdens forced their son to recant his story, the smear campaign against me on social media began with a flourish.

"There!" I said, sitting on my laptop in the living room. "Pastor wrote this fake public apology to me and 'whatever he's done to hurt me.' It's been shared fifty-three times. Nevermind that he never actually contacted me privately to apologize. He really owes the apology to Chase Derden anyway, but the public apology makes him look like the innocent victim being the bigger person. I've been blocked or unfriended by at least a dozen people. Not even the cowards who contacted me privately after Pastor announced his engagement to Cynthia will defend me. They're scared of being cut off from SBC."

Coming up behind me, Ted closed my laptop without so much as a glance. I whirled around at him, surprised and angry.

"Don't you want to see what they wrote?" I demanded.

"No," he said, "and neither should you. Rebecca, I think you should take a permanent hiatus from social media."

"Why? I have a right to know what these jerks say about me!"

"Rebecca, why do you care if people who sit under that fraud believe the slander he puts online? They have to believe his lies, or they would have to take a long, hard look in the mirror. Stop torturing yourself with this."

"That's funny coming from you," I said bitterly.

The color drained from Ted's face as he backpedaled away from me. "Stupid people spreading even stupider rumors is not the same as me blaming myself for what happened to Annie!"

Realizing my massive blunder, I wanted to apologize, but Ted left the room and slammed the bedroom door.

I hated the impotent rage I felt. My teeth gnashed at the injustice of having my reputation smeared by the man guilty of his own, phony allegations. My obsessive need to check the latest slander sucked all the time I normally spent in prayer.

You've become your father.

"I have not!" I hissed to that voice in my gut. "I am nothing like that narcissistic freak show!"

You're worshiping their hatred, Rebecca. Why not rather be wronged? Why not rather be mistreated?

"This isn't justice, and You're just sitting up there doing nothing to stop it!" I said angrily to God. "I did what you asked me to do. I shared my story. Nobody believes me, and I just look like the crazy, godless adulteress! Where are You?"

Moses and Aaron.

"Yeah, what about them?" I said petulantly.

I received no answer. Mad and frustrated at the Lord, I eschewed my usual, evening devotionals and binge watched Crossbow instead. I sat like a zombie in front of the television until midnight. Eventually, Ted asked me to come to bed, but I just shook my head. He gave a resigned sigh and closed the door with a thud.

The silence lasted well into the morning after I chose to sleep in the guest bedroom. Ted dressed and left before I woke up, and I felt myself slipping under a black cloud of depression. Nobody at work ventured anything beyond small talk given our matching scowls.

"I knew they got married too fast," I overheard MacKenzie say. Her voice carried over from the lounge area of the break room into the adjoining kitchen where I prepared my afternoon cocoa.

"Baby on board?" asked Lexie Arterton, Kyle's replacement. "Deondre, didn't you say that?"

"No, that girl lives and breathes her Bible," he said on a mocking laugh. "Margolin probably married her so she'd give it up."

The other two gossips gasped.

"I'm just saying," Deondre gabbed on, "my man's been hot for her for a while. Rebecca played it smart and held out until she could get his money too."

I placed a trembling hand over my mouth in horror.

"Ooh, did I tell you about Goldstein?" MacKenzie said.

Deondre sounded annoyed at the mention of Kyle. "What about him?"

"Well, you know how he always goes to *Los Bravos* on Taco Tuesday, right?"

"Yeah," Lexie drawled.

"He's got a new girlfriend, and she looks like an alcoholic version of Rebecca. Creeped me out!"

"No way!" the other two gossips exclaimed in salacious delight.

"Two empty margarita glasses, and she'd already started on a third," MacKenzie said. "Goldstein looked miserable. I don't know why he keeps torturing himself. What's so special about Rebecca anyway? I mean, she's not *that* pretty."

While Deondre and Lexie argued a few merits in my favor, I shut my ears off to the rest of their brutal dissection. I turned my back to the lounge area, bracing myself against the counter. Unbidden thoughts of revenge pushed their way in, and I envisioned myself splashing cocoa all over the Culver vipers. My hand slowly encircled the styrofoam cup.

I didn't realize Ted had entered the room with me until I felt his hand on my shoulder. "We need to talk," he whispered close to my ear. "This isn't working out."

Jason had uttered the same phrase nearly four years earlier, and a shiver of dread ran through me. My anger dissolved, and my arms dropped lifelessly to my sides. Like a lamb led to the slaughter, I followed Ted silently as we took the elevator down to the lobby. He found the same alcove where I had confronted him about his morning shaving habits.

Too emotionally exhausted to launch at him about how he had stolen my innocence, my trust, and any shred of a heart I had left, I let the tears roll down my cheeks. I succumbed to the overwhelming misery and defeat I felt.

"Rebecca, I—" his voice cut off. "What? What are you doing?" Ted said, his voice trembling. "Stop it!" he said louder.

"Isn't this what you want?" I yelled, clawing at my own arm. "To see me kill myself just like everyone else does? Just say it, Ted! I'm a worthless, home wrecking, piece of garbage who makes your life miserable. All I am is gossip fodder for people too bored with their own, stupid lives. Maybe I should just go walk into traffic."

Ted grabbed a hold of my shoulders, pinning me in place. "Rebecca, stop it! What are you talking about?"

I struggled against him, almost relishing the pain I caused myself. "Isn't this what all of you psychos planned all along? Convince Rebecca she's loved, then laugh at her expense? Did you ask my father or Pastor for the perfect time to say 'this isn't working out'?" I spat, throwing those four odious words back in his face.

Ted's eyes widened in shock before understanding replaced it. "Rebecca, I'm sorry I gave the impression—"

"Gave the impression?!" I shouted, still trying to break free.

"Do we have a problem here?" our building security guard, Leonard, asked. "Mr. Margolin, it looks like the lady wants you to let her go."

"Leonard, this is my wife," Ted said through gritted teeth. "It's not what it looks like."

"Oh, it's exactly what it looks like!" I fired back. "My husband couldn't wait to tell me our hasty, three month marriage isn't going to work."

"Rebecca!" Ted exclaimed. "I never said that at all!"

"Let her go, Mr. Margolin," Leonard said sternly.

Having no choice but to release me, Ted relaxed his grip. I jerked my body away from him.

"Rebecca, this isn't you," Ted said, his voice quavering. "I...I don't know what's going on, but I would never want you to harm yourself, and I don't want our marriage to end. I love you."

"Yeah, I've heard that before," I said bitterly. "Everyone says they love me right before they plunge the knife in my back."

Leonard looked between the two of us. "Do I need to call for backup here? I don't feel comfortable leaving the two of you alone right now."

"I have to go back to work," I said resentfully. "Deondre needs a proposal before two. That's, of course, assuming he's done telling the office about my brilliant scheme to withhold sex from Ted so I could get his millions."

"He said what?" Ted barked.

"You heard me."

"Is that why you were so upset in the breakroom?" he asked. "Then, I came up behind you and...oh, Rebecca! Honey, I'm so sorry! Maybe you're the one better off without me!"

The emotional fog slowly lifted, the stinging pain on my arms reminding me of the complete, public spectacle I'd made of myself. I turned to face Ted, tears in my ears met by the moisture shining in his own.

Piping up, Leonard said, "Look, I'm no marriage expert here, but y'all really need to see a counselor or something. Miss Rebecca, please get some peroxide on those cuts. I need to get back to my station, but I hope you two can work this out."

I ran into Ted's arms and sobbed. He stroked my hair and apologized over and over.

"What is happening to me?" I said, staring into golden hazel eyes. "Ted, this isn't who I am."

"I know, sweetheart," he said, holding my face tenderly. "I don't understand why you've been dragging your heels about seeing a professional counselor, but I think you should. You need to hear how sick these people are from someone trained to spot it. That sociopath and his minions wanted to shame and slander you into silence."

"So, what's this part that isn't working out?" I asked through my tears.

"The part about us working together, sweetheart. Phil nearly decapitated me after we came into the office this morning. My own father has never lectured me like that. I walked into the break room, and I saw you shaking. I meant to tell you one of us should change companies. I stupidly picked the worst possible way to say it."

"So, you don't want to end our marriage?"

"No!" he said. "I love you. I made a commitment to you. I don't care that I said those vows in front of a judge rather than a rabbi."

"Or a pastor," I joked, sniffling.

"I've had enough of those to last me a lifetime."

I smiled for the first time all day. "Fair enough."

"There you are," Ted said, planting a light kiss on my mouth.

"I'm deleting my social media accounts as soon as I download everything for the police. You know, in case they need it."

"Rebecca, you talk so much about trusting God and how I can't do His job. Do you think it's possible that you've put the outcome of the SBC scandals on your own shoulders?"

"What do you mean?"

"Whatever we might suspect Pastor Sociopath of doing, I have no doubt his real crimes are ten times worse. Sweetheart, it's not your job to expose all of them," he said.

"God told me to speak up, Ted. Why tell me to do that if He wasn't going to punish Pastor for all of his lies?"

"Maybe to get you free from that black hole and move on with your life. I'm not telling you to forgive them or let it go like it never happened. Eventually, their behavior will catch up to them, but the burden for making that happen doesn't belong on your shoulders."

"So, I just let the rest of the world believe their sick lies in the meantime? I can't knowingly allow other people to be manipulated or abused by keeping my mouth shut. Ted, that's not right!"

He took a deep breath before replying. "Rebecca, you spoke the truth. You didn't remain silent. You did your part by going to the police. You did your part by confronting your sister about your father. What the rest of the world chooses to do with the truth is their responsibility, not yours. You can't force them to see it, especially when they don't want to. Look, they even tried to kill Charles Hastings for making things worse with Pharaoh in that old Passover movie."

My blood ran cold. "What did you just say?"

"Sorry, I assumed you've seen *The Ten Laws.*"

"No, I have. I just mean the part about Moses. You're right. He tried to do right by God's people, and they just complained and tried to kill him a few times. They hated their slavery, but later on, they whined about going back to Egypt. They preferred their present misery over an unknown future."

"You got all of that from a movie reference?"

"It's from the Bible, Ted. Your Bible. The Torah. God told me, 'Moses and Aaron' yesterday, but I didn't stop and think about what it meant because I was so angry at Him." I covered Ted's hands on my face with my own. "Thank you."

CHAPTER 33

"I'VE SPOKEN WITH DEONDRE, MACKENZIE, AND Lexie," Phil said from behind his desk. Ted and I sat opposite of him in matching wing chairs. "I've warned MacKenzie several times about her chronic gossiping, and she now has a record in her file from Bonnie. To her credit, Mac didn't seem happy about it, but she understood."

"Thank you, Phil," I said.

"However, the two of you need to consider how you handle marital conflict going forward. Your relationship affects the company, but your marriage takes priority over either of your jobs. I mentioned this to Ted earlier today, and I think one of you should seriously consider changing employers. I don't want to see your marriage suffer because I selfishly want to keep you both here."

Phil leveled his gaze at both of us. "If you two can keep the extracurricular stuff at home and maintain a professional envi-ronment, I'll do my best to curtail the gossip. My concern is that because of Ted's status here, Rebecca becomes the easier target. Our dear girl has experienced more than enough trouble to last a lifetime."

"Agreed," Ted said.

"So that's it? I'm fired?" I said, panicked.

Ted grabbed my hand between the two chairs and turned his attention to me. "Most of the associates gossip or complain about me behind closed doors. To my face, however, they have to show a semblance of respect. They won't show you that same courtesy, Rebecca. I could make a few phone calls to friends at another brokerage and get you lined up with an even better package than what Culver gives here."

"You really are that good," Phil said with a fatherly smile. "You were long overdue for that raise anyway."

Too overwhelmed by the day's events, I stood up awkwardly, and slipped out of Phil's office. I nearly sighed as I submerged into a veritable bubble bath of proposals on my desk. My new coworker, Taylor Ross, leaned over my shoulder, hazel green eyes full of concern as she placed a marked up document draft on my desk.

"Anything I can do?" she asked.

I shook my head. "I guess you've heard the rumors."

She shrugged. "People talk. People are also stupid. Don't listen to them."

"Easier said than done."

She glanced back at Eric, our other trainee, noting the bop of his head to whatever EDM trance music blasted into his ear buds.

"You can't control what people think about you, Rebecca. Even if you get the chance to speak up and tell your side, people still believe whatever they want to anyway. You know I speak from experience on this one."

"I know," I said, meeting Taylor's eyes and recalling the

heart wrenching story she had shared over lunch a few days earlier.

"People like Deondre and MacKenzie will always spew their nonsense around the hive," she said with a note of annoyance, "but anyone who actually knows you will never believe it. The truth always finds a way to come to light, no matter how ugly. I held onto the last few verses from *Ecclesiastes* for a long time."

I winced, recalling Taylor's painful revelations. "How did you survive everything?"

"Still surviving," she said through a stretched smile. "Some days, I remember everything like it just happened. Other days, it feels like somebody's else's life. Oh!" she exclaimed, noticing my arms. "What happened? That looks awful!"

Hiding them quickly under my desk, I choked back the tears I refused to show anyone at Culver. "I don't want to talk about it."

Taylor raised an eyebrow but didn't pry. She reached her petite arm around my shoulders to embrace me. "Go easy on yourself, Rebecca, and know that I'm praying for you. If I can do anything else, please let me know."

I pushed the edges of my mouth into some semblance of a smile, and Taylor nodded in understanding. She patted my shoulder one last time before plopping back down at her work station next to a completely oblivious Eric. I almost admired his ability to tune out the rest of the world.

The remainder of the work day and commute passed by in a blur. Ted whipped up chicken and rice on the stove while I padded through our house in a daze. As I surveyed my beautiful surroundings, I felt oppressed by a mantle of self-loathing and shame.

"Who are we kidding?" I announced.

Ted turned to look at me over his shoulder. "What are you talking about?"

"This," I said, gesturing between the two of us. "This was a mistake. I've completely ruined your life, and you'll wake up one day and hate me for doing it."

Ted turned off the gas range and made a beeline for me. "Okay, what's going on, Rebecca? We had a fight today. You've already apologized to me, and I told you I forgave you. I'm watching you slip away from me, and I don't understand why."

"Aren't you humiliated to be seen with me?"

Ted raised his eyebrows in shock. "Why would you think that?"

"How many people witnessed my total meltdown today, Ted? When are you going to wake up from fantasy land and realize you've married a completely broken woman with no hope of recovery?"

"You know I don't believe that," he said, hands on either of my shoulders. "You are not a hopeless case, Rebecca, but you have to let go of this fear that I'm going to abandon you."

"Ted, the story of my life reads like a saga of rejection and eventual disposal. I watched you in the kitchen, humming and so happy, and I felt like an outsider looking in on a life that belongs to someone else."

He ran his hands soothingly up and down my arms. "Nobody stuck a gun to my head and forced me to marry you, Rebecca. I told you I knew I wanted to marry you last spring, and I meant it."

"Ted, I acted like a complete lunatic today! Look at my arms!" I said, viciously pulling up my sleeves. "What kind of sane person does something like this? We're supposed to be blissfully happy, except I know I'm making your life miserable. I almost cost you your job today."

"Whoa, whoa, whoa," he said. "Do you think Annie and I lived some kind of conflict free existence? That we never had an ugly fight?"

"I'm not talking about that," I said, referring to her death.

Ted's mouth thinned. "Neither was I."

"Oh," I said quietly.

"Rebecca, I love you. I'm not going anywhere. I will keep telling you that until you actually believe me. I am not your father, your brother, Pastor Sociopath, or Jason. I'm your *husband*. I committed to being here for the long haul, and that's not something I did lightly."

"I'm sure Ashley felt the same way when she and Pastor exchanged their vows," I said bitterly.

"How do I help you, Rebecca? How do I break through this wall of self-pity you're camped behind? It's like you want me to give up so you can be right about all of these lies you believe."

"They're not lies!" I roared. "People love me for a season, Ted. They get bored, life gets hard, or they realize I'm a complete basket case, and then they leave. Why should you be any different?"

The answer to my question came when Ted took two weeks off of work, and Phil issued me a mandatory leave of absence to deal with my demons. Ted also promised me a visit to Cordele to meet my grandparents, Louis and Tabitha Wasserman. He said if gaining some kind of closure regarding the Ivy family helped with my healing and recovery, he would support me. For my part, I agreed to see a counselor and stop pretending I could handle a lifetime of brainwashing and emotional torment all on my own.

Once MacKenzie got a hold of an online post from SBC with my name tagged in it, I could no longer hide my past at Culver. Mac had the decency to let me know about it, but she never looked at me the same way again. Only Phil, Miss Belle and Taylor seemed immune to the rampant office gossip about me, and they openly spoke out against the rumors. The fiasco cemented the final nail in my career at Culver Incorporated. Ted presented me with the possibility of staying home for a while and finding an identity outside of work or my old churches.

"You've been given this blank slate. You may as well take advantage of it," Ted said as we began the hour long drive up to Cordele.

"Ted, I don't even recognize my life anymore."

"Isn't that kind of the point?"

I sighed. "I guess so."

"How are your arms? Did the aloe help?"

I rubbed them unconsciously, wishing away the thin, pink stripes testifying I had reached my absolute breaking point. "I still can't believe you want to stay married to me."

My husband looked over at me, troubled. "You have to stop this, Rebecca. You haven't had to think about an RFP or a benefits guide for ten days. There's also been no psycho pastors showing up at the office, no gossiping coworkers, and no pitying looks from Miss Belle or Taylor. Enjoy your freedom."

"I feel adrift, Ted. I truly believed that if I spoke up, then justice would happen. Instead, it's been nothing but attacks on my character, losing the few friends I thought I had, and not knowing which end is up. Nothing makes sense anymore. Instead of being in control of anything, I'm just along for the ride. Literally," I quipped, gesturing to his car.

A side of Ted's mouth lifted. "What gave you the impression you had control over any part of your life anyway?"

"*Touché,*" I smirked.

"This marriage is for better or for worse, Rebecca. I um,

didn't mention this before, but I prayed to God after we had that huge fight in the lobby."

"You did what?"

He grinned sheepishly. "Yes, your agnostic at best husband prayed to God. And not just to God, but to Jesus."

My lips formed the "Oh" shape my voice couldn't quite articulate.

"Obviously, you're surprised."

"How...why...I mean...I've been such a horrible witness! I can't imagine anybody looking at my life right now and feeling inspired to know Jesus. I'm a mess!"

"But you're *my* mess, Rebecca Joanne Margolin. And since you talk to Jesus so much, I asked Him how I could help you. I asked if He gave me a second chance since I couldn't save Annie."

Tears pricked my eyes. "Did you get an answer?"

Ted smiled, glancing over at me briefly before returning his eyes to the highway. "It's where I got the idea to see your grandparents. I didn't experience a burning bush like Charles Hastings, but the thought just popped in my head. I think the Wassermans have the answers to these lifelong questions of yours."

"Ted, you know that Charles Hastings isn't actually Moses, right?"

"I think you're missing the point here, Rebecca. In fact, I thought you might be kind of excited about this."

"I'm more curious to hear what you think about it," I said. "This is a huge step for you, Ted."

His mouth curved into a smile with glittering gold. "I have a sense of peace I've never felt before. The only other time I felt something similar was after our first lunch at Le Petit Versailles.

I had finally let myself hope there could be a relationship outside of wishful thinking."

"Wow."

"Tell me about it. Never thought I'd ask Jesus for anything."

Considering Ted's words, my thoughts turned inward. "I've been so angry at God, so mad at how everything worked out with SBC. I feel like He tricked me or something."

"Rebecca, do you really think God gets His kicks by watching you suffer? You and my mom talk so much about God's love and counting all of the blessings in your lives. How can you say that if you really believe God sits up there waiting to smack you down like Bernard Ivy?"

I sat stunned for a moment, my heart pierced by the truth of Ted's words. Silently, I repented for my own lack of faith. I mourned how far I had drifted from the truth because of my frustration and pain. "Am I going to make it to the other side of this, Ted? Maybe not tomorrow, but one day all of this hurt will go away?"

"Rebecca, you've suffered a lifetime of abuse and neglect. Your feelings were ignored by person after person claiming to love you or protect you. Recovery won't happen overnight. I never thought I'd say this, but Annie's death may save your life. Losing her taught me I will never let go of the woman I love again. Not when it's within my power to save her."

Megawatt would not be restrained. To be loved like that seemed more fantasy than reality. Ted's eyes sparkled brilliantly, and he maneuvered the car easily off the highway and onto side streets leading to my grandparents' home. We stopped in front of an adorable bungalow nestled in the midst of an active senior community.

I bundled deeper inside of my winter coat as we walked past snow covered hedges.

"You ready?" Ted asked.

I nodded with a nervous smile.

Ted knocked firmly on the front door.

A stoop shouldered, elderly man appeared before us. His white hair was slicked back neatly, and he wore sweatpants and a matching state university sweatshirt.

Glancing over at Ted and me, he said, "Look, if your other Jehovah's Witnesses friends sent you here because we gave the last group tea and cookies, please tell them we said 'you're welcome,' but we're really not interested."

I grinned. That's when Louis Wasserman really looked at me. He stumbled a few steps back into the doorway like he'd seen a ghost.

"Tabby!" he yelled loudly.

A muffled response came from within.

"Tabby!" he called again, this time more urgently.

"What!" an elderly female voice said from behind him. "Did those JW's come back looking for snacks?"

"Look!" Louis hissed near her ear, gesturing toward me.

If Ted wanted a flash-forward of his new bride when we turned old and gray, she stood before us in a pink house coat, leopard print slippers, and curly hair cropped close to her head.

"Who...who are you?" she said, looking me up and down, then touching her own face.

"I'm Rebecca, Bernard and Deborah's daughter. I'm your granddaughter."

CHAPTER 34

TED CAUGHT THE SWOONING TABITHA WASSERMAN while Louis continued to stare at me like a specter.

Ted spoke up first. "We weren't sure you would believe us if we called on the phone, but the resemblance between Tabby and Rebecca just confirms everything."

"How...how did you know my name?" she said weakly.

Snapping out of his daze, Louis said, "Because I called for you, Tabby." Turning to Ted, he said, "Please, let go of my wife. This is a very cruel joke to play on two elderly people."

I looked meaningfully at both Wassermans. "My mother lied to me about the two of you, even gave me phony names when I asked. I've wanted to meet you my entire life, and I need to know what happened between her and my father."

If possible, Louis' posture became stiffer. "I have nothing nice to say about Bernard *Lucifer* Ivy. If you think I'm going to sing his praises, you have another thing coming, missy."

Ted looked at me with a raised eyebrow.

"Lucifer, huh?" I said.

"I didn't stutter, did I?"

Smiling at Lou's spunk, I replied, "We're definitely talking about the same person. I have an older brother and a younger sister. My father's a monster, and I've never understood why he always singled me out over my siblings."

Tabitha's hand came over her mouth. "You have...there are more of you?"

I smiled gently. "Yes. I have an older brother named Daniel, and a younger sister named Ada."

"And do they look like you as well?" Tabitha asked.

I shook my head. "Daniel looks like a mix of my parents, but Ada doesn't really resemble anyone."

"Grandchildren," Tabitha whispered to Louis.

"Not that we ever knew about it," he muttered back to her.

"Do you remember Phyllis and Harold Margolin?" Ted asked.

The eyes of both Wassermans became huge orbs on their tiny faces. "How...How do you know them?" Tabitha said. "Lou, this is almost too much. I need to sit down."

"Could we visit with both of you? Just for a little while?" I asked.

"How did you find us if your mother gave you fake names?" Louis said suspiciously.

"Eleanor," I said. "I used the very persuasive art of Jewish guilt, and she finally told me."

"But they didn't raise you Jewish, did they? Not high and mighty Pastor Lucifer," Louis spat.

"No, they didn't," Ted answered for me, "but I'm Rebecca's husband, Ted Margolin. My parents are Rose and Steve Margolin. Phyllis and Harold are my grandparents."

"Well, I'll be," Tabitha said. "You took after your father in looks, but hopefully not in personality. I always thought of

Steve as a *nebbish*, you know, a mama's boy. Phyllis never had a kind word to say about your mother, but I liked Rose. I don't think many people cried when your grandparents left the synagogue. No offense," she said, patting Ted's hand.

"None taken. I wasn't very fond of my grandmother either."

"And your parents are still married?" Louis asked Ted.

"Miraculously so," I said. "Rose became a Christian after Ted was born. Steve finally stood up to his mother."

Louis looked me over, this time assessing me as Rebecca rather than the image of his wife from fifty years ago. "We've been standing here almost freezing off our *tuchus* long enough. Come on inside. We have some cookies left over from those JW's. You two aren't JW's are you?"

Ted and I shook our heads.

"Not that I mind the JW's," Louis said, opening the door wider to let us in, "but we've already heard the *spiel*. They're lovely people, maybe a little *meshuggeneh*, but you know I don't like to say unkind things about people."

"Except Lucifer," Ted said close to my ear.

I snickered quietly as we followed the Wassermans inside. Admittedly, I expected to find the smell of mothballs, but they kept the home clean and well furnished. Wondering at the lack of photos, I remembered that Eleanor and Bruce chose not to have children. As for Deborah Wasserman, she all but died the day she married Pastor Lucifer.

"We can eat in the kitchen or in the living room, whichever you'd prefer, dear," Tabby said, patting my arm. "Oh, would you like to see an old picture of your grandfather and me? It's a little unnerving how much we resemble one another, Rebecca."

"Sure," I said, eager to learn as much as I could.

My grandmother produced a wedding photo from the mid-1950s. She couldn't have been more than nineteen or twenty, my grandfather nearly the same age. I gasped at a near replica of myself.

Ted whistled from above my shoulder. "That...that is amazing. Rebecca, that looks like *you.*"

"I hope you can understand why Lou reacted the way he did. It's been a while since I was such a looker."

I continued to stare at the beautiful woman in the photo, forcing myself to accept the painful truth that my parents had lied to me regarding my appearance. I marveled at the spectacular woman dressed in white, realizing she could pass for my identical twin.

"What happened with you and my parents, Tabby?"

My grandmother exhaled a heavy sigh. "I wish Deborah had never married that pompous *macher.* He didn't look at you like a person, but like what he could get from you."

"Sounds like our guy," Ted said dryly. He placed a comforting hand on my shoulder. "Tabby, can you and Lou tell us about the past? We're happy to fill you in with details from the present. I have some questions to ask about my own parents too."

"What do you say I order us some Chinese food?" Lou said, glancing at the mantle clock.

"At two in the afternoon, Lou?" Tabby asked.

He shrugged. "We're going to be talking for a while. I have a lot of questions to ask also."

Four hours later with empty cartons from the Imperial Dragon littered on the table, we finally got to the business at hand.

"So you never liked him?" I said, referring to Pastor Lucifer.

My grandmother blew a raspberry. "Even at twenty years-old, Bernard Ivy strutted around like a peacock, looking down his nose at me and Lou because we're Jews. If that man is supposed to represent Christianity, you can tell Jesus I say no, thank you."

I smiled sadly. "I get it, Tabby. I could never please my father, and I grew up constantly walking on eggshells. He and my mother found fault with me no matter what I did."

Lou frowned. "That sounds like your father's influence. We told Deborah we didn't like how Bernard eyed her like a piece of meat while preaching to me and your grandmother about holiness and Jesus. We only met his parents at the wedding, but we could see they raised him to be a chip off the old block."

"This is all new information for me," I said. "My mother told me his parents passed away not long after Daniel was born. My father never spoke of them."

"Well, we wouldn't know, *bubbeleh,*" Tabby said with a tinge of bitterness. "As soon as we paid for the wedding, we got a single page letter from Deborah saying that unless we accepted Christ as our Lord and Savior, we were going to hell. She said it didn't reflect well on her beloved, pastor husband to have heathen in-laws."

Ted and I sat in stunned silence.

Lou gestured to the two of us, "Yup, that's about the same face we made too."

"Do you still have the letter?" Ted asked.

"No, we finally got rid of it," Tabby said. "We held onto it for so long, especially when Eleanor told us your mother and father had some marital problems. God forgive me, but I hoped she'd finally leave that *nogoodnik* and come to her senses."

My voice came out nearly an octave higher than normal. "Marital problems?"

"Sure," Lou said. "The relationship between your mother and Eleanor always seemed strange. Even as the baby, Deborah called the shots. Deborah always got Eleanor in trouble by putting her up to something. Later, Eleanor came complaining to us. She still does, but not nearly as often. We've asked Eleanor a thousand times if your mother had children, and she just pursed her lips and then threatened to leave if we asked her more questions. The marriage problems came from a slip of the tongue. I think Eleanor secretly hoped your mother would leave him too. Lucifer alienated Deborah from everyone outside of that cult he calls a church. Please, tell me you got out of there," Lou said beseechingly.

"I did. Unfortunately, I wound up in another place just as bad, if not worse."

I shared my SBC story with my newly discovered grandparents. Ted filled in the gaps when emotions ran too high for me to speak. Tabby and Lou seemed sad, though not surprised. Tabby shared her own experiences with my father and their final confrontation on my parents' wedding day.

"I just remember the smirk on his face," Tabby said. "Jews don't believe in the devil and hell and all of that Christian mishigas, but I'm telling you, if Satan has a smile, your father wore it the day he told me Deborah belonged to him. He promised I would spend the rest of my days regretting how I interfered in their relationship. Two weeks later, we got the letter."

Ted's colorful response received an approving grunt from Lou.

"We only lived an hour away!" I said, aggrieved. "I can't believe my mother lied about you all this time. All the years lost!"

"Such a *shanda* what they did to all of us," Tabby said, shaking her head. "But you're here now, bubbeleh, and we can't wait to hear more about the two of you. I never imagined being related to Phyllis Margolin, the only woman ever born with two faces." At Ted's grimace, she said, "I know, I know, listen to me go on with my own *lashon hara* talking about her. Please understand, Phyllis wasn't a nice woman. Not unless she had a lobotomy or a come-to-Jesus. No offense, Rebecca."

"None taken. What's a lashon hara?"

Tabby smiled indulgently. "Look at this girl, wanting to catch up on a lifetime of Yiddish. I can't tell you what it does to my heart to know I have a granddaughter, one even more beautiful than I used to be. It's probably not right to take joy in *that man's* suffering, but to know you're here defying him makes it that much sweeter. You understand my meaning, right, bubbeleh?"

"We can thank Pastor Lucifer for that at least," Ted said, "because he's the reason we got married and the reason we're here."

We sat and talked with Tabby and Lou, forever known afterward as Nana and Papa, well into the night. They offered to let us stay overnight, but Ted promised them we'd visit again and bring his parents too. I couldn't wrap my brain around how both my mother and aunt came from such loving parents, yet turned out so rotten. Equally as stumped, Nana and Papa suggested my mother had finally met her match in my father. They said my father viewed Deborah Wasserman as a conquest more than anything else.

"Your Nana nearly choked me on my fortune cookie," Ted said on the drive home.

"No kidding! Pastor Bernard Ivy lives a lie as an anti-Semitic, self-hating Jew whose parents changed their last name from Levy to Ivy."

"I mean the part where *my* father secretly kept in contact with my grandmother even though he told Mom he cut things off," Ted said with a frown. He glanced over at me. "It's certainly been quite a day for revelations, hasn't it? Anything you need to share, Rebecca?"

I chuckled. "No little Margolin in there yet," I said, tapping my stomach. "Just a whole lot of egg drop soup and chicken lo mein."

"All joking aside," Ted said, "I'm concerned about pregnancy, hormones, and how it will affect you, Rebecca. I know we both want children, but I wonder if there's ever going to be a right time."

"We still haven't discussed how we would raise our kids, Ted. Would they be Jewish? Would they be Christian? Would we try to do a happy medium with Messianic? I just don't know which option works best for us. I loved every second at Nana and Papa's house. I loved all of the Yiddish and looking at all of those old photos. Did you see how meticulously Nana keeps her record books? Ted, I want our kids to know their history, where they come from."

"But you also want them to know Jesus," he said pointedly, "and honestly, I'd like to learn more too. I'm not saying I want to sign up for church choir, but I asked Jesus for help, and He answered me. Rebecca, this is the happiest I've seen you since everything hit the fan with the Derdens. You look like you have hope, and not just hope that a certain deviant sees justice."

"I got a new beginning, Ted. I get to write my own family history instead of the lies my parents told me. Our kids will grow up knowing they're Jewish, because they are. Before you even say it, they're going to learn about Jesus too. He's the Jewish Messiah and the King of the Jews. I know we can make this all work together."

"What do you think about looking for a church?" he said.

"Seriously?"

Ted exhaled slowly. "Yeah. I have a lot of questions, and I

don't think Rabbi Epstein can answer them. Mom definitely had his number, and your grandparents sure knew the what's what of everything going down at Temple Beth Tefillah thirty years ago."

I reached over to hold Ted's hand. "Thank you for not giving up on me and for praying for me, Ted. Of all the unexpected blessings God has given me this past year, you were the biggest, my dear. He gave me a husband, parents, grandparents, siblings, and someone who finally makes me laugh instead of cry all the time." Megawatt slowly emerged on my face like an unwrapped present. "How about I express my gratitude when we get back home?"

I didn't need to see Ted's face in the dimly lit car to know his golden eyes glittered. The engine quickly revved, and the car moved noticeably faster back toward our house.

CHAPTER 35

"Rebecca!" Ted called distantly through my sleepy haze.

"What?" I rasped.

"I just checked my phone. I have five missed phone calls, two from my mother, and another three from Titus. Apparently, Chase Derden attempted suicide last night. Titus said he tried to overdose on pills"

I bolted straight up. "Are you sure?" I said, pushing tangled curls from my face. I read the frantic text message from Rose over his shoulder.

Ted, I've tried calling you and Rebecca several times. Titus Locke phoned us when he couldn't get a hold of either of you. He needs Rebecca to contact him immediately to give an additional statement.

I looked up at Ted. "Does this mean what I think it does? Are they opening an investigation into Pastor?"

My husband shrugged. "Sweetie, you know as much as I do. How old is Chase?"

"I think he's sixteen. He was fourteen or fifteen when I saw

Pastor and Cynthia abuse him. His parents made him lie and take back the story. I can't imagine what the poor boy must be going through."

"Enough to make him want to end his life," Ted said grimly.

"Ted, are you willing to pray with me? For Chase? That his parents will pull their heads out of their own denial and wake up?"

"I don't really know how to pray, but I'll hold your hand and sit with you."

I smiled. "It's a start."

The mighty Ted Margolin attended his first prayer meeting with just him, me, and Jesus. As angry as he ever saw me ranting about one of my family members or SBC, he'd never seen me go to battle in prayer. I called out demons by name, rebuking and cursing them back to the pit of hell. I begged the Lord to protect Chase, to comfort him and restore everything stolen from him. I prayed for breakthroughs in the case, for the darkness and secrets to give way to the light shining down on them. I raged, I prayed through my tears, and I finished by praising God, singing hymns and songs I remembered from childhood. By the time I finished, I felt like I had spent ten rounds in a boxing ring. Warm flecks of gold glowed beautifully at me.

"You're amazing," Ted said reverently. "Now, I understand why these bozos want to destroy you. They're petrified of Rebecca the warrior."

Megawatt appeared. "What do you think of the warrior?"

"She's pretty hot."

I laughed. "I'm being serious, Ted."

"So was I! The fire and passion you have when you talk about Jesus inspires people. You don't play at religion like Lucifer Ivy or Pastor Sociopath. You talk about God like you personally know Him. When you pray, I can envision angels getting up to answer whatever you've asked God to do." Pausing at my expression, he said, "Why are you looking at me like that? Did I botch up my Christian-ese?"

"No, honey," I said. "You've encouraged me more than you know. It's hard to keep praying and trusting God when it seems like evil goes on unchecked."

"I know you don't believe in clichés like 'everything happens for a reason,' but do you think Chase pulled a stunt like this to get the attention of the police? Titus said as long as Chase is a minor, his parents have the ultimate say in what happens with criminal proceedings. A situation like this gets law enforcement, and certainly CPS, involved."

"Ted, it makes for a great movie plot, but we have a high schooler who experienced more trauma and abuse than many adults ever see. I wish we could visit Chase for moral support, but the very least I can do is provide him with the validation he deserves with law enforcement."

Following a phone call with Titus Locke, I made a final call to Culver and informed Phil I would not be returning to work. I thanked him profusely for hiring me and for all he'd done for me. Phil reassured me of his confidence in Eric and Taylor, and it provided the closure I needed that the Culver marketing department would survive without me. I sent private emails to Miss Belle and Taylor offering to keep in touch.

Detective Nichols and another officer assigned to the case, Detective Roberts, came by for additional testimony. They asked me about the SBC youth group, my experiences as a college student there, and my observations as an adult. I offered as many names as I could, mostly the former teens who had left and never darkened the doorway of SBC again. The detectives also wanted the names of those who still attended as adults.

I suggested they talk to Ashley in hopes she'd reveal Pastor's more private matters, specifically the strange secrecy he demanded from his upper tier leaders. Detective Nichols said they couldn't discuss any details of an ongoing investigation, but he encouraged me that justice would prevail. Rose sat with me during the interview with Ted still at work.

"Jesus knows what He's doing, honey," she said, closing the front door once the officers had collected all of their necessary information.

"I know, Rose. Waiting and not knowing makes it harder."

"Honey, you have to rest. The fate of that congregation or even Pastor What's-His-Face doesn't rest on your shoulders. The Derden boy found a way to speak up and be heard. That's already huge. I would never wish what happened to him on anybody else, but if there are others, I hope his courage helps strengthen them to come forward. These perverts never just target one person but always have several lined up. It's pathological, and it's sick."

"Rose, the detectives really made me wonder about the teens I grew up with at SBC. I had so many friends who came and went. One day, they were active in the youth group, and then they just disappeared. From the pulpit, Pastor always praised the youth who stuck around after college. He'd slaver all over them with public compliments, but looking back, it was really just about Pastor praising *himself* and SBC. He made it sound like SBC was set apart from other churches because the kids came back, but it was really only a fraction of them."

"And now, you're wondering how many other victims he's abused over the years," Rose said, the look of disgust on her face mirroring my own.

I sighed. "Pretty much."

"I'll tell you, Rebecca, I've been through a lot in my sixty-three years around the sun, but I sit and think about all you've endured, and I can't even fathom how you've survived half of it. For most people, they have one or two crazies in their lives, the meddling mother-in-law, the negative congregational experience, or the psycho ex. Honey, you just got hammered from every side, didn't you?"

"So it would seem."

After a long pause, both of us temporarily lost in thought, Rose got up and walked toward the kitchen. "Can I fix you anything, honey? Ted always keeps this place so well stocked. Maybe a grilled cheese sandwich with one of those fancy, European flavors I never pronounce correctly?"

I laughed. "Grilled cheese sounds amazing. There should be a loaf of rye on the island and muenster in the fridge."

"Muenster on rye? That's Steve's favorite too."

I joined Rose as she expertly set up shop. "Speaking of Steve, how is he doing? Ted didn't mince any words with his father, did he?"

"Oh, please. *I* had plenty to say to my husband after Ted finished. He was the warm up act. I never understood why Steve acted so squeamish talking about Phyllis all these years later. I get that it's his mother, but he told me from his own mouth how offensive he found her behavior."

"But she's still, mommeleh," I said mockingly, rummaging through the cabinets for plates.

Rose buttered a side of bread, then another slice. "It seems silly to be mad at my husband twenty years after the fact, but I am. I thought we had put all the lies and secrets behind us. How many slices of cheese do you want, honey?"

"Two," I answered, pulling them from the package and handing them to Rose. "And what did Steve have to say for himself? Nana called him a nebbish, but I have a hard time picturing Steve that way."

Rose chuckled mirthlessly. "Oh, believe me, honey, he could act like a confident man one second, and then Phyllis would reduce him to a sniveling weasel as soon as she pulled on the old guilt strings." She turned her attention to the frying pan. "You want this bread toasted or charred?"

"Charred."

She grinned. "Me too. Where were we?"

"Sniveling weasel?"

"Oh, yes," she chuckled. "I struggled for so long trying to raise two children and a husband to boot. If I had known Phyllis was still manipulating things on a smaller scale, I probably would have confronted her myself. That scared Steve half to death."

"Why?"

"After all the years of biting my tongue at her ridiculous behavior, I would have finally unloaded on Phyllis the same way I took Steve's head off time and again."

I smiled. "I'm just imagining all five feet of you letting Steve have it. The cowering giant."

Rose cackled mischievously. "I won't deny it, honey. I can laugh about it now. It certainly wasn't funny back then. To Steve's credit, he apologized for hiding his relationship with Phyllis after I ripped him a new one."

"Does he still keep in contact with his mother?"

Rose shook her head as she flipped the bread over in the pan. "No. He eventually realized his mother is toxic, but he still makes excuses for it. He wants to believe she suffered a traumatic childhood growing up during the Great Depression rather than stop and ask why difficult circumstances excuse his mother from treating people like human beings. Intellectually anyway, he understands her behavior is wrong, but he doesn't want to accept that it's her issue. The loyal little boy still wants to believe mommeleh was a victim somehow. I guess it's better than nothing, but I wish Steve could fully break free of her influence on him." Glancing down at the skillet, she asked, "How's the doneness on this for you, honey?"

I inspected the delightfully blackened but not quite charcoal pieces of bread in the pan. "Perfect. Plate it up."

"Speaking of congregations, did you ever hear anything else from Lucifer or good ole Aunt Ellie?"

I shook my head. "I have no idea about them, but Ada called me last week. She even left a voicemail, which she never does."

"Have you listened to it? What did she want?"

"I don't know. I didn't want to deal with any Ivy family drama after meeting my grandparents. My last conversation with Ada was not a pleasant one."

"Ted mentioned it. He also told me you more than held your own," Rose said as she and I sat down with our sandwiches.

"I stood up to my baby sister instead of letting her steamroll me. It felt amazing to rediscover my backbone. Beyond that...mmm, Rose...oh my goodness. Wow! Okay, I need to shut up. This sandwich is amazing!"

My mother-in-law laughed as she sank her teeth into her own grilled cheese. Her contented sigh matched mine.

"Sometimes, it's the simple things," I said, waving half of my sandwich in the air. "Just bread, butter, and cheese."

"My food always tastes better in Ted's kitchen. Any ideas why?"

I shrugged, not wanting to waste an open mouth talking when it could be better spent inhaling one of the most delicious grilled cheese sandwiches in recorded history.

"Rose, teach me your ways," I said.

"The secret ingredient is always love, honey."

"That's not what you slipped into your world famous pancakes," I said, grinning.

Rose wagged a finger at me. "That secret lives and dies with you, Rebecca Margolin! Half the fun is knowing Ted will never guess. Do I have your word on that?"

"If you share one more sandwich with me, you've got a deal."

I kept Rose's secret, and she helped me keep one from Ted when he arrived home from work one early, March evening.

"Surprise!" I said.

Ted kissed me hello before looking over the dining room table decorated with candles and a plethora of traditional, Ashkenazi Jewish goodies courtesy of Rose and Nana.

"Are we expecting an army?" Ted said, eyeing the casserole dish full of apple raisin *kugel*, a platter of chicken *schnitzel*, and another of roasted beets. "Is that matzah ball soup I smell?" He wrapped an arm around my shoulders and led me to the bubbling stockpot of Jewish penicillin on the stove.

"Sorry about the mess," I said sheepishly. "I hoped to get everything cleaned up before you got here. I wanted it to look like the food miraculously appeared."

"What's the big occasion? Passover isn't for another month, and we still haven't heard anything about the Derden case other than Chase and his brother now being in protective custody."

"*Purim*," I said.

Ted looked at me questioningly. "This must be where my newly discovered Jewish wife teaches me about a holiday I never paid much attention to growing up."

The oven timer chimed in agreement.

"Rebecca!" Ted exclaimed. "When did you find time to do all of this?"

"Your mother came over with Nana, so I wasn't totally alone. Rose handled most of the cleanup. I couldn't pull all this off by myself."

I added sizzling butter to the menu as Ted's smoldering look sent an electric pulse through my fingers down to my toes. Before I suggested foregoing dinner in lieu of "dessert," our real dessert beckoned again from the oven.

"The cookies!" I exclaimed, rushing to the oven to pull them out.

Ted glanced over my shoulder. "Triangle jelly cookies?"

"*Hamantaschen*! Nana says her recipe makes them less dry than the standard ones, and we had fun making the fillings." I laid out my last set of triangle-shaped cookies with five dozen already cooling. "We've got apricot here, and then there's prune, and one more batch of chocolate fresh out of the oven."

"I hope we have help to eat all of this food," Ted said incredulously.

I grinned. "Amanda is coming over tomorrow with Blakely and little Asher. Addison has a ballet recital, or Jen and Barry would have come over with the other kids. I think your parents are going to stop by because Steve complained your mother never makes kugel anymore."

Ted's smile diminished. "He has no right to complain about anything right now."

"Your mother forgave your father, and she's the one married to him. If she can let it go, why can't you?"

"Can we talk about this later?" Ted said, kissing my forehead. "I know you put a lot of effort into tonight, and I'd rather hear about a Jewish holiday than talk about my father or my grandmother. Deal?"

"Deal."

CHAPTER 36

"IF I HAVE THE STORY STRAIGHT," MY HUSBAND SAID, relaxed in his chair with the top three buttons of shirt undone, "this is another Jewish holiday where they tried to kill us, we won, and let's eat?"

I chuckled. "Seems like a recurring theme with the Jewish people, huh? Impending doom followed by impending food. Do you ever wonder why God has specific food tied to the holidays He wants us to observe?"

"You're asking the self-professed agnostic at best?"

I shrugged. "Different perspective."

Ted paused a moment before answering. "Certain foods can cause triggers. I can't eat matzah ball soup without thinking of Passover seders at my parents' house, for example. But tell me again why Purim means eating cookies shaped like the hat of a genocidal anti-Semite?"

"Have you ever read the story of Esther in the Bible, Ted?"

His expression suggested I would have seen an airborne fleet of swine first.

"Fine, fine. It's in the Old Testament. Does that help?"

His face did not alter.

Giving a resigned sigh, I said, "It's tradition to read from the scroll of *Esther* on Purim anyway, so why don't we do that tonight?"

"You have a scroll?" he said drolly.

"No, smarty pants, but I have my Bible. You said you wanted to learn more about Jesus. Today's a great opportunity."

"What does Jesus have to do with cookies?" he said, polishing off another apricot hamantasch.

"I already laid out why Jesus is the Jewish Messiah of the Old Testament."

"Which, as you know, went completely over my head, but we'll let that go for now. I don't remember much from Hebrew school anyway."

I walked over to the living room with my Bible already open on the coffee table. "Why don't you come join me over here?"

"Assuming I can pull myself out of this chair. I think I gained fifteen pounds tonight."

"Yeah, yeah, quit your bellyaching, and get over here."

Ted laughed. "You might not be wrong about the bellyaching. I don't think I've ever eaten that much, even at Thanksgiving. My compliments to all three lovely chefs." He kissed the top of my head as he sat down next to me on the couch.

"Let's take it from the top," I said, flipping to the first chapter.

Our reading and discussion of the book lasted well into the night. Ted asked many questions, some I could answer, others I told him I'd have to research and get back to him. I explained the backstory of Haman, the villain, the descendant of Agag whom King Saul should have killed six hundred years prior to Esther. I explained why the Jews weren't living in

Israel but modern day Iran during the time of Purim. I enjoyed seeing Ted's brilliant mind put all of the pieces together.

"The odds of this are astounding," Ted said. "You said Saul came from the tribe of Benjamin and was supposed to kill this King Agag, right?"

"Right."

"But he doesn't, eventually loses everything to David, and then this Mordecai guy and his cousin show up centuries later, also from the tribe of Benjamin. These two finally deal with Agag's descendant. Did I miss anything?"

"Nope. Rose and Nana told me when they retell the story of Esther in synagogue, everyone boos when they hear the name Haman."

"They boo? Seriously?"

"Yeah, check out chapter nine over here. Part of the Purim celebration involves blotting out the name of Haman. People either boo, or they rattle these bad boys," I said, shaking my Purim *gragger*.

"Lovely," he deadpanned, "and wow, that thing is loud."

I smiled at the little contraption in my hand, a rectangular noise maker designed to swivel on a stick and create ear splitting sound. "Your mother said you and Jennifer played with these as children."

Ted took the gragger from my hand, eyeballing the tiny, metal toy. "I have vague memories of this thing. Maybe Jen remembers. To think, we do all of this because of one Jewish orphan and her righteous cousin. That's pretty amazing."

"Esther risked everything to protect her people, even unto death. She knew God placed her exactly where He wanted her, as Mordecai put it, 'for such a time as this.' She faithfully accomplished what needed to be done."

Golden eyes glowed warm at me. "She sounds a lot like you."

I blushed. "Hardly! I haven't saved an entire people from annihilation."

"Rebecca, you risked your reputation by exposing Pastor Sociopath. Hopefully, you set Chase Derden free from all of the SBC chazarai. For that matter, I hope the pew warmers in that place get freed from their own, wicked Haman."

"Wow," I said, stunned by the similarities.

Ted continued, "Sweetheart, most people keep quiet and would rather let someone else take the punishment for being the whistleblower. They whine and complain about problems while ignoring their own culpability to speak up. You didn't do that. You stood up for what was right because it was right, and they tried to obliterate you for it. As far as I'm concerned, you're just as much a hero of your story as Esther is of hers."

I promptly smothered my husband with enough holiday kisses to render us both breathless.

Much like the Biblical story of Purim, more secrets came forth, but they arrived in the form of pounding on our door the following morning.

"Do you think it's one of the pastors?" I said quietly. I feared I could be heard even through brick walls. "Jessica would never stop by this early, and she went missing after she started dating that married lawyer from work."

"Stay here," Ted said, placing a hand on my leg. "I'll go see who it is. Get ready with the phone to call 911."

I nodded and waited.

"What are you doing here, Ada?" Ted's gruff voice demanded at the front door.

"I need to talk to Rebecca. I know you guys hate my guts, and I have no right to ask, but I have nowhere else to go."

"I wouldn't put it past your family to concoct some scheme to ruin your sister's life. How did you find out where I live?"

"Look, I just need to find my sister, okay? They said she doesn't work at Culver anymore. I asked if they knew about a guy named Ted, and they gave me your name. The police charged my father with assault and attempted battery, and I need to tell Rebecca. She won't return my phone calls."

"While I can't say I'm surprised, what does that have to do with your sister?"

"Because my dad thought the woman was Rebecca. I don't know if all that religion finally made him go mental, but he tried to smack some lady in the middle of a grocery store last month. The woman's husband beat him up. Some kids filmed it on their phones, and the video went viral. My mother won't leave her room because of the embarrassment, and they wired my father's jaw shut because the guy broke it with his fists."

I skidded to a stop behind Ted as Ada finished her tale. Peeking at her from behind my husband's tall frame, my sister looked the most mainstream I'd seen her since high school. With the blue dye gone from her hair, facial piercings removed and tattoos covered up, she looked like a grown up version of the younger sister I had adored until my parents groomed her into their image.

"Rebecca?" Ada said, spotting me. "You guys live together? I didn't think you...oh," she said, as Ted and I both held up our left hands. "Um, congratulations. I know I owe you guys an apology. Rebecca, I probably owe you a few thousand for everything I've done."

"What do you want, Ada? Why come over here with some family sob story? Do you guys expect me to swoop in and pick up the pieces? You're crazy if you think I'm going to testify on

Lucifer's behalf or lie to the police that he deserves father of the year."

"Did you just call him *Lucifer*?" Ada said, eyes wide.

"Sure did. Oh, and by the way, our grandparents live about an hour away in Cordele. Mom's parents. The ones she lied to us about our entire lives."

"They're not dead?"

"Did she tell you that?"

"No, I just always assumed they'd died since Dad never talked about them, and Mom cried any time I asked. Did you meet them?"

Ted interrupted before I could answer my sister. "In the interest of not subjecting Rebecca to any more gossip or nosey neighbors, I'm inviting you in, Ada. If you pull any stunt or attempt to manipulate your sister, I'm calling the police. I have no problem locking you up along with your psycho father for harassing my wife. Are we clear?"

Ada nodded. "Aunt Eleanor is furious at Rebecca about I don't even know what, and Daniel can't be bothered. Apparently, the baby wasn't his, so he moved in with his friend, Gooch, and decided to fry some more brain cells. If it makes you feel any better, Rebecca, you got your happily ever after while the Ivy family fell apart."

I folded my arms over my chest. "I don't take delight in the misery of others, Ada. I'm sad for all of you, but you're not roping me back into the seventh circle of hell you guys call a family."

If physically possible, Ada's eyebrows would have lifted straight off her forehead.

Ted leaned in close to my ear. "I'm going to go clean myself up. Don't go past the living room until I get back." He opened the door just wide enough for Ada to slip in.

As Ted attended to his morning grooming, I watched my sister take in our home, her eyes resting on the mantle. She walked toward our wedding photo.

"Beautiful picture," she said absently, lightly fingering the frame. "You guys look really happy. Who took the shot?"

"My father-in-law."

"Oh. So you guys just got married?"

"Right after Thanksgiving."

"Right after...wow, that was fast," she said, looking me up and down. "Obviously, you're not pregnant, not that I think you'd do something like that anyway."

"Good," I responded tightly.

Ada sighed wearily. "When everything happened with Dad, it didn't make sense why he assaulted some stranger. Mom tries to paint it like they targeted dad for being a pastor, especially since he's eating through a straw right now, but those kids caught everything on camera. At first, Dad yells at this woman and calls her Rebecca. He spouts off a bunch of Bible-y sounding stuff before he finally calls her a whore. The husband steps in because Dad is acting like a complete whacko, and then Dad tries to hit this lady."

I covered my hand with my mouth.

"All of that got me thinking, Rebecca. Did Dad ever hit you? I mean, as an adult?"

"All the time, Ada. If he couldn't get his hands on me, he threw things at my head. That didn't stop after we grew up."

Ada nodded solemnly. "After I saw the video, I began to remember. There were slaps from behind closed doors and Mom singing to me to drown out the sound of you crying. She called you the wicked daughter and called me the good one. She told me you got what you deserved by not honoring your father, but she would never punish her beautiful girl like that."

My brain flashed to childhood, adolescence, and adulthood. I recalled countless instances of Bernard Lucifer Ivy screaming in my face, his twisted features bent in a rage. I remembered the sickening sound of his palm landing against my face. I never knew the extent of my mother's willful compliance, and bile rose in my throat at her cruelty.

"He really did abuse you, didn't he?" Ada said quietly. "And all the times we just picked you apart...and...and I helped him. It made me feel good to see Dad proud of me, even though I knew how much he hated me being a lesbian. No matter what I did, if I started talking about you and your issues, he'd forget all about mine."

"Yes," I said, encouraged by Ted's strong hand on my shoulder. "All of you took sadistic pleasure in torturing me and ripping me apart. You'd make me cry and then humiliate me for it. I willed myself into believing God wanted me to suffer like that, never realizing some pervert pastor used that same, misplaced martyrdom to trick me into sleeping with him."

Ada's gaze shot toward me, her show of contrition immediately forgotten. "I knew it!"

"You knew what?" Ted said darkly.

"Rebecca, you've been in love with that pastor since you started going to SBC. You really did try to break up his marriage, didn't you? Dad had you pegged all along!"

"That's ridiculous," I said angrily. "I loved my pastor like a father figure, not like a boyfriend."

"Rebecca, you constantly gushed about 'Pastor this' and 'Pastor that.' Your entire life revolved around that church. Mom was convinced you were sleeping with him, especially since Dad sleeps with all of his First United groupies."

"What did you just say?" I said, sure my ears had deceived me.

CHAPTER 37

"YOU DIDN'T KNOW?" ADA ASKED, SOMEWHAT annoyed. "Mom doesn't care anymore because it means Dad leaves her alone. She almost left when she found out about the first one."

"The first one?" I repeated in horror. "You mean there's more?"

"Rebecca, were you completely blind?" Ada said. "Didn't you see the way Dad looked over half the women in that place?"

"I must have been too busy trying to worship the Lord," I said in a choked voice. "I didn't realize Dad used First United as his personal brothel."

Ada rolled her eyes. "Don't make it all melodramatic, Rebecca. He's a human like anybody else."

My hands trembled from rage and adrenaline. "Our father has publicly abused and humiliated me for supposedly bringing shame to the Ivy family. Meanwhile, he's been the philandering hypocrite all along!"

Ada threw her hands in the air in exasperation. "Rebecca!

What is your problem? I never would have said anything if I had known you were going to spaz out about it."

"Ada, don't you remember what happened last March?" I said, stunned and appalled by my sister's nonchalance.

"Should I?" she said.

I struggled for self-control at her faux incredulity. "Ted and I told you what happened in the farmer's market. Dad showed up at my office regurgitating all of Pastor Sociopath's lies that I tried to seduce him. He begged me to renounce some Jezebel spirit."

Ada's mouth thinned. "That sounds like something stupid Dad would say."

"So, the Jezebel thing bothers you, but you have no problem with our father screwing every female in First United?" I demanded.

"Just a minute!" Ada said. "Dad doesn't go around acting like some high and mighty saint like you do, Rebecca. I never said he sleeps with every woman there."

"Just half of them," I said, throwing Ada's words back in her face.

"Won't you even try to listen?" she said.

"Listen to what?" I snapped. "Don't try to justify his behavior, Ada."

"I'm not justifying anything. I said Dad is human. I never said he's perfect."

Acknowledging my sister's uncharacteristic willingness to budge, I inclined my head for Ada to continue. Ted's arm slid around me, and his eyes met mine in concern, no doubt from the steam pouring from my ears.

"Dad sleeps in his home office," Ada said quietly. "He and Mom don't share a bedroom."

My jaw dropped. "Since when?"

"Since forever, I guess."

"Why didn't I know any of this?"

"You know how Mom and Dad love their little secrets."

Appalled, I said, "How can Mom stand being married to him? He made her cut off her own family to marry him, and then he cheated on her. Doesn't she hate him for everything he made her give up?"

Ada shrugged. "You can ask her yourself. They worked out a deal a long time ago. As long as Dad lets her buy whatever she wants without complaining, Mom doesn't snitch on him."

I briefly closed my eyes, stunned and sickened by every new piece of information. After a calming breath, I glanced over at my sister, astounded by her acceptance of the situation as anything other than a tragic farce.

"Rebecca, why are you looking at me like that?" she finally asked.

"Like what? Like I think you're absolutely crazy for thinking this is how normal people behave?"

She sighed in frustration. "I really thought you knew. Mom and Dad got so mad about you leaving First United because they thought you'd air their dirty laundry to get back at them. They thought they'd lose the church."

"They mocked and belittled me for over a decade," I said, dumbfounded. "They treated me leaving like I'd committed some heinous sin. They deliberately tortured me, and all to protect themselves."

Hurricane Ted was not finished with my sister either. "Ada, did you know about your father's infidelity back at the farmer's market? When you accused Rebecca of being a homewrecker?"

My sister squirmed.

"You did, didn't you?" I said. "You kept that smug, little look on your face while knowing our father committed every atrocity you accused *me* of doing. You projected all of his disgusting sins onto me and then called me crazy."

Ada shook her head. "It wasn't like that, Rebecca. Yeah, I knew Dad had his affairs, but I never expected that kind of stuff from you. I know it sounds hypocritical, but I already knew Dad's private life didn't match his public one. It only seemed right to get you off your high horse when Dad told me about you and your old pastor."

"*My* high horse?"

"Fine," she said, rolling her eyes. "I know I said a couple of mean things, but I didn't know Dad went to your job and said all that Jezebel stuff."

"What do you mean you didn't know?" I shot back. "We had just told you what happened. You couldn't have cared less."

"You're right, Rebecca, I didn't care. I honestly didn't even remember you saying anything until you brought it up just now. I was mad at you for walking away from me and didn't pay much attention. Happy?"

"Why are you here, Ada?" Ted said, finding my hand and squeezing it for moral support. "You said you had nowhere else to go, but don't think for one second that you can stay here with us. You also won't find any sympathy for Bernard Ivy in this house."

"Is that why you came here, Ada?" I said. "Mom kicked you out because you won't cover for Pastor Lucifer?"

"Stop calling him that! It creeps me out."

"My house. My rules," I said. "If you don't like it, you can leave. I watched Pastor Lucifer turn my own brother and sister against me, watched all of you laugh at my expense. Your personal preferences are the absolute least of my concerns right now."

"I just want to understand what's going on," Ada said. "I

haven't seen this side of Dad before. He said he stopped by to wish you a Happy Thanksgiving, but you refused to open the door for him. It really hurt him, Rebecca. I want to know if that's why our father suddenly started acting like a crazy man."

"Suddenly?" I gaped. "Because passing yourself off as a servant of the Lord while fornicating with the women in your flock qualifies as *normal* these days?"

Coolly, Ted said, "Ada, your father left a note on Rebecca's car threatening that she couldn't hide from him forever. He said she would pay for besmirching the Ivy family name. He didn't stop by for a friendly house call, no matter what sob story he invented later. The police have that note in custody. Regardless of the assault case being one of mistaken identity, your father fully intended the harm for that poor woman on your sister instead."

Ada looked back and forth between the two of us. "You guys have absolutely no compassion, do you?"

"Compassion?" I said, enraged. "What kind of compassion did any of you selfish jerks ever show to me? How about when I was engaged to Jason, and all of you tore me apart at Thanksgiving? How about Dad's sadistic delight in that failed relationship and then listing off all of my worst qualities to you? He called Jason lucky to escape being married to me. Do you remember that conversation, Ada? Because you laughed and agreed with Dad, adding a few more flaws to his list. You don't get to come into my home and lecture me about *compassion* when you've never shown an ounce of it to me!"

"I told her it would be a waste of time," Ada muttered.

Ted immediately caught onto the implication of my sister's words. "Should I go ahead and call the police now? Is your mother outside too?"

"Mom was hospitalized, okay? She begged me to find you."

"What do you mean by hospitalized?'" I said.

"I mean, they locked her up in the loony bin. She was screaming at Dad, threatening to kill herself because of everything he's done to her. The neighbors called the cops because of all the noise. Mom went voluntarily, but she won't stop until she gets you back, Rebecca. She said you're the only one who can fix this."

"Fix what exactly?"

"I don't know!" Ada said, exasperated. "She won't tell me anything!"

"If she thinks I'm going to help exonerate Pastor Lucifer from the prison cell he deserves, she's in for a rude awakening."

"Look," Ada said, her patience at an end, "will you help or not?"

My icy glare matched the frost in my voice. "There's the door Ada. Don't ever darken it again. I will give you the benefit of calling the police after you leave, but if you, or any of those other sick *mamzers* show your faces at my door again, I will not hesitate to have you thrown in jail. Are we clear?"

"What did you call me?"

"It's Yiddish. Learn it. Both of our parents are Jewish and lied to us about it."

In all the times my sister ever called me crazy, I knew she meant it in the truest sense of the word as she slammed her way out of our front door.

Hours later, the Margolin clan descended upon us for Purim, though I felt more pensive than festive.

"Never a dull moment with you two, eh?" Rose said, helping herself to another chocolate hamantasch. "And you have no idea what your mother wants?"

I shook my head. "Ted and I both think she's going to pull her usual, 'woe is me' shtick for attention. Whenever my father took his abuse too far, my mother found ways to make me responsible. She played the mother guilt card like a true professional, maybe even better than Phyllis Margolin."

"You know, it's possible they knew one another. Steve remembers your grandparents from synagogue, but not your mother. Did she go by a nickname as a child?"

"You're asking the wrong kid. Apparently, she tells all of her secrets to Ada."

"Are you going to tell Tabby and Lou?"

"Tell them what, exactly? That Lucifer got the butt kicking he deserved because he confused some stranger with me in the food store? That their daughter, who cut them off almost forty years ago, got committed to a mental hospital? That she finally went completely bananas having to cover for my father's litany of indiscretions?"

"Honey, I say this in love," Rose began.

I frowned. "Conversations that start this way rarely end well, Rose."

A wry grin appeared on her face. "Humor me, okay? I don't mean this as a criticism, just concern."

I folded my arms over my chest. "You want to tell me I'm being too hard on my family? Unforgiving? Not Christlike enough?"

"After all of the mishigas I've dealt with on my end, do you really think I would say something as stupid as that? Honey, I can't even bear to think what could have happened if your father actually found you in that grocery store rather than that lady and her husband. My concern is all for you, Rebecca, not a single one of them."

I sighed. "What's your concern, Rose?"

"Bitterness, honey. You're angry. You absolutely have every right to be. Even God says that we can be angry, just don't sin."

"So, how exactly am I sinning, Rose?"

She raised up her hands in innocence. "Honey, I'm not saying you're sinning right now. I just don't want to see all of the anger harden the beautiful heart you have. Like I said, it's just a concern, not a rebuke."

My eyes narrowed. "I know you've been through your own mishigas, Rose, but I don't appreciate you projecting your own experiences onto me. I'm not you, okay?"

"I'm just trying to help," she said, defensively.

"Is everything all right in here?" Ted asked, noting the tension between his mother and me as he approached.

"You tell me, Rose," I said icily.

My mother-in-law seamed her lips. Shaking her head, she mumbled, "Shouldn't have brought it up. Nevermind. Please excuse me."

Ten minutes later, the house cleared of its guests, and we still had enough food left for an army. Unfortunately, neither Ted nor I possessed much of an appetite. Instead, we put in a phone call to Titus Locke and confirmed the assault charges pending against one Bernard Daniel Ivy. Two days later, Bud Riley, of all people, contacted me via DM on social media to fill in the missing puzzle pieces.

Dear Rebecca,

While I understand I may be the last person you want to hear from, you're the only member of the Ivy family with any sense. I'm dying from stomach cancer. The doctors can't explain why nothing will work to treat it, but I think we both know the real reason. You may think it's only fair given all that I've done to hide your father's sins, and you'd be absolutely right. I need someone to know all the things I know, someone who will do something

with the information, not just hide it for fear of shame or embar-
rassment. If you get this message, please know it is not a trick.

Your parents have no idea I'm doing this. The Lord is telling me
my days are short, and this is the last thing I need to do so I can
finally end this agony in my gut. I think it's the guilt that's been
eating away at me all of these years. I am in bed most days with
my hospice nurse, but I will gladly record or sign whatever you
need me to. Please just think about it. I'll understand if you want
nothing to do with me or want to leave this part of your past
behind.

-Bud

After reading and re-reading the message several times, I
showed it to my husband. "Am I hallucinating, Ted, or does this
say what I think it does?"

Ted looked over my shoulder as he read from my laptop
screen. "I'm speechless. I don't know what's going on with your
father or with Pastor Sociopath, but it looks like karma finally
caught up with them."

"Not karma, honey. Justice. God's justice. I have to know,
Ted. Bud may have more answers than my mother, more
answers than anybody other than God Himself about what my
father's done."

"Are you sure you want to handle that much ugly, Rebecca?
I'm glad you patched things up with my mom, but it will be a
lot of information to deal with."

You shall know the truth, and the truth shall set you free.

The voice of God encouraged me to face the darkness, to
hold up a shining light and send it scattering. Regardless of
whatever I chose to do with Pastor Lucifer's secrets, they would

no longer remain secret. As one of many victims I knew my father abused in some fashion throughout his lifetime, I decided to start the biggest and loudest war cry for every single one of them. Whether silenced by fear, shame, bribes, or misplaced guilt, I had a message for all of them: it wasn't your fault.

CHAPTER 38

OFFICIALLY, TITUS DID NOT ACCOMPANY US TO BUD Riley's house as law enforcement but as moral support. We trailed just behind Detective Martinez who handled the assault case against my father.

Bud lived in the same house I remembered from First United leadership meetings. The hospice nurse let us inside, and my eyes doubled in size as I took in the dilapidated state of Bud's once pristine home. The emerald colored carpets remained untouched since the early '90s, just faded with wear and time. A thick layer of dust covered the infamous dining room table where First United's business dealings went down.

"Bud is resting upstairs," the nurse said. "He told me to expect the police, but please tell me you're not going to arrest him! I don't know how much longer he'll be with us."

"We're here to collect a statement, ma'am," Detective Martinez replied. "We believe Mr. Riley has some information to help us in an ongoing investigation."

"Oh!" the nurse said in immediate understanding. "I only

met *that man* one time, and may I never see that snake again! He yelled and screamed like a demon at poor Bud. Called him every curse in the Bible while looking like the devil himself. He threatened to suffocate poor Mr. Bud with a pillow until he saw me calling 911."

I described my father, and the nurse confirmed his identity. Detective Martinez took down a formal statement from her as additional evidence. I walked slowly through the house as ancient memories resurrected like corpses from the grave.

"I'll have to give a tithing message again," my father grumbled to Bud.

I stood just outside the doorway, my brother and sister playing with the other elders' children as they unanimously agreed none of them wanted to be around "fat Rebecca." My mother and the other women lounged in the Riley's basement making full use of their wet bar. Hoping to find solace in the refrigerator, I stumbled upon my father and Bud in quiet conversation.

"Bernard, the people already complain about how many times you mention tithing from the pulpit. Rich Nelson wants to know why you need so many meetings with his wife about the new members luncheon."

My father dismissed Bud with a wave of the hand. "He should feel lucky his wife is finally being loved the way a woman really deserves."

"You told Rich he needed to serve more in the church and recommended him for head usher duties. He brayed like a donkey how Pastor Ivy called him a natural leader with real potential to do things for God. How does that help Barbara Nelson's marriage when you add extra duties to her husband's plate?"

"We all have potential for the Lord," my father sneered.

"Barbara came to me crying how unloved and neglected she feels. As her pastor, I knew the best way to handle the situation meant having Rich be about the Lord's business rather than serving the almighty dollar."

Bud exhaled a slow sigh. "Spare me the song and dance, Bernard. We both know why you made him head usher. It had nothing to do with saving their marriage or helping Rich serve Jesus more than his job."

Unmoved, my father retorted, "The woman has lusted after me since they first set foot in the church, Bud. Do you see the way she hangs onto my every word? I can't help it if she shows more appreciation than my own wife. I'm a man. I have needs."

"Bernard, you said that about the last three women."

Unfortunately, I picked the wrong time to sneeze.

"Rebecca!" my father roared, spotting me immediately. "You're supposed to be outside with the other children!" A backhand across the face sent me sprawling to the floor.

"You heard nothing!" he screamed as he towered over me. "Do you understand? *Nothing!*"

Whimpering from the pain in my cheek and the shame of his tirade, I nodded dutifully.

"Do you know the hardship of having this disobedient, little hellion running around, Bud? Look at her!" he yelled, pinching my side and the excess weight there. "The fat pig came sniffing around the kitchen looking to stick her nose in the trough."

"Bernard," Bud entreated. "She's just a child."

"A *fat* child," my father said, looking down his nose at me. "Get off the floor and stop your sniveling, Rebecca Joanne. You can think about what you've done by waiting for us in the car."

"Bernard! We'll be here for another two hours!" Bud said.

"Two less hours for Miss Piglet to stuff her face might be

two pounds she actually loses." Turning his attention back to me, my father yelled, "Go, Rebecca!"

I picked myself slowly off the floor, checking the side of my mouth for the occasional blood Bernard Ivy put there.

For a parting death blow, my father added, "Look at you, big as a house in that dress. You look like you could go without eating for two weeks, not just two hours."

Bernard Ivy turned his back on me, dismissing me like a wad of gum on his shoe. He resumed his conversation with Bud Riley as though nothing happened, as though I merely imagined the vengeful monster and my swelling lower lip. With the crippling load of shame and humiliation on my back, I trudged to the car and sat.

I sat for three and a half hours in the dark.

All the way home, my mother railed at me for scaring her half to death when they couldn't find me. My brother and sister smirked while my father chimed in about my rebellious ways and how I'd shamed and dishonored both of my parents. He called the thought of losing me unbearable, enjoying sympathetic pats from my mother as the crocodile tears wet his cheeks. My four-year-old sister demanded to know why I liked to make Daddy cry.

Touching that same door frame over twenty years later, my body jerked with a current of electricity. The deliberate, insidious torture my father inflicted upon me fueled a rush of rage.

"He has to pay," I growled.

"Rebecca?" Ted said, concern in his eyes. "You look like you've seen a ghost."

"Not a ghost, Ted. I've seen the devil, and he lives inside of my father."

"What did you remember happening here?"

So I told him.

Ted felt the word "devil" was too light a description for the darkness dwelling inside of Pastor Bernard Ivy, and he added some words of his own. Titus found us a few minutes later to inform us we could meet with Bud.

We entered the surprisingly clean master bedroom, Ted's hand securely holding mine. Opened curtains and copious sunlight revealed a bedridden, shriveled prune who hardly resembled the robust man I recalled from childhood. Bud looked as though the life had literally been sucked out of him. All that remained was paper thin skin, veins, and bones.

"Bud?" I said.

His glassy blue eyes opened slowly. Though his body seemed more than ready to heave its last breath, once he recognized my face, a spark of life flickered.

"You came," he breathed.

"I did. What do you need to tell me?"

"So many memories. So many I wish I could forget," he moaned.

"Like the night my father beat me and banished me to the car?" I said, my anger barely restrained.

Bud shook his head. "Oh Rebecca! I wronged you. I should have said something, not just that time, but so many others. Your father was a monster."

"He still is a monster," Ted corrected. "And we haven't met. I'm Rebecca's husband."

"Good," Bud said, looking at our joined hands as we stood over his bedside. "This girl deserves protecting and to be loved the way her father never could. Bernard hates Rebecca because she looks so much like his mother-in-law. Deborah begged him for years to see her parents, but your father said no. She wanted to love you, Rebecca, but your father didn't allow it. You reminded Bernard too much of her mother. He forced Deborah to choose between him and you."

"Why are you trying to paint my mother in some kind of sympathetic light, Bud? She played her own emotional torture games with or without my father's presence."

Bud closed his eyes slowly then reopened them. His next breath came out as a ragged sigh.

A strange look passed over Detective Martinez's face. "What's the rest of the story, Mr. Riley?

Glancing from Detective Martinez then back to Bud, I finally noticed a framed picture on Bud's night side table.

Of my sister.

"Did you molest Ada?" I gasped, not even sure where the words came from. "Why do you have her picture here, Bud? Is that why she became a lesbian? To escape the pain of any man who could hurt her the way you did?" At his silence, I yelled, "Why do you have a picture of my sister instead of Candace and Vincent? Why aren't *your* children in this photo?" I slammed the picture frame down, cracking the glass.

Ted laid a calming hand on me. Close to my ear, he said, "Are you really sure you want to do this?"

"Answer the question, Bud!" I persisted. "Why do you have—"

"Because she's my child!" he blurted out. "Candace and Vincent are on the other nightstand."

"Excuse me?"

"Your mother was so miserable being married to your father. He wanted nothing to do with her after you were born, even less when you didn't seem to lose your baby weight like your brother. You know your father obsessed over appearance. He had your mother constantly on a diet, trying to be good enough for him, trying to keep his eyes from every other wife in the church, even some of the college girls."

"Were any of them underage?" Detective Martinez asked.

Bud shook his head. "No. Bernard mostly targeted the married women because they wouldn't talk. He knew their husbands wouldn't believe them even when a few spoke up. Bernard had this way of captivating people, of making them feel special and important. He found the unloved or unnoticed wives while keeping the husbands busy with church business. He expertly doled out the praise, and they all came back for more."

Infuriated, I spat, "That disgusting fraud got up in the pulpit and shamed the congregants weekly for not doing more volunteer work in the church. His education director was a single mother whose daughter dressed in rags half the time, but my father still squeezed her for money. He conflated serving God with serving First United and then twisted Bible verses about God's judgment if people didn't obey."

"God forgive me, Rebecca, but I couldn't leave your mother to that man. Every time I watched her or your father preen over my sweet Ada, when I watched them turn her into a little demon just like Bernard, there was nothing I could do. God only knows what Bernard would have done to your mother or Ada if he found out the truth."

"What about Rebecca?" Ted demanded. "Where were you all the times they humiliated and abused her because she looked like someone she'd never even met? Where was all of this compassion and fatherly concern back then?"

The answer dawned on me before Bud could moisten his parched lips to reply.

"What did my father hold over your head to keep you quiet,

Bud? I doubt my mother was your only affair. How many others?"

"One other," he admitted, "and it happened early on. Edie practically worshipped your father, and she ate the slop right out of his hand. As far as I know, he never touched my wife, but Bernard ran her ragged with one thing or another. I asked Bernard to back off and let someone else handle things because of the toll it took on our family. Instead, he introduced me to Linda Phillips, another First United marriage victim whose spouse seemed more married to the church than to her. We found solace in each other's arms for a time, but when Linda's marriage fell apart, she confessed our relationship to Bernard. Your father used that ammunition to keep me quiet about his own philandering. He called me a hypocrite and told me I'd destroy Edie and her walk with Christ if she thought of your father as anything less than the man of God he pretended to be."

"Unreal," Ted muttered.

Eyes clear, Bud's gaze bored into mine. "Your father took a sick delight in watching people jump to do his bidding. He sat like a king on his throne while the loyal subjects sniped against each other, always hoping to look better in his eyes. They all wanted to hear their beloved Pastor Ivy sing their praises from the church stage. Bernard knew these people's weaknesses, and he exploited them. Once he caught wind of my relationship with Linda, he told me I could help build the church and atone for what I'd done, or he would turn me into a public spectacle and a cautionary tale. Forgive me, but I gave way to pride and fear to protect myself. It cost me everything anyway."

"Mr. Riley," Detective Martinez interrupted, "we need information specific to an incident where Mr. Ivy attempted to assault a woman thinking it was his daughter. We're hoping you can help us establish a motive for why he specifically targeted Mrs. Margolin. He left a threatening note on her car over Thanksgiving."

Bud's expression hardened. "That's because of what Rebecca knows about the pervert over at Sycamore Bible Church."

CHAPTER 39

"The plot thickens," Titus said under his breath.

"Locke, you're working the Derden case, right?" Detective Martinez asked Titus.

"Nichols and me," he replied. "I can handle this part of questioning. Rebecca is long overdue for this explanation from Mr. Riley anyway."

"This is officially on the record," Detective Martinez said, pulling out his digital video camera. "Given your unfortunate condition, I want to make sure we record everything in case it's deemed admissible as evidence."

Bud gave a rasping chuckle. "You mean, if I die before I see that man brought to justice? I understand your meaning perfectly well, Detective. What do you want to know?"

"Did Bernard Ivy know about Chase Derden or any other minors possibly endangered?" Titus asked.

"I know they talked when Rebecca left the other church.

Bernard gave him a lecture saying, 'Keep it in your pants and at least make sure they're legal age, you idiot.'"

I gasped.

"Were you present when this conversation took place?" Detective Martinez said. "How long have you been in bed like this?"

"My body started to give out six months ago. If it wasn't for the cancer already killing me, Bernard's insane demands would have done it. It took this wonderful young lady reading him the riot act to make him leave me alone," Bud said, lifting a frail hand toward his hospice nurse.

She smiled back with tears in her eyes. "And I'd do it again too, Mr. Bud."

"So, when did this phone call between the two pastors take place?" Titus asked.

"Eighteen months ago," Bud said. "Unusual for Bernard, he put the call on speaker phone. He seemed distracted with his own scandals at the time. One involved his son's girlfriend and an abortion Bernard paid for with church money. The other was an affair with the choir director. She joined a long list of women promoted to leadership positions so Bernard could have easy access and excuses to meet alone or after hours without raising suspicion."

Having hit my limit, I backed up slowly. Ted helped me sit at the foot of the bed and kept his hand on my shoulder. I grabbed onto it for dear life. Tremulously, I said, "I always knew there was something wrong with my father. I've known my whole life, but this is so cold. So calculated. Like he has no soul."

"Your father sold his soul to the devil a long time ago," Bud said before succumbing to a violent coughing fit.

The nurse appeared at Bud's side to check his pulse and

offer him a glass of water. Sure enough, there sat the picture of Candace and Vincent.

"What do you mean he sold his soul?" I asked.

"How much do you know about your grandparents?" Bud said after he had sufficiently recovered.

"My father's parents, I'm assuming?"

"Yes. I wish I could paint a picture of a troubled childhood, to give some kind of sympathetic plight to explain his behavior, but I can't. As an only child, Bernard's parents worshiped the ground he walked on. They raised him very similarly to Ada, let him believe the sun rose and set on him. His father worked as a door-to-door salesman before he realized he could make more money leading a church. Bernard would clap his hands together and laugh at the so-called *wisdom* of his father. He referred to the First United members as stupid sheep more often than not, and he viewed himself as above them. Bernard couldn't really be bothered to help unless it served himself in some way too."

"What about my mother?" I said.

Bud's expression softened noticeably. "Deborah loved people. But vanity was a weakness of hers, and your father knew it. He invented all sorts of lies about your mother to get these women into bed, and they looked down their noses at Deborah because of it. When she mentioned it to Edie or your father, they called her paranoid or too sensitive. When Deborah found out about Sadie Jorgenson in the late '80s, she threatened to leave your father. Even Eleanor tried to talk her into leaving and reconnecting with your grandparents."

"What does this have to do with Rebecca's old pastor?" Detective Martinez said. "How does this connect to Bernard Ivy targeting his daughter or the Derden investigation?"

"It's a complicated web of lies, Detective. It takes a while to unravel. You have to know the history to understand the present."

Ted's warm hand squeezed my shoulder. "How are you doing?" he asked.

I nodded. Bud took it as a sign to continue.

"Sadie Jorgenson has a daughter named Evelyn. Evelyn married a man named Luke Derden. They have two boys, Chase and—"

"Tyler," I said, finishing for him in disbelief.

Ted pieced the puzzle together. "So Bernard Ivy had an affair with Chase Derden's grandmother?"

"Yes," Bud replied as a pin drop could be heard in the room. "If Sadie got word Bernard's daughter caused a police intervention in this situation with Chase, she would have gone after Bernard out of spite. That affair did not end well. Not that many of them did."

"Did Pastor Ivy ever force himself or coerce these women into a sexual relationship?" Detective Martinez said, camera pointed at Bud.

"Not to my knowledge, Detective. He deceived and manipulated the women, but he knew well enough to steer clear of the ones who did more than just play at being Christians. Bernard knew which women would be rightly outraged by his inappropriate attention."

"Tell me more about Sadie Jorgenson," I said. "What made her different? What information does she have that incited my father to attack my doppelgänger in a grocery store?"

"Your father called Sadie his ice princess. Even though he thought of himself as wooing these women like Solomon and the Shulamite from the Bible, Sadie resisted him for a while. Or at least she pretended to. We all knew she wore the pants in her own marriage. That miserable little worm, Larry Jorgenson, lucked into marrying a woman far too good looking for him."

I rolled my eyes.

"It may sound sexist to you," Bud said, "but you had to see them together. Sadie never hid her contempt for Larry, so we figured she married him for money or because he let her get away with whatever she wanted."

"She sounds like the female version of my father."

"Precisely. Bernard wanted a challenge. He thought he would play her like he did his other women, but Sadie played him instead. She blackmailed your father for $100,000."

Detective Martinez and Titus perked up at the mention of money.

"Did you just say $100,000?" I croaked. "How? Why?"

"Sadie wanted secrets. I thought of Samson and Delilah when Sadie whined to your father that he didn't trust her. Meanwhile, your mother stayed busy with you and Daniel as small children, and your father took full advantage of it. For the members, he always put on this song and dance of being some tireless servant for First United. In truth, your father passed off the bulk of his duties to his flunkies or one of his revolving door of elders. Unless, of course, he could enjoy a public appearance where he received praise or potential new members."

"What information does Sadie Jorgenson have on Bernard Ivy?" Detective Martinez asked. "She apparently had plenty to lose if he exposed their affair. How did Pastor Ivy cover up $100,000 or explain the disappearance of that much cash?"

"Sadie discovered the fraudulent use of First United tithes. Bernard uses the church credit card to pay for everything down to his socks and toothbrush. She also knew how it would devastate Deborah if she found out about Bernard's infidelity. Sadie threatened to tell Deborah more than once, and for the first time, Bernard became the puppet on the string. He took out a home equity line to buy her off and get the Jorgensons out of town. Your mother never really questioned the bookkeeping of the church, but when she got a notice from the mortgage company saying they were approved for a loan she knew they didn't need, she confronted your father about it. He tried to convince your mother he never slept with Sadie and that he gave her the hush money to leave town and not sully the work of the Lord. Your mother finally saw through his facade. Deep down, I think she knew all along."

"But she sold her soul too, Bud. She knew about every affair afterward. My sister told me that as long as my father let her buy whatever she wanted, my mother didn't care about the physical aspects of their marriage. They had Ada four or five years after all of this happened. How can you tell me my father has no idea Ada isn't his biological child?"

Bud's expression turned mournful. "For all of Deborah's bluster, she could never resist your father. Not when he turned on the charm and acted like he did in the early days of their marriage. She fell for it every time because she wanted to believe that was the real Bernard Ivy."

"So bringing this back to the ongoing Derden case," Detective Martinez said, "Pastor Ivy realized the connection between Chase and Sadie somehow—even though you claim she left town almost thirty years ago. Are you alleging Bernard Ivy would threaten or use force against Rebecca Margolin to keep her from testifying in the Derden molestation case? That he wanted to shut her up, through whatever means necessary, to keep Sadie Jorgenson from catching wind of it? It's a huge stretch, Mr. Riley."

"He bought Sadie's silence, Detective, but I never said they stopped seeing each other."

"What about protecting his secrets?" Detective Martinez said. "Your testimony is that Pastor Ivy bribed her because she knew too much."

"Bernard always has to win. Always. He can't stand the fact Sadie Jorgenson thinks anything differently of him than what he wants her to believe. She may be the only person other than Deborah or me who knows more about what Bernard has done. She knows about the financial impropriety, the womanizing, the sham performance he puts on as a man of God. Deborah only learned these things by accident. At this point, she just buries her head in the sand and lives in a fantasy world about what her husband is capable of doing."

"Yet she found comfort in your arms," I said, my eyes running over the bony limbs that once boasted muscle and strength.

"Is this you?" Ted asked, taking note of a picture on the long dresser behind him. He passed it to both detectives before allowing Bud or me to see it.

The picture showed the man I remembered from childhood and adolescence. Bud had classic, all-American good looks with striking blue eyes, dark blonde hair, and a broad, muscular frame.

"What happened to Edie and the kids?" I said, searching for any signs of my sister's face in the thirty-year-old picture of Bud and his children.

"Edie was cleaning out the attic and stumbled on a trunk of antiques from my mother after she passed. When she asked why Ada Ivy looked exactly like my aunt, I told her the truth."

"Did she know about my father and his affairs?"

"She suspected, but I did my best to cover for your father or tell her she imagined things. I've told so many lies in my life-time, Rebecca. I hid your father's sin until this cancer finally began eating away at me. His sin became my sin, and I'm sorry for all I did to you and your family. I'm sorry for the pain I caused you, for the pain I could have prevented by holding my pastor accountable like any other man. I failed your entire family, and I hope one day you can forgive me."

"Tell me more about the connection between Pastor Ivy and Sadie," Detective Martinez said. "Let's assume he buys her off, but he just can't seem to resist her. Wouldn't she be upset about her grandson's abuse? What difference would it make who identified the perp?"

"Sadie threatened to go to the IRS a few years back and expose everything at First United. Even if the government couldn't do anything, she knew what the scandal would do to Bernard. He covets the prestige of his reputation more than anything else. He relies on the income generated from First United to finance his lifestyle." Ruefully, Bud added, "Or poten-tially buy off anyone who might go public with his private dealings."

Detective Martinez was ready with his next question. "So what happened after Sadie's threats?"

"Blackmail attempts went back and forth. Lawyers got involved briefly, but in the end, they both realized they had too much at stake if they exposed one another. For Bernard's daughter to come forward with allegations causing shame to the Jorgenson family would seem like a slap in Sadie's face and an end to her ceasefire with Bernard. Sadie detested Larry, but she practically worshiped her children. To see them in pain or distress would send her over the edge."

"But cheating on their father for over thirty years wouldn't cause them pain?" I said incredulously.

Ignoring my comment, Bud went on. "The Jorgenson kids held their father in the same esteem as their mother. Nobody seemed surprised when Larry Jorgenson mysteriously vanished twenty years ago. They treated it like good riddance to bad rubbish, especially when Sadie got the insurance money."

"This sounds like a *novela*," Detective Martinez mused. "Let's stop recording for now while I radio over to our missing persons division." Turning to me, he said, "I tell you what, Mrs. Margolin, you sure hit the bottom of the barrel with this bunch."

Hours later, Ted and I sat at our kitchen table with untouched lo mein still residing in its China House takeout bag. Neither of us could muster the words to describe all we'd learned about the Jorgensons, my parents, or even Bud and Edie Riley. Bud told us my mother didn't bother to deny her affair with him when Edie confronted her, wrongly assuming Edie had already slept with my father. Unwilling to admit she'd been wrong, my mother made things worse by accusing Edie of jealousy. Bud said that's when Edie left with the children, and his fifteen years of stomach pain began.

Bud laughed mirthlessly at the irony of being another Larry Jorgenson, the miserable worm held in contempt by his wife and family. He claimed his relationship with my mother ended after Edie left, though he clearly still pined for her. With deep sadness, Bud recalled how my mother bemoaned the pain of seeing him bedridden and said she'd pray for Bud rather than continue to visit him.

As blind as he accused my mother of being regarding my father's malignant narcissism, Bud remained willfully obtuse to the same selfishness afflicting Deborah Ivy. He bore no ill will at my mother's fleeting concern for his health, and he pardoned her of all wrongdoing. Bud called my mother "too sensitive for real life." Ted told Bud my mother's excuses all reeked of cow excrement.

When questioned about Pastor Sociopath, Bud knew nothing of any predatory designs on me, personally. He said Pastor had confessed to the Derden incident with my father, implied there were other victims, and he wanted to know the best way to hush me up. Also made clear, Pastor Sociopath seemed to know of my father's sordid history. Bud speculated Evelyn knew about the affair and tipped off Pastor Sociopath somehow. As I recalled many tear filled conversations where I bared my soul to my old pastor, he undoubtedly picked up on the double life he shared in common with my father.

I could only hope they shared a cell block together one day too.

CHAPTER 40

BUD RILEY PASSED AWAY THREE DAYS AFTER HIS recorded confession. Never one to shy away from a juicy church scandal, the press soon caught wind of the charges against both pastors in the following weeks. They gleefully ambushed current members with microphones in their faces as they exited Sunday services. To my utter disgust, Evelyn Derden spoke directly to the camera, begging for justice for her son and demanding that Child Protective Services relinquish their "unjust imprisonment of my boys." She followed with a shameless plug for her online account to cover her supposed legal fees.

Even more astounding was the near $20,000 raised by people too kind hearted and trusting to stop and ask why CPS removed the boys from her custody in the first place. Luke Derden stood several feet behind his wife as she gave almost convincing, doe eyed pleas to "bring Chase and Tyler home."

"There! Did you see that?" I said, freezing the frame on our DVR.

"What?" Ted asked.

"Luke Derden actually rolled his eyes. He looks completely disgusted with the entire charade."

"Not that it stopped Evelyn from selling herself as a mother on a crusade to protect her children from an overreach of government authority. How wonderful for her to reap a small fortune at the expense of her children while claiming it's all to help them."

"Like mother, like daughter," I said.

"Speaking of," Ted said over his glasses, "aren't you supposed to be meeting up with your own mother soon? Why aren't you dressed?"

"Because I don't really want to go. Because I don't want to pretend I enjoy drinking coffee at seven o'clock at night. But mostly because I know she's going to lie or try to manipulate me."

"The police have your father in custody since the judge denied him bail. That's one less thing to worry about."

"I just don't know if I'm ready to face her, Ted."

"I offered to go with you when you first mentioned it. That offer still stands, Rebecca. I know your counselor thinks you're ready to put all the ghosts to rest, and I agree. You've come a long way in establishing boundaries and accepting that *their* shame and guilt are *their* issues to deal with, not yours to take on."

I sighed. "I guess. What do I do if my mother comments on my weight?"

"Tell her to kiss your—"

"Got it, thanks," I said, holding up my palms.

Ted took one last look at the frozen shot of Evelyn Derden before exhaling in disgust and shutting off the television. "Just when you think they've got one psycho off the street, another steps up to take their place. Hopefully, your mother will help put a big one in prison."

I wondered how different my mother looked since the last time we spoke nearly two years earlier. My last conversation with her and my father had erupted into an epic blow out at the Ivy Castle. I'd overheard yet another instance of Bernard Ivy's cruelty at my expense.

"You're overreacting as usual," my mother chided me. "I'm sure your father and Ada weren't laughing at you or your break up with Jason. Honestly, Rebecca! Do you have nothing better to do than manufacture drama?"

"I didn't imagine what I heard," I said tautly.

My mother waved me off with a flick of the wrist. "Beggars can't be choosers after thirty, darling. Your father is just concerned about your future. Have you tried that Jewish dating website I suggested? I've heard that some Jewish men even prefer a heftier figure."

"Heftier like you?" I said, too furious to hold my tongue anymore.

My mother's eyes bugged in her skull. "What did you say to me?"

"Oh please, Mom. You throw up half of what you eat to stay thin. It's no secret that your trip to the 'secluded health spa' last year was actually surgery to repair your esophagus."

"Eleanor!" my mother gaped. "I can't trust her with anything!"

"You know what, Mom, I like to eat. Jason didn't seem to mind I wasn't an anorexic twig."

"Oh, really?" she said, quickly regaining her composure. "I don't see your knight in shining armor now, Rebecca. I've told you a thousand times that men are visual creatures. If you don't watch your weight, you'll never get a man. You'll certainly never keep one," she said, pinching my cheek for good measure. "You could have such a pretty face, Rebecca. Just make sure to keep up with your waxing because I see all of the hairs on the side over here."

I jerked away from her. "Do you enjoy making me feel like garbage, Mom?"

"Rebecca!" she said, placing a hand over her heart. "What a horrible thing to say to your own mother! You know I'm only trying to help you."

"By making me feel as worthless as possible?"

"I can't believe you would even think such things of me," she said dramatically. "What kind of a daughter accuses her own mother like that? I know I never talked to mine that way."

No longer affected by her histrionic behavior, I merely raised an eyebrow. "Oh, really, Mom? When did you last speak with Leah Shapiro? I assume my grandparents are still alive, right?"

"How dare you presume to lecture me about anything, you ungrateful cow! After all your father and I have done for you? Who do you think paid for your college tuition?"

"I did!" I shouted. "You and Dad didn't pay a dime. I got that scholarship myself!"

She sniffed indignantly. "Well, who put a roof over your head those first two years? Are you going to pretend it doesn't cost a small fortune to feed that bottomless stomach of yours?"

"I paid you rent! You give money to Ada and Daniel without batting an eyelash, but you made me pay you to live here!"

"Well, who financed your laser hair removal?" she said coldly.

"As a college graduation present! Just what every kid entering the workforce needs," I snapped.

Incensed that pushing all of my old buttons no longer worked, she called in the cavalry.

My father.

Even with the shouts and curses raining down at ear split-ting decibels, I finally stood my ground. When Bernard Ivy's hand came up to strike my face, I did the absolutely unthink-able: I ducked.

I fled the Ivy Palace for the last time, done with the lot of them. Yet there she sat, Deborah Rachel Wasserman Ivy, coffee cup in hand, looking me up and down as though no time had elapsed.

"Don't bother with how happy you are to see me because we both know you're not," I said. "Tell me what you want so I can tell you 'no,' and let's just move on with our lives."

"There's no need to be so snippy, Rebecca. I am still your mother after all."

"In name only."

Hurt crept into her green eyes, Ada's eyes. It reminded me of Bud's confession, and the pangs of bitterness and betrayal swirled in my stomach.

"What made you hate me so much, Rebecca? All I ever did was love you and help you be the best you could be. You treat me like I'm some kind of ogre. Like I'm—"

"My father?" I said tersely. Though tempted to respond to the flagrant lies and emotional strings my mother tugged on, it suddenly dawned me that she wanted an outburst. If Deborah Ivy could rile me up, she would use that as proof of her false accusations against me. She'd make herself the victim one last time.

I smiled coolly at her. "What do you want?"

Her eyes fell upon my left hand. "When did this happen?" she said, gesturing toward my ring. "My daughter gets married, and you don't even have the decency to tell your own mother?"

"He's Jewish," I said. "Just like you, just like Tabby and Lou

Wasserman, and amazingly enough, just like Bernard Levy, er I mean, Ivy."

My mother's eyes widened to twice their normal size. I watched her squirm as she struggled to deduce how I'd acquired so many secrets.

"Do you plan to tell Ada about her father?"

"What are you going on about now, Rebecca? Ada knows they locked your father up in jail on these ridiculous charges."

"You mean as ridiculous as Bud Riley being Ada's biological father? How about Sadie Jorgenson and the $100,000 mortgage fraud Dad committed to get her out of town? Do you know how many years of prison you get for lying to the bank about what you do with their money? Do you know the government doesn't approve of laundering funds through your 501c3 to buy off your mistress?"

My mother's jaw fell open.

Going for broke, I said, "Let's not forget the stupid sheep who bankroll your so-called housing expenses year after year. Do you think the church would like to know how their 'giving unto the Lord' financed your face lift, your breast lift, your esophagus surgery, and way too many facial fillers? What about the bogus Christian conferences that are nothing more than a free vacation paid for by the parishioners? Do you honestly believe God's curse is on *them* for what they do with that tithe money?"

"For God's sake, lower your voice, Rebecca Joanne!"

"For *God's sake*, Mom? How about you cut the games and the pathetic charade you ever cared about me. Did you think all of these secrets would stay hidden forever? Bud died of stomach cancer because he hid the Ivy family secrets."

"And he couldn't hide them for just a few more weeks!" she said petulantly. "Everything would have been fine if that weasel could have kept his mouth shut! He owed your father and me his silence one last time."

"You're unbelievable!" I said. "Do you even live on this planet, Mom? How can you seriously believe the problem is Bud exposing your lies rather than you actually committing crimes?"

My mother sniffed haughtily. "I'm not even going to dignify that with a response. You have no idea how hard it is to be in full time ministry."

"What about Dad? Do you think he'll go down without taking you with him? He'd turn on you in a heartbeat if he thought he could get less jail time."

"We need to trust the Lord in all of these matters, Rebecca. Besides, your father has connections in the district attorney's office. With the way you've so cruelly shut us out of your life, your father just needed to teach you a lesson. No jury in the world would convict him of a broken heart. You earned every measure of discipline your father ever gave to you. If that maniac in the grocery store only knew the pain and embarrassment you've caused the Ivy family, he would have landed those punches on your face instead of your poor father's. He would have begged your father for your address!"

I needed no further proof my mother possessed zero maternal instinct beyond the sugary spectacle she performed for the praises of others. Rather than agony or grief, however, I finally felt free. The chains and shackles of performance, of striving to earn love that never existed, snapped off in an instant. My final, family ghost vaporized under the shining beacon of truth. The urge to leap from the table and do a victory dance nearly overcame me.

Then, I spotted him.

The undercover cop.

I watched as the officer whispered discreetly toward his

jacket lapel while feigning interest in a mystery novel. An over-whelming sense of peace flooded me. I could almost sense the angelic hosts marching into the room.

I turned megawatt on my mother. Dazed, she frowned slightly.

"Something wrong, Mom?"

"No, you just reminded me of someone else. Why are you smiling anyway? Didn't you hear what I just said?"

Megawatt went supernova. "Dad wasn't targeted for a hate crime by some rabid anti-Christians, was he, Mom? He thought he was going to teach me a lesson by verbally and physically assaulting me in public, but he just picked the wrong person instead. You know he tried to assault me last year at my job, right? Didn't exactly go as planned then either."

"The Bible very clearly says we are to discipline our children, Rebecca. I would hardly call that a crime. You and your flair for the dramatic," she said on a tinkling laugh.

"Child Protective Services calls what you and Bernard did to me *abuse*. Given that I am a fully grown adult, they call attempting to physically harm me *assault*. The countless bruised and bloody lips I suffered goes under the category of *battery*. We can add it to Dad's growing list of criminal accomplishments."

"Your father is not a criminal!" she said in outrage. "He's just a very misunderstood man."

"Who can't keep his libido in his pants," I fired back. "How many marriages did he ruin, Mom? How many families of First United did you and Bernard Ivy destroy by sowing your sin and dysfunction into them? These people trusted you, and you both took advantage of them. You stole from them. You used them up and spit them out when they failed to meet King Bernard's insatiable demands."

"I've heard quite enough," my mother said icily, standing up and smoothing out her designer ensemble.

"I assume the church paid for all of that too," I said, eyeing her from head to foot.

"Your father and I earned that money. We've sacrificed so much to get to where we are."

"Wrong! You've sacrificed many people to get where you are."

Leaning in close, my mother said, "So you know, Ada has been sitting in the corner recording all of the vicious lies you've said about me. She told me your husband is loaded. Be prepared for a defamation lawsuit, Rebecca Joanne. We will *ruin* you!"

Not missing a beat I announced loudly, "I'm so glad my sister is an accomplice to the corruption too, Deborah Ivy. After all, when someone admits to fraud, collusion, child abuse, money laundering, and fabricating a temporary insanity plea in an assault and battery case, it must be wonderful knowing you've shown your true colors to both of your daughters and an undercover officer as well."

As the final *coup de gras*, I added, "And if you think Ada won't roll on you either, you've got another thing coming. After all, you and Dad raised her to be just as selfish as the two of you."

Flashing a smile to my sister, mostly so the plainclothes officer could identify her, I walked straight out of the coffee shop and toward the unmarked van in the back of the parking lot. Ted came around the side to embrace me, and I collapsed as a weeping mess into his arms.

"You did it, Rebecca," he spoke into my hair. "You did it."

Nodding wordlessly, I cried tears of joy and grief as Ted continued to rock me gently in his arms. The parking lot quickly became abuzz with flashing blue lights and cell phone crazed customers livestreaming the spectacle to social media. Picking up the story, the local news media showcased one homemade video after another of Deborah and Ada Ivy, beloved mother and daughter of First United Church of Hillcrest, arrested on charges not even a procedural crime drama could pass off as believable entertainment.

CHAPTER 41

ROSE WORKED LIKE AN ARMY GENERAL PREPARING for the massive, Margolin family Passover seder two weeks later. After seeing the amount of work involved, course after course with ceremonial food, appetizers, soup, entree, sides and multiple desserts, I silently thanked God for the wisdom of my husband telling me to sit back and observe before attempting to pull off my own seder.

"Make sure you get an extra bowl for the kid table *charoset*," Rose said, directing Jennifer toward her stash of service ware in the dining room hutch. "You know how much the kids love anything with apples and honey. Amanda, I got the pink horseradish for the little ones and the white kind for everyone else. Are your children finally eating gefilte fish and chopped liver, or should we skip them straight to the soup?"

"Mom! Chill out," Jennifer said with a laugh. "It will all get done."

"Your father ate brisket yesterday thinking it was extra. I'll have to chill out later."

"Mom, you made enough for an entire country," Amanda said with her head buried in the fridge. "I don't think Dad even put a dent in it. Where's the horseradish? I can't find it."

"On the door," Rose replied, opening up the oven. She pulled back the foil on her dishes to check on them. "Nana, I think I can squeeze your potato kugel in here."

With a tolerant smile, Nana produced a tin full of Jewish potato goodness and handed it to my laser focused mother-in-law. "Rose, darling, I think Rebecca and I are going to finish setting the table. Too many cooks in the kitchen can create a little chaos."

Rose dismissed us from her domain with a slight nod. Nana and I happily escaped the pre-seder tension.

"To think I wanted to take this all on myself," I said. "I had no idea how much work went into a seder."

"Most of it's for your benefit, bubbeleh. Rose wanted to make the seder extra special since it's your first real one," Nana said. She moved around the table and rearranged Amanda's place settings. Biting my lip from laughing, I hoped Amanda wouldn't take offense.

"I told Rose that she didn't need to go to any extra trouble on my account," I said. "I've been to seders before with the Goldsteins."

"Goldsteins Schmoldsteins, they're not your family."

I shared a meaningful glance and a quick side hug with Nana before Rose issued another edict from central command. Calling from the kitchen she said, "Can you pull a *haggadah* for each of the adult place settings, Rebecca? They should be in the middle drawer of the credenza."

"Got it!" I said and exchanged a silent chuckle with my grandmother.

I handed a stack of the Passover booklets to Nana, who

looked over the haggadah before placing it down on the table. "Rexwell Home," she said, glancing at it. "We all had these in the 1960s. Imagine a coffee maker printing a Passover booklet!"

I smirked, setting a haggadah at the head of the table. "I thought the youngest child asked the four questions. How did I get nominated for this? Shouldn't Riley or Jordyn be singing?"

"They have plenty of years to do it again, bubbeleh. Also, Rose asked me if you prefer blackberry or concord Mandelwitz wine. They both taste like cough syrup to me, but it's tradition. What I wouldn't give for a nice chianti though."

I hurried into the kitchen to produce a different bottle.

"Grape juice, Rebecca? Why aren't you drinking wine?" Nana's voice trailed off as she solved the mystery herself. Her dark eyes glowed at me, and I beamed at her. "I know that smile well, *sheyna meydeleh*. Whatever you do with my great grandchildren, please don't spoil them. If you spoil them when they're little, you'll spoil their entire lives. Oy, that we suffered forty years never knowing you or your siblings because of how we raised your mother!"

I patted her shoulder gently. "You can't change the past, Nana. At a certain point, everyone is responsible for their choices, no matter how wonderful or terrible their upbringing."

"Don't you ever wonder what life would be like if your parents had been kind, decent human beings instead of the ghouls on the nightly news?"

"Halloween is six months away," Ted said, entering the room on the tail end of Nana's comment. "Let's save the talk of goblins and monsters for late October."

"Ironic, since they scheduled my father's arraignment the day before Halloween," I said.

"What about the Derden boy?" Nana asked, "or for that matter, the other fifteen children who came forward?"

"Investigation is still in process, Nana, but Detective Nichols and Martinez convinced Cynthia to turn on old Pastor What's-His-Name when they threatened to indict her as a co-conspirator. I hate that she's getting away with her part, but hopefully, it puts that deviant behind bars for good. Even Pastor Shipley came out of the woodwork to testify."

"Isn't that the guy who groomed Pastor Sociopath for the job?" Ted asked. "Rebecca, you said he got ousted pretty quickly all those years ago. Do you have more to the story?"

"*Feh*, too many names for my old head to keep straight," Nana said with a dismissive wave. "I'm going to check on Rose and see how her matzah balls turned out. The key is light and fluffy," she said, smacking her lips. "Your grandfather likes them like a lead ball, but then, his mother was never much of a cook, may she rest in peace."

Ted and I chuckled as Nana exited the room.

"How do you want to tell them?" Ted asked, golden eyes sparkling.

Megawatt appeared.

Sizzling butter answered in response.

Some forty minutes later, I began my singing in Hebrew, "*Ma nishtana halaila hazeh mikol haleilot...*"

"Lovely!" Nana exclaimed, clapping her hands once we'd recited all four questions. "Beautiful job, bubbeleh!"

Papa nodded in agreement.

Steve eyed me admiringly, chest puffed out, and he whispered something close to Rose's ear. She grinned back.

"Why *is* this night different from all other nights?" my husband said, translating the Hebrew with a mischievous tone.

"Ted, what's going on?" Amanda asked as she nursed Asher at the table.

With a blindingly beautiful grin, my husband reached into

his coat pocket and held up our positive pregnancy test. Bedlam promptly ensued.

After hours of laughing, singing, and rejoicing, we lay in bed later that night with Ted resting his head against my belly. He said, "Do you have any names picked out?"

"I don't know why, but my gut says it's going to be a girl."

He lifted his head slightly to meet my eyes. "Why do you think that?"

I grinned. "If we take my grandmother's first name with your mother's name in Yiddish, we get Tabitha Raisa. It seems fitting somehow."

Ted laughed.

"Of course, Nana will start another lecture about how Ashkenazi Jews name after deceased relatives and then list off all of her cousins again."

"Then Mom will chime in how the Sephardic Jews name after the living, and why not try a different Jewish tradition."

I chuckled as I shook my head. "I can't remember the last time I had so much fun watching two Jewish grandmothers go head-to-head about something neither of them have any control over."

"Especially if it's a boy in there," Ted said, his eyes nearly as golden as the moment I informed him of our winter arrival.

My thoughts turning serious, I said, "How do we protect our child from all of the Pastor Sociopaths and Lucifer Ivys of the world? Do you ever wonder about that? What about the victims of both churches who now have no place to go with their grief and anger?"

"I'd say the vitriol they've posted on social media goes a long way in making sure no one trusts either of those psychos again, Rebecca. I'm sorry Ashley caught so much of it from the former SBC faithful."

I sighed. "I'm not quite as sorry as you are, Ted. Ashley turned a blind eye to his affairs with women in the congregation. Whatever threats Pastor Sociopath made to keep her from leaving, Ashley still chose to remain in that marriage and maintain the facade. I can't imagine the devastation to both Connor and Olivia, but how much worse did she make it for herself by refusing to come forward? She looks complicit in the eyes of everyone."

"A lot of people said the same thing about you, Rebecca. They wanted to know why you didn't talk to the police about your father or Pastor Sociopath years ago. How do you know he didn't victimize Ashley the same way? What if he brainwashed her into believing everything was her fault?"

"But I did speak up, Ted. Ashley refused. She refused thirteen years ago when Pastor assaulted his first victim. Ashley refused when he slandered her to the church. She refused even after the police got involved. How many crimes could Ashley have prevented if she had more integrity than fear? I remember my one night in their home so vividly, Ted. She even tried to warn me about Pastor, but she maintained their happy little image right up until he left her for Cynthia. She willingly chose to be his victim. The rest of us had no say in the matter."

"She's certainly sharing in his disgrace now. The same people who attacked you on social media for marring the reputation of SBC and its beloved pastor are the same people claiming if Ashley had simply done her job in the bedroom, none of this would have happened."

I exhaled in disgust. "I just don't understand how they keep making excuses for the real criminal in all of this. They'd rather blame Ashley, me, Chase Derden, or anybody else rather than accept the truth about Pastor Sociopath. You can shout it from the rooftops, but some people will always choose the comfort of their denial over the harsh reality they were duped. No wonder God calls pride an abomination before Him."

"Permission to change the subject?" Ted asked. He sat up and wrapped his arm around my shoulders.

I snuggled into his chest and lay my head over his heart. "By all means. We had a wonderful seder with our family, and I'd hate to ruin it getting worked up over that other chazarai."

I heard the smile in Ted's voice. "I grew up in a Jewish home, but you're the one who sounds like you've been speaking Yiddish your entire life."

"What can I say? Between your mother and my Nana, I've got two amazing teachers."

"It seems even more crazy to tell you I really enjoyed the church service this past Sunday."

"That's not crazy, Ted. It was a beautiful service. The speaker based his sermon on Scripture, and everybody thinks it's awesome we're Jewish. What's not to love?"

"If I'm being transparent, I feel guilty."

"Why?"

"Because of the shtick my father hammered into me about not being Jewish and believing in Jesus."

"Which, obviously, is not the case," I said, gesturing toward myself.

"Not the same, Rebecca. You didn't grow up Jewish."

I picked up my head so I could meet his eyes. "Help me understand this, Ted. You told me how much you hated going to synagogue as a kid. You've told me on numerous occasions that celebrating Jewish holidays was more about family togetherness than anything religious for you. What changed?"

He took a deep breath. "I don't know, Rebecca. I think about the kind of legacy we're leaving for our child. There has to be more to Judaism than saying a few prayers or going through the motions at synagogue. You grew up as a Pastor's Kid, and I feel like you've got a better grasp of who you are as a Jew than I do."

"The *yiddishe bubbe* helps," I said. "What a treasure to finally meet my grandparents!"

"That's just it, Rebecca. You already know more Yiddish than I do. You took on this heritage without a second look back, and it's like you've lived this way your entire life. Meanwhile, I've got a blown up poster of me somewhere in my parents' basement from my bar mitzvah, and I feel like I know absolutely nothing."

"I think I'm beginning to understand, Ted."

"Well, can you help me figure it out?" he asked good naturedly.

I smiled. "My experience with Judaism wasn't cultural or familial. I didn't grow up this way at all, but every time I learn something about Jewish history, a holiday, or a story from Nana and Papa, I connect with God in a deeper way. When I read about Moses, Esther, or even Jesus, these aren't just Biblical heroes to look up to, but part of my bloodline now. Did you know God chose the Jewish people to be a sign to the entire world that He's God? The fact that we exist proves He is who He says He is."

"And yet you believe in Jesus," Ted said matter-of-factly.

"They're not mutually exclusive, no matter what your father or anyone else says."

"How do we make this work, Rebecca? How do we raise this child or any others that God sees fit to give us?"

"That's a pretty interesting question coming from the self-professed agnostic at best."

"I'm not agnostic anymore, Rebecca. I can't be after everything I've seen happen. The way He brought us together is nothing short of miraculous. I'd have to be an idiot not to see that."

"And as we established a long time ago, you are not an idiot."

He grinned. "So, what do we do?"

"We start by praying, Ted. We ask God how this works for us. We focus less on what everybody else has to say about the right way to do things, and we trust God to lead and guide us. In the meantime, we let tomorrow worry about tomorrow, and we just focus on today."

He placed a soft kiss on my lips. "I think I can handle that."

EPILOGUE

WHEN YOU UNDERGO THE TASK OF REWRITING YOUR own story, you no longer drift through life limited to what someone else assigns as your "place" within it. Even though I had deemed myself the Culver fairy godmother, little sprites named Miss Belle, Taylor, and even Phil, helped orchestrate one of the best, surprise baby showers I'd ever attended. The irony of standing in that Culver break room with pink and blue streamers everywhere, of seeing Rose, Amanda, Jennifer, and Nana seated at the same table where I used to eat my lunch and read my Bible daily put a smile on my face.

I wished Jessica could have been there, but Nathan's recent engagement to a much younger girl at his synagogue left my best friend angry and bitter. Still, I invited her to the baby shower and then rolled my eyes at her paper thin excuse. Jessica's married boyfriend served not only as a rebound from Nathan's betrayal but as a way to shield herself from me. Knowing how I felt about the relationship, Jessica found ways to invite Patrick along so she could get out of seeing me. Kyle, meanwhile, continued on his own, self-destructive journey. Eventually, I resigned myself to pray for both Goldstein twins and trust God with the outcome. I had a feeling the Lord wasn't finished with either of their stories.

"So cute," Amanda said, taking in all the decor and adjusting Asher on her hip. "Can you believe this boy is thirteen months already?" Asher gurgled on cue.

"I think it's ingenious you planned the shower and the gender reveal at the same time," Jennifer said, flanking me on the other side. "Since nobody knows what kind of clothes to buy, they actually bought things off your registry. I wish I'd thought of that a million and one years ago when I had mine."

"All your brother's idea," I said, "and we liked the idea of a surprise."

"It doesn't hurt that Jen and I have enough baby clothes to pass on for the next thousand years," Amanda quipped. "I know we're done having kids, and I cannot wait to unload all of those bins of clothes on you and Ted. Hopefully, the seasons match up."

"Between the two of us, I think we'll have you covered," Jennifer said. "Plus, you know Mom can't wait to go to Mercer's and buy up the entire baby department."

I laughed. "Fine with me. One less thing for me to worry about."

"Here it is!" Ted announced, carrying a Georgie's cake carefully into the room. The absolute joy radiating from his face sent a wave of love through me. The baby happily kicked in response.

Phil clapped Ted on the back once my husband set the cake down on a table. "I couldn't be happier for you, Margolin. I know you've waited a long time for this."

"Aw, they're making nice," I said, laughing with Amanda and Jennifer.

Ted walked over to me and planted a non-appropriate-for-work kiss on my mouth. "Because I can," he said with a wink.

"And that would be why we're gathered here today," Phil said to the room at large.

Ted and I both groaned.

"Couldn't resist," Phil said, grinning. "Now, get over here and cut the cake. This was our biggest office pool to date, and the winners get free lunch on me tomorrow. Of course, Baby Margolin receives all the proceeds. I'm pretty sure we cleared most of the items off your registry, Rebecca," Phil said, gesturing to the mountain of gifts on one of the side tables, "but maybe there's some new baby gizmo you guys haven't picked yet."

"Ready?" Ted said, grinning down at me.

The moment we cut into the cake, my father pled guilty on all counts to shorten his prison sentence and prevent more secrets coming to light in a public trial.

But I didn't care.

The moment we rejoiced with our friends and family eating brightly colored cake, Chase and Tyler Derden reunited with their father. He divorced Evelyn, exposed her affair with Pastor Sociopath and subsequent publicity fraud, and he took the boys to live near his family in Colorado.

But my mind overflowed with thoughts of decorating the baby's nursery.

Rose rubbed her hands together gleefully. "To Mercer's I shall go. Nana, did you remember the coupons?"

"As if I pay full retail for anything," she scoffed. "Lead the way, Rose darling. If it's one thing a yiddishe bubbe knows how to do, it's how to shop for her great-grandchildren."

I grinned at Ted.

So much joy.

Too much to contain.

It took over an hour to open all of the gifts, Ted's brilliant idea ensuring we wouldn't need a car seat, crib sheet, bouncer, baby swing, or high chair for the very foreseeable future. We had traded in my car for a minivan a month earlier, and it was the only way we got everything home in one trip.

I stared at the open doorway of our former guest room, now nursery, packed to the gills with baby paraphernalia and a disassembled crib requiring an engineering degree to construct. When Ted arrived next to me, I smiled up at him, then retrieved a gift bag from the white changing table.

"What's this?" Ted said as I handed him the bag. "I think we've got enough presents in here to last this kid until college."

"I was walking around the baby store last week, and I felt a nudge from the Holy Spirit to buy them. You'll see why when you open the bag."

Golden eyes sparkling, Ted reached in and pulled out two, wooden block letters.

"Ted and Rebecca?" he said, holding them up.

"Tabitha Raisa," I replied, megawatt in full supernova effect.

ACKNOWLEDGMENTS

Tina Adams for reaching out in an online author group, offering to edit when I had no idea how I would ever afford it, and for all the words of encouragement, guidance, and sisterhood along the way. You were truly a godsend.

Hannah Linder for your patience with me as a first time author tweaking this cover, taking all of my suggestions, and then not being mad when we went right back to your original design. The learning curve for self-publishing is huge, and you were a total champ. You truly live up to your name as full of grace.

Nicole and Bruce for those hours on the phone providing accurate information on reporting child abuse. Thank you for helping me separate cop show drama from real life.

For all of the friends, baristas, and complete strangers who offered their services as beta readers or simply confirmed why this book needs to be on the market. Thank you for giving me the courage to put Rebecca's story to print.

Lydia and Amy who provided honest feedback, couldn't wait to read the next books in the series, and talked with me about these characters like they're real people. Thank you for confirming I'm doing exactly what I'm supposed to be.

Kimberley for walking with me through the process, holding up my weary arms, and your prayers of faith. You are such an incredible mother and woman of God.

My precious girls who already want to be authors themselves and have been there with Mommy through rejection letters, cover art, and praying for breakthrough. You have been my biggest cheerleaders, and I will always be yours.

My darling son and rainbow baby, your hugs are healing and your smile lights up the world.

My Lord and Savior who took words forged out of brokenness and despair and transformed them into a source of light and hope. You make *all* things beautiful.

COMING 2021

BOOK 2 IN THE BEAUTY FOR ASHES SERIES:
EX NIHILO: LEARNING TO LIVE AGAIN

Devastated from loss and a broken marriage, Taylor Ross had closed off her heart in order to survive. All of that changes when the infamous Kyle Goldstein challenges Taylor to see the man beyond the office gossip. At the same time, Ian Horner has never hidden his admiration for Taylor. Even after their awkward first meeting at church, his steady faithfulness cannot be ignored. As Taylor allows her heart to beat again, feel again, and break again, she must also confront the pain of her father's abandonment twenty years earlier. Threats both old and new press in, and ancient family secrets refuse to remain hidden any longer. Taylor knows that God can make something beautiful out of nothing (*ex nihilo*), but can she set aside her past in order to embrace everything her heart has ever wanted?

EXCERPT FROM EX NIHILO

My comatose heart first showed signs of awakening one warm, March evening following a particularly hideous day at work. When I had accepted the job a year earlier, they told me I had large shoes to fill. I just never expected the shadow of Culver Incorporated legend, Rebecca Margolin, to completely overhaul my life.

"Another day, another dinner alone outside of the office," I said in sarcastic self-loathing. I inched a second chair closer to me so I could prop my aching feet. "How many more months before they finally hire someone to replace Eric? I'm too young to feel this old."

A burst of noise caught my attention as a group of heavily made up, party girls sauntered by. Once the sun dipped below the horizon in Parkview, our uptown office location transformed from a bustling workplace into an evening hotspot. Pulling off from behind the crowd, an inebriated woman stumbled toward the door of the restaurant while her exasperated boyfriend trailed just behind her.

"Why are we even here?" she whined, groping for the door handle. Her marked resemblance to my former coworker left my jaw on the table. Although Rebecca Margolin and I worked at Culver together for just a short time, a friendship had bloomed due to common suffering as well as faith in Jesus. Trying to make sense of the situation, I realized I would never see Mrs. Margolin publicly intoxicated, let alone with a man other than her husband.

The woman's boyfriend seemed familiar, but I couldn't quite place him. Our eyes met and his narrowed slightly, confirming my sense of déjà vu. Unsettled by my reaction to his intense blue gaze, I quickly averted my attention back to my dinner container.

"Do I know you?" I heard him say, suddenly standing above me.

I gulped before responding. A litany of food allergies meant I had to choke down a dry salad. I took a sip of water before meeting those powder blue eyes again.

"We...um...haven't dated or anything, have we?" he said, speaking quietly lest his intoxicated lady friend overhear us. Oblivious, she managed to enter the restaurant unassisted, mincing her way to the counter before careening into it. I cringed in embarrassment while her apathetic boyfriend continued his perusal of me.

"Do you think I'd talk to you if I knew you dumped me for some babbling drunk?" I said.

Rather than the expected offense at my impertinence, the familiar stranger actually smiled. Dozens of overheard conversations from my coworkers, Deondre, MacKenzie, and Lexie finally clicked into place. Bearded, blue eyed mystery man no longer remained a mystery.

Armed with far too much information to find him attractive,

I managed to defy the odds anyway. He glanced down at my open Bible on the table then back up sharply, as if seeing someone else. Or more accurately, the woman resembled by his drunken imposter.

"How...how do I know you?" he asked again, his eyes scanning my face for some shred of recognition. "I know I've met you somewhere."

I shrugged innocently. If I didn't open my mouth, I wouldn't have to lie.

Blue Eyes raised a dark brow at me, unrelenting in his quest to discover my identity. Unfortunately for Kyle Goldstein, I found nothing attractive about cheating boyfriends, especially after my one and only failed relationship. Moreover, if even half of MacKenzie's tales regarding her former coworker held true, I'd be better served hiding the source of our mutual acquaintance.

"Five minutes for fresh chicken fingers," Rebecca clone announced from the door with a giggle, "but I can't open the sauce packet. Stupid sauce!" She let the door slam shut as she staggered back inside.

"Seems like you've had enough sauce already," I muttered.

Kyle surprised me with humor in his eyes and a knowing glint.

"How is everyone at Culver these days, Taylor?" he said, unraveling the mystery of our association. "I'm sure they keep you buried and overworked in the marketing department."

I responded with a sunny smile. "We've had some turnover lately, but nothing I can't handle. Our top producer and his wife just had a baby, so as you can imagine, we've had lots to celebrate."

I gauged Kyle's reaction to see how my news landed, but his expression remained sardonic. "Turnover, hmm? Is that why you have a bowl of rabbit food for dinner at nine o'clock at night?"

My mouth opened and shut at how easily he perceived the situation.

The slight smile on his face reached his eyes. "I heard Phil fired the snowflake they hired along with you when they replaced Rebecca."

"You're the expert on replacing Rebecca," I said.

"Hit a nerve?" he asked, his eyes flicking over me.

Accustomed to most men dismissing my petite frame and mousy hair and eyes as too childlike, I kept my ego in check. Kyle Goldstein's interest in me resulted from nothing other than morbid curiosity. "I'm shocked you even know my name, Goldstein. Congratulations."

A flash of white teeth appeared along with a very attractive smile. "Obviously, you remembered mine. Must have made quite an impression on you."

I smirked. "Oh, people still talk about you at Culver."

"Ah," he said in understanding, "and you enjoy all of the juicy gossip just like the rest of them, right?"

"You tell me," I shot back. "How did you know about Eric getting fired? You left Culver a year and a half ago. Nobody even called him a snowflake until he got that stupid haircut and a series of unfortunate tattoos."

"Like you said, people talk," he said with a grin. "Curious to hear what they say about you, Taylor?"

I stood up from my chair, not very intimidating as I barely squeaked over five feet tall, but my temper compensated for my lack in stature. "I've put up with a lifetime of manipulators trying to screw with my head, so don't delude yourself into thinking you have an easy win here. If you have something to say, Goldstein, then go ahead and say it. Otherwise, let me enjoy my dinner in peace."

"It's Kyle," he said.

I raised an eyebrow.

"I hate being called Goldstein. I don't work at Culver anymore, and I want nothing to do with that place."

"Yet, you still keep tabs on everything going on in the office. You knew about Rebecca and Ted's baby, and you knew about me working alone in the marketing department. You seem to have at least one foot firmly planted there."

"Like you said, people talk," he parroted.

"Apparently, they talk to *you*. Quite a conundrum for the man who claims he wants nothing to do with the place."

Powder blue eyes assessed me again, and I shifted uncomfortably. With his drunk girlfriend pitifully attempting to shove napkins and ketchup packets into her to-go bag, Kyle Goldstein's seeming interest in me turned my stomach. No matter what I thought of the woman teetering on stiletto heels at the restaurant condiment bar, I would never wish the pain of an affair on anyone.

The outside door opened and closed with a decided thud as Kyle's girlfriend rejoined him, her arm looping through his.

"Kyle," she whined nasally, "stop talking to the librarian and let's go! I can't get the lid off my coffee."

Kyle inclined his head and offered me a wry smile. Evidently, he found Rebecca clone equally as cringeworthy, but he turned his attention to her anyway.

"Nice talking to you, Taylor," he said.

I rolled my eyes and sat down, daring to glance back up once I felt sure they'd both departed. Kyle aided his swaying, mess of a girlfriend down the street, and I jerked in surprise at his soothing tones. Kyle's enigmatic behavior stirred feelings in me I didn't care to identify.

"Librarian?" I finally said, touching my chin length bob. "I look like a librarian?" Rebecca clone's passing remark cut deep.

Throwing away my trash, I located Clara, my favorite Chick-A-Yum employee. Hers was the familiar face whose work shifts often coincided with the nights I just didn't want to make another bowl of gluten free pasta.

"Clara, can I ask you something?"

"Sure, *mija*."

"Do I look like a librarian?"

"No," she said in heavily accented English, "you look like the girl from the cartoon doggy show. The one always losing her glasses when they solve mysteries."

I inwardly groaned, disheartened to hear I gave off the book-worm, nerd vibe even to people who liked me.

"Thanks," I said, though I didn't mean it at all.

I trudged my way back to the parking deck, lost in thought and not expecting to encounter Kyle Goldstein a second time in one night.

"Heading home?" he said, coming along beside me.

"Are you stalking me?"

"No. Well, maybe."

"Where's your Rebecca clone?" I said with saccharine sweetness.

Kyle's face pinched tightly, clearly not enjoying the reference. "Sent her home. The vomiting usually commences in a few hours, and I didn't feel like hanging around for that."

"Nice."

"You don't like me," he said, brushing past me to blockade any forward progress.

I glared at him. "Very perceptive. Now, why don't you leave me alone?"

Kyle held my gaze, and I silently cursed my weakness for blue eyes. Smirking, he said, "Don't pretend you didn't enjoy our little banter outside of the restaurant."

"I don't flirt with other people's boyfriends," I snapped. "Get out of my way, Goldstein."

"It's Kyle," he said, "and are you planning to beat me up, Taylor? I'd like to see you try."

"What information can I possibly supply for you about Rebecca that you don't already know, *Goldstein*? She's happy, she's in love, and she's a mother. Are we done here?"

"What did she tell you about me?"

"Why do you care?" I said, exasperated. "Look, it's been a long day, and all I want to do is go home. I have pepper spray in my purse, and so help me, if you don't move, I will not hesitate to use it."

Though not overly tall by male standards, Kyle still towered over me. "You haven't told me why you don't like me."

I looked up into his eyes, again annoyed with the surge of attraction I felt. I vowed to start another fast from my litany of Austen remakes and romantic comedies. His lazy smile indicated he noticed my reaction to him.

"You're cute, Taylor."

"You're gross, Kyle."

"You don't look at me like you think I'm gross."

"You have nice eyes, okay? Also, you're a selfish pig, at least to hear your former coworkers tell it. I can't believe you're hitting on me after sending your drunk girlfriend home. I want no part in whatever sick game you have going on here."

"Her name is Heather," he said coolly, "and I didn't send her home just to talk to you, so don't flatter yourself."

I pursed my lips and raised an eyebrow. "Not buying a word of it, Goldstein."

"Not that it's any of your business, but Heather and I broke up more than a year ago. I found her completely wasted after happy hour today, and I brought her to Chick-A-Yum to get food and coffee. End of story."

"Things didn't look broken up with the way she hung all over you."

"She could barely walk in those shoes. Of course, she held onto me! Do you believe everything you see, or do you bother to ask questions, Taylor? You seemed smarter than that."

"Don't insult my intelligence by literally *insulting my intelligence*," I fired back.

"I'm not the villain you seem to think I am, no matter what rumors you've heard," he said.

My eyes glanced over the vacated parking garage and Kyle's annoying presence still in it. "Like I said, don't insult my intelligence."

"You don't believe me?" he accused.

I held his gaze, no longer shaken or ashamed by my initial attraction to him. Confessing it somehow made it easier to overcome. "Not a word."

Kyle said, "MacKenzie Pascale is a gossip and loves inventing Lifeline movie drama. Whatever she doesn't embellish, she'll flat out lie about. Sometimes, she provides useful information, but mostly you learn to take it with a grain of salt." He handed me a business card. "Call me sometime if you ever want to find out the truth."

"And what about the things Rebecca's told me?" I said, unable to help myself.

CPSIA information can be obtained
at www.ICGtesting.com
Printed in the USA
LVHW022338220920
666822LV00001B/28